D0064119

Area around Franklin

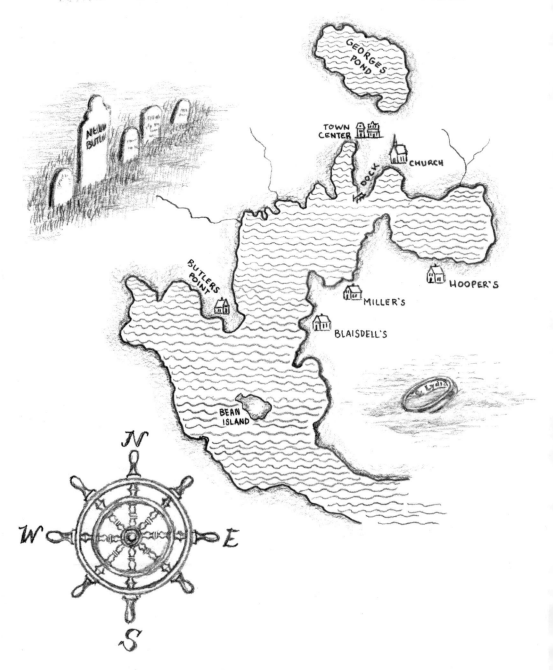

BASED ON A TRUE STORY

The Gathering Room

A TALE OF NELLY BUTLER

Michelle E. Shores

The Gathering Room: A Tale of Nelly Butler
Copyright © 2022 Michelle E. Shores

ISBN: 978-1-63381-330-4

This is a work of fiction. Names, characters, places, and incidents either
are the product of the author's imagination or are used fictitiously, and
any resemblance to actual persons, living or dead, is coincidental.

Designed and produced by:
Maine Authors Publishing
12 High Street, Thomaston, Maine
www.maineauthorspublishing.com

Printed in the United States of America

In memory of Remy, for his loyal companionship,
his reserved demeanor, and his unconditional love.

CHAPTER ONE

April 1797
Franklin, Maine

George Butler felt the ship shudder beneath his feet as it slowly eased against the wooden pilings. Several men scurried over the railings onto the deck below, lines of heavy rope trailing behind them. He watched as they worked to tie the lines and secure the vessel. From across the ship's deck, he saw his wife Nelly approaching him, their daughter Edna beside her clutching her hand.

"Is this home, Momma?" he heard the small child ask.

Nelly smiled at her and nodded. "Yes, this is home." She could barely contain her excitement. Moving back home had consumed Nelly ever since she had learned she was with child.

"Papa! Papa!" Edna shouted. "This is home!" The little girl's excitement mirrored her mother's.

George smiled at her, trying to shake off the feelings of foreboding that were rippling through him. "Yes, it is." He bent to scoop her up in his arms. As he buried his face in her soft blond curls, he whispered, "And may God watch over us."

Nelly had heard him. He wasn't exactly sure he had tried to keep his voice quiet. Maybe he wanted her to overhear him. Well, she certainly had, for now she turned on him in full fury. He felt her words before he heard them.

"George, you have done nothing but brood ever since this ship left Bangor. Please do not ruin this for me." She laid a hand on her bulging stomach. "We have come home. Home to have our son," she said, pointing toward the shoreline, "right here in this town, on that point, like your father did before you. What's done is done and in the past." She leaned in close to him. "We are here, and you will be happy with this decision, for my sake."

1

He didn't utter a word. His mind raced with the thoughts of the things he knew that Nelly did not. His stoic silence only angered her more.

She huffed and reached over to set Edna's bonnet on her head. She pulled the child from his arms and set the little girl on her feet, then grabbed for one of her hands and started across the deck. Edna stumbled a few times before gaining her equilibrium and righting herself as she followed her mother. Nelly headed straight for the gangplank that had been lowered. She could see her parents waiting for them on the dock.

"Nelly! Nelly!" Her mother Joanna was shouting and waving. "Look, David! That must be Edna! Over here! Over here!" she cried.

Nelly's father, David Hooper, had seen the exchange between George and his wife. Although he could not hear their words, he could read the body language between his daughter and son-in-law. The fact that George remained steadfast on the ship and did not follow Nelly down the gangplank spoke volumes to him. Something was not right.

"Odd that he stands there still, isn't it?" a voice spoke from behind David. He turned to see George's father Moses standing there. The Butlers had just arrived, and George's mother Sarah had joined Joanna, along with a few other women, in flocking around Nelly and Edna.

"Yes, I was just thinking that myself. Did you see the exchange of words between them?" David asked.

"No, we were just arriving," Moses replied. "What did they say?"

"I could not hear the words exactly, but I'm pretty sure she gave him a good dressing down."

They both chuckled as they walked toward the group of women. George was making his way toward them, instructing a crew member on the items of luggage and packing crates that would need to be off-loaded before the ship's return to Bangor in the morning.

"Father!" George exclaimed as he identified Moses in the crowd. George embraced his father, pounding him on the back. He greeted David with a hearty handshake.

"Son, it is so good to see you. Everyone is healthy, I trust? The journey not too hard on Nelly?"

"No, not at all. The Penobscot was clear of ice and rushing rapidly, so we made excellent time to Bucksport before turning east for home. Fair winds and fine travel, as they say!"

"Excellent." Moses seemed pleased with this. "And that little one there must be Edna."

"Yes, come, I shall introduce you both." They joined the women and other family members who had all gathered around Nelly and Edna. George lifted the little girl into his arms.

"Edna, these are your grandfathers. This is Grandfather Butler, and this man here is your Grandfather Hooper." The men smiled as they were introduced. "Now say hello," George instructed Edna.

Edna dipped her head shyly into George's neck, peering out at the two men sheepishly around the edge of her bonnet. Everyone laughed. David reached out and touched her small hand.

"'Tis fine, child, you will have plenty of time to get to know us. We are all together now."

The many family members gathered around cheered, and there were more embraces and well-wishes. The women all cooed over Nelly's pregnancy. There were several who were certain it was a boy and several others who were certain it was a girl. In the flurry of family love and activity, George could feel himself relax. His mood began to lift. Maybe everything was going to be all right after all.

+———+

Farther down the bay, Lydia Blaisdell sat at the water's edge. The granite rock she leaned against was protruding into her back, but she hardly noticed. She had watched the packet ship from Bangor glide into the bay. She knew he was on that ship. No one needed to tell her. She had sensed his presence. As the ship had sailed past, she had hidden behind the rock. Peering over it, she had tried to get a glimpse of whoever was aboard. She couldn't identify anyone specifically, but it didn't matter. She knew he was there.

Earlier that morning, for no particular reason, she had been drawn to the shoreline by a force she could not understand. She had spent the morning picking among the stones and beach debris left over from winter. Then she had seen the ship, and she had known.

She felt the peace of the past two years melt away, the odd feelings rushing in again. Her hands began to tremble. She tried to make them stop, fearful that the shaking would bring on another one of those fits that so scared her mother. She was older now, nearly twelve. Her mother had said she would outgrow the fits. She hoped that would be the case, because they left her weak and exhausted.

From her vantage point across the bay, she could not make him out specifically. She could only see the movement of people as they clustered on the docks, the men moving up and down the gangplanks, and the usual dock activity. She watched as the sails were gathered in and lowered, leaving the mast bare against the spring sky. She wondered if George were here on business. How long would he stay? Would she have an opportunity to see him?

"He is here."

The sound of the voice startled her so that she almost jumped up. It was supernatural and vibrated through her body. She looked all around her, but she was alone on the beach. No one had spoken. Lydia thought for a moment that she might have just imagined the voice, but in her heart, she knew. It was all starting again. She tossed the stone into the water, watching the ripples reach out in ever-widening circles. She wanted to escape the voice but knew that it would follow her as it had in the past. She stood with her fists clenched at her sides and screamed out at the water, "I know!" Then she sank back onto the rocks, sobbing. "I know. I know." Inside, Lydia was torn with emotions.

"And she is with him."

Lydia slowly raised her head as the tears streamed down her cheeks. She could see the dock begin to clear of people as the group moved away toward the center of town.

"She is with him," the voice repeated more forcefully.

Lydia slumped to the rocks and let out a scream that reverberated around the bay like the ripples around a stone.

CHAPTER TWO

Two Years Earlier
Spring 1795

As his boat cleared the narrows and entered the bay, George saw the pines standing tall on Butler's Point. George could see his parents' house on the slight rise just before the terrain dropped off to the rocks and beach below. His parents, Moses and Sarah Butler, had come to Franklin in 1766, five years before George's birth. They had been the very first family to settle in this area. His mother had spoken often about the difficulties of traveling from their home in South Berwick and taking care of four young children in the wilderness. They had settled on the neck of land that jutted out between Egypt and Taunton Bays. Everyone called it Butler's Point. It was good land. Moses was a farmer. Over the past thirty years, he had cleared the pines, opened up the natural meadows, and made a nice little home for his family. The town of Franklin had grown up around them, and on the other side of Taunton Bay was the town of Sullivan. There were many people settled here now. Fishing and shipping were the prime means of commerce in the area.

George had never been interested in farming. Despite his older brothers all taking up land in the area, George had taken to the sea early. He loved the sea. Whereas his brothers saw it as just the backdrop of their home, George saw it as a gateway to worlds unknown. To adventures waiting to happen. He had first set sail at the age of sixteen onboard a ship bound for Barbados. He had learned things the hard way. After taking a few knocks, he finally got a small sloop of his own. He was now Captain George Butler, master of his crew of five sailors. He was returning home after his own first successful run to the West Indies.

He hadn't seen his parents since last fall, choosing instead to winter over in the tropics rather than attempt to sail home during the winter months. He was eager to get caught up on the news of the family. His sister Mercy had been expecting another child when he had left. He wondered now if it was another son for her and her husband. They had six already!

But foremost in his mind was Nelly Hooper. Last fall, they had struck up a friendship—well, he would like to think it was more than just a friendship. She was a good woman from a fine family. Her father, David Hooper, had served in the war with his father. Nelly, he was hoping, hadn't taken a fancy to anyone else over the winter.

"Well, hello there, Captain Butler!" a voice shouted out to George as he stepped onto dry land for the first time in weeks. It was Abner Blaisdell, another Revolutionary War solider who had brought his family here from the town of York. He was a man of little consequence. George wasn't exactly sure what Abner did to sustain his family, although he mostly mended fishing nets. He wasn't as prominent as George's father in town affairs, that was for certain. His family kept mostly to themselves. They were a strange lot, devoutly religious, but some said that was to hide things they didn't want others to see about them.

"And what is the word from the outside?" Abner asked him.

"The usual. Politicians are lying. Business is bad, and the religious folk think we are all going to hell in a handbasket!" he joked.

Abner laughed heartily. "I suppose things never change, do they? Did you happen near York, by any chance, on your way up?"

"No, I'm afraid I did not. Passed right on by. I put in at Cape Elizabeth instead. Why, are you looking for news?"

"Yes, my son had been in York a few weeks ago. Said there was an awful sickness going around. Many in my family were stricken. I was just looking for news of my parents. Aged as they are, you know, I worry about them."

"Completely understandable," George said. "I'm sure they are fine. Word would have been sent if things were really bad, no?"

"Yes, my brother especially would have gotten word to me somehow. Ah! I see that your trip to the Indies was profitable!" Abner said, pointing as George hefted his heavy satchel over his shoulder.

"This? Oh, mostly gifts for the family." Abner's comment made him uncomfortable. "You'll excuse me, Abner, but speaking of my family, I'm eager to get home."

"Of course, of course! By all means, do not allow me to prolong the separation any longer!" And with that, Abner bowed to George and turned away.

⊹————⊹

Lydia Blaisdell watched her father closely as he spoke with Captain Butler. Sitting high on the bank above them, her feet dangling over the edge of the downed birch log she sat on, she remained out of sight. Captain Butler was the handsomest man she had ever seen. He towered over her father. His browned skin, weathered just a bit by the sea air, was in sharp contrast to his shoulder-length golden hair. Whereas most of the men in town wore their hair either plaited or hidden under a powdered wig, Captain Butler left his loose under his tricornered hat.

She watched as he shifted the weight of his heavy satchel, his muscles rippling under the arms of his shirt. She had spent hours imagining herself as Mrs. George Butler. Everyone in town knew he was becoming a very successful mariner. She had heard her father speak of Captain Butler to her brother Paul several times, always with admiration. The young lady who landed him as a catch was certainly going to be the talk of the town. Lydia wanted nothing more than to have that be her! At only ten years old, she was more than ten years his junior. She didn't think she had much of a chance of wooing him away from the other girls more his age—unless she resorted to trickery. Now that was an evil thought! She chided herself for even considering such a thing. Her father warned her constantly on the perils of evil thoughts. She was drawn to Captain Butler in a way she could not quite put a finger on. She felt her hands begin to shake as she watched him. Surely this was a divine message to her.

The thought had just entered her mind when she noticed her father walking away from Captain Butler. They parted and headed in opposite directions. She watched the captain as he headed west, knowing full well he was headed for Butler's Point to see his family. She jumped down from her log, hiked up her skirts, and dashed into the trees. Her plan was formulating in her head as she ran. She followed the old footpath that paralleled the road for a short distance. This trail would come out on the main road just where Captain Butler would turn off to reach his parents' house. If she could just run fast enough, she could get ahead of him and be there waiting.

Breathless and exhausted, she broke through the trees right at the fork in the road. She looked both ways quickly but didn't see anyone. She sat down on the side of the road and loosened her boot just a bit. She spit in her hands and dabbed some of it on her cheeks, then picked up a handful of dirt. Closing her eyes tightly, she tossed the dust toward her face. She ran her fingers down her cheeks hoping to give the illusion that she had been crying. She pulled her bonnet askew a tad, and her tableau was complete. She waited. It wasn't long before she saw the tall, strong figure of Captain Butler approaching from the direction of town. "Oh, the web we weave when first we practice to deceive," she whispered to herself under her breath.

＋———＋

Head down, striding forward, George had one thing on his mind—home. He could hardly wait to see his mother. Of course, a hot meal and a good soaking bath wouldn't be bad, either. He wanted to talk to his father about the success of his trip. He hadn't been completely honest with Abner Blaisdell on the contents of his satchel. It had been a fruitful trip, and he wanted his father's advice on what to do with his newly acquired wealth. With thoughts of his future filling his mind, he almost missed the sounds of crying. He lifted his head, and that's when he saw her—a young girl sitting in the dust on the side of the road cradling her left foot.

"Miss, are you all right?" He took the last few steps toward her. Setting the satchel down, he placed his hand on her shoulder.

"Oh! I seemed to have twisted my ankle. It's terribly painful!" Lydia cried. She looked up into the face of Captain Butler and tried to appear stricken and weak.

"I see that. Captain Butler at your service, ma'am."

Lydia felt her heart leap in her chest, and she thought she was going to faint. Oh, if only she could! That would certainly add to the drama and couldn't do anything but help her cause.

"Miss Lydia Blaisdell, sir. I thank you so much for your kind attention." She fluttered her eyelashes a bit before demurely glancing away.

"Blaisdell, you say? Are you relations to Abner Blaisdell, by any chance?" George asked her.

"Why, yes, sir. He is my father."

"Ah, I was just speaking with him in town," George said. "Well, we must get you up and out of this dust. You will certainly ruin that lovely dress you have on. Can you stand?"

"Oh, I think not, sir!" Lydia replied. "It is much too painful."

George thought for a moment. His satchel was much too heavy for him to attempt carrying them both. He glanced around. They were still a good half mile from his parents' house, but it was also about the same distance back to town. Off the road a few paces, he noticed a large boulder.

"Miss Lydia, would you excuse me for a moment?" He stepped into the woods and placed his satchel behind the boulder. Should be safe enough here, he thought. I'll only be gone for an hour or so.

Coming back onto the road, he looked down at the small girl sitting in the dirt. She was but a waif of a thing.

"All right, then. I just happened to see your father in town not more than quarter of an hour ago. I believe if I carry you back straight away, we should be able to locate him. Here, let me help you up." He bent down to scoop her up.

"Back to town?" Lydia exclaimed. This wasn't at all part of her plan. She was hoping, this close to his parents' house, he would take her there to be mended by his mother. This would give her the opportunity to meet his family and plant the seeds of her plan with them as well.

"Why, yes, of course, back to town. Your father must surely still be there. If we hurry, we can catch him." He lifted her up and steadied her. "Can you walk at all?"

With her indignation in full bloom, she almost forgot that she was supposed to be injured. She quickly lifted her right foot and held it aloft. "Oh, the pain!" she exclaimed.

George eyed her suspiciously for the first time. "Was it not your left foot you were cradling when I first approached you?" He raised an eyebrow as he asked the question.

Lydia quickly put her right foot down and lifted her left. Crumbling a little as she spoke, she muttered, "Oh, I do believe I've injured them both!"

George quickly grabbed her before she could fall into the dust again. "I see," he said. "I believe you certainly think you have!" He scooped her up, placing one arm under her knees and the other around her shoulders. "Come along, Miss Lydia, let us go find your father."

Luckily for George, Abner Blaisdell was standing outside of the Wayside Inn with his son-in-law Atherton Oakes. "See, Miss Lydia, there is your father right there."

Lydia hadn't looked up from her folded hands during the whole embarrassing walk back to town. This was not going as she had planned, and she was sulking and infuriated.

"Abner! Look what I found on my way home. I believe this young lady belongs to you." George stood in front of Abner, hoping he would take Lydia off his hands.

"Lydia! What on earth? I thought you were with your sister!" Abner exclaimed. He relieved George of his burden, cradling Lydia and looking into her face. "What has happened, my dear?"

Lydia refused to answer. Her scowl grew deeper. She clenched her fists in anger. She could feel a power inside of her growing.

"I found her on the side of the road on my way to my parents' house," George explained. "Said she had twisted her ankle. Although I'm not really sure if she knows which one she injured." He winked at Atherton and smiled.

"On the way to your parents' house?" Atherton said. "Lydia, what were you doing way out there? You were supposed to be with Hannah getting cloth."

"That's right, she was!" Everyone turned to see Lydia's sister Hannah approaching the group. "The little creature vanished not long after you left us, Papa. I've been looking for her for close to thirty minutes."

Lydia rolled her eyes. This was going from bad to worse. Hannah and Atherton had just gotten married last week. Hannah being a married woman made Lydia feel more infantile!

Lydia wiggled uncomfortably in her father's arms.

"Well, I shall leave you in the safety of your father's family, Miss Lydia. Good day!" George bowed graciously, if not a little over dramatically, at Lydia and turned to leave.

Lydia watched his back as he walked away, seething. She couldn't believe her plan had turned out this way. "Oh, for goodness sake, Papa!" she said. "Put me down!"

Her father set her on her feet, and she marched off in the direction of their own home, stomping out her frustrations with each step. Abner, Hannah, and Atherton exchanged glances of amusement.

"I do believe our little sister has designs on the captain," Hannah said.

"Unfortunately, I think you are right," Abner mumbled.

CHAPTER THREE

Later that afternoon

"So do you feel this West Indies route will continue to be profitable?" Moses Butler asked his son as he sat behind his desk. George and his father had been locked in the older man's study for over an hour, the stacks of coins George had brought home laid out on the desk between them.

"Obviously, it can be," George replied. "There is huge demand in Boston and in Philadelphia for products from the Indies. Not just rum, although that is most of it."

Moses lowered his lids as he eyed his son. "I'm not keen on making a living off of the vices of other men," he said. "We have always been honorable men. Evil begets evil, George."

"I understand, Father, but we've also never been very pious. If there is money to be made, I intend to make it. Farming does not interest me. I can make more in one trip to the Indies than a farm can earn in several seasons. I would like to continue this course for a while."

Moses tapped his fingers on the desk. There were certainly a lot of coins there.

"How long do you intend to continue this sowing of your oats? Do you not wish to settle down? Find a wife, start a family? You certainly cannot expect a wife to follow you around the world on a ship."

George knew this was ultimately how all the conversations with his father ended. George was the baby of the family. All of his siblings were married and had started families of their own. They had blessed his parents with numerous grandchildren. All of them were clustered there on Butler's Point. He knew what his father wanted. George needed to take his place in the family structure and follow suit. This is what his father had envisioned for his children when he chose this neck of land.

"Well, I was thinking about that," George said.

Moses sat up a little straighter. His eyes brightened, and he leaned forward. "You were?"

"Yes. I have spent the winter thinking about a wife. I wouldn't mind a wife. Wouldn't mind having children. I thought if I could find someone suitable, someone who wouldn't mind my being gone, that I could possibly have the best of both worlds."

Moses slumped back in his chair. "My son, it is very unlikely that you will find a good woman who will let you leave her. They are interesting creatures. Happiest when they are telling a man what to do!" He sighed. "That's impossible to do when your husband is on a ship and you are on land."

George laughed. He had to admit his father was right. His mother was always nagging his father about this and that. His father mostly just took it and smiled.

"They care, therefore they nag. Am I right?" Moses said when he saw George's amusement.

"Yes, that would seem to be the case." George shifted in his chair. "Last fall, I spent some time with a lady I became fond of. She's from around here. Said she wouldn't mind staying close to home. Her family is here and all."

"A local girl? Is it anyone we know?" Moses asked.

"I think you are pretty familiar with the family." George smiled. "I am considering Nelly Hooper." He watched as his father smiled broadly.

"David Hooper's daughter?" He said. "Wonderful! I will be anxious to hear how this unfolds." Moses sat a little straighter in his chair. His eyes bright with enthusiasm.

George smiled, he knew this news would please his father immensely. Now he just had to speak to Nelly himself.

+ —————— +

Nelly sat in front of the window, darning a stocking. The spring sunlight was streaming through the window, making her task that much easier. She hummed a hymn to herself as she worked. She really didn't mind doing needlework—anything to help make things easier on her mother. Poor Joanna Hooper was forty and pregnant with her ninth child. As the oldest daughter, Nelly, along with her sister Sally, was expected to help their mother with all of the younger children.

At twenty-one, Nelly should have been having children of her own. Most of the girls her age had at least two or three by now. But Nelly was choosy when it came to picking a husband. She wanted a man who was already pretty confident in himself. She wanted someone she could spend hours talking to. Not like her parents, who sat inches from each other in matching chairs but rarely spoke. She wanted a husband who could fill the void of long, cold winter nights with good conversation. Someone like—well, like Captain George Butler.

Nelly had met Captain Butler the previous fall at a barn raising. George's father was an old friend of her father's, as they had fought together during the Revolution. Since the Butlers lived in Franklin and her family lived in Sullivan, they had never gotten to know each other very well—that is, until the barn raising.

Nelly had spent the day with the other women cooking over the open fires, keeping the smaller children out of the way and generally picking up on all of the gossip. She had seen George arrive with his father and brothers. He stood well over six feet tall. His shoulder-length blond hair was tied back with a leather strap, but it was still loose and wild. He was clearly used to hard work and not the least bit afraid of heights. He scurried to the top of the barn rafters easily and stayed there most of the day. He held fast to the beams with his muscular thighs, as she imagined he did aboard his ship as well.

When it came time for the noon meal, she handed out biscuits to the men. He smiled at her when he approached. She went to place a biscuit on his plate and her hand brushed his. A jolt of energy passed through her body with such force that she shook. She looked up, and their eyes locked. He had felt it, too. What was that? Neither of them moved until someone farther down the line cleared their throat and shouted, "Let's keep it moving, Butler!" There were laughs and guffaws. Nelly felt her face turn red. George looked mortified. He moved on without saying a word.

The other girls had noticed, too. Especially her sister Sally. "Did you see the way he looked at you?" she whispered, coming up beside Nelly.

"Shhh, stop it," Nelly shot back. "Someone will hear you."

"Hear me?" Sally said. "I think everyone here is talking about you and Captain Butler! It was pretty obvious there was something going on there."

Nelly couldn't help but agree. What was that jolt? It was otherworldly. Not anything that she had ever felt before. Was this what love felt like? It couldn't be—she didn't even know the man. Love was a feeling that was built over time, not something that happened instantly. But what could explain that feeling? It had rattled her to her very bones, and she knew that he had had the same feeling. The men had resumed their work, but she kept a closer eye on Captain Butler now. He was keeping a closer eye on her as well. Their eyes frequently met from across the way. She would always blush and look away first.

Once the work was wrapped up, everyone prepared for dancing. Nelly saw Captain Butler walking straight toward her. She felt her palms get sweaty, and she looked around frantically for something to pick up, anything to keep her hands busy. She settled on a dishrag that had been draped over a few dried-out goldenrod stalks.

"Miss Hooper, is it?" he asked with the most distinctive voice she had ever heard.

"Yes, but by all means, call me Nelly," she replied, giving him a slight curtsey.

"Nelly? I was told your name was Eleanor," he said with a slightly puzzled look on his face.

"Oh, it is! But my family all calls me Nelly. I don't mind if you do as well." She blushed.

"Why, thank you. I'm George. George Butler."

"I know." She smiled. "Captain George Butler."

"Yes." He smiled in return. "Care to walk with me for a while?"

They walked around and around the Widow Cook's field so many times they wore a path. Respectfully, Captain Butler always kept her within sight of her parents and the other townsfolk. He was easy to talk to. It seemed like they had known each other for many years. She told him about her family. How close she was to her sister Sally. She was blessed to have a close-knit family. He talked of his brothers and their wives, and the many nieces and nephews he had. She told him she loved big families and hoped to have one of her own someday. She asked him about his ship and the places he had been. After he told her of his adventures, she admitted that she was scared to death of the water and would always be happiest with her feet firmly planted on the ground. That made him laugh.

The evening had been perfect except for one small incident. A young girl had fallen out of a tree. It had happened near where Nelly and George were walking. They had seen the commotion and rushed to the scene. The young girl did not appear to be seriously hurt, but she was most certainly getting plenty of attention. Her parents arrived shortly and hastened her away. Someone had said it was little Lydia Blaisdell.

Two days after the barn raising, George had appeared at her home and asked her mother politely from the porch if Nelly would be allowed to sit outside with him for a while. With a knowing smile, her mother had agreed. He had explained that he was leaving soon. Heading to Boston and then on to the West Indies. He wouldn't be back until spring he said, but would it be okay to call again? She had agreed and then spent all winter thinking about him.

And now spring had arrived. More ships would be coming into town—how soon before George was on one of them? Her thoughts were interrupted by her sister Sally rushing through the front door.

"Nelly!" she shrieked. "Captain Butler is back!"

Nelly jumped up quickly, her sewing basket spilling to the floor. "Are you sure?" she asked Sally.

"Absolutely sure! Several in town are saying they saw his ship arrive yesterday morning. And everyone is talking about Lydia Blaisdell!"

Nelly was lost in her thoughts of what to do first when she realized Sally was babbling on about someone other than Captain Butler.

"I'm sorry…everyone is talking about whom?"

"Lydia Blaisdell! Are you not listening to me at all?" Sally sounded frustrated. She bent to help Nelly pick up the sewing basket and its contents before continuing on. "Apparently, Captain Butler was seen with her in front of the Wayside Inn. Mary Card saw the whole thing!"

Nelly rolled her eyes and sat down in her chair again. "Mary Card is the world's biggest gossip, Sally. I wouldn't believe a word she had to say."

"Well, believe it or not, it's your choice, but everyone says that little vixen Lydia is trying to snatch Captain Butler up for herself!"

Nelly burst out laughing. "Are you completely serious? She's only a child. I hardly think the captain would be much interested in a child bride." Nelly's mind returned to her earlier memory of Lydia lying on the ground under the tree that she and Captain Butler had walked under only moments before. How old was that girl?

"Well, according to what everyone is saying, the dear captain carried her up to the steps of the inn, handed her to her father, and winked at Atherton Oakes. After a short discussion, he left, and Lydia stood and walked away. Why would a man carry a lady, even a young one, to the presence of her father if she was perfectly capable of walking? Unless it was symbolic of some deeper meaning."

"Oh, Sally, I truly think you are touched in the head!" Nelly said. "She's just a child!"

Nelly thought on this for a while. Captain Butler certainly wasn't in a hurry to marry; everyone knew that. It was possible he was considering Lydia, maybe not soon, but in the future. But no, he had specifically come to Nelly's home to ask to call on her again when he returned. He wouldn't have done that if he was seriously considering little Lydia as a potential bride. Or would he?

"Nelly, are you listening to me?" Sally asked.

"Um, what?" Nelly replied.

"I said that Mary made a convincing argument when she pointed out that Captain Butler sought out Lydia Blaisdell rather than you on his first day back in town."

Well, that point was undeniable—he had seen Lydia first. Nelly slumped down in her chair.

CHAPTER FOUR

The following day

After a good night's rest and a long-overdue bath, George felt he was ready to present himself to Nelly Hooper. The woman had consumed his thoughts the entire winter. He was eager to talk with her again and see if he still felt the same way as he had last fall—and to see if she felt the same way about him. If everything was still as he remembered, he would waste no time in speaking to her father. He wasn't the type to dally over things. If he was seriously going to court Nelly Hooper, he wanted her father's full permission.

As he put on his waistcoat, he tucked the small comb he had purchased for her into his pocket. It was a dainty, beautiful comb made from a carved conch shell. He had wrapped it in a piece of muslin to keep it safe on the journey home. He hoped she would like it. He hoped, too, that she wouldn't think him too forward for presenting her with such an expensive gift.

"Heading out?" his mother asked as he walked through the small kitchen. She was standing before the hearth stirring the enormous black kettle that hung over the fire, doing her best to keep her skirts out of the flames.

"Yes," he replied, feeling a little sheepish.

"Heading to the Hoopers', no doubt." She straightened up and placed the large ladle on the iron hook on the side of the hearth. "Your father told me last night of your intentions." She smiled. "The Hoopers are good people, George. I'll admit I don't know much about their oldest daughter, but they are salt-of-the-earth types. No flibber-tigibbets among them."

"Flibbertigibbets?" George laughed. "No, they certainly aren't that!" He kissed his mother on the top of the head as he turned for the door.

The half-mile walk into town went by quickly, as his mind was on other things. Nelly Hooper, mostly. However, his next voyage was competing for attention as well. He had to form a crew. Reuben Gray would certainly be back aboard as his first mate. Some of the others he couldn't be as sure about. He'd have to get the word out that he was looking for new crew.

At the center of town, he passed by the large white church, the heart and soul of the community. Standing just outside the door was the Reverend Crawford. The reverend was from down the coast a ways, from Warren specifically. It seemed like the town was always getting new preachers. No one seemed to stay long. Crawford had been here for several years which was almost a record.

"Good day, Reverend," George hollered out, raising his hand in greeting.

"Oh, Captain Butler! I was just thinking of you," he replied and hurriedly stepped down the stairs, coming toward George with earnest. "How good it is to see you safely back in port, dear man!"

"Why, thank you." George bowed with respect to the elderly clergyman.

"And I trust God kept you well over the winter?" Reverend Crawford eyed George's tanned face.

"Ah yes, there is nothing like a winter full of sunshine rather than snow. I hear you folks were socked in pretty bad this past season."

"Yes, Old Man Winter surely showed his teeth! Will you be joining us for services this Sunday?"

"Most assuredly!" George replied. His mother had read the Bible to him as a child, and they had always attended the services when a preacher was in town. But no one would call the Butlers a devout family. One particular denomination was as good as another, Moses had always said. The fire-and-brimstone feelings of the past few years had not convinced his father of anything different. George's own beliefs were pretty much in line with his father's. If there was an afterlife, no one had ever come back to talk about it. So he wasn't sure God cared too much which sect you aligned yourself with. He believed in living a good life, and he hoped that would be enough. But if he were going to settle down, to take a wife, he would need to attend church services to become a respected man in the community. That much he knew. The church was the epicenter of the social network for the surrounding towns.

"Good, good," the older man replied. "I'll look forward to seeing you." He patted George on the arm as he turned to walk away.

George continued through town, speaking to this one and that one. It seemed that everyone knew he was home, a testament to the fact that word traveled fast in the town. He walked on through town and made his way to the eastern side of the bay. The road here passed land that was more open and barren than on the western side, where he lived among the tall pines.

As he approached the Hoopers' white clapboard home, he saw Nelly. She was on the side of the house near the well. The sleeves of her dress were rolled up, and she was leaning down into the well, hand over hand, pulling a bucket of water up from the cool depths. George watched her for a moment. She was beautiful. Certainly not a delicate flower by any means. A good strong woman, but still feminine. He liked that about her. She could tackle the job of keeping house without wilting away.

As Nelly lifted her head out of the well, it took a moment for her eyes to adjust from the darkness of the well to the bright light of the yard. Setting her bucket down, she saw George standing there.

"Captain Butler!" she exclaimed. She quickly rolled her sleeves down and tried to stuff the loose strands of hair back under her cap. "I did not know you were here. How long have you been standing there?"

"Uh...not long," George stammered. He was embarrassed that he had been caught watching her and even more embarrassed by the physical reaction she had caused within him. "Please, call me George." He turned to look at her. "When I saw you in the side yard, I came to speak with you...but I...I hope you will forgive me for not letting you know of my arrival."

"No, no, it is fine," Nelly tried to reassure him, but her heart was pounding in her chest. He was so handsome. It took her breath away just to look at him. She felt her palms starting to sweat.

"Please, follow me. I should be a better hostess!" she said, quickly wiping her hands on her skirt as she turned, smiling at him.

He followed her back around to the front of the house and inside. Nelly's mother, Joanna, was just making her way down the stairs. She looked pleased to see George.

"Please, Captain Butler, let me offer you a seat in the parlor." She smiled. "Nelly, go make a pot of tea." She shooed her toward the kitchen and walked into the parlor. George followed the older woman and took the seat she offered.

"I understand you had a successful voyage, Captain," she said.

"Yes, it was very profitable. It didn't take long for word to get through town, now did it?"

Joanna laughed. "No, the women do a great job of communicating! We heard last night that you were home. Will you be heading back out to sea again soon?"

"My plans are to be in town for a few weeks and let my crew rest. I'm thinking some shorter runs between here and Bagaduce or York. Maybe a run to Boston. I've set my first mate looking for some cargo between here and Machias."

Nelly entered with the tea and set about settling the cups. George smiled up at her. She returned the smile, and he felt that same jolt he had felt last fall. Things had not changed!

Nelly's mother felt the energy between the two and knew that she should leave them to themselves. "Well, I shall let you two get reacquainted. It has been a long winter!"

The younger couple smiled awkwardly at each other. It was obvious that neither one really noticed if Joanna was there or not, so she stepped out without another word.

+———+

George and Nelly talked for hours. The tea was soon forgotten and cold. The shadows shifted around the room as the time passed. They were completely unaware of its passage.

Nelly absolutely loved the conch shell comb he presented her with. "I was hoping you wouldn't think me too forward for getting you a gift," he said.

"Oh, it's beautiful! I don't think even my father would be concerned about it. It is lovely!" She smiled. "I thought of you all winter myself." She got up and reached into her sewing basket. From the bottom, she pulled out a stark white handkerchief. In the corner, the initials *GB* were embroidered in navy blue thread. She handed it to him.

"It is lovely, Nelly. Did you do the work yourself?" He rubbed his thumb over the stitches.

"Yes, I did."

George reached for her hands. "Nelly," he said as he held them in his own, "I would like very much for permission to court you. Would you mind if I asked your father?"

Nelly felt her heart leap inside her chest. She looked up into his eyes. They were just as she had remembered them. Blue as the seas he sailed on and deep as the oceans as well. She pulled her hands back slightly.

"May I ask one question? I ask that you give me an honest answer."

George nodded.

"Are you planning on courting anyone else during the few weeks you will be home?"

George was stunned by this question. Anyone else? How could there be anyone else? This woman had consumed his thoughts day and night for several months!

"Now you have me at a disadvantage, Miss Hooper." He stood and stepped to the window. "Have I led you to believe that I am a cad? That my intentions are anything but honorable?"

This hurt him. She could see it. Nelly felt bad for even mentioning it. Curse the women in town and their idle gossip!

"I'm sorry, George," she said, standing and approaching him. "It's just that…well, there was talk from town. I fell victim to it. My apologies."

"Talk? What kind of talk?"

With a heavy sigh, she told him of Mary's tale. Of his conversations with Abner Blaisdell. Of being seen with Lydia. Of her fears that he was considering a child bride.

He began to laugh as he reached for her hands. Holding both of them in his, he stared down at her.

"Miss Nelly Hooper, I can most passionately assure you that I am not the least bit interested in Lydia Blaisdell. She's a sweet child, but that is all she is, a child. My days have been filled with thoughts of you since we parted last fall. During the nights, you walk among my dreams. I have no time nor interest in considering anyone else. Does that answer your question?"

She nodded.

He cupped her face with his weathered hands. "Let's go find your father."

CHAPTER FIVE

On Sunday, George and Nelly sat next to each other in the same pew—the equivalent of a public announcement that they were officially courting. From her seat farther back, Lydia could see them each time they bent their heads to whisper something to each other. Whatever Reverend Crawford was extolling on today, Lydia was not following it. She could not believe this was happening. Anger filled her soul. She felt consumed by it. She felt it surging through her veins with each beat of her heart. She could hear it in her ears. It was palpable. How could this be happening and in church, no less? Had she not received a message that she was to be the wife of George Butler? She felt something every time she saw him. Wasn't that a message from God?

She shifted on the hard pew, trying to escape the anger boiling inside of her. No, this was all wrong, this couldn't be happening this way. She clenched her fists in her lap, tightening every muscle in her arms until she began to shake. This aroused her mother, who glanced down at her, scowling. She shook her head silently as if to warn Lydia to be still. But the anger was so strong she didn't know how she could ever be still again.

After services, many of the young ladies gathered around Nelly. George begged off and said he would meet her later. He stopped and spoke with her parents. He was just turning to leave when he saw Lydia Blaisdell staring at him. There was no way to avoid her, as she was between him and the door.

"Good day, Miss Blaisdell," he said as he tried to walk by her.

"Good day, Captain Butler." She smiled and curtsied.

"I trust that your ankle is better."

"Yes, much. Thank you again for your kind assistance."

"Well, a gentleman could never leave a lady in distress!" He turned slightly, indicating that he wished to pass by her and head for the door. She stood stock-still.

"How long will you be in town, Captain Butler?"

He shifted his weight onto the balls of his feet, anxious to get beyond her. "Oh, a few weeks at least." He glanced back to see if Nelly was aware he had been stopped by Lydia.

"Will you be seeing much of Miss Hooper during your stay, or have you other plans?" She looked at him with her large brown eyes.

He felt annoyed at her assertiveness. "I intend to, yes." He stared back at her. What an impertinent little child! She did not avert her eyes but instead continued staring at him with a face of stone.

"Lydia, do come along and leave the good captain be." Her mother spoke from behind her, taking her by the hand and dragging her away. George stood rooted in his spot as Lydia left with her family. She refused to break eye contact with him until she finally could not crane her neck backward any farther and was forced to move on.

"I don't believe I've ever seen a young girl so lovelorn as that one!" Reverend Crawford said with a touch of gaiety in his voice.

George turned and looked at him. "Lovelorn? Do you think so?" George replied.

"Oh yes, Captain Butler! That little lady there has claimed you in her heart." He chuckled.

George watched Lydia until he could no longer see her. He hoped that's all this was, a childish infatuation. But something in the way Lydia had spoken to him made him sense danger—as if at that moment, she had changed from a little girl lost in a child's fantasy to an adversary.

＋———＋

George and Nelly spent as much time together as they could. Most of their time together was spent at the home of her parents. He wanted nothing to indicate to David and Joanna Hooper that he was anything less than honorable when it came to their daughter. On occasion, they did get to spend time alone. One sunny day, George took Nelly for a boat ride in his small rowboat. She brought a basket of bread and meat, and they found a flat rock along the shore. They sat eating and talking, enjoying the warmth of the sunlight.

George knew he had to get back to sea. If he didn't keep his crew, they would sign with someone else. He didn't know how to tell Nelly that he had to go. But before he could talk to her about that, he had other more important details on his mind.

"Nelly?"

"Yes?" she said, not opening her eyes. She was stretched out beside him on the rock.

"I have to go back to sea soon."

"I know." She didn't move and spoke so matter-of-factly that it startled him.

"Well…" His voice trailed off.

She sat up and looked at him. "Well, what?" she asked softly.

"I would…" He gulped down the words and then started again. "I would like it very much if you would consent to be my wife." He let out a long sigh. It had been harder than he thought to say it out loud. In his heart, he wanted nothing more—he knew she was the woman he wanted to spend the rest of his life with. But actually putting the feeling into words had been the tricky part.

Nelly sat looking at him for several seconds. Then she leaned forward and kissed him ever so gently on the lips. He felt the warmth of her breath. That jolt of excitement he always felt when she was near passed through him.

"Captain Butler," she whispered, "I would be honored."

He drew her into his arms and held her close. The water lapped on the rocks below them, the seagulls screeched overhead, and a light breeze whispered through the pines. It seemed as if all of nature was announcing their news to world.

✦———✦

George was nervous about asking for the blessing of Nelly's father, but David gave it gladly. He liked George. He thought very highly of him and felt he would be a good provider for his daughter. Still, he played the stern father when George approached him. They sat in the parlor, and David let George stammer on about his devotion to Nelly and how he wished to care for her. David asked him lots of questions about his shipping business and how often he expected to be at sea. He reiterated that he wasn't comfortable with his daughter being left behind while her husband traveled the world. George assured him that his goal was to devote more of his business to shorter runs, which would mean being gone a few days at a time rather than months.

After a time, David stood, clasped George by the hand, and placed another on the young man's shoulder. "You have my blessing, George. Now go and share the news with Nelly. I'm sure she's eager to know." David had never seen a young man jump up from a chair so quickly.

"Thank you, Mr. Hooper, thank you!"

CHAPTER SIX

May 1795

Moses Butler invited the whole Hooper family up to his place on Butler's Point for a large dinner. Here the news of the intended marriage of George and Nelly would be shared with the rest of the family. Most of George's siblings were in attendance. George's mother, Sarah, was in her glory with the twenty or so grandchildren all flocking around her. She was truly blessed to have all of them live in close proximity, if not right on, Butler's Point. Still, it was a great treat for the children to be with all of their cousins at once.

The Hoopers brought Nelly's sisters and brothers with them. Also with them was the newest addition to the family. Nelly's mother had given birth to little Eliza just a few weeks ago. She was wrapped in a swaddling blanket, and Joanna held her tightly as she sat in the wagon next to David. Eliza was a sickly little baby, and Joanna wasn't keen on this overnight stay with a newborn.

When the Hoopers arrived, they found tents of all shapes and sizes staked up on the large open meadow that fanned out between the house and the shoreline. There were dozens of children running here, there, and everywhere.

"Oh my!" Joanna exclaimed to David.

"There, there, Mother," he said as he patted her knee. "This is the blessing that awaits you as our first daughter prepares to marry. Soon our home, too, will be overrun by the pattering of little feet of grandchildren and the squealing of laughter!" He smiled at her.

Nelly and her sister Sally rolled their eyes at each other. "Father!" Nelly exclaimed. "Will you at least let me get married first?" she laughed.

"Aye, I will, Nelly. But the captain comes from a large family, and it won't be long before you will be adding to it!" he said with a wink.

They all dined outdoors on baked fish, fiddleheads, and asparagus.

In the evening, the large table was moved, and a fire was started in the open pit.

The young people all sat gathered around the fire, talking. Nelly's brother Hart was pushing dirt around with his boot and listening to the chatter.

"Did anyone else hear about Lydia Blaisdell?" he said, looking up.

"What about her?" George asked as his gut clenched. He just didn't like the way he felt whenever the subject of Lydia Blaisdell came up.

"Well, she nearly burned her house down."

"Oh, Hart," Nelly said, kicking him in the foot. "We really don't need to be talking about Lydia Blaisdell tonight, do we?"

George's sister Mercy was just walking back to the group after breaking up a fight among the cousins. "Are you talking about the fire out at the Blaisdell place?"

"Yes, Hart was just mentioning something about that," Sally said. "I hadn't heard anything."

George's brother Peter gave him a slug in the shoulder. "Little Lydia Blaisdell…madly in love with the captain is what I heard." There was a round of laughter.

"Hart, you said there was a fire?" George leaned in to hear all the details.

"Yes, it happened a few days ago. She was out in the yard hanging laundry with her mother. Her brother had just come back from town with the news of George and Nelly's intentions. As he and his mother stood talking, the sheets on the line burst into flames."

There was a collective gasp from several in the group who hadn't heard the story yet. George felt his stomach tighten into a knot.

"How do sheets just burst into flames?" Sally said.

Nelly rolled her eyes. "Clearly, they don't. Look, Lydia is a troubled child. She is known for trying to get attention."

"I'll agree that she has done things in the past for attention," Mercy interjected, "but wet sheets don't burn, Nelly."

There were several in the group who nodded their heads in agreement. Hart spoke up. "A few folks in town say it's the work of the devil.

They say Lydia is upset that George chose Nelly and the devil has gotten into her heart."

A heavy pall fell over the group as everyone tried to digest the details of the story. George was lost deep in his own thoughts.

"Maybe I should go speak with her—make peace, as they say," he suggested.

Nelly looked at him. "Oh, George, that would be a marvelous idea! She is, after all, just a child. Our first loves are always the most tragic, are they not?" She looked around the group. There was mutual agreement to her statement, and conversation started drifting into a different direction.

Peter leaned over to Hart. "Do you think it's the devil?" he asked quietly.

Hart watched his sister with her future husband, their faces illuminated by the firelight. "Wet sheets don't burn."

CHAPTER SEVEN

The following day

George wasn't sure what he was going to say to Lydia. What could he say that would help to diffuse this situation and yet not hurt the poor child's feelings? He made his way to town quickly, but once there, it was hard to walk more than a few paces without someone stopping him. Ever since his and Nelly's marriage intentions had been posted in the town square, he had been smothered with congratulations every time he got near the place. Today was no different. Between tipping his hat to the ladies offering their well-wishes or stopping to hear the advice of the old men, it was well into the afternoon before he arrived at the Blaisdells' door. Knocking, he expected to see one of the womenfolk answer the door, but instead Abner himself appeared.

"Well, Mr. Blaisdell, I'm glad you are here!" he said.

"Captain Butler, pleasant to see you as well. What brings you to our threshold?"

"I was wondering, sir, if I might speak with Lydia."

Abner's face turned an ashen white at the mention of his youngest daughter. "Well…she is…I mean, she has taken a bit ill, sir. I'm not sure she can see visitors at this moment."

"Abner, please! Do come back!" a voice hollered from inside the house. "I need your help here."

"If you'll excuse me, sir," Abner said before quickly turning to go back inside. George could hear scuffling and groaning. There appeared to be some discussion, but he couldn't make out the words. He stepped to the side of the door and peered into the front window. There he saw Mrs. Blaisdell on the floor cradling Lydia's head in her lap. The child's face was twisted in agony. The fingers of her hands were curled tight into her palms. Her legs were rigid and jerking.

"Abner, do something, please!" Mrs. Blaisdell urged.

"I do not know what needs to be done!" he replied.

At that moment, the child's mouth opened and she spoke. In a halting, gasping voice, she announced, "He is here."

George stepped back away from the window. He should go. This was obviously not the time to have a discussion. As he prepared to leave, Abner came back to the door.

"Captain Butler, will you please come in a moment? Lydia is quite ill, but I believe that your presence may make her feel better. Please, come this way." He indicated that George should enter the front room.

As George entered, he beheld the same scene he had seen from outside the window. Lydia was clearly having a fit of some kind as her body continued to jerk and thrash despite her mother's best attempts to hold her still. There was foam forming around the corners of her mouth, and her eyes were rolling back in their sockets.

Mrs. Blaisdell looked up at him. He couldn't tell if she was pleading for help or if she felt uncomfortable that an outsider was witnessing a private family affair. He was certain that she did not share her husband's feelings that George was going to make the situation any better.

"Lydia, dear," Abner said, kneeling down next to his wife, "look, Captain Butler has come to see you."

Abner motioned for George to kneel down and say something to the child. Stiffly, he knelt.

"Lydia, it's true I'm here—it's me, Captain Butler. I came to see you today, but I am sorry you are ill."

With the words barely out of his mouth, the child's eyes flew open, her back arched, and all of her limbs stiffened straight. Spittle shot out of her mouth as she made a gurgling sound. George wasn't sure, but he could have sworn that the child's body actually lifted off her mother's lap. Mrs. Blaisdell screamed as Abner grabbed Lydia and lifted her into the air by the shoulders.

"Breathe, child, breathe!" he shouted, shaking her. A few more gasps could be heard coming from Lydia, and then she went limp.

"She has died!" Mrs. Blaisdell shouted, struggling with all of her skirts to get up off the floor. George reached to take the child from Abner as he collapsed into a chair. Cradling her in his arms, George could feel her breathing.

"No, she is breathing. She is fine," he said, trying to reassure and calm both parents. "It's a fit of some kind. It will pass." He continued to pace the room, holding the small body of the little girl carefully against his chest.

"What was she doing when this happened?" George asked. He had seen a sailor having a fit like this once, but the cause was thought to be the heaving of the ship.

Both Abner and Mary looked at each other, neither one wanting to speak.

"Tell me, what was she doing?" George demanded.

"We were sitting at that table going over her lessons," Mary said, "when all of a sudden she looked at me and said, 'He is coming to speak to me.' I asked the child what she meant, and she said, 'Captain Butler is coming to me.' And then she collapsed onto the floor and started shaking."

The words hung in the air. George looked down at Lydia resting in his arms. How had she known? There was no way word could have gotten to her from Butler's Point ahead of his arrival. It was only family around the fire last night, and they were all accounted for when he had left Butler's Point. The Hoopers had all headed home as well, but he doubted very much that any of them would have tried to stir up trouble by coming here first.

Lydia stirred in his arms. Her eyes fluttered and then slowly opened.

"Captain Butler?" she said.

"Yes?" he replied.

"You have come to tell me of your reasons for marrying Nelly Hooper, have you not?"

Stunned, he could not reply.

"Lydia!" her mother said with indignation. "How dare you speak to Captain Butler in such a manner?" She reached to take Lydia from his arms, but George turned slightly, indicating he wasn't finished.

"Yes, Lydia, I did. I thought that if I spoke to you myself that it would calm your heart. But it appears someone has told you of my plan ahead of time."

"No one told me," she replied, looking straight up at him.

33

"Well, then, how did you know I was coming? Your mother told me you informed her of such."

Lydia blinked her eyes a couple of times as if she were trying to clear her vision. "The voice told me."

"The voice? Whose voice?" George asked.

"I do not know. It is a voice that speaks to me sometimes."

George gently placed her in a chair in the room and kneeled down in front of her. "Ah, I see," he said. "Is it really a voice you hear, Lydia, or are these just the wishes of your heart?"

He could see her thinking that over for a moment, and then she said, "It is a voice that speaks to me just as you are speaking to me now. Sometimes it sounds like the rushing wind, and sometimes it speaks."

George began to see that she really was a troubled little girl, just as Nelly had said. He patted her knee a couple of times.

"Lydia, sometimes when we want something so badly we can create ideas in our heads that aren't real. I know you like me in a way that is a lot more than just friends. I know that you might even think you love me and that someday we will get married." George shifted his weight and glanced at Abner. This was an incredibly awkward conversation to be having. "But I am not the man for you. Miss Hooper and I are much better suited for each other than you and I would be. Do you understand that?"

Lydia continued to stare at him with those enormous, vacant brown eyes.

"In a few more years, a very nice fellow will come along and sweep you off your feet, and you will forget all about me. All right?" He took out his handkerchief and wiped away the tears and saliva that had stained her face. "You'll see." He rose, making eye contact with Abner, who nodded his approval.

"Captain Butler is right, Lydia. You must stop all of this nonsense at once." Her father spoke to her in a very stern voice. His tone startled Mary and George alike, but Lydia seemed unfazed by it.

"Well, I will be going now," George said, turning to head for the door. At that moment, he thought he heard a sound like a rushing wind. He turned and looked back into the room, but Lydia sat still in her chair.

"Thank you again, Captain Butler," Mary said. "Our best wishes to Miss Hooper and yourself on your impending marriage."

Tipping his hat to her, George was about to reply when he caught sight of a pewter cup flying across the room. "Watch out!" George hollered as he ducked. The cup went through the window, shattering it and sending shards of glass everywhere. Lydia still sat perfectly still and expressionless in her chair, but George could see that her fingers were gripping the sides of the wooden seat and beginning to shake. A candlestick quickly slid across the table and landed on the floor.

Mary jumped up in panic. "Pray, Abner, pray!" she screamed as she fell into her husband's arms.

As more and more objects began to fly around the room, George heard Abner speak. "Lord God, our savior and protector, deliver us from this evil that has entered our home!"

The flying objects chased all three of the adults from the room, and they stood in the entryway. Only Lydia remained unmoved in her chair. George could see her among the midst of the chaos as more and more objects flew through the glass windows. The doors on the cupboards in the room were banging open and shut. Books were falling from the shelves, and their pages were ripping out by themselves and flying about the room as if in a cyclone.

As George stood dumbfounded at the scene before him, he watched as Lydia's chair rose off the floor and floated in the air. There was clearly a good foot or more of empty space under her. Mary gasped and fainted, crumbling to the floor. Abner continued shouting his prayers of deliverance toward the tumult. In an instant, Lydia's chair fell back to the floor with a thud. George heard a deep growl start within her throat. He watched as her mouth opened and a sound unlike any other he had ever heard came forth. It was deep and guttural, certainly not the voice of a female child.

"I will be the wife of Captain George Butler!" it growled at him. And with that, he felt the most powerful force he had ever experienced press against his chest. It pushed him back toward the open front door. He stumbled and fell, hitting his back hard against the doorjamb.

Lydia was still staring at him, her eyes dark and wild. Her mouth was open, but the sound coming from it could only be described as unearthly. George regained his footing and stood looking one last time at the scene before him—a possessed child, a praying father, and an unconscious mother lying in a heap on the floor. He turned and ran.

CHAPTER EIGHT

The home of David Hooper

Nelly heard someone running up the lane toward her house, their footfalls fast and heavy. She looked out the window and was surprised to see George heading straight for the house.

She got up just as he burst through the door.

"George! What on earth is the matter?"

He grabbed her and nearly crushed her in his embrace. He buried his face into her hair and began to sob.

"My land sakes alive, George, are you weeping? What happened to you?" She pulled herself free so that she could get a good look at him. What she saw frightened her. George was a powerfully strong man. Built for the sea, he had endured many hardships and seen many things. His normally reserved demeanor was gone, and he could only be described as distraught.

"Sit, sit," she urged him. "I will get you some tea."

"I don't want any tea. I only want you," he pleaded with her. "I have never in my life witnessed anything…" He broke off and sobbed again. "I just need to know that the world is all right. That we are all right." He took her by the hands and kissed her hard on the lips.

"Oh!" she exclaimed. "George, you are truly frightened. You have got to tell me. Where have you been?"

"The Blaisdells' house," he said. "I went to talk to Lydia."

"You did? Well that's good, isn't it?" She ran her hand down the side of his face and felt the cold sweat that still lingered there.

"No! It was awful. It was a very bad idea for me to go there. And now I don't know what to think of it all!"

"Think of what?" Nelly said.

George then began to describe for her the scene he had found when he got to Abner Blaisdell's house and what transpired afterward.

She listened, rubbing his hands the whole time with her own. When he finished, he sat back in his chair, exhausted.

"So do you think the rumors are true? The child is possessed?" Nelly asked.

"I don't know," George sighed. "It would seem that way, but then again, maybe she just has a really bad temper." He tried to make light of it to calm his fear.

"Do you really believe you saw her chair float off the floor?" Nelly asked. That was the most unbelievable part of the story for her. "Was there any way she could have maneuvered the chair so it just looked like it was floating? Chairs don't float, George."

"I know. Maybe in all the chaos I thought it was floating, I don't know. But things were flying all over that room like a whirlwind. That I'm certain of."

Nelly had never seen George so frightened. "I feel badly that I was the one who told you that you needed to go out there. I should have just kept my opinions to myself."

"No, it was good that I went. I said what needed to be said. Whether she believed me or not, it needed to be said." He kissed Nelly again on the lips, softer this time, with love rather than desperation. "It will be good when I can call you Mrs. Butler." He smiled at her.

"Oh, really?" She smiled back. "And why is that?"

"Because then the only little children we will have to worry about will be our own!"

She smiled at him and held him until the memory of what he had witnessed seemed less frightful and he felt ready to head for home.

<hr/>

After George left, Nelly was alone with her thoughts. What had happened out there that had scared him half out of his wits? He said Abner and Mary were both present. Could it be that they were involved in this, too? Was this a plot hatched by the parents that used Lydia as the pawn? George was a very well-off sea captain with nothing ahead of him but a bright future. Were the Blaisdells trying to trap him into marrying their daughter? There was too much talk in town—first about

38

George being seen with Lydia when he arrived home. Talk of the devil and burning sheets, and now this. Her head spun with all of the possibilities. She had to find her sister and talk this over with her.

"She did what?" Sally said as she rose from weeding the garden. There was incredulity in her voice. She shielded her eyes from the glare of the sun as she looked at Nelly.

"That's what George said," Nelly replied. "Said it was utter chaos. He was clearly shaken by the experience. So now I'm wondering if the Blaisdells are just behind this whole thing. Maybe Lydia is just a pawn in some elaborate scheme to trap George into marrying their daughter."

"I wouldn't put it past them!" Sally said. "It has to be a trick. I mean, chairs don't float, and George isn't exactly the kind of man to lose his head and see things that aren't real." She threw another weed over the fence. "It's got to be a trick or something."

Nelly spoke her thoughts out loud. "George was really frightened. Was that the plan? To scare him into believing that Lydia would make herself sick if he didn't marry her?" She looked at Sally, who was nodding in agreement.

"That's what it sounds like," she said. "I'll talk to girls in town about it. We'll get to the bottom of this!"

CHAPTER NINE

June 1795

Mary Blaisdell stood over the hearth stirring the pot of beef stew she had set to making that morning. The house was quiet, at least for a while. She had sent all the children out to pick strawberries. With a quiet house, her mind drifted to Lydia and what could possibly be happening in her life.

As a toddler, Lydia hadn't spoken much. Instead, she would stare intently at you with those large brown eyes. There was something behind those eyes, but Mary could never understand what. It was awful to say, but there were times when she felt spooked by her own child. That look that Lydia could give you turned your blood to ice water in your veins. Then this whole thing with Captain Butler had started. Why the child had fixated on that man Mary was unsure. It was as if she did not realize that he was a man and she was a child. Certainly many men had taken child brides in the past, but Lydia wasn't a stunning child or set to inherit anything, either. There wasn't much there for a man to want to commit to while she was so young.

The talk around town was starting to get to Mary. She had actually heard people say they thought the devil was in Lydia. The idea was ludicrous. Lydia was just a child with a serious case of infatuation. She just wanted attention, preferably from Captain Butler, but if not him, then anyone would do. Take the burning sheets incident. Naturally, Lydia would have been upset about news of Captain Butler and Nelly Hooper's marriage intentions. It probably bothered her that her own family members had been talking about it. So she set the sheets on fire to stop the conversation. Right? It certainly had done that! There had been no more talk as she and Abner had struggled to get the sheets off the line and plunged into the washing tub.

It was Hannah's husband, Atherton, her own son-in-law, who had first mentioned that Lydia might be talking to the devil. Mary was certain that it was also Atherton who had taken the story to town, interjecting his own personal opinions, and now everyone knew. She shook her head and sat down at the table, looking out the window. *Wet sheets don't burn.* No matter how many times she turned it over and over in her head, it still came back to that fact.

She tried, as she had on so many occasions since that day, to remember Lydia's every move. They had been doing the washing. The fire was going under the tub so that the water was good and hot. The line was in the same area as the washing tub but not close enough for the sheets to touch the flames. Although there was a slight breeze that day, it wasn't enough to blow embers from the fire up onto the sheets hanging on the line. So Lydia had to have taken an ember or a partially burned stick out of the fire and touched the sheets. Right? Wet sheets don't burn, she heard the logical side of her brain say.

And there was certainly no explanation for the episode when Captain Butler came to the house. That had been the most terrifying incident yet. At first she had thought maybe Captain Butler was right, that it was just a fit. She had heard about people having fits so it wasn't that strange. But what had followed was beyond belief—the damage that was done and then Lydia and her chair lifting off the floor. No, there was no explanation for that! After it was over, Abner had forbidden her and Lydia from ever mentioning it again. There would be no talk of the evil that had passed through their parlor that day, he said. Not a word. Nor would the name "Captain George Butler" ever be allowed to be spoken in their home. When Abner said enough was enough, he meant it. Lydia had been exhausted afterward. Mary had put her right to bed. Lydia had no memory of the things that she had said to Captain Butler or of what had taken place. In fact, her daughter seemed frightened when Mary told her what had happened.

Mary shook her head. She had no idea how to stop this or even what it was that was tormenting her youngest daughter. Her heart broke for Lydia, but on the other hand, she was aware now more than ever that a part of Lydia didn't belong to her—that her daughter was, in fact, controlled by a force that Mary knew nothing about, and that was unsettling.

CHAPTER TEN

July 1795

George was walking out to the end of the dock when he heard his name.

"I say, Captain Butler!"

He turned and saw Samuel Ingalls fast approaching.

"I say, Captain, do wait up!"

George sighed heavily. He really wanted to be going. He was making a run to York, and when he returned, he and Nelly would be married. So the sooner he got this started, the sooner he could be back home.

"Samuel," George said as he shook his hand. "What can I do for you?"

"I understand you are heading to York."

"I am, I am. Is there something you need?"

Samuel pulled a letter from his pocket. "I was wondering if you wouldn't mind delivering this for me."

"I would be happy to, Samuel," George replied.

"Thank you! My father has been ill, and I want to try and cheer him up with news of my family here."

"Well, that is a fine idea, Samuel. I'm sure it will cheer him up!"

"I understand that you will be married upon your return."

"Yes, I will." George smiled.

"Well, it will be a good thing all around. Might put that Blaisdell girl and all of her troubles to rest once and for all. Have a safe trip, Captain!" Samuel hurried off.

George placed the letter in his jacket pocket and hoped that would be the case.

Not a peep had been heard from Lydia in the past two months. The gossips were still rehashing all of the old tales. The more spiritually minded of the town gossips were convinced that Lydia was possessed by an evil spirit and that the devil was at work in the Blaisdell household. The less fanatical were in agreement that it was all a hoax of some kind. But George didn't believe the intent was to trick him into marrying Lydia. He had seen her parents just as scared as he was that day at their house.

Thankfully, things had quieted down, and he and Nelly had made great strides in planning their wedding. They were to be married next month, and the day could not come fast enough for him.

Stepping aboard his ship, he inhaled deeply, filling his lungs with the salt air. It felt good to feel the movement of the ship beneath his feet.

"Captain!" his first mate Reuben Gray shouted. "Welcome back!"

"Aye, Reuben, it is good to be back. How's the crew? Did you find us some good men this trip?"

"Yes, I believe I did. I'll gather them up for you, sir, so you can take a look. And if you don't mind my sayin', congratulations on your upcoming nuptials." Reuben's face widened into a big grin as he elbowed George in the ribs.

"Why, thank you, Reuben. She's a good woman. I feel honored that she has accepted me."

"And an honor it is, sir. Word is Nelly Hooper is a very picky lass when it comes to men. You must be pretty special."

George slugged him in the arm and headed for his quarters. "Just gather the men, Reuben. I want to be under sail in no less than hour."

———

The crew of six stood on the aft deck. Three of the men were returning from previous runs. Elijah Hutchings and his brother Daniel had both proven themselves indispensable in the past. Nathan Bowden had agreed to return as cook.

"Nate, glad you're with us," George said, patting the man on the back. "The thought of having to eat Reuben's cooking would have kept me ashore!" There were snickers among the men.

Reuben spoke up. "Sir, I take offense," he said, feigning indignation.

George continued on down the line. The other three men were unknown to George but apparently had come well recommended. George walked past each man.

43

"What's your name, lad?" he asked the youngest of the three.

"Oliver Bateman, sir," the boy replied.

"How old are ye?"

"Sixteen, sir," Oliver replied, trying his best to appear taller.

"Exactly the same age I was when I first went to sea. Have you sailed before?"

"Yes, sir. I sailed with Captain Jonathan Buck last year."

"You did? Well, that is very impressive. I suspect Captain Buck taught you many things. He is a fine mariner. Welcome aboard."

"Yes, sir!" Oliver replied with a smile.

The second man was much older, closer to fifty if he was a day. He was of slight build but had strong, muscular arms.

"And your name?"

"Theo Smith, sir, of Ellsworth."

"Ah, the Smiths of Ellsworth!" George exclaimed. "Are you familiar with Asbury Smith, by any chance?"

"Yes, sir, he's my mother's second cousin."

George shook his head, laughing. He wasn't about to try and figure that one out. The Smiths had bred like barn cats, and you couldn't toss a stone in Ellsworth without hitting one or someone they were related to.

"Well, if you are half the man Asbury is, you'll do. Welcome aboard!"

"Thank you, sir," Theo replied, bending slightly at the waist.

The third man stood watching George approach. He was of medium build and height with an exceedingly fair complexion. His hair was jet black, parted at the side and swept high off his forehead. He was in his mid-thirties or so, and his face had that angular look of one who has missed a meal or two once too often. His cheekbones were high on his face, and the skin was stretched taunt over them. His lips, pressed tightly together, formed a thin line. But all of this was just a backdrop to the piercing blue eyes that sat deep in their sockets. To George, it appeared as if his eyes were placed too close together. His Romanesque nose was just a bit too large for his face. His overall appearance was skeletal. That was the only way George could think to describe it.

"And you, sir?" he asked the man.

"Jeremiah Sprague," came the reply.

George knew he had heard the man speak, but he wasn't sure he had seen his lips move. "I don't believe I've seen you around here before. Where do you hail from, Jeremiah?"

"Machias," he replied curtly.

"I see. I have heard of Spragues up that way. What brings you down the coast?"

"I was looking for work, sir." Jeremiah stared intently at George. There was just something awkwardly unsociable about this fellow.

George held his gaze for a moment and then turned to walk away. "I see. Well, uh, welcome aboard."

They were well underway when Reuben entered George's quarters. "You wanted to see me, sir?" Reuben asked.

"Yes. Who is that Jeremiah Sprague, and why is he on my ship?" George said, turning in his chair.

"Sir? He came highly recommended. He's a fine sailor."

"I'm sure he is, Reuben. You've never hired anyone who wasn't, but that man has something about him that I do not like. Don't you see it?"

"Oh, I'll admit, sir, that he is a tad bit gangly and awkward-looking. But I wouldn't let his looks bother you, sir. He's a good man."

George wasn't convinced. "Watch him, Reuben, just watch him."

+———+

The trip to York passed almost without incident until their last evening aboard ship. As George lay sleeping in his quarters, he dreamed of Nelly. He could see her standing near a well dipping her bucket into the fresh, clean water. The sun shone all around her, glinting off the blond highlights in her hair. In his dream, he reached out to touch her. To pull her closer to him. He tried and tried to reach her, but she was always just a little bit too far away. He tried walking toward her, but she seemed to get farther out of reach. She vanished into the shrubbery, and he followed her. Then he was walking toward her in a meadow. He could see her white gown fluttering about her ankles as she ran through the grass. She kept turning and looking at him. Laughing, she continued on. He tried hollering for her, but she would not wait for him. He struggled on, trying to reach her as she headed toward the seashore. Just as she reached the rocks, he was able, at last, to grab her arm. She turned to look at him, and when she did, he beheld the cold, white face of Jeremiah Sprague.

"Arrrgh!" he shouted as he sat bolt upright in his cot. Sweat was streaming down his chest, and his breathing was rapid. "Jesus Christ Almighty!" he said to himself as he regained awareness of his surroundings. Gripping the sides of his cot, he tried to control his breathing. "Air, I need air," he said. He slid into his trousers and threw on a jacket. Leaving his quarters, he made his way to the deck. Leaning over the railing, he watched as the moonshine played across the waves lapping the sides of the ship. He tried to shake the image of Jeremiah from his mind and the feeling of uneasiness from his bones. "What was it my mother always said? If you dream about someone, it's because they are thinking of you," he muttered out loud.

"Sir?"

The sound of another voice in the darkness jumped him. "Who goes there?" he shouted, his heart pounding in his chest.

"It is I, sir. Jeremiah." As if he had been a part of the darkness itself, Jeremiah suddenly appeared beside him out of the inky shadows of the ship.

"What are you doing out here?" George demanded.

"I have the first watch, sir. I heard your steps on the deck and approached to investigate. Who were you speaking to?"

"No one. I'm here alone. I just had a terrible dream and came out to get some air. I was speaking to myself."

Jeremiah leaned against the railing of the ship. "Ah yes. Wedding nerves, maybe, sir. Begging your pardon for speaking of your personal affairs."

Jeremiah didn't strike George as the gossiping type, so how had the man known of his impending marriage considering he was from out of town?

"And what might my personal affairs be?"

"That you are to be married on our return. But not to the woman who wants to be your wife." Jeremiah said it so matter-of-factly that George didn't know how to respond.

"I do not know what you mean. I am to marry Nelly Hooper, and I'm more than certain she wishes to be my wife."

"Oh indeed, sir, she does. But there is another who wishes to be your wife as well. She, too, will call herself such someday."

George felt his chest tighten at this comment. Lydia was to be his wife?

"Is that so?" George replied. "And how would a fellow from Machias know so much about my private affairs?"

"All one has to do, sir, is listen. There is much talk in diverse places about you and a young child who has a familiar spirit."

"A familiar spirit? Possessed, is that what you mean?" George's mind flashed back to that day he had gone to the Blaisdells' house to speak with Lydia. What had he seen that day? For sure it had scared him, but he wasn't about to admit that to anyone, certainly not to this drifter!

"Some might call it that, sir."

"Well, I'm afraid you have been misinformed. If you are referring to Lydia Blaisdell, she is but a fawn of a child and will never be my wife. She has a small infatuation with me that has been blown out of proportion by the town gossips. You will do well, Mr. Sprague, to steer clear of them the next time you are in town. Is that clear?"

"Yes, sir. Goodnight, sir." He turned to walk away but stopped. "Sir, it is true. When you dream of someone, it is because they were thinking of you." And with that, he melted into the darkness from which he had come so silently that George was sure he could not hear his footsteps on the decking.

CHAPTER ELEVEN

Ashore in York, George headed straight for the office of Chase & Nichols. He needed to settle up on the cargo and payment for this load of barrels he had brought down. The bell above the door tinkled as he opened it, the clerk at the desk looking up.

"Can I help you, sir?"

"Yes, Captain Butler from Franklin. My crew is unloading our cargo now at the wharf. Could I speak with Stephen Chase to settle up?"

"Of course."

The clerk got up, parted the curtain that partitioned off the room, and disappeared. George glanced around at the many crates and boxes stacked up against walls. The August sunlight was streaming through the windows, and he could see the dust sparkling within its rays.

"Captain Butler, sir?" The clerk was indicating that he should follow him beyond the curtain. George entered and saw Stephen Chase seated at a richly dark stained oak desk.

"Come in, come in," he said, rising to shake George's hand. "It's a pleasure to see you, Captain Butler! What did you bring for me today?"

"I've brought a load of barrels made from the best wood the Downeast can offer." George loved this part of his business. The sales, the negotiating to find a fair price. It was like a chess game of the minds.

"I see." Stephen sat back at his desk, making a tent with his fingers and resting them against the tip of his nose. He studied George momentarily. "Dry or wet?"

"Dry. Thought you could sell them farther south for the tobacco that seems to be pouring out of Virginia these days."

"I thought you were leaning more heavily on the rum trade?" Stephen asked him. "At least, that's what I've heard lately."

"I am still invested in that area as well," George replied. "However, I had some pressing matters at home to tend to, and I didn't want to make a long run just yet."

"I see." Stephen shuffled through some papers on his desk. "Are the barrels unloaded yet?"

"My crew is working on that now," George answered. Stephen lifted a small handbell from his desk and gave it a ring. The clerk from the front responded immediately by parting the curtain.

"Nathan, will you go check on the barrels that Captain Butler has brought from Downeast? Give me an accurate count and description of the condition, please."

"Yes, sir." The young man bowed slightly. "The name of your ship, sir?" he asked, directing his question to George.

"The *Schoodic*. We docked third ship in on the main wharf. My first mate's name is Reuben Gray."

Taking note of the information, the clerk scurried away, leaving George and Stephen alone again.

"So I hope your family matters are not of the distressing kind."

"Oh, not at all." George smiled. "I'm to be married on my return!"

"Well, congratulations, sir," Stephen smiled. "It is a sign of God's favor that a man is capable of marriage. I trust she is a fine woman?"

"Yes, she is, and of a fine family as well."

"Do I know them?" Stephen asked. "Is her father also in shipping?"

"Hooper is the surname. Her father came from Saco. He served with my father in the Revolution. Her father farms, but her brothers are getting into fishing."

Stephen shook his head. "I do not know any of the Hoopers from Saco. Fishing, you say? Dangerous work."

"Yes, many in our area are now running out to Georges Bank. They say the fish are very plentiful there. But I don't think it is any more dangerous than running a British blockade into the West Indies, do you?" George smiled as he spoke.

"Nay, I guess you are correct. Nor any more dangerous than fending off the pirates that infest those waters."

"How is that situation progressing? Have there been any improvements?"

"Unfortunately, no. They are getting more and more brazen as the rum traffic increases."

George took all of this in. It was his plan to head straight for the West Indies this winter. There was money to be made down there for sure. But his mind turned to Nelly, and his adventuresome spirit was reigned in with thoughts of her being left a widow shortly after their marriage.

Stephen and George continued their conversation of piracy and the perils of the open sea while waiting for the clerk to return. Once he did, George was able to negotiate a fair price for the barrels.

"You were surely correct, Captain, in the quality of these barrels," Stephen said, glancing down at the notes his clerk had brought back. "Who did you say made them?"

"I don't believe I did, sir, but they are made on the banks of the Narraguagus River just up the coast a bit from me in Milbridge."

"Oh yes, Milbridge. I've heard of it."

"Made by a man named Bailey. A very fine cooper."

"That he must be, as I've never seen my clerk write a report such as this. I would certainly be interested in more of these barrels on future trips you make this way, Captain Butler." Stephen handed him a small canvas bag full of coins.

"I will keep that in mind, sir." George bowed politely, placing his hat on his head. "It has been a pleasure doing business with you, sir."

"And I with you. Good luck in your nuptials, and give my best to the future Mrs. Butler."

George stepped back out into the sunshine, feeling the heft of the bag in his coat pocket. With what he owed Bailey for the barrels, and paying the crew, he would still have sufficient funds to pick up the very important items he hoped were waiting for him at James Barrows's shop. Turning, he hurried in that direction. He entered the shop just as a small band of children were racing out the door. He lifted his arms up and out of the way, trying to avoid being trampled.

"Whoa!" he said, laughing. "What's all the excitement about?"

Mr. Barrows looked up from the counter. "A stick of sugarcane. Causes a raucous every time!" he laughed. "Well, well, Captain Butler, I was wondering when I would see you. Your items have been here for several weeks now." He winked at George as he turned to the shelves lining the back wall of his shop. He shifted a few items around, moving things here and there until he withdrew a good-sized pine box from the shelf.

George could hardly contain his excitement. Shortly after Nelly had agreed to marry him, he had sent word to an associate in Boston. He had listed explicit instructions on the items he wished to purchase, requesting them to be sent to Mr. Barrows's shop in York. And now here they were, and he was seeing them for the first time.

Mr. Barrows used a small wedge to pry open the lid on the top of the box. Squeaking with the sound of dry wood, the lid gave itself up, revealing a mound of hay inside. Mr. Barrows pushed the box toward George.

"By all means, sir, you may have the honor," he said.

George reached into the box and felt around inside of the hay. His hand grasped the cool, hard feel of porcelain, and he withdrew the piece carefully. It was a small cuplike vessel with curving handles on both sides. The piece was ivory and decorated with a lively scene in blue of birds flying over a path of garden stones. In the distance, a ship at full sail could be seen. On one side of the vessel, a small spout started at the bottom of the cup and extended up in a gentle curve. This enabled the drinker to drink the contents from the bottom of the cup first. George held it up, admiring its beauty.

"I don't believe I've seen a finer posset cup than that," Mr. Barrows said. "How many in the set?"

"Six," George said, gently setting it down and finding the other five among the hay. The cup or "sack," as it was called, was specifically made for the drinking of posset, a strong alcoholic drink served at weddings. A posset required a special drinking vessel because of the layers within it. The top layer, or the "grace," was a creamy foam that could be eaten with a spoon. The middle layer was a smooth and spicy custard, and at the bottom, a very pungent alcoholic liquid would settle. Thus the need for the spout. George checked all six pieces carefully to make sure there were no chips or cracks. They were fine.

Mr. Barrows whistled between his teeth. "Six is a fine set, sir, very fine. Is this a gift for a family member?"

"You might say that," he said. "I am surprising my bride on my return home."

"Well, blessings to you then, Captain Butler. I had no idea. Who is the lucky woman?"

"Nelly Hooper, David's daughter."

"Ah yes, I remember David Hooper well. Is it possible that his daughter is old enough to marry?"

George blushed a little. "Yes, she is, and I am very honored that she has accepted my request."

Indicating the posset set, Mr. Barrows said, "Do you have a ring? You know many couples now are tossing a ring into the posset. The lucky one to find it will be the next one to the altar."

"I had heard of that, but no, I did not purchase a ring," George said, reaching deeper into the box. "But I did get these." He pulled out a pair of gloves. Made of delicate ivory muslin, they were fingerless gloves with a separate extension for the thumb. Stunning in their appearance, they had heavy embroidery around the cuff. The small blue stitches made a graceful pattern that resembled waves. On the inside of each cuff was embroidered the initials *N. B.* and the year 1795.

"Do you think she will like them?" George asked Mr. Barrows.

"Wedding gloves are always a wonderful gift." He smiled. "And I like the touch of the wave pattern. Very appropriate given your occupation, sir."

George repacked his items carefully into the box and watched as Mr. Barrows gently tapped the nails back into place.

"How much do I owe you for these things?" George asked. Mr. Barrows consulted his account ledger on the desk.

"One pound, fifteen shillings," Mr. Barrows read, taking his glasses off and looking up. "That's quite a fine sum."

"Yes, it is!" George replied, shaking his head. "I believe that was a full month's wages when I started as a crew member on my first run to Barbados!" he laughed. "But my Nelly is worth every penny of it." He handed Mr. Barrows the coins he had withdrawn from his bag.

"She must be a fine woman." Mr. Barrows reached into a smaller chest located on another shelf behind him and withdrew a small silver ring. Plain in its simplicity, it was a thin band with no markings on it whatsoever.

"Here," he said, handing the ring to George. "A gift for the bride and groom. Use it in your posset." He smiled. "And give my regards to David Hooper as well."

"Why, thank you, Mr. Barrows. That is very gracious and kind of you," George said, taking the small ring. "I'm sure Nelly will be thrilled with the idea."

CHAPTER TWELVE

August 28, 1795
Butler's Point

M oses Butler reached up toward the wagon to help the older man from his carriage. Lyman Pope, magistrate for this area, was not a young man. Moses wasn't exactly sure of his age, but he had heard it rumored that Lyman was closing in on eighty years old. He certainly looked it. His skin hung in sagging wrinkles from his jowls. His long, beaked nose had a slight downward turn to it on the tip. His chin turned upward so one had to look twice to make sure that the man's nose and chin were not touching. He was missing just about all of his teeth, so his lips were drawn inward at his mouth. He was bent nearly in half as well. What he lacked in physical stature was made up for in respect and admiration from those in his community.

"Your most humble servant, Magistrate Pope," Moses said, bowing slightly as the man tried to regain his balance after his descent from the carriage. "We are honored that you have agreed to perform the marriage of my son and Nelly Hooper."

"Aye, I thank thee for picking such a fine day for it," he replied, indicating the bright sunshine and warm summer air. "If the weather had been rainy, my rheumatism wouldn't have allowed me out of bed." He took a few wobbly steps on his arthritic knees.

"This way, sir," Moses said, taking him by the arm and leading him toward a group of chairs under a large oak tree. "Can I get you a refreshment after your journey here from Ellsworth?"

"Just a dipper of cool water will be fine, thank you." He took the seat offered him in the shade. His assistant, who had driven his carriage, spoke quietly in his ear. "Yes, yes, that will be fine. And bring my satchel back with you when you come. The documents are in it," Lyman said.

The assistant, after assuring himself that his employer was taken care of, then shifted his attention to the horse. He led it out of the yard and toward the barn. There was no need to even unharness it from the carriage, as they wouldn't be there that long. The Puritan civilities of New England meant that marriages were nothing more or less than a civil contract. No pomp or circumstance. No finery or religious overtones, either. This was a brief and highly efficient legal joining of two individuals that would give the woman protection and transfer all of her legal rights to her husband. She would move from the care of her father to the care of her husband, according to the law.

The marriage ceremony today would be a quiet affair. Just a few members of the immediate families in attendance, a few words said by the magistrate, and it would be official. Later, more family members, friends of the couple, townspeople and assorted other well wishers would join them for a celebratory gathering. Then on Sunday, they would be presented to everyone at the meetinghouse for their Coming Out Sunday, and God's blessing would be bestowed upon their union.

＋━━━＋

Inside the main house the women were busy "Will you sit still for a minute?" Sally said as she tried desperately to tuck the last tendrils of hair into Nelly's bonnet.

"I can't! Look, George is coming!" Nelly said, pointing out the window of the parlor, where she was getting ready.

Her mother turned from her own preparations. "That he is! Sally, finish up, and hurry. George must have something very important to say if he's coming here!" Joanna said, hiding all of the combs and brushes that were strewn across the table. George knocked gently on the door as Sally and Joanna quickly perched themselves on two chairs, spreading their skirts and trying to act casual.

"Come in," Nelly said with just a touch of excitement in her voice.

George opened the door slowly and stuck his head in. "Is it safe to speak with you for a moment?" he asked shyly. His hair was well powdered for the occasion and tied back with a thong of leather at the nape of his neck. He looked dashing in a blue suit. Nelly tried not to stare at the way his stockings clung to his muscular calves. The gold buckles on his shoes shined as if they had just been polished.

55

"Yes, yes, it is fine. We are just about done here, aren't we, Mother?" Nelly said, indicating that her mother and sister were present and George should be mindful of his conversations with her.

"Excellent!" He smiled as he stepped into the room. "Mrs. Hooper, Sally," he acknowledged, bowing slightly in their direction. "I'm glad you are here. I would like to present a gift to my wife." He almost stumbled over the last word as his eyes met Nelly's. He looked at her so deeply and with so much affection she wanted to reach out to him and kiss him.

"She is not your wife yet, Captain Butler," Joanna said with a sternness in her voice that caused George to take his eyes off Nelly and look at her. "But I will allow it." She smiled at him and winked.

Exhaling with relief, George removed a small parcel he had been holding under his arm. Wrapped in muslin, it was tied with a blue ribbon. He handed it to Nelly.

"How lovely!" she said, taking it from him. "Did you know that blue is my favorite color?"

He smiled, glanced at Sally, and replied, "Yes, a little bird told me." Nelly laughed, catching his meaning.

She tugged at the ribbon until it came free and peeled back the layers of muslin to reveal the elegant gloves George had purchased for her.

"Oh, George!" she exclaimed. "They are beautiful!" She ran her fingers over the delicate waves stitched into the edges. "Mother, look!" she said, showing them to Joanna. "Aren't they stunning?"

Joanna reached out and touched the fine fabric of the gloves. "Yes, they are. Truly a gift of love and admiration. Well done, Captain," she said, smiling at him. "Well done."

"Well, put them on, silly!" Sally said to her sister.

Nelly slipped her slender arms into the gloves, maneuvering each thumb into the small loop of fabric meant for it. The gloves covered her forearms almost to her elbows.

"George, however did you think of such a wonderful thing?" Nelly asked him.

"A few years ago, I was in Boston and attended a wedding with an acquaintance. At those much more elaborate city affairs, gifts are given to all those in attendance. Fans, hatbands, and gloves were all bestowed on the guests by the bridal pair." Holding his hat in his hand, he glanced at Joanna. "I did not think purchasing such gifts for everyone here would be necessary."

He knew how humble his own parents were, and he was sure Nelly's would feel the same way. Joanna nodded in agreement. George looked up and met Nelly's gaze. "But I was determined to provide my wife with a piece of finery on her wedding day that she would always cherish."

Nelly leaned into him and rested her forehead on his chin. "I am honored to be the woman who can call such a thoughtful man my husband."

George reached out and embraced her just as Joanna cleared her throat.

"It was a very thoughtful gift, Captain, but let us reserve the more intimate parts of this conversation for later."

"Oh, Mother!" Sally said, rolling her eyes. She stood and embraced her sister. "I'm so very happy for you, Nelly. You truly have chosen a good one!"

George blushed. "Why, thank you, Sally." He smiled.

At that moment, Nelly's father David stuck his head in the door. "Are you ladies about ready?" he asked before realizing that George was in the room as well. "Captain? There you are! Your father has been searching all over for you. The magistrate has arrived, and if you two would like to get married today, I'm sure he would oblige you!"

<hr />

Magistrate Pope stood under the oak tree next to a small table that had been brought outside. On it were the documents that would need to be signed and filed with the courts back in Ellsworth. Two small stones had been set on top to prevent them from blowing away. Standing to one side of the table were Peter Butler and Hart Hooper. On the other side stood Sally Hooper and George's sister, Mercy. The sunlight reflecting off the waves at the end of the point shimmered like crystals. A slight sea breeze stirred the leaves of the oak, but it was not enough to really make the stones on the documents warranted. Overhead, a smattering of seagulls could be heard. It was truly a glorious day for a wedding.

+———+

Appearing first at the door to the house were Nelly's parents, David and Joanna.

"Our first child is to be married today, Jo. Where has the time gone?" David whispered to her. She squeezed his arm, indicating that she too was overwhelmed by this milestone in their lives. They proceeded toward those gathered under the tree followed by George's parents, Moses and Sarah. Once they were seated, George and Nelly stepped from the front door of the home and walked the path toward the tree.

Nelly was certain she had never seen the bay look more beautiful as it sparkled off Butler's Point. The waves lapped against the shore, creating the sound so familiar to those who live by the sea. Across the bay, she could see the houses and other buildings of Sullivan. She glanced down at her gloved hand that was entwined with George's arm and then smiled up at him.

Wasting no time, Lyman Pope spoke and brought Nelly from her thoughts. "Who present will give this woman to this man?" he asked.

David Hooper stood from his seat. "It is I," he said.

"Do you, Mr. Hooper, agree to relinquish all rights to your daughter Eleanor Joanna Hooper, who has been in your care all the days of her life?"

"Yes, I do."

Lyman turned his attention to George. "George Goodwin Butler, do you agree that Eleanor Joanna Hooper is now yours to protect, provide, and care for all the remaining days of her life or until your time on this earth ends? That you will forsake all others and the two of you shall stand as a testament of honor and dignity in this community?"

George looked down at Nelly. "Yes," he said.

"Eleanor Joanna Hooper, do you agree to leave the home of your father and take up your place with your husband, George Goodwin Butler? That you will always obey him and provide him with children for his posterity until your time here on earth shall end? That you, too,

58

will forsake all others and stand as a testament of honor and dignity in this community?"

"Yes." Nelly felt her heart thudding in her chest as the word spilled out of her mouth. That was it—she was now George's wife.

The magistrate then turned to the small table and removed the quill from the ink well.

"Captain Butler, please sign." He handed the writing instrument to George. George made his very elaborate signature and handed the quill to Nelly, who also signed before passing the quill to the witnesses.

After the marriage documents were all signed, Lyman Pope turned to address the crowd.

"Marriage is a legal and binding contract. Entered into this day before these witnesses. It is my pleasure to introduce to you Captain and Mrs. George Butler." He bowed his head toward George and Nelly and stepped backward.

Nelly's mother was the first to approach the bride and place a kiss upon her cheek. "I am so happy for you, Nelly. You will make a wonderful wife and mother."

"Thank you," she said.

Her father then placed a small and delicate kiss upon her forehead. His eyes were brimming with tears. He said nothing, instead turning and shaking George's hand very firmly. They were followed by George's parents, who also bestowed kisses on Nelly's cheek and well-wishes to the couple. Soon, the remaining family members had all kissed the bride for good luck, and George was able to look at his wife for the first time undisturbed.

"May I?" he asked her.

"I thought you would never ask," she whispered back.

He slowly bent his head toward her and let his lips touch hers. She could feel the warmth of his breath, the tenderness of his touch, and the love that was behind it all. He gently, ever so gently, kissed her, holding her by the shoulders. She felt her knees go weak, and she thought she would faint when applause erupted from the family.

"It will be a long day until we are in that bridal chamber," he whispered back, the tension clearly evident in his voice.

The mothers and sisters of the bridal pair now swung into action. There was much work to be done to prepare the food that would be served to the extended family and townsfolk who would make their way to Butler's Point over the next few hours to congratulate the young couple. Fathers and brothers hurried back and forth across the front yard, laying out planks of wood for tables and stumps for seating. Nelly's younger brothers had brought a set of ninepins to play with along with other games. They would practice marksmanship with their rifles and take part in the ever-popular stick-pulling.

In the summer kitchen, Joanna Hooper leaned over the kettle, checking to see if the cream was at the boiling point yet. Floating on the top of the cream was a stick of whole cinnamon and a few flakes of mace.

"Ready for the eggs yet, Mother?" Sally asked.

"Just about." Joanna turned to count the eggs Sally had in her basket. "That should be enough." She nodded in satisfaction.

George's mother Sarah was busily setting up platters of cooked meats, fresh-cut vegetables from the kitchen garden, and baskets of fresh early apples. "I hope we have enough food for everyone!" she said.

"Oh, that I am sure of," Joanna replied. "It's this posset I'm most concerned about. Many will have to partake of it from custard dishes!"

"That is fine, Mother," Nelly said, entering the kitchen with George. "The posset cups that George purchased were only meant to be used by the closest members of the family. Custard dishes will serve the others well enough." She gently set down the box containing the porcelain cups George had gotten while in York.

"Did we arrive in time?" George asked, fishing around in his pocket for something.

"In time for what?" Sally asked him.

Pulling the small silver ring from his coat pocket, he held it up for all to see. "For this!" he announced, winking at Sally. "They tell me the latest thing in Boston is to toss a silver ring into the posset, and whoever finds it in their cup will be the next to marry."

"You will not be throwing any trinkets into my posset, George!" Joanna shrieked, moving her body to guard her pot of boiling cream. Everyone laughed.

"Oh, Mother Hooper! It is but a small ring, see?" George passed it to her so she could see it closely. The small silver ring was unmarked and not much bigger than a coin.

"Only a child could wear a ring that small," she remarked.

"Well, I certainly hope that no child is drinking posset!" Nelly laughed in reply. As everyone knew, the alcoholic bottom layer of a good posset was meant for adults only.

"Fine, fine," Joanna conceded. "If this is what you both want on your wedding day, who am I to stand in the way?"

George gave her a quick hug. "Then by all means, Mother Hooper, you may have the honor of depositing the little ring into your brew!" He bowed mockingly at her. She laughed at him and tossed the ring into the thick cream. It made no sound as it disappeared.

"My work here is done," George said with a smug smile and turned to leave. Nelly batted at him playfully as he stooped to exit the small door out of the summer kitchen.

"I'll be out to join you in a while," she said, and he nodded and disappeared.

Sally started cracking the eggs one at time over a large wooden bowl. Eighteen egg yolks and eight egg whites. She beat them well until they were creamy. She handed the bowl to her mother, and they all watched as Joanna slowly poured the beaten eggs into the cream. Next to go in was the white sugar, a very rare treat, and a goodly portion of wine.

"Set out the cups, Nelly," Joanna instructed as she slowly grated nutmeg over the steaming liquid.

Nelly set out the six fine posset cups that she, George, and their parents would use. The rest of the table was strewn with little custard cups for the remaining guests who would wish to partake. Not everyone drank alcohol, and most only did so on special occasions such as this. She was not worried that anyone would go without.

As her mother began to pour the creamy liquid into the cups, they all watched for the little silver ring.

"Oh, Sally, I do hope you find the ring in your cup!" Nelly said, giving her sister's waist a squeeze.

There was much laughter among the women in the room.

"Misery loves company! Is that what you wish for me, dear sister?" Sally said.

"Nay, I only hope that you will find someone as wonderful as George," Nelly replied.

The last drops of the creamy custard were poured. They all reached for the cups and began placing them along the hearth stones. The cups would have to be kept warm until the custard set up. Only then would they be ready to eat.

Nelly stepped back out into the sunshine and looked around. A few guests were arriving by boat down at the dock. She could see her father helping the ladies step ashore. The town of Sullivan was just across the bay, and it was much easier to come by boat than to walk all the way around by land. The folks from Franklin would probably arrive on foot or by carriage. Soon, Butler's Point would be hosting the social event of the year. People would be talking about this for years to come.

CHAPTER THIRTEEN

Mary Blaisdell sat stiffly in the skiff as Abner rowed it across the bay. Lydia was dragging one hand through the cool water as the boat moved swiftly toward the shore of Butler's Point.

From his position in the center seat, Abner could look directly into his wife's face.

"I don't agree with this one bit, Mary, not one single bit," he said, leaning into the oars as they plunged into the dark water and then pulling backward.

"Abner, I don't think we need to discuss this any further," Mary said, tossing her head in Lydia's direction. "We owe it to Captain Butler to show that there are no hard feelings from our family and that we wish him and Miss Hooper—uh, Mrs. Butler—well."

"Well, that's all well and good, woman, but who's to say they don't hold hard feelings for us? What if we are not welcomed there when we arrive?"

"I hardly think they will be rude, Abner. Besides, we won't stay long, truly. Just long enough to pay our respects to the couple."

Knowing that he was not going to win the argument, he threw himself into the rowing, head down, a cool breeze blowing through his hair as they entered the widest part of the bay.

Lydia had heard every word of this discussion here and back home. She wasn't happy at all about going to this gathering. She had no desire to see Captain Butler and Nelly. In fact, she was going to make every effort to stay away from them while she was there—no matter what the voices in her head said. It didn't matter now. The die was cast. Captain Butler had married Nelly Hooper that morning. Her dreams of becoming his wife were over.

The boat bumped onto the shore, and Abner stowed his oars.

"Well, hello there, Abner!" George's father said to him. "Welcome to Butler's Point." He extended his hand to help Abner out of the boat.

"Why, thank you, Moses. That's very neighborly of you." Abner turned to help his wife and daughter from the boat.

"Mrs. Blaisdell, Lydia," Moses said, tipping his hat. They both curtsied slightly.

"My...my wife felt it important for us to give our best wishes to the bridal couple," Abner explained, stammering a bit. "We won't be here long."

It was obvious how uncomfortable the man was. " 'Tis fine, 'tis fine," Moses said, patting him on the back. "Go help yourself to our food. Enjoy the company of our neighbors. It is well, Abner—truly, it is well."

This seemed to reassure Abner, and his body relaxed a bit. "Thank you, Moses, truly." He reached for his wife's hand and led her and Lydia up the path toward the house.

Moses's son Peter stepped out from behind the tree, whistling for emphasis. "Damn plucky of them, don't you think?"

"Watch your tongue, Peter," Moses replied. "We shall hold no ill for any of our neighbors."

"Father, their child has familiar spirits. Whatever is within her nearly attacked George!"

Moses turned to his son. "I will not talk of that evil here nor on this day. Whatever is wrong with that child could easily be explained, I'm sure. I will not allow any of us to meddle in the town gossip. Nor will we be the subject of such. All anyone here today will see is that the Butlers welcomed the Blaisdells openly. Is that understood?"

"Yes, Father." Peter turned. "I'm at least going to warn George."

A warning for George was not necessary, as both he and Nelly saw the Blaisdells coming up the hill from the shore.

"Good God, what are they doing here?" George muttered.

Nelly saw them at the same time and sucked in her breath, reaching for his hand. "Why would they come, George? Why?"

"I don't know." His eyes focused in on them. "It appears that Lydia is not with them," he said, relaxing a bit. "Maybe they have come alone."

Nelly watched them also, and she, too, noticed that Abner and Mary were alone. She relaxed her grip on George's hand as the couple approached them.

"Captain and Mrs. Butler," Abner said as he and Mary greeted them. "Congratulations on your special day." Nelly and Mary curtsied to each other but did not exchange words.

"Why, thank you, Abner, it is kind of you to come," George said. "Please have some food," he insisted, indicating the tables covered in platters.

"Thank you. We…uh…my wife and I and Lydia…" His voice trailed off as he glanced around frantically trying to locate his daughter. "Where is she?" he hissed to his wife. But Mary, too, was turning her head this way and that looking for Lydia.

"Is something wrong?" Nelly asked, looking at George with concern on her face.

"Uh…no…we, uh…" Abner did his best to regain his composure. "Our family wishes you the best. We hope that the turbulent times of the past will now be behind us," he finished hurriedly. Shaking George's hand and smiling at Nelly, he grabbed Mary's arm and began to move her away.

"Where did she go?" His voice was harsh in Mary's ear.

"I don't know, Abner," Mary replied. "Let go of my arm—you're causing a scene!" She twisted away and began adjusting her skirts. "We will find her. She could not have gone far."

+———+

Lydia had watched the interaction between her parents and the Butlers from behind a large pine tree to the side of the yard. She wasn't going to let anyone see her, most of all George and Nelly. She skirted her way along the edge of the trees until she found a granite rock to sit on. From here, she could see several of the Butler grandchildren playing a game of ninepins. They had set up the wooden pins on a flat section of the lawn. Each one took a turn rolling a wooden ball toward the pins. After their turns were completed, they would count the number of pins each had knocked down. The player with the least number of pins was out. The pins were set up again, and play continued until only one player was left.

It didn't take long before one of the young girls spotted Lydia. Approaching her cautiously, the young girl spoke. "Would you like to play with us?"

"No," Lydia replied.

"My name is Prudy. What's yours?"

Lydia hesitated a bit but then decided the truth was probably the best. "I'm Lydia."

"Are you hungry? There is lots of food."

Lydia thought for a moment and then slid down off her rock. "I would like something to eat, yes." She walked with Prudy toward the tables.

She took a few slices of tomato along with a piece of cold meat. As she moved toward the end of the table, she spotted the little custard dishes.

"Is this custard?" she asked Prudy. "I love custard."

"My grandmother said it is just for the adults," Prudy said, eyeing it suspiciously. "I don't think we're supposed to have any."

At that moment, Prudy's cousin Nathan stepped up to the table. "It's posset," he said. He was almost fifteen years old and puffed up his chest to show the girls he knew what he was talking about. "It's got wine in it. Go ahead, have some."

Lydia set the little dish down, shaking her head. "Even I know enough not to get into the wine," she said.

"Oh, don't be such a baby," he said. "The wine is at the bottom. The top is all custard. Just eat the custard, and I'll drink the wine." He winked at her, giving her elbow a little nudge. "Besides, I heard them say there is a silver ring in the posset. Whoever finds it in their cup is going to be the next one married!"

"A silver ring?" Prudy said, getting excited. "Nathan, are you sure?"

"Yes, I am. I saw the ring myself before Uncle George threw it in the pot. I heard tell he bought the ring in Boston."

Lydia's mind began to tumble with thoughts. The next one to get married. A ring from George just for her. He had bought it in Boston especially for her…no! She would not let herself get caught up in those kinds of thoughts again.

"Ooh, a silver ring," she heard Prudy saying. "That would be a nice little treat to take home from today." Prudy reached for a custard dish. "Nathan, if I eat the custard, will you drink the bottom of mine, too?"

"Of course, Prudy!" A much bigger smile spread across his face. "But let's not do it right here at the table." Glancing over his shoulder to make sure no adults were watching, he quickly snatched two of the little custard cups and ran for the trees. Lydia and Prudy followed. Seated on the rock that Lydia had just abandoned, the girls dug into the custard with their fingers. Lydia had only managed a couple of scoops into her mouth when she felt something cold and hard brush up against her teeth. She stopped slurping and sat completely still for a moment. Was it possible that she was holding George's ring in her mouth? Prudy had finished off the custard from her dish, and Nathan was already drinking the wine down in one quick gulp. He looked at Lydia.

"Are you done yet?" he asked. Lydia nodded and handed him her little dish, afraid to speak for fear she would swallow.

Nathan looked at the remaining custard in the dish. "You didn't finish it all."

Lydia shrugged and then made a shooing motion toward him with her hands. She slid down off the rock and walked into the trees. With her back to the other two, she reached into her mouth and grasped the cold, hard piece of silver with her fingers. She pulled it out and looked at it. It truly was a silver ring!

"Lydia, what's wrong?" she heard Prudy say. She turned around and showed the ring to Prudy.

"Nathan, look!" Prudy squealed. "Lydia found the ring!"

"Well, I'll be," Nathan said as he drained the last of the wine from Lydia's cup. "Ain't that something. Looks like you are the next one to get married!" He laughed heartily because Lydia was so young. The joke stung, and even Prudy felt it.

"Nathan, stop being such a tease. Lydia, don't pay him any attention." She picked up a pine cone and threw it at her cousin. "Go on, Nathan, go!" she shouted.

Having gotten what he wanted, Nathan had no problem heading off in the direction of the other boys his age.

Prudy came to Lydia's side. "Let me see it," she demanded.

Lydia held the ring between her thumb and forefinger so Prudy could get a good look at it.

"Put it on! Does it fit?" Prudy urged her.

Lydia took the ring and slid it effortlessly onto her left ring finger.

"Sweet angels of God. It fits like it was made for you! We should go tell the others!" she announced, pulling on Lydia's arm. "This is so exciting!"

"Uh, no, I don't..."

But it was too late. Prudy had already started shouting to her other cousins, and before Lydia knew it, she was surrounded by brightly smiling faces all wanting to see the ring.

All of the little girls were atwitter with excitement. "You're the next one to get married!" they sang as they danced around her. Soon they were reaching for her hands to form a large circle of girls. She removed the ring from her finger and placed it in her dress pocket and clasped hands with the girls. They spun their circle round and round, singing, "Lydia will be married next. Lydia will be married next!" She laughed and sang with the girls until they were all dizzy and fell to the ground.

+———+

Nelly stood with some of the other women watching George and Jeremiah Bunker tackle a round of stick-pulling. For this, both men sat on the ground facing each other. Their legs were spread wide, and the soles of their feet were touching. George held a large stick horizontally in front of him by placing both of his hands close to the center. Jeremiah then placed his hands on the outside of George's hands, grasping the stick closer to the ends. On the count of three, both men would begin pulling in an attempt to pull the other man up off the ground first. Whoever did so was the winner. The men grunted and groaned in their effort, and the crowd gathered around them cheered quite loudly. Nelly was laughing and clapping her hands, hoping that

George would win. Through the din of noise, she heard a sound that caused her to pause.

"Lydia will be married next! Lydia will be married next!"

She turned away from the crowd and saw a group of young girls laughing under a big pine tree.

"What is it, Nelly?" Sally said, approaching behind her.

"I could have sworn I heard someone say 'Lydia will be married next!'" she mumbled, eyeing the group of girls. "She is here!" she suddenly said. "Look! Lydia Blaisdell is right there!"

Applause rose from the stick-pulling crowd at that moment, and Nelly saw George getting congratulated.

"Oh, I let him win!" Jeremiah was heard saying. "It is his wedding day, after all." There was much laughter from the group.

Sally was already striding toward the group of young girls.

"Sally, wait!" Nelly hollered. She then turned toward George. "George! George! Come here!" she shouted. Everyone in the group stopped talking.

"Nelly? What's wrong?" George asked.

She lowered her voice so as not to draw more attention from the group. "Lydia Blaisdell is over there," she said, pointing toward the pine tree. Sally was already talking to the girls, who were clearly very animated.

"What's going on, girls?" Sally asked, approaching the group.

"Miss Sally," one of them said, "Lydia found the ring! She's going to be married next!" They were all filled with the kind of joy that often bubbles out of young girls. Only Lydia remained stoic and silent as the others giggled and fidgeted.

"Is that so?" Sally said, eyeing Lydia coolly. "Lydia, would you like to explain how you came to be in possession of a ring?"

Lydia wasn't about to let anyone take this ring from her. She reached into her pocket and encircled the ring with her hand, feeling it burn into her palm as she clenched it tightly. She said nothing but just stared at Sally with those big brown eyes.

By now, Nelly and George had joined the group as well.

"Lydia," George said, bowing slightly. "I am glad to see you are here. I trust you are feeling better than the last time I saw you."

Again, Lydia made no indication that she was going to speak.

Nelly spoke to her this time, kneeling down so that she was more on the child's level. "Lydia, I feel honored that you have come to see the captain and me."

Only a blank stare was returned. Nelly rose as Prudy came bounding forward from the group.

"Uncle George! Uncle George! Lydia found the ring! She found the ring, so she will be the next one to be married!" Prudy's excitement could not be contained, and once it was loose it was quickly picked up by the six or seven other young girls, and the chattering and singing began again. Lydia remained silent and unmoved in the midst of the chaos.

"Girls, girls!" George said, putting his hands up to try and regain control. "What is this nonsense? Are you speaking about the ring in the posset?"

"Yes!" Prudy said, showing her exasperation with her uncle for being so slow to grasp the situation. "Lydia and I took two cups of custard. We were only going to eat the custard, Uncle, I promise," she said, trying to avoid any ramifications from their actions. "Lydia found the ring in her bowl of custard! That means she will be married next." The other girls renewed their exclamations of excitement all over again upon hearing the story spoken out loud.

Nelly reached for Sally's hand. Their eyes met, and complete understanding passed between them. Of course, it would have been nice if Sally had found the ring, but after all, it was just a party game. But to have Lydia Blaisdell, of all people, find it…there were not words to describe the shock they both felt at this turn of events.

The twittering and laughter of the girls had attracted the attention of other guests, and before long, the group surrounding them had grown larger as news spread that someone had found the ring.

George straightened and stretched his back. He was regretting his decision to join stick-pulling on his wedding day. He was about to say something to Nelly when Abner Blaisdell pushed through the group.

"Lydia!" he shouted. "There you are!" He grabbed her by the arm. "It is time for us to go now, child." He looked at George. "I am so sorry my daughter has caused a scene at your party, Captain Butler."

"Oh, it is well, Abner. She has done nothing of the sort. To be perfectly honest, she has been as quiet as a church mouse." He smiled at Lydia. "I'm afraid it is these other girls who are causing the fracas." He patted his niece on the head.

Prudy stomped her foot in indignation. "But Uncle George, Lydia found the ring! Shouldn't she be congratulated in some way?"

"Ring?" Abner looked down at his daughter. "What ring? What is she talking about?"

"Oh, I placed a silver ring in the posset this morning," George explained. "It's a party game. Whoever finds the ring will be the next to marry." He looked down into Lydia's brown eyes. "The girls say Lydia found the ring, but she has yet to show it to me."

Lydia continued to clench the ring in her hand. This was her ring—she had found it. George had purchased it just for her. She knew that had to be the truth. If she could not have him as her husband, at least she could have this ring. Her thoughts were broken by the voice of her father.

"Posset?" He shook Lydia's arm. "Child, were you drinking?"

"No," was all she said.

Prudy stepped forward at this moment. "No, sir. She and I were just eating the custard. She found the ring in the custard." Prudy stepped back and made eye contact with Nathan, who was lurking around the edges of the group. He looked grateful that his little cousin was not turning him in.

"Lydia, if you have a ring that belongs to Captain Butler, you must give it to me right now," Abner said.

"No, no, Abner. If she truly found it, then it is hers to keep fair and square," George said, placing his hand on Lydia's shoulder. "Do you really have the ring, Lydia?"

Lydia pulled her hand from her pocket and slowly opened her palm. There lay the ring glinting in the sunshine. She wanted George to see it. He had just said it was hers to keep. She wanted everyone to see that she did possess the ring—the ring that George had purchased just for her.

Abner reached out and snatched it from Lydia's palm. She squealed and began to cry. As he shoved Lydia forward and out of the group, he handed the ring to Sally.

"This ring was not intended for a child to have. I am sorry that she ruined the game for the other more eligible ladies. Good day, Captain Butler." He continued on with Lydia firmly gripped in his hands. Mary emerged from the back of the group, and the three of them quickly made their way across the yard and toward the path that led to the shore.

"Mary, I told you we should not have come," he murmured as he pushed Lydia into the skiff.

"Abner, please," she said as she followed Lydia into the boat. "Be reasonable. There was no harm done."

The guests began to murmur and talk among themselves about the abrupt departure of the Blaisdells.

With Lydia gone, all of the little girls scattered quickly to find other amusements.

"Well…now you possess the ring! By default or not, it appears it is yours! My wish has come true!" Nelly said, laughing at Sally. "George, who can we fix her up with?"

"Oh no! I'm not ready yet!" Sally said, holding her hand up and trying to slip the small ring on her finger. "Mother was right. This ring is so small it would only fit a child!"

She pulled it off and was about to place it in her pocket when she noticed something on the ring. She held the ring up so the sun was shining directly on it. Nelly and George had begun to walk away to visit with other guests when they heard Sally scream.

"For the love of God!" she shrieked, tossing the ring to the ground as if it had burned her.

Several other guests had also heard her scream and rushed to her side, as did Nelly.

"What? What is wrong?" Nelly questioned her sister. But Sally was shaking so badly that she couldn't speak.

"Water! Someone get her some water!" George yelled to the crowd. Sally was collapsing onto Nelly, and both women sank to the ground in a flurry of skirts and petticoats.

"Sally, speak to me! What has happened?" Nelly demanded.

"The…ring…" Sally spat out. "Look at it! Look at it!"

Her brother Hart had rushed to the group and spotted the ring in the dust. Picking it up, he handed it to George. "Is this what she's talking about?"

"Yes, that's it," George said. "It's the ring I bought in…" But his words were cut off as he, too, noticed what Sally had seen on the ring.

Nelly watched as his face turned an ashen white color and his hands began to shake. "George?" she questioned, watching his face. "What is it?"

"Well, I don't know exactly," he said. "I'm at a loss for words. I could have sworn the ring I put in the posset was a plain silver band."

"Is it a different ring? Let me see it," Nelly insisted.

George handed it to her slowly as if he were not quite sure he should but he didn't want to deny her, either. It appeared to be the same simple silver ring George had shown her this morning—until she looked inside. Engraved around the inside of the band were the words *George & Lydia Butler*. She looked up at her husband and down at her sister. What was this about? Then the world got black around the corners, she felt her head begin to buzz, and everything went black.

+ —— +

Dusk was starting to fall, and most of the guests had left. Joanna had taken Sally and Nelly into the house to calm them down and help them freshen up. George and Hart stood on the front porch of the house trying to make sense of it all.

"It has to be another ring," Hart was saying.

"Well, I would like to think it is," George replied, rolling the little piece of silver over and over between his fingers. His mind was trying to fathom all of the different explanations for this turn of events. "But it looks and feels very similar to the one that I brought back from Boston. The very one I tossed into the posset myself this morning."

"Maybe she brought the ring with her to the party. Had it in her pocket the whole time. You know she's had designs on you for quite some time now."

"That's true, but she is a child. Where would she have gotten the means to purchase a silver ring and then have it engraved in this town? Someone most certainly would have let that little tidbit slip." George was looking very closely at the engraving. There was no engraver's mark, yet the lettering was perfectly styled as if a professional had done the work. "No, this was not done haphazardly by a local," he said. "This is fine work."

At that moment, Nelly stepped out into the early evening light, followed by Sally.

"Ah, my bride!" George said, reaching for her hand. "I trust you are over your shock and feeling better?"

"Well, I can't say I feel better about this," she said, indicating the ring he was holding in his hand, "but I am determined to put it from my mind. It is our wedding day, George, and I do not want this to mar our memories." She kissed him on the cheek and gave his hand a squeeze.

"I can tell you exactly what all of this is," Sally said. "This is just another trick by the Blaisdells. I'll never understand! The die is cast. He's already married!" She flung her arm in Nelly's direction to add emphasis to her point. "There was nothing to be gained by this but to ruin the day for both of them." Sally stretched out her hand toward George, indicating that he should hand over the ring. "The fact that they even dared to show their faces here after that scene at their house proves they are up to no good. Decent people would have just stayed away." With her palm facing upward, she wiggled her fingers, urging her new brother-in-law to give her the ring. George glanced down at the little ring one more time and then dropped it into her hand. Closing her hand tightly around it, she stepped off the porch and headed for the shoreline.

"Where are you going?" Nelly asked.

"Come with me!" Sally shouted back. "Come help me send this little evil token back to where it belongs."

Laughing, Nelly grabbed George's hand and pulled him off the porch. Together, they made their way down the path to the very tip of Butler's Point.

"We will not let this ruin your wedding night," Sally said, holding the ring up for all of them to see. Spinning around, she faced the open waters of the bay. "We will send it to the depths of the sea so it will never be seen again!" Sally raised her arm, and with all of her might, she threw the little ring out into the bay.

"There! We shall speak of it no more!" she said with a grunt of satisfaction.

Hart turned to George, his voice low so the women could not hear. "My gut tells me it was a ring the child came with. However, if it is, then where is the ring you placed in the posset?"

"I've thought about that, too," George replied, watching his wife and her sister dance around in the grass like the little girls had done earlier in the afternoon. "But I shall not think about it anymore."

Across the bay in Sullivan, Lydia sat on a stump in her father's yard. Evening had just about come full on. From here, she could see the bonfire burning on Butler's Point and make out the shadows of a few people still milling around. Sound travels very well over water, especially at night. She could hear laughter every once in a while, which just made her feel more sullen. Pulling her knees up closer to her chest, she rested her chin on them and kept her eyes on the point. Soon she spotted a small group heading down toward the water's edge. She could hear them talking but couldn't quite make out the words. Suddenly, one woman's voice got louder and Lydia heard "never be seen again!" and then more laughter. They moved on and headed back up the path toward the bonfire.

Hunkered down on her stump, Lydia pulled her skirts tight around her legs. What a miserable day. Not only had Captain Butler married someone else, but her father had caused a scene at his wedding feast by dragging her off. The final insult had come when she had lost the ring that George had given her. Her heart ached. That ring had been hers to keep. George had said so. Her father had had no right to snatch it from her like that. Bowing her head, she began to cry. Stifling her sobs so as not to draw attention from her family just inside the house, she let the tears trickle down her cheeks onto her arms.

It was then that she first heard the noise. It was a rushing sound, not quite like the rushing of the wind she had heard at other times. This sound instead was coming from the bay in front of her. She lifted her head from her arms and saw a rogue wave rushing toward the shore in front of her father's house. The rest of the bay remained calm and unmoved except for this one pulsating burst of water. Foam rose up over the top of the wave as it crested and then crashed into the rocks just below where she sat. Sea foam sprayed up from where it had made landfall, and a flock of seagulls rose up in anger, squawking their disapproval. Out of the spray and foam, a small, shining object flew upward and landed right in front of her. Shocked, she looked down and beheld the silver ring. Reaching down, she picked it up, and in the last of the fading daylight she saw what the others had seen. Engraved around the inside of the ring were the words *George & Lydia Butler*. She sucked in her breath in amazement, blinking her eyes and checking again to make sure she had truly seen what she thought she had seen. There it was, carved into the cold, hard silver. An affirmation of what she had known all along. She would be George's wife someday.

Her eyes scanned the opposite shoreline. Let them have their party. Let them celebrate this day. Her turn would come, of this she was certain.

CHAPTER FOURTEEN

The wedding night

Nelly was jolted awake. She and George were sleeping in the rough log cabin that his parents had first built on the point when they had arrived in 1766. It offered only the slightest bit of privacy, but it was better than spending their first night as husband and wife in the Butlers' overflowing main house. It was not uncommon for friends of a newly married couple to spend the night right outside the door, shouting taunts and encouragement as things progressed. She was pretty certain nothing like that had taken place. She and George had been afforded some measure of privacy as they had enjoyed their first night together.

She could feel the heat emanating from George's body as he lay beside her. It was a comforting warmth, as the night sea air was seeping into the room through the old chinks in the log walls. Her mind reflected on her wedding night. Her mother had done all that she could to prepare Nelly, but nothing the woman had said accurately described how it had all played out. She was thankful for George's worldliness, of which she only suspected but was not sure, and for his gentle kindness. He had been nothing but a gentleman during the whole process, but she could also tell he knew his way around a woman's body. She tried not to think of the other women he had probably been with. Tried not to imagine who they were or how she could not compare. She was his wife. Not those other women who only passed through his life in a port where his ship was docked. She would be the keeper of his heart, the maker of his home, and the mother of his children. Reaching down and brushing her hand lightly across her stomach, she hoped the last of these duties was already underway. The movement caused George to stir.

"Nelly? Are you awake?"

"Yes."

"Are you all right?"

He rolled over, and she could smell the warmness of him as the blanket shifted.

"Yes, I was just thinking."

He groaned slightly and placed his arm under his head to prop it up a bit. She could tell in the darkness that he was looking at her but could not make out his expression.

"Not about that ring, I hope," he said.

"Oh no." She laughed. "That was a party game gone terribly awry, and I will not consider it again." She reached out and ran her hands through his hair and down the side of his cheek. "No, I was thinking of our children and how I hoped the first one was on its way."

"Already? Woman, we haven't even been married twenty-four hours yet! What is your rush?" He laughed so she would know he was joking, but part of him was also serious. He wasn't quite sure himself if he was ready to be a father. He knew it would come in time and hoped that when it did, he would be ready then.

"Of course I want it to happen soon!" she said playfully. "You will be gone away at sea. Are you going to just leave me here alone with no one to talk to?"

"Alone? I doubt very much you will be alone here on Butler's Point," he replied, thinking of the myriad number of his siblings and their children who came in and out of his parents' dwelling each day. "Besides, when you are not here, you will be at your father's place. Your sister will certainly keep you entertained."

Nelly pondered that for a moment and then said, "I want to keep a piece of you with me at all times." She snuggled deeper under the covers so that her face nuzzled into the hairs on his chest. She entwined her legs with his, feeling the warmth of their bodies as they touched. "Can you understand that? How having your child within me or caring for your children leaves a piece of you with me always? Besides, we may not have that much time together."

"What do you mean we don't have much time?" he asked, kissing the top of her head.

"Well, despite the obvious that you will be leaving for the winter rum run in a few months, I…well, I just feel…" Her voice trailed off.

How could she explain this to him? "What happens if you don't return?"

"Ah, I see," he said. "My practical Nelly is worried about becoming a widow on her wedding night. Am I right?"

"Well…I wouldn't say it like that!" she laughed, giving him a little pinch under the covers.

"Well, then, what would you say?"

She rose up and leaned over him. "I would say that you are the best catch a girl could ever wish for. That I am happy and proud to call you my husband. That being your wife and the mother of your children will make me the happiest woman in the world!"

As she spoke, he could feel the ends of her hair falling down and brushing against his shoulders. It tickled, but he didn't dare brush them away. He wanted to let her finish her thoughts.

"But I also know the dangers of your profession. I understand there may come a time when I stand out on the point scanning the horizon for signs of your ship that I may never see. That a day could come when I eagerly await your return to show you your son for the first time only to have you never see either one of us again." With these words, she leaned down and kissed him hard. "I fear that I will not be with you long. I cannot bear that thought. That is why I wish to start having your children immediately so that a piece of you will forever reside with me should the unthinkable happen." In the darkness, she wished she could see his face. She felt his hand caress her face, and he kissed her.

"A man must also consider himself lucky to have found a woman as devoted to him and the continuation of his family as you are, Nelly. I will never leave you, I promise." He kissed her again, harder this time. "And I'm damn sure I will work as hard as I can to give you as many children as you want." He laughed and rolled over on top her. "If it's a piece of me you wish to keep, then a piece of me you shall have."

CHAPTER FIFTEEN

The first Sunday after the wedding

Seated at his desk in his private study, Reverend Crawford checked his sermon notes one more time. He had invested far more time, prayer, and energy into this Coming Out sermon than he had ever done in the past. These sermons were usually not a time of fire and brimstone or harsh speaking to the congregation. However, this one needed to be. He had not been at Butler's Point for the wedding festivities, but news traveled fast around the bay, and he had heard all about it. The fact that Abner Blaisdell had even taken his daughter there in the first place was enough to convince him that whatever was afoot here, Abner and the rest of the Blaisdell clan were somehow responsible. The stories of the burning sheets, demonic voices, and now this ring were all anyone talked about anymore. The community was becoming polarized. It had always been a struggle to keep his flock of mixed denominations all focused on the same goal, eternal life. He now felt as if they were tearing at each other's throats over this Blaisdell nonsense.

"Arch? Will we be going soon?" his wife, Anna, hollered to him from the hallway. Her heels clicked on the hardwood floors as she approached his study.

"Yes. I believe I'm ready," he said.

Anna entered the room, struggling to place her bonnet on her head. The strings were twisted, and one hung over her shoulder. She reached back, trying to grasp it.

"Here, Anna, let me help you." He pulled the string forward so that it was within her reach.

"Thank you," she said. "Are you sure you're ready?"

"Yes." With a sigh, he picked up his sermon notes that were lying on his desk.

Anna eyed them and then turned her gaze upon him. "Do you think it will help?"

"I can only hope," he said, thumbing through the pages. "This latest incident with the ring has really set the whole town on fire."

"Oh dear!" Anna said, rolling her eyes. "Mabel Wadsworth was like a chattering old hen at the sewing circle yesterday. Telling everyone that she had firsthand knowledge that Lydia Blaisdell had made a pact with the devil himself to coerce George Butler into marrying her. She said the ring was engraved with their names by the finger of Satan!"

"Lord forgive them," Reverend Crawford said, shaking his head and reaching for his hat. "Pray, Anna. Pray for me that I will be able to set this all to rest today. That this town will heal."

"I will." She took his arm as they left their home for the short walk to the meetinghouse.

✦ ———— ✦

At the meetinghouse, Mary Blaisdell held her head high, jutting her chin out as she walked with a clipped step down the center aisle. She clutched Lydia by the arm and held her tightly to her body, trying to protect the child from the stares and whispers as if they were daggers being thrown in their direction. Abner had absolutely refused to accompany her to meeting today. However, she felt that being in the Lord's house on the Lord's day was what everyone needed to see Lydia doing. All of this talk about the devil was absurd.

"Good morning, Sister Blaisdell," Abigail Abbott said as Mary and Lydia slid into their pew in front of her.

"Good day to you, Abigail," Mary nodded.

Abigail reached over the pew and touched Mary's shoulder lightly. "I am so sorry for all the talk around town," she whispered. "I am so glad to see you here today. I was fearful that you would not come."

Mary's back stiffened in response. "I thank thee, Abigail, but really, there is nothing to talk about. I don't know why everyone has turned their hatred on my daughter." Mary considered Abigail an acquaintance but not a good friend. They mostly saw each other in meeting or occasionally in town. She wasn't about to imply to Abigail that any of the talk about this ring was true. After all, she had seen

Abner return the ring to George Butler before they had left. Who knew if George had done something with the ring to incite all of this talk himself.

"Truly, Mary, you have my sympathies," Abigail was saying. "To have half the town saying your daughter has made a pact with the devil must be terribly upsetting."

Mary turned in her seat so that Abigail could see the indignation on her face. "Please, Sister Abbott, if you must talk about my daughter, do so in truth. There is no pact with the devil. The ring was a simple party game that Lydia inadvertently stumbled into the middle of. I have heard what they are saying, and it is simply not true. Abner retrieved the ring and gave it to Sally Hooper, and we left Butler's Point. Although I did not behold the ring closely, I can assure you that had the devil truly engraved Lydia's name on the ring, Abner would have seen it. Perhaps Captain Butler should be held responsible for what is on that ring, not my child!"

Mary nodded curtly to emphasize her point and turned back around in her pew. She fumbled with the pleats in Lydia's skirt, trying to smooth them out as if this, too, would smooth out the whole affair. She looked into Lydia's deep brown eyes and her heart ached for what this child must be going through. As her mother, it was her place to defend her child, and defend her she would.

"Furthermore, Sister Abbott," she said, turning back around, "everyone should be asking themselves—who had access to an engraver? A ten year-old girl or a sea captain just back from a trip?" Mary held Abigail's eyes, daring her to disagree with her.

"Mary, my apologies if you thought I had any ill will for your family. I truly did not. I only spoke to inform you that you have a friend in me if you need one." She leaned back.

Lydia watched her mother's face remain stiff and unmovable.

"Thank you, Sister Abbott," Lydia replied, reaching over to take her mother's hand when Mary said nothing. "We will remember you in our prayers."

Out on the bay, George dipped the oars deep into the water and pulled backward with all of his might. He felt the boat lurch forward, scrape along the bottom in the shallow water, and land solidly in the pebbles of the shoreline. He was glad he had made the decision to row his wife up the narrows rather than go with the rest of the Butler clan overland. Not only had it allowed them this private time out on the water, but they had also been able to stay abed in the log cabin a little longer. He smiled at the memory.

"We have arrived, Mrs. Butler!" he said, leaping out of the bow of the boat. With one quick jerk, he pulled the boat higher onto the shoreline.

"George!" Nelly squealed, grasping the gunwales to prevent herself from being tipped over backward and out of the boat. "Are you trying to unseat me?" she laughed.

"Nothing of the sort," he said, bending over to slip one arm under her knees and the other around her waist. "I'm just trying to keep you and all of your finery out of the tide." Lifting her high, he gingerly made his way through the rocks and up over the ledge to the path. Setting her safely down, he bowed mockingly in front of her.

"Your Highness, I have successfully gotten you ashore!"

"George, stop it!" she giggled, trying to straighten the skirts of the creamy apricot dress. "People are staring at us!" She glanced around and nodded here and there to the folks who were looking her way. "Get up, you fool!" she whispered.

Rising and stepping in front of her, he said, "Oh, let their tongues wag. Seems they will, anyway! Better that they are saying that Captain Butler loves his wife than what has been going around lately!" And with that, he kissed her hard on the mouth as he gripped her shoulders. She tried to wiggle away, but he held her firm and continued the kiss until someone shouted from up on the bluff.

"Attaboy, Captain!"

He pulled away and stepped back to see Nelly's face red with embarrassment.

"George!" She stamped her foot in indignation. "How dare you?"

"I dare because I love you, Nelly Butler! And I'd do it again if I thought you'd let me get away with it! What other time in our lives do we have to put our love on public display than our Coming Out Sunday?" he said.

"Escort me to meeting then, Captain, and we shall discuss later how I shall show my love for you." She winked coyly at him as he grasped her hand with a hard squeeze.

The two of them made their way through the shoreline path, up over the bluff and into the town of Franklin proper.

Nelly looked exquisite in the apricot dress she had chosen for this very special day. Sally had helped her freshen up the little roses along the trim and brighten the lace. The bodice was cut slim and drew in at her waist. The skirt was full, and she liked the way it swayed back and forth as she walked toward the meetinghouse. Beside her, George wore his best blue suit and cream-colored stockings. His hair was powdered. The two of them made quite a striking pair. As they proceeded down the main thoroughfare, they were joined by several others also headed to meeting.

The younger men made joking reference to their first weekend together as a married couple. There were plenty of laughs and slaps on the back for George. The women were less likely to discuss the sexual nature of the past few days and instead peppered Nelly with questions about her plans for setting up housekeeping and exactly where she would live.

Suddenly, a voice rose from the crowd. "Do you have the devil's ring with you, Captain?"

Everyone stopped as George scanned the group looking for the source of the question.

"I say, sir, show yourself!" he hollered out.

Nelly reached up and touched his arm. "George, let it be. Come along." She tried urging him forward.

"I want to know who spoke it," he said. "I say again, sir, show yourself."

Atherton Oakes stepped forward. Sensing that this may or may not go well, a few in the group broke away and headed off. Those left hanging on were individuals who were known to delight in all of the rumors around town. This was more than they could ask for.

"Atherton," George said with a slight sigh of relief. "Good man, how are you?"

Atherton was known as a bit of a rabble-rouser, but George had known him for many years and didn't exactly consider him an enemy. Atherton's association with the Blaisdell family, though, was well known. He was married to Lydia's older sister Hannah. So George was a little bit leery of the direction of this question but not overly so.

"Do you have it?" Atherton persisted.

"Let us not talk of these things today, shall we?" George said, nodding in Nelly's direction. "It is my Coming Out Sunday, after all."

"There are in many in town who would like to see this ring, Captain."

"I'm sure there are, if the rumors are to be believed—it isn't every day that one finds a ring engraved by the hand of Satan!" George attempted a laugh, shaking his head and speaking a little louder so the crowd could hear him. "But I can assure you, Atherton, none of it is true, so there is no reason to produce it."

"But it is true that you placed a ring in the posset as a party game, correct?" Atherton pushed.

"Yes, that is true," George replied.

"And Lydia was the one who found the ring and upon doing so saw that both her name and yours were engraved upon it?"

George hesitated, remembering what he saw when he took the ring from Abner Blaisdell. He really did not want to be discussing that blasted ring anymore.

"No, that is not entirely correct," he said, staring intently into Atherton's eyes. "Lydia was the one who found the ring, but she never indicated to me or anyone else that she believed it to be engraved." Not exactly the truth, but not a lie, either. After holding his gaze for a moment longer, George turned. "Come, Nelly, let us go."

"But many at your gathering heard and saw the reaction from your family when the engraving was found," Atherton shouted toward them as they walked away. George stopped and turned back, facing his accuser. Murmurs were heard rumbling through the crowd.

"Atherton, I truly do not know why you are persisting in this ridiculous line of questioning."

"Captain, surely you can understand the interest this ring has generated…" he started to say before being cut off by another voice.

"The ring is gone."

They all turned to see Nelly's sister Sally hurrying toward the group, her skirts lifted up in her hands. "I tell you the ring is gone. I threw it into the bay myself."

A collective gasp went up from the crowd that was following them.

"Did she say it's in the bay?" someone said.

"It's true," Nelly said loudly, reaching out and grasping her sister's hand. They stood as a united front against the storm. "I saw her do it."

Atherton stared at the two women, clearly trying to determine whether they were telling the truth or lying to protect George.

"Why would you do such a thing?" he asked.

"Abner Blaisdell handed me the ring as he left Butler's Point. Apparently, he considers me the next eligible maiden to be married off. It then became my ring, and I could do with it what I wanted," Sally said.

George eyed Atherton. He could see the man's mind working trying to make sense of this new piece of information.

"Atherton, whatever you are trying to accomplish by this line of questioning will come to naught," he said. "Sally speaks the truth. I was there, too, and I saw her toss the ring into the bay. It's gone."

The majority of the crowd was beginning to disperse. The young men had lost interest because there clearly wasn't going to be a scuffle, and the young ladies went off to share the latest news. The ring was gone, no one would ever know now if it was truly engraved by the finger of Satan.

Nelly and Sally continued on their way to the meetinghouse as Atherton held George's arm for one final word. In a harshly whispered voice, he said, "Captain Butler, it is my belief, and that of many in this area, that you are responsible for the engraving on that ring."

George tried to remain calm, as he didn't want Atherton to feel him shaking.

"Me? Atherton, my God, man, think through what you are saying. Why would I spend the money to engrave another woman's—no, girl's—name on a ring that I was going to use at my own wedding? It's preposterous!" George scoffed at him and tried to pull away. But Atherton held his arm tight.

"Then explain, sir, the reaction from you, Sally, and several others when you all saw the ring."

George hesitated. He couldn't explain that, for he had clearly seen his name and Lydia's engraved on the ring, but he was not going to fan the flames by admitting it to Atherton or anyone else.

"The ring is gone, Atherton. We will not be discussing this further." He yanked his arm out of Atherton's grasp and hurried to catch up with Sally and Nelly.

"Do you think that will be the end of it?" Nelly whispered when he reached her side.

"I hope so," he replied, smiling and tipping his hat to a group of older ladies along the path. "Good day, ladies," he hollered out.

"Good day to you, Captain, and your new wife," one of them said in reply.

"Thank you, Sally," George said, making eye contact with his sister-in-law.

"Let's just hope that puts an end to it," Sally said. "It is long past the time when this whole Lydia Blaisdell mess should be put to rest."

Nelly said a silent prayer that her sister was right as the three of them climbed the steps of the meetinghouse and went inside.

†———†

As George and Nelly waited in the vestibule, the remaining congregants made their way to their seats and got settled. Reverend Crawford stood at the pulpit at the front of the hall. Below him was a sea of faces. His flock was a mixture of Baptists and Methodists with a sprinkling of others who preferred not to align themselves with any particular denomination. By staying away from the muddy details of conflicting doctrine, he had managed to keep everyone happy for the most part.

He was looking for Abner Blaisdell, but he did not see him. Seated in the Blaisdells' pew was only Mary, the small child Lydia, her older sister Hannah, and Atherton Oakes. So Abner had chosen to keep away from everyone on the Lord's Day. Or had he only chosen to stay away because it was George and Nelly's Coming Out Sunday? Either way, it only further solidified his opinion of the man. If there was a plot to trick George into marrying Lydia, then Abner had been behind it.

Reverend Crawford raised his arms, spreading them out in a welcome. "Brothers and sisters, welcome," he said. The whispered voices quieted, and he had everyone's full attention.

"I would like to welcome you all to the Coming Out Sunday for Captain and Mrs. Butler, who were married just two days ago at Butler's Point."

Everyone in the room turned in their pew to look toward the vestibule door. George, with Nelly on his arm, entered the room and proceeded down the center aisle. As they passed each pew, the whispered well-wishes of the townsfolk could be heard. George led Nelly to the seats of honor—two huge, ornately carved chairs placed at the front of the hall to the left of the pulpit. From here, they could see everyone, and everyone could see them. They were the spectacle of the day.

"Today, brothers and sisters, I will be speaking from the verses of Luke 10:41 and 42, the story of Martha and Mary meeting our Lord and Savior Jesus Christ. I hope to share with you a little insight that you may or may not have thought of before when reading these particular verses." He paused, and then raising his arms toward heaven, he bowed his head and said, "Let us pray. Lord God, hear our words this day as we welcome Captain and Mrs. Butler into the soul of our community. May they always feel welcomed here, Lord. May their path through life be free of hardships that would cause their hearts to falter. May they have strong faith in Your everlasting love for them. And may they always feel the love and support of this, their spiritual family. In the name of Jesus Christ, amen." He raised his head to a chorus of "amens" from the congregation and reached for his notes.

"When the Lord arrived at the home of Martha and Mary, He did not come alone. With him were disciples and followers, people of every persuasion. Not all of these people were interested in things of a spiritual nature. Mixed among those seeking the teachings of Christ were individuals there to collect gossip that they could then spread throughout the towns. There were seekers of truth and seekers of deceit. While there were many who wanted to support the Savior, there were also many who wanted to make things difficult for Him."

Reverend Crawford knew this was a stretch for this particular verse, but he hoped he was sounding convincing. He turned the page on his notes and continued.

"With a multitude to feed, Martha immediately set about getting her house in order. Mary, on the other hand, went directly to the Savior and sat at his feet, waiting to hear the truths that he would speak. The scriptures tell us that Martha busied herself with food preparations—surely she had help and did not try to do this all alone. There must have been other people with her in her kitchen or workrooms. What were these people talking about as they prepared the meal?" He stopped here and looked out over the faces. Were they following him? He hoped so.

"I'm sure some were excited about the truths that they hoped to hear from the Savior. But were there also some there who said unpleasant things about the Savior? The scriptures are silent on this, but we know human nature. When you have a controversial person in your midst, there will always be different opinions. So I do not believe it is a stretch to think that there would have been varying opinions on exactly who the man seated in the next room claimed himself to be."

Reverend Crawford continued, "We know from the scriptures that Martha went to the Lord and complained about Mary's lack of help in preparing the meal. She wanted her sister with her, but Mary was with the Savior, listening intently to His words. She was not in the workrooms listening to the idle chatter of the others. The Lord's reply to Martha's complaint is very direct and straightforward. He said, 'Martha, Martha, thou art careful and troubled about many things.'" He lifted his head to make eye contact with a few in the audience. "What things do you think were being said in the workroom that were troubling Martha? Ponder that for a moment, and think how the words that come forth out of your own mouths might be causing trouble for someone else."

He paused, letting that sink in, and then he continued. "The Lord then said, 'But one thing is needful and Mary hath chosen that good part.' What part was that?" He removed his spectacles for a moment so he could address the congregation without reading from his notes. "Many times when these particular verses are spoken of, we think of Martha being caught up in the things of the world. The day-to-day tasks we all must complete. We think of Mary as sitting at the feet of the Lord, feasting upon His Word. Many a minister has used these verses to urge you to spend more of your day focused on the spiritual aspect of your life rather than the daily tasks of living. But today, I want to challenge you to think of these differently."

He went on, "What if the good part that Mary had chosen was to avoid the gossip that was taking place in the other room? What if these verses have nothing whatsoever to do with womanly chores and duties but rather convey a very important lesson that we all need to learn? We must not gossip. We must only open our mouths and let our voices speak words that are uplifting and kind for our fellow man." He stopped and looked down at Lydia.

"Brothers and sisters, I am not going to stand here today and pretend that I do not hear the talk that flies around this town." He turned and looked at George and Nelly. "This couple has chosen each other. They are right for each other. God has placed them together. One only has to look at them to see the deep love and affection that they have for each other." He smiled at George and Nelly and then turned back to the congregation. "I know that there are some in this town who would have preferred if these two had not married." His eyes traveled to the Blaisdells' pew. How he wished it were Abner sitting there, but it was not going to alter what he had to say. Let Mary Blaisdell take these words home to her husband, if need be.

"There are some in this area whose hearts are set on the riches of the world, and that clouds their minds and brings evil into their lives. This evil has spread outward and is now affecting our whole community. On both sides of this bay, people have taken up sides against their brothers. Tongues wag in constant motion with this story and that. With each and every telling, the stories become more elaborate and far-fetched until at last there is talk of demons and pacts with the devil." He thumped his fist down hard on the pulpit. "I will no longer tolerate such talk!"

Lydia sat in stunned silence at what she heard. She was but a child and sometimes the things that adults said were hard for her to follow, but that was not the case in this situation. She knew exactly what Reverend Crawford was saying and who he was saying it about. This was about her and George. The pounding of the pulpit was scaring her, and she leaned in closer to her mother. As Reverend Crawford expounded on God's plan for George and Nelly, she felt her legs begin to tremble. She placed both of her hands on the seat of the pew to try and steady herself. Pressing down hard, she tried to hold herself still. It was then that she noticed the pocket on her skirt. It was moving about on its own, like there was a mouse inside of it. But Lydia knew there was no mouse in her pocket. Instead, she knew what was in there. The ring. She had kept the ring with her every day since it had flown out of the bay. She had placed it inside her pocket before heading off to meeting with her mother. And now, the louder that Reverend Crawford got, the more the ring jumped around in her pocket.

Raising his voice even louder, Reverend Crawford continued with his sermon. "As the mouthpiece of the Lord in this corner of His vineyard, I proclaim to you today that just as Jesus spoke to Martha and said, 'Mary hath chosen that good part, which shall not be taken away from her,' I say to you that this man and woman have chosen the good part." He raised his hand and pointed directly at George and Nelly. "They will not be separated, and this woman's husband will not be taken from her and given to another!"

With that, he slammed his fist down hard on the pulpit once again.

The ring flew out of Lydia's pocket.

"Oh no!" she screamed, jumping up and grasping the air as the ring flew across the room. Mary reached for her daughter, not knowing what was happening. At the sound of Lydia's voice, many in the room turned and looked in her direction until the sound of clinking silver could be heard from the pulpit. All heads spun around to see the tiny silver ring spinning slowly around in a circle before coming to rest right in front of George's feet.

For a few seconds, there was absolute silence in the meetinghouse, and then chaos erupted. Women fainted, and men began hollering. There was much finger-pointing as to who was the culprit who had thrown a ring at George.

"What a horrible prank!" Nelly exclaimed.

George bent down and picked up the ring. It didn't take him long to recognize it was the little ring that Sally had thrown into the bay two evenings prior. No, this was not a prank. This was the same ring he had brought home, to be put in the posset. He felt a knot form in his stomach as he turned the ring to see inside the band. There were the words he did not wish to see. His and Lydia's names. Only this time, there was something else engraved on the ring. The room was erupting around him as everyone tried to talk over one another. He steadied his shaking hands so he could see the ring more clearly. Inside the band of the little silver ring was engraved *George & Lydia Butler*, as before, but now George saw the year 1800 was engraved as well.

Standing, feeling his legs begin to shake, he scanned the pandemonium below him, trying to find the small child. There she was, standing next to her mother. His eyes locked with hers. She held his gaze. It was as if the space between them had quickly been swallowed up, and he felt as if he were standing right in front of her. She knew he had the ring.

"George? Is it the same ring?" It was Nelly's voice that brought him back.

"Uh…no. No, it's just a cheap pewter thing," he said, stuffing the ring deep inside the breast pocket of his coat. "Look, we have to get out of here. Now!" He grabbed Nelly's wrist and helped her down onto the floor in front of the first row of pews.

"George, over here!"

He turned and saw his brother Peter standing next to a side door that was propped open.

"Come, Nelly, this way." He pulled her along with him as they made their way out of the meetinghouse. A few hands reached out, grabbing at him.

"Was it the ring, Captain? Was it the ring?"

Reverend Crawford was still pounding on his pulpit, hollering, "Brothers, sisters! Please stop this nonsense!"

All George wanted to do was get his wife away from all of this. Away from Lydia. Away from whatever evil was building itself within that little girl and trying to suck him in. As he and Nelly burst out into the sunshine, he scooped her up into his arms.

"I will never let anything hurt you. Do you understand me?" He pressed his face to hers and kissed her hard on the lips. "Never."

"George!" Nelly sputtered under the pressure of his mouth. "George! You're frightening me. Stop! Put me down."

He glanced back over his shoulder. He could see people pouring out of the front and side doors of the church. His brother Peter was talking to a group of men and pointing off in the direction of the road back toward Butler's Point. Good! Maybe that would give him and Nelly time to get over the edge of the bank and into their boat. He could always count on Peter to think quickly in a tight situation.

"George!" Nelly said again. "I really wish you would put me down!"

"Not yet," he replied. "I want to make sure we are safely away."

His feet were slipping in the loose pebbles as he tried picking his way down the steep bank. Twice he thought he was going to fall, but he regained control of himself and kept his balance. He could see his skiff bobbing slightly in the shallow waves. Placing Nelly in the bow, he looked one more time over his shoulder. "Quick, get to the stern!"

As she scrambled forward, he gave the boat a shove and jumped in. Finding his place in the middle seat, he grabbed the oars and propelled the boat farther out into deeper water. Quickly pulling on the right oar, he spun the bow of the boat toward the east.

"Where are we going?" Nelly asked.

"They will be expecting us to head straight for Butler's Point. So we will go to your parents' home instead."

She could see his muscles straining under his coat as he plunged the oars deep into the water and pulled backward. They were making quick time, and it didn't take long for him to get the boat out of view of the town and headed east through the narrows. George slowed his rowing a bit once they were safely out of view.

"George?" Nelly asked, reaching forward to touch his arms.

He lifted his head and looked at her.

"Nelly, I never want to lose you," he said, staring intently into her eyes.

She held his gaze, feeling the boat's slow forward momentum even without his efforts. She felt, more than saw, the tall pine trees drift past.

"Lose me?" She was shocked by his response. "Dear husband, I believe it is I who is more in fear of losing you."

He dug the oars in deep again and pulled back hard. His brows furrowed, showing not only his efforts in rowing but also his exasperation with this situation.

"We need to get away from here," he said. "And we'll be better for it the sooner that we can."

CHAPTER SIXTEEN

Nelly's parents were only slightly surprised to find the newlyweds at their house when they arrived home from the meetinghouse. Nelly sat at the small writing table while George stood looking out the window. It was evident that the two of them had been in deep discussion and had stopped abruptly when the rest of the family appeared.

"Are you two all right?" Joanna gasped as soon as she saw them in her drawing room. "I was so hoping you would be here. Half the town has raced to Butler's Point looking for you."

"Yes, and it wouldn't surprise me if the other half decided to look for us here," George said, not taking his eyes from the road.

"Indeed," David said, opening a small chest on the mantel. He withdrew his firing pistol and began priming it with ball and powder.

"David!" Joanna reacted. "You do not think that it will come to that, do you?"

"I certainly hope not, Joanna, but I will not allow Abner Blaisdell and his riffraff of a family to cause us any trouble here." He jammed the ramrod deep into the barrel of the gun to make his point.

"What do they have to gain by all of this?" Joanna asked. "George is married now. Certainly they must understand that."

"Oh, they understand it, Mother," Sally said, entering the room. "Now I believe they are just angry and trying to stir up trouble."

"That's exactly what it is," Nelly replied. "When we arrived at the meetinghouse, the whole town was talking about that silly little ring. To have someone in the congregation throw a ring at us was no more than an attempt to keep the talk going."

Sally was nodding her head in agreement. "The ring is at the bottom of the bay where it belongs. This is nothing more than a prank."

Nelly was warming to this conversation dramatically. She stood and walked to her husband near the window. Slipping her arm around his, she said, "George, you see, there is no reason to be so upset. Sally is right—things will calm down eventually. This is not the time for quick decisions. We should think this through."

"Decisions?" Joanna asked. "What decisions are you considering?"

For the first time, George turned from his place at the window and looked at his in-laws. In a stone-cold voice that sent a shiver up Nelly's spine, he said, "Father Hooper, may I have a few words with you alone?"

David nodded, stood, and walked to the door. With his hand on the doorknob, he opened the door wider. "Joanna, take the girls upstairs."

"George?" Nelly said, looking up at him.

"Go, Nelly. Go with your mother and sister." He looked at her gravely, and she knew not to disagree. He kissed her gently on the cheek. "It will all be all right, I promise."

Gathering her skirts, Nelly headed for the door. She followed her mother, who had already risen. Sally was the last to exit. Still single, and probably destined to be so for many years, she had a defiant streak. It only took a glare from her father, though, to get her out the door. David closed the door quietly and turned to his son-in-law.

"Is there more to this than the ladies know?" he asked. It was obvious George was very upset about this situation despite the fact the women wanted to make light of it.

"Yes," George said, sitting down. "I'm not totally convinced this is all just an act."

"How so?" David asked him.

George hesitated, wondering if he should tell David about the ring or not—or, for that matter, if he should tell him any of the things he had seen happen with Lydia Blaisdell.

"Father Hooper…I…well…it's just…" he stammered.

"Son, just speak your mind, please."

George sat bent over, staring at his hands. He looked up as he spoke. "I've seen things at the Blaisdells' that I don't want to speak of, but because of them I'm not totally convinced this is just a prank."

"What kinds of things?"

"Evil things. Or maybe not. Maybe the child—Lydia, I mean—is just ill." He ran his hands through his hair, showing his frustration.

"And there is more. The ring, the one that was tossed at Nelly and me." He looked at his father-in-law gravely. "It is the one from the posset."

David stood staring at him, tapping his loaded pistol methodically against his thigh. "How can that be? Sally threw it into the bay, didn't she?"

"Yes, she did. I saw her do it with my own eyes."

"Then it can't possibly be the same ring, George. Surely you are mistaken."

"No, I am not. I am certain." George stared long and hard at David, then reached into his breast pocket to withdraw the ring. "This is the same ring Sally threw into the bay, and yet here it sits in my hand. Is this not evil, Father Hooper? Is this not something I should protect your daughter from?"

"Lord God, save us!" David exclaimed as he sat down next to George. "How can this be?"

"I don't know. I honestly don't know," George said, quickly putting the ring back into his pocket. It was incredible enough that the ring had returned. That should prove his point well enough. David did not need to see the additional engraving that had appeared. That was something George would show to no one. "What I do know is this evil is seeking out Nelly and me. Whether it truly is the devil or simply an elaborate hoax by the Blaisdells, it will not stop as long as Nelly and I are here." He took a deep breath and plunged on. "That is why I have spoken to Nelly about taking her with me on my next voyage."

"Voyage?" David exclaimed. "You mean to say you wish to take my daughter to sea?"

"Yes, I know that is quite unorthodox, sir, but I cannot leave her here. Not with all of this happening. I would fear for her life."

"I cannot agree to this. I simply cannot." His father-in-law was sputtering as he placed his pistol on the mantel and began to pace around the room. "A woman's place is not on a ship, George. You of all people should know that."

"I do, but I also know that my wife's safety may be dependent on her being with me. For that reason, I cannot leave her behind."

"She may be your wife, but she is still my daughter. I am perfectly capable of keeping her safe while you are away."

George stood, shaking his head. "No, sir. I don't believe you are." He reached into his pocket and withdrew the ring one more time. "This was at the bottom of the bay!" he shouted.

David stepped quickly in front of him. "Keep your voice down, boy, or the women will hear you!"

"You have to listen to reason," George hissed. "My wife. Your daughter. This evil is trying to get at her. Get at me. We have to leave this place. I will not leave without her, do you understand that?" George was shaking with a combination of rage and fear. "I am taking her. Either with your blessing or not. We will leave in the morning."

He turned to make his way to the door, but David rushed before him and reached it first, blocking his exit. "George, I cannot let you take my daughter to sea. Let me think for a moment."

George waited, staring at him.

"Take her to York. She can stay with my brother while you are gone. But for the love of God, please do not take her to the Caribbean," David pleaded.

This was a development that George had not thought of. Would he feel safe leaving Nelly with people he did not know? They were, after all, her family. He exhaled and spoke.

"I did not realize that you had a brother in York. I still am unsure if leaving her there would be safe. Too many in this area have ties to York. I do not want it known where she is."

"She has never been to York. No one will know her—or you, for that matter."

"Well, I have done business with a merchant there, Stephen Chase."

"Oh," David replied, looking down at the floor.

"I have only met the man once. If I do not make an attempt to contact him while in town, and we place Nelly with your brother under a different name, it just might work," George said, sounding mildly intrigued by this thought. "But no one, and I mean no one, in this town must know. They will all be told that she is going to sea with me."

David was nodding in agreement. "I will write a letter to my brother immediately telling him to accept the both of you into his home." He hurried to the writing desk. He withdrew a foolscap of paper and began dipping the quill in the ink.

"And what name will we use?" George asked.

The scratching of the quill stopped momentarily as David thought. "Daniel and Mary Lee," he finally said, bobbing his head in satisfaction.

"Daniel and Mary Lee?" George asked. "Who are they?"

"Daniel was a man I met along the St. Croix during the Revolution. Pembroke, I believe, he was from. Nice enough fellow, but there was always something shifty about him in his mannerisms. He and his family have relocated to St. Andrews, New Brunswick. More than likely because he was a spy! No chance of anyone in York knowing that name."

George smiled. This might actually work!

Dear Brother James,

I hope this letter finds you and yours well. As you will have noticed, the presenter of this missive is a young man and his new bride. The bride is your niece, my daughter, Nelly. She is your kin, and I am sending hope and prayers that you will accept her into your home as your own at this time. For you see, the young man is a sea captain about to leave on a six-month voyage. Due to some very trying circumstances here in Franklin, it is impossible for him to leave her behind. His first decision was to take her with him; however, I cannot allow that. It is my wish that you will keep her within your household while he is away. However, due to the fact that there are many connections between York and Franklin, we cannot let anyone know she is with you. I trust that you will understand the seriousness of this situation if I tell you they must interact with you and the townsfolk under the assumed names of Daniel and Mary Lee. Please, dear brother, do not tell even your own wife of her true identity. Her mother, sister, and everyone here will be under the impression that she is traveling to the Caribbean with her husband, as abhorrent as that sounds. Tongues cannot wag more than they already are! But that is a story for another letter. I just need to keep her safe while her husband fulfills his obligation on this voyage. I am certain that upon his return he will undertake another line of employment where he can be more readily available to her. I thank you in advance for helping me with this and keeping it all confidential.

Sincerely,
Your humble and grateful brother David

Joanna Hooper nearly fainted when she heard her husband tell her that he was allowing Nelly to sail to the Caribbean with George.

"Well, I never!" she said, storming about the kitchen.

Sally sat with her mouth agape. "Father, are you serious?"

David cleared his throat. "Uh, yes. George will leave in the morning with Nelly."

Nelly leapt up from the bowl of peas she was shelling, rushing to his side. "Father, you were my last vestige of hope for some sanity in all of this! Certainly you do not want me to sail aboard a ship."

"It is not a matter of what I want, Nelly. It is a matter of what your husband deems is best for you. He is your keeper now. He has stated his case, and I cannot argue with its points. You will accompany him on his voyage to the Caribbean so as to remove you both from this situation with the Blaisdells."

Nelly spun to face George. "You, you…! Aargh!" she screamed as she ran from the room.

Sally snickered. "First fight."

"Sally, that is enough!" said Joanna.

George turned, shaking his father-in-law's hand. "Thank you. This is for the best, I know it is."

"You do not have to reassure me, son," David said, nodding in the direction that Nelly had fled. "But I think if you do not wish to sleep alone in the hayloft tonight, you might try and reassure her."

✦ ———— ✦

"Nelly! Please, open the door." George stood outside of the small gardening shed that Nelly had fled to. She sat in a pile of skirts and petticoats in the corner. Dust particles danced on the rays of sunlight that shone through the cracks in the old door. She could see George pacing on the other side as the light shifted and changed as he moved about.

"Nelly…this is breaking my heart. Please open the door. At least let me talk to you." He leaned his head against the door, feeling the cracked paint press into his forehead.

"You can talk to me through the door," she snapped back at him in anger.

"No, I do not want to talk to my wife through a door. You are my wife, are you not?"

"I was this morning, but now I don't know what I am. As your wife, I should be privy to decisions that involve me!" she huffed.

"I had to make this one alone. It is far too serious of a situation, and I could see that you and Sally are just treating it lightly."

Nelly stood and reached for the handle of the old door. Flinging it open, she caught George completely by surprise. He had been leaning with all of his weight on the door and when she opened it, he fell into the shed, collapsing on her.

"Ahhh!" she hollered out, feeling all of his weight suddenly pressing down on her. His face was a few inches from her.

"Well, I must say you certainly changed your mind quickly!" He kissed her gently on the lips and then more forcefully as he felt her respond. She moaned. "There, see, you are not nearly as angry as you thought you were."

She was breathing heavily from the shock of him falling onto her. Or was it the closeness of him? She loved him so that the physical touch of him made her weak.

"George…" she started to say, but he stopped her with another kiss.

"Shhh. Just this once, can't you trust me?" He kissed her again.

"Are you really that concerned about a little girl?" She looked up into his eyes.

He stared back at her for a long moment, then rolled over and sat up. Grasping her by the hands, he helped her to a sitting position. Kissing the backs of both her hands, he looked at her.

"I do not believe it is just a little girl. There is more happening here. Whether it's her family behind it or something else, I do not know. But I do not intend to let it threaten my wife or my happiness. We will leave here. Give things time to calm down. Distance and time usually solve most everything."

"But George, my sister is here. My friends are here. I was hoping to start work on turning that old cabin into a home for you. I cannot do that bobbing about the ocean on a boat!" She reached down and placed her hand on her stomach. "And what if I am already with child? I will be terrified to be alone at sea with a ship full of men rather than here with my own mother nearby." Tears began to fill her eyes.

"I do not wish to delay our family, Nelly, but I doubt much you are with child after only a couple of nights. And even if you are, we will return home long before you shall have to give birth. I promise." George smiled at her, knowing full well that even if she were with child, she would not be aboard a ship but safely tucked into her uncle's home in York. But that was a conversation that would wait until later. "You'll see, all will be well." He looked into her eyes, hoping for a sign of encouragement.

"Captain Butler," she replied in a stern voice, "when I agreed to become your wife just a few short days ago, I agreed to do so no matter what life would throw at us. I agreed that I would trust you and confide in you and love you all the days of my life." She swallowed hard and stood. "I did not at that time think that it would mean I would also become part of your crew, but sir, if that is what is required, then I shall do it!" She curtsied before bowing her head and looking at her shoes.

"Goodness gracious, Nelly." George started to laugh as he scrambled to get up from the shed floor. "You will never be part of my crew! You will always be my first mate!"

She stood on her tiptoes and kissed him. "I'm sorry I was disagreeable. I was just immensely shocked by this turn of events, that is all. It actually might be exciting to sail the world with you."

George smiled to himself. Perfect! Now that he had convinced her to go to sea, he would have to convince her to stay in York with strangers for six months. Being married was turning out to be more difficult than he had imagined!

◆———◆

The following day Reuben Gray was shaking his head as he stood on the deck of the *Schoodic*. He was watching the tableau in front of him with all the suspicion of an old seaman. Nelly was crying hysterically as she said her goodbyes to her mother and sister. Off to one side stood her father with George's parents and various other family members.

"Bad, bad luck to take a woman to sea," he muttered under his breath. "Let alone one who is bringing that much misery with her."

"What's that you say?"

Reuben jumped when he heard George behind him.

"Aye, nothing, Captain. Just, if you don't mind my sayin', it's bad luck to bring a woman aboard."

George eyed the man coolly. "There will be no more talk of that. Do you understand?"

Reuben understood and nodded. "Yes, Captain. My apologies for speaking out of turn."

George gazed over the bay. "Now let's get this ship underway. We are losing the tide quickly, and I don't want to be stuck in the narrows on a sand bar." Turning, he walked toward Nelly and the rest of the family. Placing his hand around her waist, he spoke to them all. "It is time."

"Goodbye, my dear." Joanna hugged her daughter one last time and turned away into the arms of her husband.

"Goodbye, Mother," Nelly whispered softly.

Leaning in to kiss her sister, Sally gave her hand a squeeze. "Come back to us in the spring glowing with a child, okay?"

"I will, Sally. I love you."

The Butlers all stepped up to wish their goodbyes to Nelly as well. George's father whispered quietly in his ear as he clasped his hand in farewell. "Keep her safe, son. If any harm befalls her, the Hoopers will never let us hear the end of it."

George smiled. He had not even told his own parents of the plan to leave Nelly in York.

After all the goodbyes were said, George walked Nelly up the gangplank and they both stood at the rail waving. George's men quickly untied the ship, and she lifted with the tide. The sails unfurled and began to blow in the breeze, and they were soon on their way. George kissed Nelly gently on the cheek.

"You stay and watch as long as you need to. I've got work to do." He squeezed her arm in parting. She stood there watching while the dock and her family got smaller and smaller. Eventually, she turned away from her past and toward what would become her future. The mouth of the bay and the wide Atlantic Ocean lay in front of her, and she knew it was time to think about her next adventure.

CHAPTER SEVENTEEN

October 12, 1795
York, Maine

Although this letter indicates it comes from Mary Lee, I assure you, my
dearest mother, that it is I, your daughter Nelly, writing to you.

I would hope that by now Father has informed you of my whereabouts
to help ease your mind. If not, then let me be the first to tell you. I am living
in York with Father's brother James and his family. This appears to be a plot
hatched by Father and George. I am living here under the name of Mary Lee.
All of those tears you shed on my shoulder at my parting were for naught, as I
am merely two hundred miles or so down the coast. If Father has not told you
of this, then by all means show him this letter so he will explain to you why
he did this. George did his best to explain to me the necessity of doing it this
way. He has assured me that if he could have canceled his Caribbean trip, he
would have. However, he felt the money to be earned by making a run that
way one more time was worth it. He said it will set him up well to become
established in another trade upon his return in the spring. I must trust in
my husband and his decisions. I miss him terribly. Watching his ship sail out
of the harbor a little over a month ago was heart-wrenching.

I am settled well here with Uncle James, although it is quite odd to have
everyone call me Mary. Even James's wife Eliza has not been made aware
of my true identity. They have a lovely, large home that sits high on a hill
overlooking the harbor. Eliza and I spend most of our time out on the wide
porch. We hang the laundry there, as well as sit in the rockers to do the
sewing. The view is expansive, and one can see all of the activity coming and
going into the harbor. York is certainly a much busier place than Franklin!
I have been getting to know my cousins and the rest of the family, although
they do not know who I am truly. It is not a bad "prison" to be in. I would
rather be with my husband working on starting our family. We were

apparently unsuccessful in doing so in the short time we spent together as husband and wife. I will hope for better results in the spring. I must close. The page from the ship heading Downeast just arrived and needs to take this letter with him. Write to me often, Mother, only remember to address your letters to Mary Lee at the home of James Hooper.

With love and kindness, your daughter Nelly

November 1, 1795
Franklin, Maine

My Dearest Nelly,

Or should I say Mary? With such joy and gladness I received your letter dated October 12th. No, your father had not informed me that you were in York. The look on his face when I took your letter to him was incredulous. He had to read your letter twice himself before he believed me. He was greatly concerned that this might destroy all of the effort that he and George had put into getting you away. However, I showed him the outside of your letter with the signature of "Mary Lee" and the wax seal that had been unbroken. That seemed to assuage his fears a bit. We agreed that I would wait a couple of weeks before replying so as not to seem too eager to anyone who might take notice.

Your father also explained his reasoning for hiding you in York, and I have to say I agree with him heartily. Not only are you safer there than on the high seas, but this town has been transformed since you and George departed. The Blaisdells have kept nearly to themselves down in the lower end of town. We see Abner, Mary, and the children at meetings on Sunday, but they do not speak to us nor we to them. Sally and I went to see George's mother Sarah the other day. We had a very lovely visit. During that time, she, too, indicated that George was right in taking you with him and getting out of town. Of course, she still thinks you are with him! She said she has heard nary a peep of gossip about the goings-on at the wedding feast or anything associated with the vixen Lydia. I would have to agree with her. Out of sight and certainly out of mind has calmed everyone down around here. There is one thing of interest that I am sad you are not here to see. Sally is being courted by Moses Wentworth! He is a fine gentleman who has started a farm just outside of town. I wish you were here to share in her joy, but I know having you there in York is for the best. My love for you is eternal, my child. Until we can speak face-to-face again....

Your loving Mother

December 25, 1795
St. Mary's Parish, Jamaica

My Cherished Wife,

I hope this letter finds you well. I have struggled these many months without your kind and generous heart near me. Many times I questioned my own decision to leave you behind. For how much sweeter my life is when I am in your presence. However, if I needed any more reminders of how unsafe this would have been for you, I need only look out the window. I am spending this Christmas Day ashore in Jamaica, but I am not sure if I am safer here or aboard the *Schoodic*. War has torn this area asunder, as the Maroons are engaged in their second battle against the British. Most of the fighting is inland a few miles in the heavily forested mountainside. However, at certain times you can hear the crackle of gunfire and cannon. The town is teeming with British soldiers marching through the streets in formation. All of this I would not want you to see. So I am thankful I left you safely in York with your uncle.

I think of you often, my love, and hope that my child stirs within you. I cannot wait for this journey to be over. I promise you I will never leave your side again to undertake any form of business pursuit that would keep me from you. This line of work appealed greatly to me as a bachelor. Knowing I have a wife at home makes it less exciting. I am anticipating an arrival date of mid-April providing we can skirt the winter storms. Be looking for me then, my love.

Your husband, George

February 26, 1796
Charleston, South Carolina

Dearest Wife,

I am sending you a quick and short note. As you can see by my letterhead, we are safely making our return thus far. I was able to pick up a second cargo to carry to a merchant in Bangor for a very fair price. I will speak more on that when we are together. However, it has slowed us down considerably. We are holding over here to get a few supplies and let the men rest. I do not expect us to reach York by mid-April as I had first hoped. The merchant from Bangor has agreed to carry a message to you in York, as he is traveling back on a smaller and faster ship. I hope this finds you well, and I long to be with you. By the time this reaches you, it shouldn't be much longer. I can't imagine I will be more than a few weeks behind this fellow.

Until we meet again, all my love, George

March 10, 1796
Franklin, Maine

My Darling Daughter,

I thought I would send you a quick note to let you know that Sally and Moses were married on Wednesday past in a quiet and private ceremony here at the house. It was a glorious day with the late winter sun shining brightly and early songbirds twittering around the yard. Sally spoke several times of her wish that you could be present. It was all I could muster to remain quiet on our secret. Moses is a fine man, and your father and I are both pleased with this union. His farm out near the pond is of a goodly quality, and I'm certain that he will provide for Sally well. Those in attendance for friends were Samuel and Sarah Simpson, Mary Card, Margaret Miller, Sally Martin, and Rev. and Mrs. Crawford as well as many of our family. We served

108

venison in abundance to all those who attended. It was a cheerful afternoon spent with good friends and family. Please give of our love to George when you are reunited. Until we may see your face again and hold you close to our heart, I will be your forever devoted mother.

April 27, 1796
York, Maine

Mother,

I just received your letter, and I am trying to contain my emotions. How wonderful to hear that Sally and Moses were wed! I am saddened that I wasn't there to be a part of it, but I can certainly understand her reluctance to wait until my return. Please give them both my love. I now long to be home more than ever. What a wonderful thing it would be for Sally and I to start our families together and be raising your grandchildren close to you. I hope that this will be the case very soon for both of us.

You will be greatly pleased to know I got yet another letter from George yesterday! He was in Charleston, South Carolina, of all places. A very nice gentleman named Cyrus Arnold arrived at our doorstep, with the letter in hand, looking for "Mary Lee." After we were seated comfortably in the parlor, he related to me how he had met George in Charleston and learned of my "imprisonment" here in York. He got quite a bit of humor out of being let in on the secret. He seems like a very nice fellow. He said George and his crew were doing fine when he last saw them. Mr. Arnold is from Bangor, and he indicated that he and George had discussed future business dealings. I will keep you informed for certain. Upon parting, Mr. Arnold stated that George should be no more than two or three weeks behind him. I shall keep an ever-present eye on the horizon from the front porch now. I know that when I finally see his ship sail into the harbor, I shall faint. Never have I thought that I would miss anyone so much as I have missed my husband. Of course, I miss you and Father as well! Give my love to everyone in the family and to our dear friends, too. You made no mention in your last letter of Lydia or any of the Blaisdells. I trust that they are truly no longer a care in anyone's lives and this is the reason for your omission rather than something sinister. I hope we are together again soon.

Your loving daughter Nelly

May 10, 1796
Franklin, Maine

Dearest Nelly,

By the time this letter reaches you, I hope you are reading it in the arms of your husband. I hope you both will take comfort in the news contained within this letter. I wanted to reply as quickly as possible to try and ease your mind regarding the Blaisdells. I did not mention them in my last letter because they are of no interest to anyone. All is quiet here in Franklin. Lydia has nary been seen since last summer. It's as if everyone just plain forgot you and George ever existed! Most of the talk in town is about fishing. More and more families are moving here with their men going out to sea. The meetinghouse is full to overflowing on Sundays now. Reverend Crawford said he was thinking of holding two services soon—one in the morning for the folks from the upper part of town and one in the afternoon for those in the lower part. If that happens, we will rarely see the Blaisdells anymore as they would be attending a different service time from us.

Sally and Moses have moved out to his farm by the pond. I wish you could see how happy she is there. She is planning on a large garden and has begun her early plantings. As I write, I know that it's possible George is with you and you two will be deciding on what your future holds. Remind him that your mother loves you dearly and looks forward to the day when he brings you back. The Blaisdell affair appears to be completely behind us now, and we would love to have the two of you close by. You may come home!

All my love, Mother

June 27, 1796
Bangor, Maine

My most honorable Father and Mother,

I have safely returned from my voyage. If you have not heard from Nelly's parents yet, you may not know that she did not accompany me to the Caribbean. Nor did I ever intend for her to do so. David Hooper suggested I leave her in York with his brother, and that is where she spent the winter under the assumed name of Mary Lee. This was to prevent detection from any of the numerous folks in Franklin who have connections in York. I am sorry I had to mislead you, but I felt it was best for the safety of my wife and my own mental well-being. It was, and still is, my greatest desire to keep myself and Nelly removed from the Blaisdells and their ilk.

Over these many months at sea, I have thought often of the things that transpired with Lydia, and I have come to the conclusion that I do not share Nelly's belief that it was all the workings of a little girl with an infatuation. Because of that belief, I have decided that Nelly and I will not be returning to Franklin. Instead, we have settled in Bangor. This is a bustling, growing town, and I have made excellent business connections with gentlemen in this place—particularly one, Cyrus Arnold. I sold the Schoodic and have invested my profits into a business venture with Arnold. We have opened a mercantile shop, Arnold & Butler, on City Point specializing in West Indies goods. Mother, I know you will be slightly disappointed in me that I continue to seek my fortune in the rum business. However, rum sells fast and well here in Bangor. We barely can keep enough supply on hand for the demand of the grog shops here. Lumber is the name of the game in town, and rum is the lubricant that keeps it all moving.

Nelly and I have taken rooms at the Rose Inn up on the hill. It is a lovely little place with views of the river. She has settled in well and is keeping herself busy with the many women's groups that have organized here in town. She is particularly drawn to helping the poor and less fortunate young children. I am saddened to tell you we are still as yet unable to produce a child of our own, so she is embracing the motherless and downtrodden to ease her pain. We would love to have you, and as many of the family as able, make the trip to see us. I have been told that there is a good road running from here to Ellsworth. The terrain consists of a small section with numerous hills, but for the most part the thirty-odd miles are level and wooded. I hope you will consider discussing the matter with Nelly's parents as well. On some days, I am concerned about her as she struggles to stay cheerful.

Your loving son, George

CHAPTER EIGHTEEN

August 1796
Bangor, Maine

Nelly walked quickly out of the room, silently closing the door behind her. She hurried down the hallway, her soft-soled shoes not making a sound on the wide-plank floors. She needed air, fresh air. She burst out onto the porch of the small rooming house and leaned over the railing, inhaling deeply. She stared down into a patch of black-eyed Susans that swayed in the slight breeze blowing off the Penobscot River. She was in Joppa, a small neighborhood south of the Kenduskeag Stream, on the outskirts of Bangor. Whereas City Point, on the northern shore of where the Kenduskeag met the Penobscot, boasted successful businesses, fine markets, respectable neighborhoods, the plains along the southern side had collected the shanties, boarding homes, grog shops, and brothels. Her work with the Women's Compassion Society often brought her over here to assist the women and children. She would bring clothing, baskets of food, sometimes even small toys. Often, her work was to provide a caring touch or lend an ear.

Today, she had come with the midwife Lucy Giddings to a rooming house run by the Widow Hatch. The message said to come quickly. Nelly knew when she started over that more than likely, she would see a child born today. Another child. Not her own child, but that of some other woman who did not struggle as she did. She almost told Lucy she couldn't go, but she had changed her mind and accompanied her. Now she wished she hadn't.

She had not witnessed the happy birth of a new child to a loving and devoted mother. Instead, she had watched the woman endure intense pain only to deliver a blue baby, a dead little boy. Shortly after, the mother herself succumbed to the same fate. In her death throes, she had stared into Nelly's eyes.

"It didn't cry! Tell me it is dead. Please, dear God, let it be dead."

Shocked at the woman's reaction, Nelly took her hand. "Yes, ma'am, he did not make it. He never took a breath."

"He?" the woman had gasped out. "Praise God another one did not take a breath in this world." She laid her head back on the pillow, struggling to breathe. Nelly looked down at Lucy, who was frantically trying to stop the blood that was gushing all over the bedding. She heard a gasp and looked back at the woman. She was gone. She had died holding Nelly's hand. Died thankful that her baby was dead. Right there in front of Nelly, who wanted nothing more than to have a child of her own. This woman had praised God that hers was dead. Nelly couldn't take it. She let go of the woman's hand and ran from the room.

Nelly heard the screen door open and turned to see the Widow Hatch approaching.

"How is she doing?" she asked Nelly.

"The baby was born blue. A little boy. Very small. Probably wouldn't have made it, anyway."

"Ahh," the widow said, shaking her head. "Probably for the best. Another mouth to feed and all."

"She won't be worried about that," Nelly replied. "She died as well. Lucy said something about a rupture. There was a lot of blood."

"Died? Oh my! Whatever will we do? That does complicate matters some!"

"What do you mean?" Nelly asked.

"That woman had another child. A little girl. I had my daughter Sissy take her up to her house when I noticed the woman was starting her pains. Not good for children to hear their mothers scream, you know."

"Another child? Well, certainly her husband should be located immediately."

Widow Hatch took Nelly gently by the arm. "My dear, I don't believe a woman of her kind would have a husband such as you and I would." She gave Nelly's arm a squeeze.

"What do you mean? She had two children, certainly she has a husband. How else would she have gotten…" Nelly's voice trailed off.

Since coming to Bangor, she had heard of the women who provided comfort to the men who left for the woods or came up the river on the ships. All of this was such a far cry from the peaceful shores of the bay in Franklin.

Nelly sat down in the small chair on the porch. "Widow Hatch, she kept asking me if the child was dead. She actually begged God for it to be so. And when I told her it was and the poor thing had been a boy, she praised God that another one hadn't taken a breath in this world." Nelly looked up. "She did not have much love of men, did she?"

Widow Hatch took the seat next to Nelly and patted her hands.

"No, my dear, more than likely she had been ill-treated by many of them. If she even knew who the father of that small dead boy was, it's unlikely he would have claimed him, or the mother, as his own. She and the boy are in God's rest now and far better off."

"Yes, you are probably right. But she has another child? What will become of her?"

"The poor creature," the widow said, shaking her head again. "Her mother called her Edna. Doubtful she has a father who would claim her, either. She is small, but I would guess she's not more than two years old."

"Do we know anything about this woman? Is she from around here? Does she have family we could take the child to?" Nelly asked.

The widow was shaking her head emphatically. "I don't know much. She only arrived a few weeks ago. She told me her name was Martha and that her husband had brought them to Bangor because of the lumber. She said he had already gone north and she needed a place to stay until she had her child. She must have thought me a ninny. Most men aren't headed to the woods in late August. They won't start that way for a least another two months, maybe more. And any man worth half his weight in beans would have never let a woman so close to her confinement, and with a toddler in tow, be out looking for accommodations on her own. No, I knew her situation when I saw it."

"Why did you take her in?" Nelly asked.

"The little girl. She has the most angelic face. Like a cherub. If ever an angel child has graced this earth, it is that one. I couldn't turn her away. So I told her mother absolutely no gentleman callers. She guffawed at that and promised there wouldn't be. I told her I wouldn't be minding the child if she went gallivanting off without it. She agreed. She paid for a month up front, so I let her stay."

Nelly thought for a moment. There was no way of knowing where this woman came from or even if Martha was her real name. "Can your daughter Priscilla keep the child?"

"Oh heavens no! She's got seven of her own! Not to mention this child is of miserable stock, Miss Nelly. Her husband would have a fit!" Widow Hatch laughed.

Just then, Lucy stepped out onto the porch to join them. "We'll need an undertaker, Mrs. Hatch." She said wiping her bloodied hands on her soiled apron.

"Not to be uncharitable, Mrs. Gidding, but who's going to pay him? The woman had no husband or any kind of family to speak of."

Lucy raised her eyebrows and glanced at Nelly. "Well, that explains her comments to us, doesn't it?"

"Yes, that's what I realized as well," Nelly answered. "And she has a daughter."

"Another one?" Lucy looked shocked. "Oh dear!"

As Lucy and Widow Hatch discussed how to get the woman's body, and that of her son, removed from the boarding house and who exactly was going to pay for it, Nelly's mind focused on the little motherless child. What if she had come today, not to witness a birth, but to find a child of her own? Was it too soon to assume she was barren? She and George had been married a year, but he had been gone more than six months of that time. Had they just not tried long enough? Maybe she should wait. Give them more time to try. She should think this through carefully. What would George think if she brought home the child? A child of a prostitute, no less! Would he accept it as his own? He wanted a family as much as she did, but he often talked of "their" children. Little Edna wouldn't be theirs. Would the memory of the hateful face of the mother as she lay dying, praying for the death of her baby, be with Nelly forever? Or could she replace it with happy memories of a happy child?

"Widow Hatch, the Women's Compassion Society will cover the cost of the undertaker and a burial in an unmarked grave for the two of them if you find the child a home. It seems like a reasonable compromise," Lucy stated in her firm tone.

"Oh dear, Sissy's husband is not going to like this one bit!" the widow was exclaiming, hanging her head and placing her hands in the pockets of her apron.

"I'll take the child," Nelly heard herself say.

"You'll what?" Lucy asked incredulously, spinning on her heels.

"Land sakes, child, are you serious?" said the widow, looking up with relief.

"Yes. I said I will take the child. I have no children, and I could care for her."

"Nelly, think about what you are saying," Lucy said, taking her by the arms and shaking her. "This is a child. It's a lifelong commitment. And a child with a questionable background, no less! Nelly, it is one thing to help these people, but it's never a good idea to bring them into your home!"

Nelly looked down at the dead woman's blood that was now staining her wrists. Lucy followed her gaze and quickly removed her hands. "I'm sorry," she said.

Nelly thought she could feel the blood absorbing into her skin and mixing with her own. A child of this woman would be a child of hers. "Lucy, those are vile words to say. If we are truly compassionate, then our compassion should extend beyond what is convenient for us. This child may be a product of her mother's choices, but in no wise should that be an indicator of how the child will turn out. I said I would take the child, and I meant it. It is the least I could do for a woman who had suffered so much in her life. George and I will give the child a better life so that she will never have to know the hatred that her mother knew."

"Miss Nelly, you are a true Christian," Widow Hatch said, giving her a hug. "I will go and get the child from Sissy right away." She hurried off the porch and toward her daughter's house.

"I hope you know what you're doing," Lucy said.

Nelly was certain she did not.

George looked down at the sleeping child who now lay in their parlor. His brow was furrowed with the thoughts that ran through his head. He knew that Nelly longed for a child just as much as he did, but to bring home someone else's? Was it right? Would this little waif fit into their lives as one of their own would?

"What are you thinking, George?" Nelly asked quietly as she entered the room.

"Truly?" he said, turning to look at her. "I'm not sure what to make of it. What did you say her name was?"

"Edna."

He sat down in the chair opposite the child, continuing to stare at her. "The mother...she had no family?"

"No, at least, not in this area. Widow Hatch wasn't even sure of where she had come from, either. So there is no one to send word to." Nelly had not lied to George about the child's background. She had truthfully told him the woman had been a prostitute. "Of course, as for a father..." She let her voice trail off.

"Yes, yes, of course," George said, dismissing the end of the conversation with a wave of his hand. He continued staring at the child, finalizing his thoughts before he spoke them out loud to his wife.

"Nelly, come sit here with me." He patted the seat of the chair next to his. She obliged, and soon the two of them were staring at Edna trying to figure out what to make of this whole situation.

George reached for his wife's hand and looked deeply into her eyes. "I know you want a child, Nelly. It is what I want as well. I'm doing my best to give you one!" He squeezed her hand and smiled at her. "But to bring someone else's child into our home—I never really considered it. I was certain that after I returned from sea, the babies would just come quickly on their own." He stopped.

Nelly let her eyes fall to her hand clasped in his. What could she say? This problem of theirs could easily be her fault. She couldn't let him feel as if he had failed her.

"George, it's not your fault." She looked back up at him. "I could be barren."

"Either way, whether it is you or me, we will solve the problem together. But at this time…I'm just not ready to accept a child who isn't mine. I just don't feel that we have given ourselves enough time."

Nelly's heart was crushed. She glanced at the sleeping child, her cheeks rosy and soft in the early evening light.

"With that said, she can stay," George said.

Nelly felt a rush of breath escape her lips.

"However, I will be actively asking around town to see if anyone knew the mother and where she came from."

"She can stay? We can keep her?"

George placed his hands on Nelly's shoulders to assure that she was looking straight at him and understanding every word he was saying.

"She can stay until we find her mother's family. Then she goes. Understood?"

"Yes! Yes! Oh, George, thank you so much!" Nelly leaned over and wrapped her arms around him, kissing both his cheeks.

"Now, now, just settle down. You may care for her, but she is not ours. She will leave you someday, when I find her family."

"I know, I know," Nelly said, continuing to nuzzle into his ears. She had heard what he said, but there was no chance of George finding that prostitute's family. Nelly was now a mother!

+———+

As late August turned into autumn, the days got shorter and cooler. Everyone said they could feel it in the air—winter was coming, and she was not going to be a good one. Nelly paid no mind to the weather, however. Her days were full with motherhood and the duties of caring for Edna. The young child cried often, wanting her mother. It broke Nelly's heart to hear her. During those times, Nelly would tell Edna that her real mother had gone to live with the angels and had left Edna with her. She would tell her that she could call her "Mommy" now. She would then divert her attention to something bright and pretty. Edna loved pretty things and always wanted to have ribbons put in her hair. During other times, the memory of her mother was far from Edna's mind, and she would cuddle into Nelly's side as they read a book. On their walks, Edna would hold tightly to Nelly's hand for fear of losing her, too. When Nelly rocked her to sleep at bedtime, she could feel the little body relax against her chest. She was safe and comforted, free from the memories.

For George, fatherhood had settled on him despite his best efforts to avoid it. Edna, having never had much of a father figure in her life, viewed George as a novelty. When he came through the door in the evening, she would shriek with delight and run to him. He tried not to become attached to the little thing, still determined to find her mother's family, but her chatter about squirrels, pebbles, and other such things touched his heart in a way he had never imagined it could. Eventually, he gave up and became content with the knowledge that no matter how she had gotten there, Edna was his daughter. He loved her dearly.

CHAPTER NINETEEN

December 1796

Nelly gazed down the steep hill to the city below from the second floor of their rented house on High Street. After making the decision to keep Edna permanently, they quickly realized the rooms they had taken at Rose Inn were not going to suit raising a family. George had found them a lovely home on the opposite side of the Kenduskeag Stream. From here, Nelly could see the docks along the river and watch the bustling activity of this growing city. She touched the lace curtains that adorned the window of Edna's room. Her mother had made them upon hearing the news of Edna's arrival into the family. How Nelly longed to be near her mother as she started this journey of motherhood herself. Movement outside caught her eye, and she saw George making his way up the hill toward the house. A light snow was falling but nothing severe.

"Edna, darling, come to me," Nelly spoke, straightening the bonnet on Edna's head. "There, now, don't you look pretty. Father is home!" she announced, standing back and admiring the little girl.

"Show Father," the little girl replied, running from the room. George was just coming in from outside, stomping the snow from his boots.

"Well, look at my princess!" he said, scooping up Edna and swinging her around as she squealed in delight. "That is a very fancy new bonnet you have there." He smiled at Nelly as she joined them. "What's the occasion for a new bonnet?"

Nelly smiled at him warmly and took his arm. "Well, my goodness, can't a lady have a new bonnet without there being a special occasion?"

"Yes, yes," he replied, setting Edna down and removing his coat. "Let me look at you again."

Edna stepped back and lifted the very outer edges of her long skirt just enough to let the toes of her black shoes peek out and then bowed in a very elegant curtsy.

George clapped his hands and laughed out loud. "My dear, you are a very proper lady! What a fantastic teacher your mother has been!" He lifted the little girl with one arm and encircled Nelly's waist with the other, squeezing them both tight.

"I doubt very much a man could be happier!" he said, kissing Nelly lightly on the cheek.

"Me too!" Edna begged, turning her cheek toward him.

"Well, of course!" He gently kissed her as well.

"George, I actually do have something to tell you," Nelly said as they moved into the parlor.

George eyed her suspiciously and set Edna down. "Nothing of a serious nature, I hope."

"Oh, it is quite serious." She seated herself on the settee and patted the empty space beside her. He slowly lowered himself.

"Has there been news from home? Is everyone all right?"

"Home," Nelly repeated, tilting her head a little and giving a small smile. "Funny you should mention home, because Franklin has been much on my mind over these past few weeks." She reached down and took both of his hands in hers, looking deeply into his eyes she spoke with excitement and strength.

"George, I am with child, and I want to go home."

George felt the world tilt slightly as his mind tried to register the words that Nelly had just spoken to him. He looked from his wife to his daughter and back again.

"What did you say?" he asked. "You are…"

The words were left hanging in the air. He was afraid to say them out loud for fear they would not be true.

"I am with child, George," Nelly said, smiling again. "I am certain. I've waited several weeks to tell you so that there would be no doubt."

Still unsure of what to say, George pulled her to him and squeezed her tight.

"Me too!" Edna shouted as she tried squeezing into their embrace. Both of them started laughing as George picked up the little girl and placed her on his lap.

"By all means, Princess! Come sit here with the family." George looked into Nelly's eyes, which were brimming with tears. He kissed her on the cheek. "When?"

She laughed. "Near as I can tell, after consulting with Lucy about these things, the end of June sometime."

George stood, and Nelly could see his mind working.

"June," he mumbled, rubbing his chin.

"I'd like to go home, George," she stammered, smoothing out Edna's skirt as the girl slid from Nelly's lap to the empty space on the settee. "I want to be with my mother and my sister—you know a woman needs her family at a time like this."

"Yes," he replied, still deep in thought, "you mentioned that. However, I'm not sure if that is feasible, my dear." He turned and looked down at her. "We just rented this house. I have my business interests here in the city. I just can't up and leave Cyrus with all of the work." He walked across the room, staring out the window at the docks. "There is so much opportunity here." Turning, he stared intently at her, and she held his eyes with her own. He lowered his voice as if he did not want Edna—or anyone else, for that matter—to hear what he was going to say next. "And, of course, there is still the Blaisdell affair to consider."

"Oh, George." Nelly stood and walked toward him. "Are you still wrestling with that demon?"

George bristled at her choice of words and turned back toward the window. "Nelly, please…" he said.

"No, I suffered long enough with Lydia Blaisdell nearly ruining my wedding day. I will not tolerate her being a part of each and every decision we make. George, look at me." She raised her voice, causing Edna to stop fiddling with the ribbon on her new bonnet and stare at her parents.

"Franklin is my home. I want my child born in Franklin. Not here in this lumber town of brothels and grog shops. At home. On Butler's Point, just as you were. Certainly you would want that for your son, too?" she asked rhetorically. "Over the last year and a half, I have questioned my mother several times regarding the Blaisdells. She assures me that no one speaks of the rumors surrounding our wedding. She says the Blaisdells keep mostly to the eastern side of the bay. They are only seen at meeting. If there is any talk regarding them at all, it is that Abner Blaisdell has increased in piety. His devotion to the scriptures and daily prayer is all that one hears of them. Surely you cannot find fault with any of that."

George looked at Nelly for quite some time. He stared into the beautiful eyes that had captivated him from the first moment he had met her. He glanced at Edna, who had realized that there was no immediate concern regarding her parents' unusual conversation and had gone back to her blocks on the floor.

"I will consider it," he said simply. Straightening his waistcoat, he gave her one last look and walked from the room.

George sat in his study with the door closed. The early darkness of winter had settled over the room and his spirit. He could hear Nelly chatting with Edna in the kitchen area as she worked to prepare their evening meal. He felt the weight of this decision pressing him into his chair. Before him on the desk sat his lockbox, the key inserted in the brass lock, the lid open. Beside it lay a small leather pouch. The drawstring on the pouch had been loosened, and the object inside had been removed and placed on his blotter.

Slowly, almost with trepidation, he reached his hand out to retrieve the item. In the flickering lamplight, it looked as if his hand were shaking. He pulled his hand back, holding it to his chest. Was he shaking? No, it must be a trick of the light on his eyes. He took a deep breath and reached his hand out again. Grasping the item between his thumb and index finger, he lifted the ring closer to him. The ring from the posset. The very item that had so marred his wedding day and then mysteriously found its way back to him during the chaos in the meetinghouse. He stared at it. *George & Lydia Butler 1800* was still engraved deeply into the ring. He read it, feeling a shudder run through his body.

He set the ring back down on the blotter, still staring at it. What kind of evil was this? Nelly's argument that the gossip in town had quieted and the Blaisdells were of no consequence to life in Franklin currently held little weight as he looked anew at this ring. His original intention of staying away from Franklin until well after 1800 had seemed a plausible plan. He had not taken into consideration that if Nelly became pregnant, she would want to return home. Pregnant. His wife was with child. His child. Finally. Oh, the joy that this thought brought to him! A son. He was certain his wife would bear him a son and felt his joy should be all-consuming right now. Instead, he was torn with fear. Fear? Yes, fear was what he was feeling. How could he tell Nelly that it was impossible for them to return to Franklin? Staring at the inscription on the ring, his heart was wrenched with anguish. What did the future hold for Nelly? For him?

"Aargh!" He slammed the palms of his hands down on his desk, the ring jumping with the force. He hung his head as he felt hot tears spill from his eyes. The sound of voices from the kitchen suddenly stopped, and Nelly's footsteps could be heard coming quickly toward his study.

"George?" She tried the door, but he had locked it. "George, are you all right?" She jiggled the knob several times. "George, let me in!"

George lifted his head and stared at the ring. He thought to pray, but he wasn't sure even that would help him. He was desperately trying to hold back his emotions. The love for his wife burning deeply in his chest.

"George? George?" Nelly's voice from the hall kept intruding on his thoughts.

"I'm fine, Nell," he finally managed to say. "I'll be out shortly."

"Let me in," she insisted.

"No, please. I need to be alone right now."

Nelly stopped jiggling the doorknob, and her footsteps retreated toward the back of the house.

George sat back in his chair. How was he to manage this? For the sake of their unborn child, he wanted Nelly to be happy and content. However, for the sake of their unborn child, and himself and Edna, he needed Nelly to be safe. He was almost certain that Franklin was not safe. The child Lydia Blaisdell. What he had witnessed at the Blaisdell house that day. The ring. The spectacle of their Coming Out Sunday. All of these things pointed to the very real possibility of danger if he took his family back to Franklin. Not to mention that his business dealings with Cyrus Arnold were here in the city. Was it possible to keep his hand in the business from Franklin? And if not, could he take to farming on Butler's Point after all of this? He glanced around at the fine home he had secured for them on High Street. It was a proper frame house with wide-plank floors, a fireplace in every room, and views of the river. He would have to take Nelly back to that little log cabin. There was no time, with the dead of winter upon them, to build her a proper home to have the child in. If they returned, she would have to do her lying-in in that cabin. Had she thought of that?

He reached out for the ring once more, his confidence building as he made his decision. Picking it up, he only gave it a cursory glance as he dropped it back into its leather pouch and pulled the drawstring tight. No, he was the husband. He was the man who made the decisions that best suited this family. When Nelly agreed to become his wife, she had become his responsibility. He placed the pouch back in the lockbox and closed the lid. She was his wife and she would obey his decisions, whether she liked them or not. He turned the key in the brass lock and heard it click securely. He removed the key and placed it in the drawer of his desk. Pushing his chair back, he stood and placed the box in the cabinet behind his desk. He had made his decision. Under no uncertain terms was he taking his family to Franklin.

CHAPTER TWENTY

February 1797
Franklin, Maine

Mary Blaisdell slowly shut the door to Lydia's room and quietly retreated down the staircase. She found her older daughter, Hannah, sitting in the large kitchen in front of the fire.

"How is she?" Hannah asked.

"Oh, I suspect she'll pull through. The fever is still high but not nearly as high as it was before." She sat down at the table and placed her head in her hands. "Where is your father?"

"In the front parlor. He said he was going there to read scripture and pray." Hannah took a deep breath, wanting to say more but not knowing how to put it into words.

Mary glanced at the doorway, trying to decide if she wanted to go join him or stay there with Hannah. She chose the latter. There was no need to bother God, although Lydia was quite ill, she did not think she would die.

Hannah stood. "Can I get you a cup of tea?" she asked her mother.

"Yes, that will be good. Thank you."

Mary was quiet for a while, lost in her thoughts of Lydia. Losing children was commonplace, and many of her friends had lost their dear little ones. But thus far, Mary had avoided that calamity. She had even lived through giving birth to twins with both of them surviving. She had to admit that God had watched over her children thus far.

Hannah set the cup of tea down in front of her. "God is good, Mother, don't fret. He will protect Lydia," she said, taking the seat opposite her mother. "And us."

Mary hesitated before speaking. "I hope so. Lydia is…well, Hannah, you must admit Lydia is a different child. The happenings and all." She looked intently at Hannah, seeking confirmation.

"It is true. I don't always understand her. Sometimes I think she is ill, and other times I think she is possessed by a spirit."

"Shhh!" Mary hissed. "Do not speak of those things out loud. It will attract Satan for sure." Mary reached across the table and clutched Hannah's hand. "We cannot ever say those things. Do you understand?"

"Yes, Mother," Hannah said contritely. "I'm sorry."

The two women sat in silence. Mary thought about the things that had happened to Lydia in recent years. Certainly, George Butler and his wife leaving town had helped. Lydia had been a wonderfully happy child since then. No more episodes. No more bizarre occurrences. Lydia had clearly been infatuated with George. Could that young love, so improperly placed, have been the source of her problem? It certainly appeared that way. Nothing in Lydia's character lately indicated that she was possessed by an evil spirit. No, there would be no more talk of that. Even the townspeople had let that rumor go.

Hannah suddenly spoke. "Mother, there is something I need to tell you."

"What might that be?" Mary asked, looking at her daughter.

Hannah leaned forward slightly, as if she really didn't want to say the news too loudly. "George and Nelly Butler are moving back to Butler's Point. They will be here in a few weeks."

Mary froze in her chair, staring intently at Hannah. "Who told you this?"

"I saw Nelly's sister, Sally, while I was in town picking up the things you sent me for," Hannah said. "She said Nelly is with child, and they are to come home."

"Come home? Why? Why would they need to do that?" Mary's mind was rushing with thoughts. How would this affect Lydia? Her child, even at this moment, was lying upstairs with a raging fever. Lydia must not be told of this development. She must not.

"We must not speak of this to Lydia. Do you understand?"

Hannah nodded silently.

"I want her to get through this sickness without any thoughts on her mind. Especially thoughts of George Butler!"

"I'm sorry, Mother, maybe I shouldn't have told you."

"No, you did the right thing. But I do not want this spoken of in this house again."

"Yes, Mother."

"They will arrive in a few weeks?" Mary questioned her daughter.

"Yes, apparently they have been living in Bangor. George needs to settle up some business affairs, and then they will return to Butler's Point."

Bangor? Mary thought they were in the Caribbean. Had the Butlers lied all along about their whereabouts? What did all of this mean? For Lydia? For their family?

"Maybe I will go pray with your father."

She rose, leaving the tea untouched.

CHAPTER TWENTY-ONE

March 1797
Bangor, Maine

"Oh, Nelly, I cannot believe you will be leaving us!" Lucy Giddings exclaimed as she watched Nelly place porcelain cups into hay-filled boxes.

"Lucy, it's not like I'm going to the end of the earth. Franklin is just a short trip down the river."

"Down the river and then Downeast," Lucy replied. "I so wanted to be there for you when you have the baby. Will you be able to find a decent midwife in Franklin?"

"My mother knows of a fine woman, Mrs. Mary Bragdon. She has delivered many babies in Franklin very successfully. I will be in good hands." Nelly smiled at her friend.

Lucy fiddled with some hay that had fallen to the floor. "George does not seem happy to be leaving."

Nelly stopped and sat down rather abruptly. "No, he is not. Is it that obvious?"

Lucy smiled at her. "Yes, yes, it is. George is normally a very jovial sort of fellow. Lately, though, he seems aloof. I have heard it from several associates in the city. Seems everyone who enters the store can see it."

Nelly was concerned. This was not how she had expected the impending birth of their first child to be. She and George had had a terrible disagreement about the return to Franklin. For the first time in their married life, they had raised their voices at each other. It seemed that as vehemently as she wished to return to Franklin, he just as vehemently opposed it. His initial argument had focused on the Blaisdell child, but when he saw that didn't matter to her, he switched gears. He lamented the financial loss he would take by selling out to Cyrus. She countered with evidence that living on Butler's Point would not cost as much as renting this fine house in the city. He told her she would not be comfortable giving birth in that musty old log cabin. She reminded him that his very own mother had given birth to him in that cabin! He stated he wasn't even sure he could be a successful farmer or produce enough to sustain them. She told him she was at peace with him returning to the sea as a ship's captain if he so chose. Once home among their families, and with Edna and a new baby, she would not be so lonely if he were gone.

It was at that point that the yelling started. He had no more logical arguments left, so he resorted to plain male stubbornness. He was the man and had decided they would not be returning to Franklin, so she just needed to stop asking and be an obedient wife. She, in turn, resorted to female theatrics and began crying. This went on for days, and it was clear that sooner or later, one of them would have to give in. In the end, it was George who could no longer stand the emotional drama and caved in to her wishes.

"Well, we did have several very heated arguments over the subject. I can't say it was a mutually cheerful decision," Nelly admitted.

"Odd that a man would not want to return to his family with a wife carrying his child. Seems to be the kind of thing most men are proudest of. They strut around like roosters crowing to the world 'Look what I have wrought!'" She brought her hands up, tucked them under her armpits, and flapped her bent arms like a chicken, making Nelly laugh.

"Oh, Lucy, I will miss your sense of humor," she sighed. "George has his reasons, I guess, and it's not without compromise on my part, either."

"What do you mean?" Lucy asked.

"For him to agree to take me home, I had to agree to stay on Butler's Point until after the birth of the baby. I cannot go into town at all. Not even for Sunday meetings."

"Are you serious, Nelly?" Lucy exclaimed. "That's like a prison! Why on earth would he want to keep you restricted like that? Can you not even go and see your own family?"

"No, I cannot leave for any reason. It won't be so bad. Butler's Point is very large, and many people will come to visit us, I'm sure.

My family will call often." She tried not to show her own trepidation at the thought. "Besides, it will only be for a few months. My lying-in is only three months away now." She laid her hand on the bulge of her stomach and smiled.

"Well, you are a far better woman than I. That just sounds utterly ridiculous to me. Who is he hiding you from?"

Nelly hesitated but then decided there was no point in keeping it from Lucy. "There was a bit of drama regarding a young girl in town. She apparently took a liking to George and convinced herself that he would marry her. When that did not happen and he married me instead, there were some unfortunate incidents that arose. It was all very disturbing, but things have quieted down now and I'm sure she has seen the error of her ways—although George isn't so sure. "

"Another woman?" Lucy placed her hand at the base of her throat in shock. "George hardly seems the type!"

"Not another woman, Lucy—a small child, really. She was only ten years old."

"Oh, well, that does make a difference," Lucy said, regaining her composure. "How could a child cause so much turmoil that George would not want to return home?"

Nelly picked up another cup and continued her packing. "This is no ordinary child, Lucy," she said.

CHAPTER TWENTY-TWO

April 1797
Franklin, Maine

George stood on the newly arrived packet ship from Bangor and watched his wife being greeted by her family. He had been unable to stop her determination to return home. He felt as if his ability to control his own destiny was being ripped from him. How could he protect his own family if his wife was fighting against him, too?

He tilted his head back to stretch the tension from his neck and then scanned the eastern shore of the bay for the Blaisdells' home. He couldn't make it out, but he knew it was there. He knew she was there. Just as he knew the inscription on that ring read *George & Lydia Butler 1800*. The date was three years hence. The question of what could possibly transpire in the next three years filled him with dread. He would not be controlled by Lydia, the Blaisdell family, or by Satan himself. If it was a war to save his family they wanted, then he was prepared to fight them for it—whoever or whatever that force might be.

Down on the dock, George and Nelly were surrounded by their families as they made their way to the wagons. Everyone was chattering away at how beautiful Edna was. How healthy and fine Nelly looked so late in her pregnancy. What a joyous time this was to have the family all together again. George began to relax slightly. Maybe things would be all right. If the situation started out on the right foot, maybe it would continue that way. He reached out and took Nelly's hand to help her into the wagon.

"Nelly, I'm sorry," he said, smiling at her.

He didn't need to say more—she knew what he was apologizing for.

"It's all right, George. Everything will be fine, you'll see." She kissed him and stepped up into the wagon. George lifted Edna up and handed her to Nelly. "There you go, my little princess. Just a short ride, and the day's travels will be over."

"Home?" Edna asked.

"Yes, home at last," George replied. He climbed up onto the wagon seat next to his father, glancing back at his wife and daughter. He let out a small sigh.

"Ready, son?" his father asked.

"Yes, we are ready to go home," George said with just a glint of happiness rising in his voice.

Moses was lifting the reins, getting ready to slap them against the horses' rumps, when they heard it. The sound reached them slowly at first and then washed over them like a wave. The scream of a child. Everyone looked out into the bay, where the sound had come from.

"What in the name of heaven was that?" Moses exclaimed.

George kept staring down the bay. He knew. He couldn't see her, but he knew she was there. It was starting. Though the scream itself had died away, George could feel it burning in his chest like the fire of a branding iron. It was Lydia.

He slowly turned to look at Nelly, his eyes boring into her. She stared back at him. If she knew, she made no indication. She just stared at him, willing the wagon to move forward.

"Let's go, Father," George said to Moses. "Take us to Butler's Point."

Moses slapped the reins, and the wagon lurched forward. Nelly's family, the Hoopers, started in behind them. There would be much merrymaking at Butler's Point tonight between the two families, George thought. He hoped it would help to wipe away the fear that was building inside of him.

+———+

Abner Blaisdell, Lydia's father, heard the scream from his study. He knew immediately that it was his daughter. His wife jumped up from her sewing in the next room and rushed to him. Standing in the doorway of his study, Mary looked ashen with fear.

"Abner!" she cried. "It's Lydia!"

They both ran outside toward the sound of the scream.

"I think it came from the beach," Mary said. They ran down the short path through the thick hemlocks and out onto the rocky beach. There was Lydia, crumpled in a heap among the rocks.

"Lydia?" Abner exclaimed, rushing to his daughter. He scooped up her limp body.

"Is she breathing?" Mary asked.

"Yes." Abner sounded relieved. He gave the child a shake. "Lydia, open your eyes. Look at your father, child."

Lydia's eyes flew open, and her body stiffened like a board. Mary watched as the child's mouth opened but no sound came out.

"No! Dear God, please protect us. No!" Mary shouted. She knew it was another of Lydia's fits starting. The child's body began to shake as Abner held her. Guttural sounds emanated from deep within her throat. Her eyes rolled back in her head.

Abner leaned over Lydia's body. "Father in heaven, protect this child from the evil of Satan that has possessed her." He kept repeating it over and over, rocking back and forth while his daughter thrashed and tossed in his arms. Eventually, the thrashing stopped and her body relaxed.

"Why? Why?" Mary muttered, crying. The fits had stopped. Lydia hadn't suffered one in nearly two years. Why were they starting again?

Then the voice spoke from within Lydia's throat. It was the same voice they had heard many times when Lydia had fits. It was deep, haunting, and unearthly, and it certainly did not resemble Lydia's natural voice at all.

"He is here," the voice said.

Abner and Mary exchanged fearful looks. From Mary's position on the beach, she could look up the bay toward the town dock. It was then that she noticed it for the first time. The ship. Sails down, masts bare. It was the packet ship from Bangor. Mary fell back, leaning against the rocks. She felt exhausted. Hannah had been correct. The gossip she had heard in town many months ago was true. George and Nelly had returned. She had tried so hard to keep the news from Lydia and was fairly certain she had succeeded. She had forbidden Hannah to speak of it ever again. She had not allowed Lydia into town unaccompanied.

How had the child known? She glanced down at her daughter. Spittle ran out of the corner of Lydia's mouth.

The voice spoke again. "He is here."

"Satan is again with our daughter," Abner said to Mary.

She looked at him in horror, fearing he was correct. "She is a child, Abner. Only a sweet, innocent child." She started to cry. "If there is any fault for this, it lies within the breast of George Butler."

"George Butler?" Abner exclaimed. "He has been gone these two years, and we do not speak of him any longer."

"Yes, but he's home," Mary said, pointing to the ship. "Clearly, he brought his evil with him!"

Abner turned and looked over his shoulder in the direction Mary was pointing. He saw the ship.

"God have mercy," he said as he bent over his daughter, praying and lamenting.

CHAPTER TWENTY-THREE

Butler's Point

The frame house on the edge of the water at Butler's Point was overflowing with people that night. Hoopers and Butlers of every kind mingled in and around the rooms. Nelly felt so much comfort at the nearness of her mother and her sister, Sally. The women were all gathered in the drawing room. Edna was seated on the floor playing with rag dolls that her grandmothers had made for her. Although Nelly assured herself that things were going to be just fine, she felt a shudder run down her back at the thought of that scream. She knew that George would think it was Lydia. Every ship heading to Franklin had to pass by the Blaisdell property on the east side of the bay. The child must have been there. Must have seen the ship. But how could she have known George and Nelly were on it?

"Have you thought of names for your new baby yet?" George's mother, Sarah, asked Nelly, jarring her from her thoughts and bringing her back to the warmth and love of the room.

"Oh, well, naturally, if it's a son, he will be George like his father," she said. "As for names for a girl…" She reached out and took her mother's hand, giving it a slight squeeze. "I was thinking of either Abigail or Eliza."

Joanna drew her breath in sharply and smiled at her daughter. She thought back to the two little angels she had given birth to who had not lived. Eliza had been born the year after Nelly, and Abigail had been born the year after Sally. Neither one had been fit for this world. To perfect, she had always told herself.

"That would be a wonderful gesture," she said.

"Those are delightful names!" George's mother Sarah replied. "What do you think, Edna? Would you like a sister or a brother?"

"A sister!" the little girl announced, pressing her rag doll to her chest and kissing the top of its head, causing the women to laugh at her antics.

Standing in the doorway of his father's study, where he had gathered with Moses and David, George watched his wife and daughter across the hall. Slowly, he closed the door and turned to face the two men.

"What is the serious nature of this meeting?" Moses asked. "I trust nothing is wrong with Nelly and the baby."

"Oh no," George reassured him, "Nelly is fine. Very healthy. She has a good friend in Bangor who is a midwife, and she assured both Nelly and me that the pregnancy is progressing fine. The baby seems well, and she has no worries as to the delivery."

"Good, good," Moses nodded. "Then why do you seem so sullen? I thought I would find you more joyous to be back among family."

George sat down. "It is the Blaisdells that I wish to discuss."

"Blaisdells? You mean specifically the child Lydia?" his father said.

"Yes."

"Son, all of that happened nearly two years ago. There has nary been a word spoken of it since your departure."

"That's just the point, Father! Now that we are back, I do not want it all starting again!"

"George," Nelly's father, David, interjected, "I understand how disturbing the events surrounding your wedding were. I agreed with your need to send Nelly to York and keep her hidden there. But as your father said, that is in the past. There have been no further strange events here with that child."

George felt frustrated. These were the two men he relied on the most, and he couldn't make them understand what he knew.

"But we are back now. You heard that scream today after we arrived. That was Lydia."

Moses and David exchanged looks.

"You cannot seriously believe that," David said. "George, many more people live around the bay now. It is spring. Children play outside—they laugh, they run, they chase each other, and often, they scream."

"David is right, son. What makes you think the scream was from Lydia? Surely she had no idea you were on that ship."

George ran his hands through his hair. "Ugh! How can I make you understand? I just know it. I don't know how or why, I just know it was her." He looked up at both men, the strain clearly evident on his face. "I need to protect my wife."

"Protect Nelly? From what?" David asked.

"From Lydia. Or from whatever evil is within that child." George stood up, pacing the room. "You have to believe me. I need to protect Nelly. I need to keep Lydia away from my wife!"

"Son, please sit back down," Moses urged him. "You have worked yourself into a state." He pulled open the lower drawer of his desk and removed a small flask. After pouring a small amount of amber liquid into a pewter cup, he slid the cup across the desk toward his son. "Drink this and try to relax."

"Rum?" George asked, taking the glass. "Father, I didn't think you were a drinking man."

"I'm not, but I keep some here for medicinal purposes, and this appears to be such an occasion."

George took the cup and swallowed. He felt the burning warmth of the liquid as it penetrated his throat. He coughed a couple of times and sat back down.

"I just need your help in keeping Nelly safe, at least until after the baby is born. She and I discussed this before we left Bangor. I want her to stay here on Butler's Point until after the birth of the child. She is not to go to town for any reason. Not even for meetings. David, if you and Joanna or any other members of the family wish to visit with her, you must come here. I will not tolerate any chance meeting with Lydia or any of the Blaisdells out on the roads, either."

"And Nelly agreed to this?" David asked.

"Yes. It was the only way I would agree to bring her back home. Coming home was not my idea—it was hers." George drained the last of the rum from the cup and set it on his father's desk. He looked hard at both men as they silently evaluated his demands.

Moses leaned back in his chair. He studied his son. The strain of something was clearly evident in him. Something lay heavy upon his son's mind.

"I felt the York solution was a bit drastic but willingly agreed because of the ruckus surrounding the wedding," he said slowly. "However, I cannot see the logic in this latest demand. There is no evidence whatsoever that Nelly is in any danger."

George jumped from his chair, nearly knocking it over. "The scream! My God, Father, did you not hear that child scream today?"

"Settle down, settle down. And do not take the Lord's name in vain in my house, understand?" Moses was beginning to feel anger rise within his own breast, and he stood to confront his son. "This is not some rum-running grog shop on the river in Bangor."

George bristled at this and threw his arms up in the air. "That bothers you, doesn't it, Father? That I made my money on the West Indies trade?"

David stood up and stepped between father and son. "I think we all need to calm down and keep this discussion on the topic of Nelly. Sit down, both of you."

George and Moses returned to their chairs as David continued to speak.

"George, clearly you are troubled. We can see it plainly on your face. I noticed it immediately when you arrived at the dock today. I saw Nelly speaking with you before disembarking from the ship. Something was not right between you two." He placed his hand on George's shoulder and looked straight at Moses.

"We may not understand his reasons, Moses, but he is Nelly's husband. He is man of his own house, even if he has come back to live within yours."

Moses nodded slightly at this statement.

"Nelly's lying-in time is shortly approaching, and I do not think it will be too troublesome to have her remain here on Butler's Point until that time comes. Particularly if she has already agreed to George's conditions, who are we to not support this as well?"

George exhaled loudly and visibly relaxed. "Thank you, David, truly."

Moses sighed audibly, looked from his son to his friend. "I will abide by this if Nelly has agreed to do as much. It will be hard to explain to the rest of the women, though. How do we accomplish this without appearing to everyone in town like lunatics?"

"We will just say Nelly wishes to remain here at Butler's Point because she is close to her time," George said.

"Fair enough," Moses replied. "David?"

"Yes, I think that will do. Now we just wait for June."

No one moved, each lost in his own thoughts. Moses and David were concerned for George's state of mind. George was concerned for Nelly.

———

Back in the drawing room, the women were discussing what items needed to be sewed for the new baby when they heard a loud crash and raised voices coming from Moses's study.

"My sakes!" said George's mother, placing her hand upon her chest. "What is happening in there?" She stood as if to move toward the door when Nelly reached out and grabbed her wrist.

"Please, Mother Butler, don't disturb them. Let them be." She looked around at the group of startled women and sighed deeply. "George has been terribly on edge lately. I'm sure he's discussing the matter with the men he trusts most."

"But must they do it so loudly?" Sally asked. "Doesn't sound peaceful."

"Men rarely discuss things the same way women do," Nelly laughed. Several of the other women laughed as well. Sarah, still standing, continued staring at the door of her husband's study. Nelly gave her a small tug on the sleeve. They made eye contact, and Nelly whispered, "It will be all right." She smiled at her mother-in-law. Since no further sounds came from the study, Sarah slowly returned to her seat.

CHAPTER TWENTY-FOUR

Returning to the log cabin the day after their arrival brought back a flood of memories for Nelly. This had been her first home as a wife, although their time there had been brief. Here she and George had known each other for the first time. Here they had tried desperately to create the child they both wanted so badly. She rested her hand on her stomach. It may not have happened when they wanted it to, but it did happen. Soon she would have the child in her arms.

The snow still clung to the edges of the woods around the cabin, but in the clearing, it was warm and sunny. It was a good day to tackle getting settled in. George had gone with Moses farther inland to look at a piece of property he was considering buying. Moses had described it as good, solid farming land. There was a pond and a natural meadow. Nelly knew George's heart was not in farming. He had adjusted to the mercantile life in Bangor well enough, but it was the sea that he loved. Franklin already had a town center with a handful of shops that served the needs of those in the area, but it did not have that boomtown feel that Bangor had. For now, there would be no opportunity for George to open a shop here. Farming was the only answer.

Nelly stared at the pile of packing crates that had been moved to the side of the cabin. They had been placed under the overhanging eaves to protect them in case of rain. Luckily, the weather had held, but she couldn't let the crates sit there long. How was she going to get all of that in the tiny cabin by herself? She placed her hands on her hips and arched her back. The baby was sitting heavily on her spine. As she stretched, it kicked in protest.

"Sorry, little one, Mother needed a stretch. Go back to sleep."

"Hello at the cabin!" a voice suddenly called out.

"Hello, I'm here!" she shouted back into the pines. Coming out into the clearing, she saw George's brother Peter with his wife and several of their children. Edna, still unsure about all the new people she was meeting, hid behind Nelly.

"It's okay, Edna, these are your cousins," Nelly told her, ruffling her hair. "They were here yesterday, too."

The group had reached the cabin, and Peter was surveying the crates.

"George said you might need a little help unpacking."

"Oh, that would be splendid. Thank you!"

Peter's wife, Polly, pushed two of her children forward. "Nathan, Elizabeth, go play with your cousin Edna."

The two children looked shyly at Edna and then stared down at their feet as they dug the toes of their shoes into the dirt.

"Edna, why don't you go play with your cousins so Mama can get some work done on the cabin?"

"No," Edna pronounced firmly and buried her head into Nelly's skirt. There was a scattering of laughter from the adults.

Nelly pulled her daughter out from her skirt and took her by the hand.

"Come this way." She led Edna and urged Nathan and Elizabeth to follow as she walked toward a fallen pine tree on the edge of the clearing. "See how many pinecones there are on this tree," she instructed, pointing.

The children all nodded as they surveyed the cones that clung to the branches of the tree. The tree had fallen sometime during the winter.

"Can you pull the cones from this tree and make a pile of them over there?" Nelly asked, pointing to a few granite rocks a short distance away. A large iron triangle with a hook hanging from its center stood over the rocks, indicating the spot where the cooking fire would be. "I will need these cones to start my cooking fire after we get the cabin set up."

Edna took to the idea quickly, wanting to help her mother in any way. She started pulling cones from the tree and carrying them over to the rocks. Nathan and Elizabeth were quick to join in, and soon all three of them had forgotten their shyness and were working together. Peter had begun prying the tops off the crates, and Polly was already removing the hay to reveal Nelly's dishes and cookware. With so much family around, it wouldn't take long for the cabin to be set to rights.

Polly began to chatter about all the local news as she and Nelly carried items into the cabin and found places for them. Her voice carried on nonstop like the clucking of a chicken. Nelly was barely able to get a word in. She smiled to herself and wondered how Peter, so quiet and reserved, dealt with this on a daily basis. Polly chattered on.

"And there will be a sewing circle next Tuesday at the meetinghouse to make clothing for the Leighton family," she was saying. "They are the new family that moved in on the eastern side of the bay. They lost their cabin and all of their belongings last week in a fire. Shameful, just shameful. I think it would be great for you to come and sew with us." She stopped and looked at Nelly, waiting for a response.

Nelly thought about her promise to George to stay on Butler's Point. "Oh, Polly, that sounds like such a wonderful thing for all of you ladies to be doing, but I'm going to stay close to home until after this baby arrives." She placed her hand on her stomach for added emphasis.

"Oh, pish posh!" said Polly. "You've got weeks to go before you need to worry about staying close to home! You really need to get out to socialize. You wouldn't believe how many people have settled on the eastern side of the bay since you left."

"Yes, I remember hearing about that in the letters I received while we were away. I think that's wonderful."

"All the more reason for you to come to the sewing circle. Meet some of the new ladies!" she said as she placed the folded linens into the rough-hewn storage box built into the wall of the cabin.

"Really, Polly, I'm happy to just stay here until my time has come. I don't feel much like socializing with my body all plumped up and aching half the time." She sighed dramatically and arched her back for effect. "I think I'll sit down to rest for a minute, if you don't mind."

"Oh, you poor dear!" Polly was immediately thrown off topic and shifted her attention to the care of her sister-in-law. "I've been talking away and not paying attention to how hard you've been working! Let me go get you some water." She was off like a shot and out the cabin door toward the well.

Nelly smiled as she watched her go. Polly had the attention span of a squirrel, for sure! When she returned with a dipper full of water for

Nelly, she was babbling away about the children and the pile of pine cones they had made. This led her onto the topic of her other children, and away she went, bouncing from one topic to the next and thankfully not mentioning the upcoming sewing circle again.

⁜ ──── ⁜

George and his father had spent the better part of the day surveying the land he was considering to purchase. The spring air smelled of mud and grass, and the sun felt warm upon his face as they made their way through the natural meadow to a small hill. They had already ridden on horseback through the trails of the wooded portion of the land out to the pond. It was of good size, with clear water and several areas along the shoreline that were pebbly. The pond was fed by a brook that tumbled and bubbled over rocks on its journey. George wasn't sure of its source, but it guaranteed that the pond water would never be stagnant and unhealthy. It was hard to tell from horseback, but George was sure there would be fish there as well.

They now guided their horses through the meadow toward a small hill. Despite the spring season, the land appeared to have drained well, and there were only a few low spots to contend with as they trotted along. From the hill, George could see out to the bay about five miles in the distance.

"Good land, isn't it?" his father said.

"Yes, so it makes me wonder why no one else has purchased it yet. There is an abundance of wood, and the meadow is just prime for planting with very few rocks to remove. The pond provides fish and other game for hunting. There is certain to be several areas to place a well and numerous level areas to use as a building site. So why is it not taken?"

Moses laughed and pointed out to the bay. "That's why. The emphasis now is on building up that area."

"I don't understand," George said.

"Thirty years ago, many of us left Berwick, York, and the surrounding towns to come to the western side of this bay. It just takes one man to find a decent spot, and he sends word back to his family. Before you know it, everyone in that area is flocking to the new opportunity."

Moses gazed out to where he could see Butler's Point jutting out into the bay. "When I first laid eyes on the point, I had the same reaction as you do to this land. How was it possible that something so beautiful was not already taken? I realized then that the Lord intended for me to have it, and it was so."

George waited for his father to say something more, but he didn't. Moses was seemingly content to let that be the last word on how they had arrived at Butler's Point. It was the Lord's will.

"Are you saying that it's the Lord's will that I should have this land?" George asked.

"I dare not speak for the Lord," Moses replied. "I will say that the rush to buy land seems to be centered in and around the eastern side of the bay at this time. No one is looking five or ten miles inland…yet." He winked at his son.

George looked out over the land. It certainly was good land. The price was decent as well. He had the financial means due to his investments in Bangor.

"I suppose we could call that brook George's Brook," he said with a smile.

His father smiled back with a twinkle in his eye. "Think bigger, son. I'd call that pond George's Pond, too."

CHAPTER TWENTY-FIVE

Eastern Side of the Bay

The room was exceptionally quiet as Abner Blaisdell scooped more stew into his spoon. Glancing around at his family seated at the table, he could feel the tension in the room thick as the fog that rolled in along the bay. When a fog rolled in, it enveloped the pines and spruce, wrapping its tendrils around everything, smothering it with the dense grayness. That was exactly how his heart felt at this moment. The gaiety and happiness that had filled his home for the past two years was gone. In its place came that sickening feeling that something was not quite right with his youngest daughter.

His mind played over the scene two days ago on the water's edge. Remembering the haunting sound of that voice made the hairs on his arms rise with electricity. It hadn't been Lydia speaking. It had to be a spirit of some kind that had possessed her body. This spirit knew things that Lydia could not know. His mind searched through all of the scriptures he had committed to memory. Familiar spirits. That is what the Lord called them. The Lord warned his people about them. But what was the warning? He couldn't remember. He knew he had to remember. In order to save his daughter, he had to learn all he could about familiar spirits. He pushed his chair back, the scraping sound causing Mary to jump. She looked at him, questioning.

"Do not wait up for me. I'm going to town to speak with Reverend Crawford," he said, kissing her gently on the head. "I might be late."

Mary nodded. He kissed the heads of Hannah and the twins, and when he reached Lydia, he stopped.

"Dearest child, stay close to your mother this evening while I'm away." He kissed her head as well and turned for the door.

The candle flickered wildly as Reverend Crawford yawned with a heavy exhale. He attempted to cover his mouth and stifle the yawn quickly, trying not to be rude, but he wasn't successful.

"Oh, Reverend, I'm terribly sorry I've kept you at this for so long," Abner said, looking up from his deep study of the Bible laid out before him.

"No, no, Brother Blaisdell, 'tis fine. It's just been a long day. I'm here for you as long as you need me to be."

Abner had arrived shortly after Archibald had finished his evening meal. He could tell the man had a heavy heart and needed to talk. He had listened with interest at the tale the man wove. He well remembered the incident at services after George and Nelly's wedding. He knew how the talk before the wedding and after had nearly torn his flock apart. He had to admit for a time he had felt the Blaisdells were at fault in this situation by possibly encouraging the infatuation of their young daughter in hopes of securing a well-placed marriage for her. But now, as he sat across his desk from this man, hearing his descriptions of what was happening to his daughter and seeing the fear in the man's face, Archibald knew that Abner Blaisdell was not orchestrating this—he was experiencing it right along with the rest of his family. Abner was terribly concerned that his daughter had a familiar spirit and had come to Archibald to see if there was any counsel to be gleaned from the scriptures in this case. He had remembered reading about familiar spirits as a younger man.

Abner leaned closer to the candle, pointing with his finger to a scripture he had just found.

"Here, I think I finally found what I was looking for." He cleared his throat and began to read. "It's in Leviticus, in the Old Testament. Regard not them that have familiar spirits, neither seek after them to be defiled by them. I am the Lord your God. And the soul that turneth after such as have familiar spirits, to go a whoring after them, I will even set my face against that soul and will cut him off from among his people." He sat back in his chair. "That's it. That's the scripture I remember reading."

Archibald sat staring at Abner. After hearing those words, what could one say to the father of a child who most likely had a familiar spirit? The scripture was damning at best.

"Abner." He paused, not knowing where to start with his thoughts. He needed to provide solace for this man, but the Lord had spoken, and His word was His word. How could Archibald dispute the word of God? "Abner, let us not get ahead of ourselves. Lydia is but a child. I'm not sure that the Lord meant these words for a child. Children are innocence before God."

"What else could be tormenting my child, then? Satan himself? Familiar spirits know things that others do not. Lydia knew George was on that ship, and something spoke from within her to announce as much. There can be no other explanation." He exhaled loudly. "She is quickly becoming a woman, Reverend. She is twelve years old now, not exactly a toddling child. She is my daughter. I cannot turn her out. Yet how do I keep her in my own household and still obey the word of God?"

Archibald closed his eyes, sighing deeply. Opening his eyes, he spoke to Abner.

"For now, we will pray. I will pray. You will pray. We will seek the Lord's guidance and protection for Lydia." He reached into his desk and pulled out a leather-bound book, flipping through the pages until he finally lighted upon what he was seeking. "I will also pen a letter to a colleague of mine, Abraham Cummings. He is a very learned man. He served at a Baptist church in Bucksport for a time, which is how I made his acquaintance. He's serving in Freeport now. I will get word to him and see what his thoughts might be on this."

Abner reached his hand across the reverend's desk, and Archibald grasped it.

"Thank you, Reverend. Thank you."

"Abner, try not to trouble your mind too much about this. Find peace in the Lord. Let Him take care of this. Do you understand?"

"I don't believe it is that easy, Reverend. I fear the Lord has forsaken us."

CHAPTER TWENTY-SIX

Main Street, Franklin

The sign hanging above the door blew slightly in the wind. The dark-green image of a pine tree was carved in the center, and the proprietor's name, Zachariah Marshall, was spelled out in gold letters above it. The words *Land Agent* appeared at the bottom. Zachariah Marshall was a shrewd businessman, there was no doubt about that, but he covered it with a jovial personality that few people could resist. He just exuded trustworthiness whether it was earned or not.

George's father stepped before him through the door, and George followed.

"Moses! What a fine day it is to see you!" Zachariah extended his hand to both men and gave each a vigorous handshake.

"Yes, yes it is," Moses replied. "This is my son, George."

"Why, of course it is! Everyone knows of the esteemed Captain Butler." Zachariah smiled. "Your wedding to Nelly Hooper was quite the talk of the town for some time, was it not?"

George felt the smile on his own face vanish quickly. Would he never escape from this as long as he, Nelly, and Lydia lived in this town?

He chose to say nothing, and Zachariah understood immediately his faux pas. Clearing his throat, he moved on.

"So I understand your father took you up to see the acreage inland a bit. What did you think, my boy? Would you like to own it?" He sat back down at his desk and opened a ledger in front of him. Dipping his quill into the inkwell, he looked as if he were all set to finalize the deal right then and there.

George glanced at his father; they were still standing. He had never bought land before, but he was pretty sure it didn't go this quickly.

Moses reached for a chair and offered it to George, then took another from along the wall for himself. After sitting down, he spoke.

"Well, Zachariah, I believe George is interested in the land, but how about we talk this over as gentlemen for a spell first?"

Zachariah placed his quill back in the well and leaned back in his own chair. "So what say ye?"

George leaned forward and spoke for the first time. "I'm interested in all the land from the surveyor's marker south of the hill heading northwest to the second marker with the brook as the eastern boundary."

"That's fine. Fine piece of land there, my boy." Zachariah smiled and leaned forward, reaching once again for his quill.

"And…" George began, causing the man to stop and look up at him, "from the second marker proceeding northeastward to include the meadow and the pond."

"Well." Zachariah spoke with a smile in his voice. "That is quite a bit more than your father and I initially discussed."

"Yes, well, after walking the land myself, I feel that I would need all of the land around the pond as well as the pond itself for what I want to do."

"Got big plans, have you?" Zachariah asked.

"Yes, for a big family." George smiled, looking at his father. "My father has the point, and I shall have the pond."

"Ah, I see. A gathering point for more Butlers." Zachariah reached for his quill again. "Well, that is a considerable amount of land you are talking about, close to five hundred acres. You should be able to fill that with quite a few children." The quill rose from the inkwell for a second time.

"And I'd like it for no more than twenty cents an acre." George smiled.

Zachariah's quill stopped in midair over the inkwell. George continued smiling as large drops of black ink dripped from the tip of the quill.

"Well, then, let the negotiating begin," Zachariah said, grinning widely and replacing the quill into the inkwell.

Lydia sat on the bench outside of the mercantile store with the twins. They were fidgeting beyond belief and couldn't be trusted to keep their hands to themselves inside the store. Lydia wasn't happy that she had been chosen as their keeper. She so wanted to be inside with the rest of the ladies. The boat from Boston had arrived last night, and she wanted to see the new items for sale. She was hoping for a new bonnet. Lydia watched the people moving about the town. Franklin was clearly the business center of the area. She watched as men stood around in groups discussing deals or local politics. Women carrying baskets moved in and out of the shops. The twins beside her were seeing who could swing their legs the fastest, and it made the whole bench move beneath her.

"Look, Lydia! My legs go faster than Eb's," Samuel screeched.

"Stop, you two," Lydia scolded. "For Pete's sake, can't you sit still for just two minutes?"

It was then that her eyes caught sight of the tall man exiting the business directly across from her. It was George Butler. He was with his father, and they were shaking hands with another man. She watched him closely. It was the first time she had seen him since he had returned home. As she looked at him, she was certain he had gotten more handsome. She was riveted by him and couldn't tear her eyes away. The twins were kicking up a dust storm now and laughing, but she hardly noticed. Her whole world was centered on the man just across the street. She heard the voice in her head telling her to speak to him. She shook her head to try and clear her mind, but the voice came back: "Tell him you know."

George and his father were finishing up their conversation with the other gentleman and turning to leave. She knew if she was going to get a chance to speak to George, she had to do it now. She had to tell him that she knew. She had to speak to him. Without thinking of the twins at all, she stood up and darted across the street. She was moving as fast as she could without running, feeling her skirts pulling on her legs with each stride. She did not want to draw attention to herself, but she did not want to lose this opportunity, either. As she got closer to them, she called out.

"Captain Butler!"

George stopped and turned around. She knew he recognized her immediately because his facial expression changed from one of happiness to one of grave concern and almost fear.

She reached the spot where he had stopped and tried to catch her breath. "May I have a word with you, sir?" she asked, adjusting her bonnet and smoothing her skirts to try and appear older than her twelve years.

"Miss Blaisdell," George replied icily, nodding his head slightly in greeting. "I'm afraid I am short on time this afternoon, as I'm anxious to get back to Butler's Point."

He did not turn away from her. She knew he was too much of a gentleman for that. But it was clear from his tone and his look that he would rather be anywhere else at that moment than talking with her.

"I understand, sir, but it will only take a moment."

"Very well. Speak," he said, narrowing his eyes.

Lydia looked at Moses and cleared her throat. "Privately, sir."

An audible sigh escaped George's lips. He looked between Lydia and his father. "Very well. Father, please?"

Moses nodded. "I'll meet you at the boat." He touched his son's shoulder in parting.

After Moses had walked a considerable distance away, George spoke. "Well? What is it you have to say?"

Lydia took a deep breath. "I know," she said and looked up at him.

"You know what?" he asked, glaring down at her.

"I know what the ring says, and I know you have it."

George's eyelids flickered rapidly for a brief second, but he maintained his composure. "And what ring is this that you speak of?"

Lydia shifted her weight slightly to indicate her frustration with him. "Captain Butler, we are talking of the ring that was found in the posset on your wedding day, the ring that was thrown into the bay and then brought to me by some unseen force. I saw it with my own eyes. It is engraved with my name and yours along with the date 1800."

George stood motionless, staring at her. She could feel his eyes boring into her. Was he going to speak? She wanted to yell out "say something!" But instead, he just turned to walk away. Lydia reached out and grabbed his arm. He flinched as if her touch had burned him. He stopped, but she continued to clutch at his arm.

"Let go of me, Lydia," he said coolly.

"Captain! Do not disregard me. I am no longer a child. I know you have the ring and you've seen it, too."

George reached up and disengaged her hand from his arm. Calmly but coldly, he spoke to her. "Lydia, do not make a scene here where everyone can see and make talk of it." He continued to stare at her but did not say a word. His face, which earlier she had thought to be so handsome, now appeared cold, hard, and almost dangerous. He turned again to leave her.

In defiance, she blurted out the deepest feeling in her heart. "Mark my words, Captain Butler, I will be your wife someday."

He slowly turned around and returned to where she was standing. He leaned in so that he was closer than he had ever been. She could feel his breath as he spoke. "Miss Blaisdell, let me remind you that I have a wife. A beautiful, loving, wonderful wife who I have begun a family with." He pulled back, staring deeply into her eyes. "And that will be the end of this discussion. Good day, Miss Blaisdell." He turned and strode off.

Lydia watched him go until he had disappeared among the crates and barrels that lined the dock. "Oh yes, I will, Captain Butler," she whispered to herself. "Someway, somehow, I will be your wife."

<hr />

Moses sat at the stern of the small rowboat watching his son pull heavily on the oars. His son was clearly lost in thought. He had not spoken a word since his private talk with the Blaisdell girl.

"Zachariah fought a tough battle, but I feel you got a fair price on the land."

George looked up as if seeing his father for the first time.

"What? Oh, I'm sorry, Father, my thoughts are elsewhere. Yes, I paid a bit more than I initially wanted to, but it was a fair deal. I'm pleased."

"Your thoughts are on Lydia Blaisdell, no?"

George bristled at the question but answered. "I wish to have no thoughts of Lydia Blaisdell, now or ever."

"I see. Would you care to tell me what was discussed?" Moses asked.

George looked at his father and stopped rowing. The boat slowed its forward progression and began to drift with the current. Moses thought his son was finally going to open up to him and explain this fear he had of the Blaisdell child. But after a moment, George started rowing again and then spoke.

"No. I will not speak of it and give it credibility."

Moses sighed. "Son, you will never find peace within your soul if you harbor trouble there. Do you understand that?"

George looked thoughtfully at his father. He knew the man was right. This knot of anguish that he was trying so desperately to bury deep felt like a millstone about his neck. But he also knew that if he spoke of it out loud, gave it credence, it could become larger than himself. Certainly, fear gripped his soul; there was no peace there. His wife was weeks away from bringing their first child together into this world. A son, he was certain it was a son. He had a beautiful daughter that the Lord had provided to them at a time when Nelly needed it most. Edna had come to them serendipitously and was now their beloved daughter. He had just purchased a large tract of land so that he could build a farm and provide for his family. His life was nearly complete in every sense of the word—except for Lydia Blaisdell. Why did this hang over him? He could not discuss this with his father, so he remained silent.

The bottom of the boat began to scrape the sandy bottom as it neared Butler's Point. George gave one last pull on the oars, propelling them into the shallow water. He stowed the oars and jumped into the water, pulling the boat closer to the rocks so his father could disembark. He held the boat steady, waiting for his father to rise. Moses still sat in the stern, unmoving.

"Father, please," George said.

"I wish you would discuss this with me before we join the others. They will be eager to hear if you were successful with the land agent, and there will be no further time for us to speak privately."

George shook his head, reaching for the rope to tie the boat to the large iron ring that was driven into the rocks. After securing the boat, he stood looking down at his father, who was still seated.

"I will not speak of Lydia Blaisdell. I will go to great lengths to protect my wife and family, whether anyone else sees the necessity of it or not. Child or no, Lydia Blaisdell carries the mark of evil within her." He turned on his heels and walked up the path toward the main house, leaving Moses to ponder his words.

CHAPTER TWENTY-SEVEN

Franklin, Maine
May 1, 1797

My Dear Sir, the Most Reverend Abraham Cummings:

I send this letter with greatest regards for your well-being and continued success working in the Lord's vineyard. I trust all is well in Freeport and the surrounding area due to your great efforts.

I write to you at this time to seek advice regarding a problem that has arisen in my flock. I was approached recently by a father who is much concerned about his daughter. She is twelve years old and appears to be possessed by a familiar spirit. There is much talk in town of events, real or imagined, that transpire in her presence. I can honestly say I am not unaware of this, as I have witnessed a disturbing incident myself. Her father, whose perspective I trust, relates tales of the child speaking in a voice unlike her own, fits of stiffness and trembling, objects flying about the house, fires starting on their own, and the child knowing things that she could not possibly be aware of.

The father is greatly concerned that she has a familiar spirit, and I cannot say I disagree with him. However, I shrink from my duty to apply the strictest sense of the law to her. I fear doing nothing will allow Satan's power to increase within my flock. This child attends Sunday services with her family, sits within the sound of my voice, and hears the words of the Lord. How can I not rebuke the spirit within her? And yet I do not wish to cause turmoil and upheaval in the town by calling this spirit out publicly. The gossip mongers are already well aware of this young lady, as there is a bit of a love triangle associated with her and two other members of the community. Nothing immoral, mind you, only a childish infatuation that seems to have gotten out of control. I do not wish to inflame that situation, either, by drawing more attention to her.

As you can see, I find myself in quite the quandary and write to you for advice and guidance. Currently, I have asked the father to continue to pray, as I am, for the Lord's help in this matter. Your words of wisdom would be greatly received here.

Your most humble servant,
Rev. Archibald Crawford

Archibald looked over the letter twice before folding it and sealing it with wax. The warm scent of melted beeswax reached his nostrils as he sat staring at the letter on his desk. Had he explained the gravity of this situation enough? Would Abraham think him a poor servant of the Lord for not rebuking this spirit immediately and casting Lydia out? What kind of spiritual leader was he if he shirked his duty at the first sign of evil? And yet, what kind of spiritual leader would he be if he could not deal compassionately with his followers? Wasn't the Lord himself a paradox of both ideals? He could deal sharply and harshly with sinners when the need arose, and yet he also treated them with loving compassion and service. How does one find that balance? How does a mere man know when to rebuke and when to succor?

Rising from his desk, letter in hand, he hoped that Abraham would have the answer.

CHAPTER TWENTY-EIGHT

May 1797
Butler's Point

Polly sat on the edge of the bed holding little Nathan's hand. He had been coughing and wiping his nose for a few days now. She hadn't really paid attention at first, as springtime colds were common, but now he was listless from a fever and had the telltale signs of the measles with the red rash spreading from his neck to his chest. She worried about the other children in her own family as well as their cousins on the point. She knew, all too well, that measles could spread quickly and take many of the children away if they were not careful. She had to get word to Nelly and the others soon. Rising, she kissed Nathan's brow and headed for the door. Nathan, Elizabeth, and Edna had been inseparable recently, and if one of them had measles, it was likely they were all going to be sickened with it.

The path through the hemlocks and pines was dappled with the spring sunshine. Polly stepped over the roots and rocks as she made her way toward Nelly's. Elizabeth was there now, and she must bring her home. The only way to stop this was to keep her children away from the other children. As Polly walked out into the clearing at Nelly and George's cabin, she could see Edna and Elizabeth playing with their dolls just outside the cabin door. Polly watched as Elizabeth reached up and wiped her nose on the sleeve of her dress, and her heart sank. Elizabeth was more than likely sick with it, too, and she was spreading it to Nelly's family.

Polly spoke briefly to the girls as she walked by and knocked lightly on the outside of the door before just walking in.

"Nelly?" she called, peering into the cabin. She paused to let her eyes adjust from the bright sunshine outside to the darker interior of the cabin. Nelly was standing at the table, kneading bread dough, her large belly protruding out and making the task more difficult.

159

"Polly! I am so glad to see you!" Nelly sank down into a chair and wiped her hands on her apron, sending little puffs of flour flying into the air. "Could you take over? I'm exhausted and can't knead that a minute longer!" she laughed.

"Well, of course." Polly went straight to work, releasing some of her pent-up anxiety into the dough as she worked it hard with her hands. Rolling it over and pressing down with the heels of her hands, she could feel the elasticity of the dough.

"Feels like you have it almost done," she said.

"Yes, probably just a few more minutes and it can be set to rest." She adjusted her body in the chair, trying to find a more comfortable position.

Polly hesitated just a moment before she spoke. "Nathan has the measles," she said, looking up from the bread and at Nelly.

"Oh dear."

"Yes, exactly. So I came to get Elizabeth. I'm afraid Edna won't have any playmates for a few weeks."

Nelly rose and got the big bowl down from the shelf. She dusted it with flour and set it beside Polly on the table.

"Here, put that to rest now," she said. "Measles?"

Polly lifted the large ball of dough, set it in the bowl, and covered it with a cloth. She dusted her hands off on the rag Nelly handed her.

"Yes. It can spread very quickly. I'm hoping by keeping them home it will spare the cousins. But I'm afraid with how much time they spend with Edna, it might be too late already."

"Edna complained of a sore throat this morning when she woke up," Nelly said. "I figured she was just getting a cold."

"Yes, that's what I thought Nathan had, too, but he's covered in the rash this morning and has a fever."

"Poor little man," Nelly said. She was concerned for Polly's child, naturally, but weighing more heavily on her mind was her own daughter and, just as importantly, her unborn child.

"Is George up at the land?" Polly asked.

"Yes, he goes there every day. Dawn until dusk. My brother Hart is up there helping him clear a building site. He has grand plans for a frame house to be built. He said he will not ask me to move from one log cabin to another, especially with a new baby. So we will stay here until a solid, respectable home is constructed." She laughed.

Polly reached out and touched Nelly's shoulder. "Well, make sure you let him know about the measles. If Edna sickens with it, he will have to care for her." Polly looked away, fearing the words she knew had to be spoken. "Measles is a serious disease for a woman with child."

Nelly looked down at her pregnant belly. "I know."

Polly moved to the cabin door and opened it to leave. "Take care of yourself, please, Nelly."

Nelly smiled, trying to cover the fear that was growing in her heart. "I will. All will be well, Polly, you'll see. The kids will be back playing together in no time." She rose to follow Polly out.

Polly spoke to Elizabeth and helped her gather her dolls and things. Neither girl was thrilled with the news that playtime was over. Edna began to cry.

"Oh, poor little thing," Polly exclaimed. "Now, don't cry, Edna. Elizabeth will come back soon."

Nelly gathered Edna into her arms. She cooed soft sounds of comfort that she hoped would quell her own rising anxiety.

"I'll send Peter over later with some quinine, in case there's a fever," Polly said, glancing at Edna and then back to Nelly.

"Thank you," Nelly said. "I'm sure all will be well. Really."

"Maybe you should get word to Midwife Bragdon," Polly offered.

Nelly nodded and kissed her sister-in-law on the cheek. "Really, Polly, I'll be fine. The children will be fine. Don't tax yourself with too much worry or you'll get sick, too."

Polly sighed. "Of all the times for this to happen." She waved goodbye and then headed off toward the path back through the trees to her own home.

Nelly hoisted Edna higher on her hip as she watched Polly leave. Edna's nose was running, but it could be from crying over Elizabeth's departure just as well as from the measles. She would not let herself get worked up into a frenzy over this. Just take things one day at a time and see what happens, she told herself.

Later in the afternoon, Nelly was just slicing the warm bread she had removed from the bake oven when George walked through the door.

"Ah, my beautiful wife and the smell of warm bread. A man cannot be more blessed." He encircled her in his arms and kissed her playfully on the neck. She giggled and tried to pull away from him.

"George, please," she squealed, laughing. Edna heard the commotion and came from the back bedroom.

"Father!" she yelled, running toward him.

"And my beautiful daughter!" He scooped her up and planted kisses all over her face, making her laugh until she started coughing. "What's this? A cough?" he asked.

Nelly looked on with concern. "It could be just a cold, George," she said, giving him a look that she hoped would convey that they would discuss it later. "Children get colds, you know."

"Yes, they do," he agreed, setting Edna down and heading toward the bucket to wash up. He then began to fill the cabin with the sound of his voice as he related to Nelly the accomplishments made at the land that day. Nelly loved to hear him talk. The sound of his voice was soothing and comforting to her after a day filled with worry. He was clearing land on the rise in the property. He said they would be able to see the bay from there. Tomorrow, Samuel Simpson was meeting them out there to divine for a well. Peter had offered to help dig it. Nelly's heart lifted as he chatted on, filled with so much excitement and enthusiasm for his latest project.

Later that evening after Edna was asleep, Nelly worked on her stitching as George read a newspaper from Bangor that had arrived on the latest ship.

"George," she spoke into the silence, "Peter's son Nathan has the measles."

George looked over the top of the broadsheet. "Measles? How did you hear of this?"

"Polly came today. I thought it was strange this morning when Elizabeth showed up without Nathan. Polly arrived a little before noon to say he was in bed with a fever and the rash. She came and got Elizabeth."

George folded the paper and set it in his lap. His mind was racing. He knew, just as well as any of them, the ramifications of this news. "Is that why you were worried about Edna's cough?"

"Yes, because this morning when she awoke she complained of her throat hurting as well. That's how it starts, you know, with symptoms you wouldn't be concerned about until you know better. And then it's too late."

"I had measles as a child. I remember all of us were sick. None of us perished from it, but I have heard of other families that were not so lucky."

"Measles is very dangerous for women in my condition, George. If Edna gets the rash, you will have to care for her. I cannot. Not without putting myself and our baby in danger."

George nodded, his thoughts on the danger for Edna now extending to Nelly. Almost instantly, an image of Lydia passed through his mind. It was gone as quickly as it came. He felt the fear returning to grip his chest, making it difficult to breathe.

"Did you have measles as a child?" he asked.

"Yes."

"Well, then, see, both of us survived it as children. Edna will, too." He reached for his paper as if that was the end of the discussion.

Nelly knew not to push it further. There was no point in debating it. The facts were there for both of them to see. She had told him, and now they would wait and see if Edna got the rash or if, in fact, she just had a cold.

CHAPTER TWENTY-NINE

Freeport, Maine
May 12, 1797

To the Honorable Reverend Archibald Crawford,

Received your letter of late regarding the young woman with a familiar spirit. I advise a measure of caution. Although one must take into account our duty as servants of our Lord and Savior Jesus Christ, we must also be wary of inciting hysteria. As you briefly pointed out in your letter, there is already much gossip about this young lady. We certainly do not need a mob reaction and find ourselves with a public flogging or worse.

Therefore, it is my best measure of advice to suggest to you that you work quietly and privately with the young woman to ease her back toward the light of our Savior through continued prayer and scripture study. If her mind and heart are filled with the teachings of the true God, there will be no room for an evil spirit to abide within her. I would also suggest her family take on an attitude of continual prayer that the entire household shall be filled with the power of everlasting salvation.

Please keep me informed on the progress of your work, and do not hesitate to contact me again if you feel you are in need of further assistance.

Yours in the Lord,
Reverend Abraham Cummings

CHAPTER THIRTY

Elizabeth had been taken to bed with the fever within days of Nathan. Peter had sent for a doctor from Ellsworth, but he wasn't sure the man would come. All work had stopped on George's land because word had come that Edna was sick now, too. Peter looked down at his son nestled in his arms. The boy was dying. He knew it. His skin was a pale, sickly white, and he already felt cold to the touch. His breath came in short, shallow gasps. He needed to let Polly see him before he was gone. She was in the next room tending to Elizabeth. He rose from his chair, carrying Nathan with him. He stopped in the doorway as he entered the small room the children had shared. Elizabeth lay on the bed, her face red from the rash and glistening with sweat.

"Polly," Peter spoke.

She turned around and saw Nathan's little body draped over his arms.

"No…no…no," she repeated as she rose to come toward them.

"Kiss him, he's fading fast. Tell him goodbye." Peter tried to sound reassuring, but his voice cracked with emotion.

Polly leaned into Peter, with Nathan cradled between them. She began to cry quietly. She kissed his cheeks and murmured to him how much she loved him. He continued to struggle to breathe, and then slowly he exhaled loudly and was still. Polly collapsed at Peter's feet, sobbing. Peter took the small boy and laid him in the bed next to his sister. Squatting down, he tried to comfort Polly.

"Polly, you need to be strong for Elizabeth. She needs you. We cannot lose them both. Do you hear me?"

Polly nodded, trying to stop the hysterics that were gripping her.

"Peter," she sobbed, "I can't. I am not strong enough for this."

"Yes, you are. Get up. I'll help you." He pulled her up and held her close to his chest. Feeling the warmth of his wife within his arms released his own emotions, and he began to cry. They held each other fast for some time before he regained his composure and took action.

"Can I leave you here alone with Nathan while I get word to Father and Mother?"

She nodded, glancing at the small boy's lifeless body lying in the bed. "He needs a shroud."

Peter went to the sitting room and removed Polly's shawl from the chair. Returning, he showed it to her, and she nodded. He spread it out over his son, covering his face as well, an act that nearly broke his heart.

Kissing Polly, he said, "I won't be long. I'll be back as soon as I can."

She resumed her place next to Elizabeth, watching her even more intently than before.

<hr>

Nelly sat in a rocking chair in the parlor of her in-laws' large house. She had been here for days now, ever since Edna had taken sick. George had insisted she leave the house. He would care for Edna himself, he said, and send word if he needed her. The parlor where she sat was on the side of the house that faced the bay. The sun shimmered off the water, casting diamond-like rays of light across her vision. Because of her position at this end of the house, she was not aware that Peter had approached from the wooded side and entered. She heard voices coming from the kitchen area and then sobbing.

Fearful that it was news of Edna, she struggled to raise herself from the chair. The child within her must be enormous, she thought, as she had never felt so big in her entire life. Maneuvering her girth about was like trying to turn one of the packet ships—next to impossible.

She moved cautiously down the hallway toward the voices. "Mother Butler?" she called. "Is there word from George?"

She stopped when she entered and saw Peter, head resting against his mother as if he were a child, sobbing.

"Oh, I'm sorry, I'll…" She turned to leave, not wanting to embarrass Peter further by intruding on his display of emotion. But then remembering his children were sick as well, she turned back. "Peter?"

He raised his head, eyes rimmed red from crying. "We lost Nathan. Just now. I've left him home with Polly, but he has to be tended to."

Sarah Butler spoke. "Nelly, I think Father is in the tool shed. Could you go and ask him to send for the reverend?"

"Yes, Mother," Nelly replied, leaving the two alone again. Her mind was tumbling with thoughts of poor Polly left alone with one dead child and one sick. This was all very real now. If Polly's child could die, then she, too, could lose Edna. George had to be told.

She made her way to the tool shed and found Moses there with his son-in-law Thomas. When the two men heard the news, they flew into action. Thomas would head to George and Nelly's cabin. His wife, Mercy, George's sister, was there helping George take care of Edna. Thomas would send her to Peter's to tend to Nathan's body. Moses would go get the reverend and get word to Nelly's parents. He had wisely suggested that Nelly have her own family around during such a difficult time. Nelly was truly appreciative of this quiet but thoughtful man.

Nelly returned to the main house. Peter was gone, and George's mother sat alone in the kitchen staring at the silver she had been polishing.

"Are you all right, Mother?" Nelly asked, sitting down at the table with the older woman.

"Yes. The Lord giveth and the Lord taketh away," she sighed.

"I imagine," Nelly said, picking up the polishing cloth and a spoon. The unspoken reality of the fate of Nelly's own daughter hung in the air.

"Edna will be fine," Sarah said, trying to reassure her.

<hr/>

Thomas arrived at George's cabin with the news. Mercy immediately left to head toward Peter's cabin through the maze of footpaths through the woods that kept them all connected.

George tried to digest the news as he sat staring at his daughter.

"How is she doing?" Thomas asked.

"The rash has spread so that it covers her whole body," he said. "She burns with a fever that I have never seen so high." He shook his head. "I will die myself if I lose her."

167

"Now, now," Thomas insisted, "let's not start that. She will make a turn here soon. I have watched Mercy bring our own children through the measles. It always looks darkest before the dawn."

"Does Nelly know?" George asked him.

"Yes. She brought news of it to your father and me. Your father has gone to town for the reverend and said he would continue on to the Hoopers' and bring Nelly's mother back with him. He felt it wasn't right for her to be without her own at a time like this. Especially since you two cannot be together."

"Of all the times for this to happen." George let his frustration show in his voice.

"Yes, it is bad timing for certain. But we must keep Nelly and that baby safe. Women will lose a child if they get the measles."

George nodded silently in agreement. Edna shifted on the bed then and asked for water. George reached for the pewter cup and spooned some into her mouth.

"See," Thomas exclaimed, " 'tis a good sign. She is thirsty!"

George took this as a good sign as well and said a silent prayer.

+———+

Within hours, Butler's Point was alive with somber activity. Word spread quickly through town, and many came to leave food and condolences at the main house. Reverend Crawford arrived to provide spiritual comfort for the grieving parents. Nelly's mother and sister both arrived, dividing their time and duties between Nelly at the main house and George at the cabin. On the following day, little Nathan was laid to rest in a small burial ground on Butler's Point. His only marker was a piece of pink granite that his father had placed over the broken earth. Polly informed everyone that it looked like Elizabeth's fever had broken, which gave Nelly hope that word of the same would come soon from the cabin in regards to Edna.

Word did come on the third day after Nathan's passing. Nelly was surprised to see George himself walk into the parlor of his parents' house where she sat with her mother. She rose to meet him, and they embraced for the first time in nearly two weeks. He held her so close and tight she could hardly breathe.

"Oh, George!" Nelly cried out, feeling almost faint from the sight of him. "Edna? She must be better if you are here." But she felt him begin to shake as sobs wracked his body.

"I could not save her, Nelly. I could not save her."

"What?" Nelly shrieked. "What are you saying?" She tried to pull away from him, but he held her ever tighter. "George, let go of me for a minute."

He released his grasp on her, and she pulled away as if repulsed by him. Joanna was there to take her into her arms.

"What do you mean? Did she not make it?" she yelled at him.

"Now, Nelly," her mother said, trying to quiet her. "Do not get upset—it's not good for the child you still have."

Nelly recoiled from her mother. Her child couldn't be dead. She had not been there. How could a child leave this earth without a mother's love and comfort?

"I'm sorry, Nelly. She's gone," George stammered. "Her fever never broke, and then the convulsions began until there was no life left in her little body." The images of what he had seen brought on another wave of sobs that burst from his chest despite his efforts to control them. He held his head in his hands and cried.

"My Edna. My little Edna." Nelly stood in shock, unable to comprehend that her daughter was truly gone. "Who is with her now?"

"Sally is there," George replied.

Joanna let out an audible sigh of relief. "Nelly, sit down. Sally will take care of her."

Nelly collapsed onto a chair and then let the grief consume her. She began to cry and cry. George felt helpless to relieve his wife's suffering, let alone his own.

<hr />

Later, George helped Nelly make her way back to the cabin so they could spend the last evening with their daughter. Sally had washed the little girl and dressed her in one of her prettiest gowns. She lay on her bed with her hands neatly folded in front of her. Her blond curls peeked out from under her bonnet. Her skin, although pale white, still bore the telltale rash of the disease that had claimed her life. Nelly sat in a chair beside the bed staring at her. She had not been there to help her pass—what kind of a mother was she?

"Nelly?" George asked as he entered the room. "Would you like to eat something?"

"No," she replied coldly.

Sally was there as well and bluntly spoke what George could not. "Nelly, you need to eat. You have to keep your strength up, as your time will be soon."

Nelly waved her hand as if trying to swat away a pesky fly. Sally rolled her eyes and stepped back, leaving the two of them alone.

"Why did you not come for me sooner?" Nelly asked George.

"I don't know," George said. "It just seemed to happen so fast. The convulsions would end, and by the time I understood what had happened, she would be having another one."

"You could have sent Sally for me."

"It was the middle of the night, Nelly. I wasn't going to risk you falling on those footpaths trying to get here in the dark."

"I never got to say goodbye," Nelly cried, as tears began to run down her cheeks. She leaned forward and touched Edna's cold face. "She never heard me say goodbye."

"Oh, Nell, she knew you loved her. She knew we all loved her."

"I hope so."

"Of course she did. That child was more loved than any child on this point. In the whole county, for that matter!" George kneeled down next to Nelly's chair. "We gave her a good life, Nell. It may have been only for a few years, but she never suffered. Never wanted for love or attention. Never went hungry or cold."

Nelly thought back to the woman who had died giving birth to her stillborn son. Crying out in her anger and hatred. What kind of a life would the child have had with a woman like that? Certainly what George and Nelly had provided was better.

"I will miss her so much, George." Nelly felt the tears starting anew. "So very much." He held her hand.

"I will, too," he said. "But very soon, you will have another baby to focus on."

"The baby will not replace Edna," Nelly said firmly.

"Of course not!" George stammered. "I did not mean that it should. I only implied that there will soon be another child who will depend on you for comfort and life, and you need to be ready to face that."

Nelly let herself cry again. George continued to hold her hand as she dealt with her emotions. Sally spoke from the doorway.

"Children are like flowers to the Lord. Some He lets stay to beautify the earth, and others He gathers home to beautify the heavens."

Nelly looked up at her sister. "That's beautiful."

†———†

The following morning, Reverend Crawford returned to the point to bury another Butler. Edna was laid to rest next to her cousin Nathan. George had made a small wooden cross and carved her name into it. Sally had helped Nelly gather some of the early spring wildflowers. They laid bunches of lilies of the valley around the base of the cross. The little, white bell-shaped flowers were as pure as Edna had been. Prayers were said, hymns were sung, and then the somber procession returned to the main house, leaving the little girl plucked from the ruckus of Bangor's hedonistic waterfront to her eternal peace alone in the woods of Butler's Point.

CHAPTER THIRTY-ONE

June 1797
Butler's Point
Main House

Midwife Bragdon had arrived quickly when word came to her. She was now sitting with Nelly in the large bedroom of the main house. Nelly and George had not returned to the cabin after the loss of Edna. Nelly could not face being alone all day in the cabin without Edna. Instead she had sought comfort with George's parents at the main house.

George sat staring out the window of the parlor. It had been hours since Nelly had asked him to send for Midwife Bragdon. The afternoon was waning fast. Across the bay, to the east, the rays of sunlight from the west were illuminating the shore. He could see that people were gathered at the Blaisdell place. He spoke to his mother, who was sewing nearby.

"Seems to be quite a gathering going on at the Blaisdell place."

"Hmm?" She looked up. "Oh, the Blaisdells. Yes, I heard that several of Atherton's family were coming for a visit. All those Oakes people are shifty characters, if you ask me." She shook her head. "Not sure what Hannah saw in that man enough to marry him."

George thought back to the last altercation he had had with Atherton regarding the ring. The ring. Thoughts of it sent shudders through his body. He stood up abruptly, as if to try and shake the feeling from him with movement.

"I've got to go find something to do. This waiting is horrible."

His mother looked up at him and smiled.

"Yes, babies come on their own schedules and not ours. Go chop some wood. Your father always did that after I had taken to my childbed."

George laughed. "Doesn't sound like such a bad idea. You'll come find me as soon as it is time?"

"Of course. The minute that son of yours makes his appearance, we will let you know." She reached up and patted the hand he had rested on her shoulder. "Now go. Men aren't good at waiting."

He bent down and kissed her on the cheek. "Son or daughter, it no longer matters to me at this point. We just need to fill the void left by Edna. My heart aches for her so much, Mother."

"I know. It seems so unfair when they are taken from us in their innocence. But it happens all too often, I'm afraid."

George glanced one more time across the bay and turned away. The last thing he wanted on his mind today was the Blaisdells.

His mother watched him head out of the backdoor before she rose and headed up the stairs.

+———+

Sarah slowly opened the door to the bedroom. Nelly was lying in the big bed with sweat pouring down her face. Sarah could hear her groans of pain. Both Nelly's mother, Joanna, and her sister, Sally, were there with her. Sarah made eye contact with Joanna and indicated she would like to speak with her. The two women spoke in whispers in the hallway.

"How are things progressing?" Sarah asked.

Joanna had concern etched in her face.

"Not well. Midwife Bragdon thinks the baby is very large. Nelly has been at this for hours, and there is little sign that the baby has moved downward at all."

"Oh dear, I was afraid of this. She had gotten so large. Is it possible that it's two babies?"

Joanna shook her head. "No, she is pretty certain there is only one."

"I will not speak of it to George just yet."

"How is he holding up?"

"Like most men, fidgeting. I just sent him out to chop wood." Sarah reached for Joanna's hand. "I will let you get back. Keep us posted."

"We will, and thank you, Sarah." Joanna silently slipped back into the room and closed the door.

The afternoon turned to evening. George took supper with his parents in the kitchen. Moses Wentworth, Sally's husband, arrived and stayed a few hours to keep him company. Joanna appeared downstairs at regular intervals with requests for more water but no news. Everyone tried to reassure George that first babies take longer. It was well past midnight when his mother urged him to get some rest. He slept in fits and starts. He could hear Nelly in the next room moaning in pain and he wanted to go to her, to reassure her that she would be all right. But his mother had warned him away. Childbed was the domain of women only, and he would be breaking a cardinal rule if he entered that room. So he remained separated from his wife for the second time in as many weeks.

With the first rays of sunlight breaking the eastern sky, George walked past the room where Nelly was. He wanted to knock on the door, to inquire, but his mother's stern warning left him standing there with his ear pressed to the wood instead. Nelly was crying, and her mother was trying to calm her down.

"I can't, Mother, I can't go any longer."

He could hear her anguish. Her voice sounded weak and fatigued.

"I know, I know. But you must," Joanna insisted. "That baby has to come out. Just relax and let your body do the work."

"I can't," Nelly replied. She cried out in pain as a spasm wracked her body.

George could listen no more. He made his way down the back stairs and into the kitchen only to find Midwife Bragdon sitting there with a cup of tea. She looked worn out and bedraggled.

" 'Tis been a long night," George said, sitting down beside her.

"Aye, it has." She eyed him carefully before speaking again. "George, 'tis not uncommon for a woman to take this long on her first child." She smiled in an effort to reassure him. "Nelly is very strong."

"Yes, yes, she is." He smiled back at her.

"The baby is very large."

"Aren't larger babies healthy babies?" he asked.

"Yes. Normally, that is good. A tiny baby can be sickly. But sometimes the babies are too big. It becomes very difficult for mothers to pass a large baby."

George looked at her thoughtfully, trying to understand the ramifications of what she was saying. She patted his hand reassuringly.

"I will know more by this evening." She stood to return to the upstairs room.

"This evening? Do you think she will still be struggling by then?" He was shocked by the thought that Nelly would suffer a minute longer, let alone another whole day.

"Yes, I'm afraid I do." And she turned and walked up the stairs.

<hr />

George spent the day outside of the house. With no fear that a birth was imminent, there was no reason to sit in the parlor for a second day of waiting. He did not travel far from the main house but rather busied himself stacking wood, fixing fencing, and rummaging around in his father's toolshed. Shortly before supper, he was summoned to the house.

Midwife Bragdon stood in the parlor with her hands folded in front of her. Seated in the room were George's parents, Joanna Hooper, and Nelly's father, who had arrived earlier in the day. Everyone looked grave. George's heart skipped a beat as he entered the room.

"Is she all right?" he asked immediately.

"Nelly continues to struggle on," the midwife replied, "but I'm afraid the baby is gone."

George did not understand her words. Gone? What did that mean? He felt his father taking him by the arm and placing a chair near him.

"Sit down, son," the man whispered gently to him.

George slowly lowered himself into the chair. "Gone? I don't understand. You were supposed to come get me when my child was born. Dead or alive, even briefly, I wanted to hold him…" He paused and blurted out, "Or her." He looked quizzically at everyone in the room. "Do I have a son or a daughter?"

Joanna stifled a cry, as it was heart-wrenching to watch her son-in-law struggle with his emotions.

"The child has died within Nelly," the midwife told him. "I cannot say if it's a boy or a girl."

"Within Nelly?" George let the words sink in. "So she has not given birth to a child yet?"

"No. The child was too big to be born, and the continued exertion of the birthing process went on for too long. The child has stopped moving, and I fear it has perished."

George leaned back in his chair in shock. First Edna, and now the loss of another child. An unknown child. How would Nelly survive this? All she ever wanted was to be a mother. Now her only children were gone from her.

George stood quickly. "I must see her myself. She will be devastated by this. So soon after losing Edna."

His father reached for him again. "Sit down, George, there is more."

George looked at him questioningly and slowly returned to his seat. He glanced around at all the faces in the room before his eyes fell on Midwife Bragdon once more.

"More? What more?" he asked of her.

"Nelly's body will continue to try and expel the baby. I cannot stop it. It is a natural process. She will continue to suffer the pains. She is beyond exhausted at this time, and I do not know how much strength she has left in her."

"This will go on?" George asked the question before his mind registered that, of course, Nelly could not live with a dead child inside of her. That at some point, the child would have to be born. "But it's too big to be born."

"I'm sorry, George, that is what I'm trying to tell you," the midwife said, softening her tone. "There is no way for Nelly to survive this. She will expire herself from sheer exhaustion before that child ever emerges."

"No! No!" George stood up and paced around the room. This could not be happening. He could not be losing his entire family. The angelic Edna. Nelly, his beautiful wife. This unknown child who represented his future. All gone? He braced himself on the windowsill, lowered his head, and cried. He could hear the midwife saying that they could send for a surgeon from Bangor, but in her opinion, Nelly would not survive long enough for a surgeon to arrive.

George raised his head and stared out the window. Before him lay the bay, the tide low and the mudflats visible. He stared absently, not recognizing the view in front of him as his mind tumbled with emotion. Tears streamed down his cheeks and sobs wracked his body, making him shake. All he had ever dreamed of. All he had planned for was gone. Death was snatching everything from his grasp. He had not been able to protect his family. He had lost.

And then she came into view. He saw her through the glass. Lydia. Slowly, she made her way down the path from her home to the edge of the beach. She did not stoop to pick up stones. She carried no basket to indicate she was digging clams or gathering berries. She just stood there. Standing on the farthest point of land that stretched into the water. The breeze blew at her skirts. Her hair, not covered by a bonnet, bounced around her face. She just stood, arms at her sides, staring across the bay directly at George. As if she knew he was in that window. Knew that he could see her. He could feel her. Sense her. A shudder passed through his body.

Mark my words, Captain Butler, I will be your wife someday. The words from their conversation outside the land agent's office weeks earlier rang in his ears. He wrenched his hands from the sill and grabbed a stack of books lying nearby. Screaming in outrage, he flung the books to the floor. The act itself startled everyone in the room. He began to tear through the room, knocking over candlesticks, sewing baskets, anything he could get his hands on. His father and David jumped up to restrain him. Both men struggled with the strength of rage and anguish that enveloped him. He continued to scream and cry out. The women scattered from the room as the men continued to try and calm him down.

"George!" his father yelled at him. "George! Get control of yourself." Both men had wrestled him to the floor and were pinning him there as his rage subsided. He continued to cry.

"You must stop this, George. Nelly needs you to be strong for her right now. Not running loose like a deranged animal."

George wiped his face with his sleeve and tried to speak. "Lydia." The word emerged from his throat like growl. "She did this."

Moses and David exchanged looks. "Lydia?" Moses asked. "The Blaisdell girl?"

"Yes," George replied. "Look out the window. She's there. She knows that I suffer."

Moses rose from the floor and looked east out the window. He saw the child standing there, stock-still, unmoving. He raised his eyebrows at David, who also rose to look.

"How odd," David murmured before returning his attention to George. "Your thoughts must be on Nelly—she needs you."

"David is correct. You have very little time left with Nelly, and you must go to her. Whatever your obsession with this Blaisdell girl is, it will have to stop right now!" George's father spoke firmly and forcefully.

George sat on the floor looking up at his father. "I have no obsession with that Blaisdell girl," he spat out. "It is she who is obsessed with me and my wife! I wish no more than to be rid of her!" He wiped his face again and rose to his feet. He stared one more time at the figure across the bay before turning and stalking from the room. Both Moses and David turned their gaze to the girl. She continued to stand there like the figurehead of a ship for a moment longer before she, too, turned and walked back up the path toward the house.

+———+

After regaining his composure and cleaning himself up, George crept up the stairs to second-floor room. Sally answered his knock at the door and let him in. The room smelled of sweat and death. Nelly lay in the bed she had taken to with so much joy and anticipation. It was now her deathbed. Lying on her back, her large belly protruded upward and stood as a reminder of what could have been but was never going to be.

The midwife offered her chair to George. "She is still suffering from the pains," she whispered. "When one hits her, give her this cloth to bite on. The pain will pass, and then she will be able to rest again briefly." Both she and Sally left the room, leaving George alone with Nelly.

Almost immediately, the pains wracked Nelly's body. George placed the cloth close to her mouth, and she bit down hard on it. Her arms were raised above her head, and her hands gripped the spindles of the headboard with so much ferocity that her knuckles turned white. George watched in amazement as her belly stiffened and rose higher in the bed. She cried out with the pain.

"Nelly! My God, Nelly," he cried. "I wish I could make it stop." He sobbed into the bedding next to her, feeling completely helpless as he watched her torment. After the pain subsided, she spoke to him.

"George?" Her voice was barely a whisper, as she had very little strength left.

"Yes, Nelly, I'm here. God, I am so sorry," he cried.

"George, the baby…it's dead."

"I know, Nelly. It's all right."

"I won't live." She said it so matter-of-factly that it shocked him.

He could not bring himself to answer. He just buried his head into her shoulder and cried. He kissed her cheek and neck. He smelled her hair, trying to savor every last memory of her. She moaned in pain again, and he gave her the cloth again until it had diminished. The pain was evident on her face, and he could hear that her breathing was labored long after the pains stopped.

"George," she whispered again.

"I'm right here," he said, leaning in closer.

"I never wanted to be apart from you. When you went to sea, I was so fearful you wouldn't return." She gasped for air, the exertion of speaking almost too much.

"Shhh, Nelly, save your strength. Don't try to talk too much."

"I have nothing to save my strength for. I must tell you this." She was cut short by another spasm of pain. This one was so strong, it nearly lifted her from the bed. She cried out, writhing as she suffered. George had to turn his head and look away. He had watched Edna suffer with the convulsions as she neared death, and now he just could not watch his wife suffer a similar fate. Death would not come easy to either of them.

"Listen," Nelly croaked out, gasping for air.

"I'm listening, go on."

"I cannot bear the thought of being without you, so I'm taking the baby with me in death. A piece of you will always be with me."

George reached for her hand, clasping it in his. "I love you so, Nelly." He could not hold his emotions in and began to cry. "Nelly, please, try to be stronger. I can send for a surgeon. We could try to save you. Please," he begged. How could this be happening to them?

"I love you, George," she whispered. "I'm so tired. I will miss you, but I need to go."

Another spasm of pain washed over her. He felt her grip on his hand tighten, but it was weakening. He watched as her face twisted in agony. What a horrible way to die, he thought. Endless pain until you can no longer endure another moment of it. Nelly didn't deserve this. No one did, but certainly not his Nelly. This would not be a peaceful passing.

"Promise me you'll never forget me," she whispered when she regained some measure of strength.

"I could never forget you," he sobbed, kissing her hand. "You were the most cherished wife a man could ever have. Our time together has been too short."

She attempted a feeble smile and opened her eyes for the first time since he had come into the room.

"I want to see you one last time." She looked him over carefully, and he saw a stream of tears trickle out of the corner of her eye. "I loved no one but you," she said before closing her eyes again. Another pain came over her, but her strength was gone. Her belly still stiffened, and she squeezed George's hand slightly before he felt her release it all too quickly. A heavy whooshing sound escaped her lips as her face slackened with relief, and all evidence of the pain she had suffered was gone.

George sat motionless, still holding her hand. The room was silent and still. Gone. His wife was gone. He was alone. No wife, no daughter, no new baby. He was utterly and completely alone. Two months ago, he had arrived home with everything, and now it was all gone. Stolen from him. Taken, all of it, like he knew it would be. Complete and total devastation had reached into his life. He laid his head down on Nelly's chest and cried.

CHAPTER THIRTY-TWO

August 1797
Burial Ground, Butler's Point

Eleanor Hooper Butler
25 Apr 1774–13 Jun 1797
Beloved Wife of
George G. Butler

Edna Eleanor Butler
1794–26 May 1797
Cherished Dau of
Geo and Nelly Butler

George looked over the two stones that stood upright, side by side in the burying lot. This was all that was left of his family. The black slate stones stood out in stark contrast to the green of late summer around them, somber and solitary in their pronouncement of the chaos that had encircled George's life. He had ordered them etched just last week, and this was the first time he had seen them.

"I'm leaving," he said out loud. "I came to tell you." He continued standing in silence, as if he were waiting for someone to answer.

"I can't stay, Nelly." His mind turned to thoughts of Lydia and the few times he had seen her in town since Nelly's passing. They had not spoken, but it did not mean the encounters had left him unshaken. He knew, all too well, the year engraved on that ring. What that now possibly meant in light of Nelly's death, he would not think about. He had to go. He could not stay in Franklin. Could not return, ever.

"I miss you," he whispered as teardrops fell onto his boots. "I have to go." Turning, he walked from the small clearing toward the path that led to his parents' house. A breeze picked up suddenly, and the pines whispered in response. He stopped for a moment, feeling the wind brush across his face, then ducked into the thick forest and headed down the path.

Lydia stepped out from behind the big pine tree where she had hidden herself when she saw George approaching. Walking quickly through the grass, she stopped just short of the stones. She glanced around to make sure that George was truly gone. She lowered herself into the grass near the stone.

"Nelly," she said in a quivering voice, "I'm very sorry. I did not mean for you to die."

———

Down at the dock in town Reuben Gray reached out and grabbed the small trunk George tossed up to him. "Is that it, Captain?" he asked.

"That's it," George hollered back. "I travel very light these days." He turned back to finish his goodbyes to his family.

"Take care," his mother said, touching his cheek. "You don't have to run, you know."

"I'm not running, Mother. Farming was never for me—my heart has always been at sea. I was willing to do it for Nelly, but now that she's…" His voice trailed off and his eyes misted over.

"Let him be, Mother," Moses said. "A man knows his limits." He reached out and shook George's hand. "Write often, and let us know where you are."

"I will," George said, shaking his father's hand vigorously. Mounting the gangplank, he took it in long strides and found his place along the rails.

"Let's go, men!" he hollered out to his crew as the shoremen lifted the ropes from the pilings. He felt the boat move beneath his feet to catch the rising tide. The sails were unfurled, and they quickly filled with the favorable offshore wind he needed to make it down the bay. Looking up into the flapping canvas, he thought of Nelly. He was not leaving her alone this time—she had the baby.

"You all right, Captain?" Reuben asked as he stepped to the rail alongside George.

"Yes. I will be, once we clear this bay." He purposefully had placed himself on the starboard side of the boat so he would not have to see the Blaisdell property as they passed out to open water.

"Truly sorry about the loss of your wife, sir," Reuben was saying. Coming from hardy Scots heritage, Reuben was a man of action more than words. George nodded in response, releasing the man from further conversation on the topic.

As the ship drifted down the bay George watched as Butler's Point came into view. He saw Peter standing out on the lawn with his other siblings and all of the grandchildren. They were all waving.

"Fair wind, my brother!" Peter hollered out.

"Aye! Thank you, Peter!" George hollered back. "Take care of the land!" George had signed his land over to Peter, at a significant loss. He had no use for it, and he never intended on coming back. He had used the meager profits from the sale to purchase this new much smaller ship. His life would be at sea from now on. Peter had insisted that the stream and pond would still bear George's name, however.

George stared at the main house, its bright white clapboards shining like a beacon on the rise above the beach. He knew Nelly and Edna lay in the woods to the left. He said a silent prayer for them and closed his eyes.

As the ship moved out through the bay, George excused himself from Reuben. "I'd like to be alone for a moment, if you don't mind."

"No, not at all," the man said, showing only a slight wariness as he turned and walked farther astern. George proceeded to the bow of the ship. He reached deep into his breast pocket and retrieved the ring. He felt the coldness of the silver as he pulled it out. It still looked very much like the small, delicate ring he had received for the posset just two years earlier. Had it only been two years? It seemed so much had transpired since then. He turned the ring around so that the sun shone on the inside. His breath caught as he read the engraving again. *George & Lydia Butler 1800.*

"Over my dead body!" he whispered as he gave the ring a mighty toss. He watched it sail through the air toward the shoals of a small island. It landed with a splash and a small ripple just shy of the eastern tip of the island. "Return to hell where you belong."

CHAPTER THIRTY-THREE

Lydia stopped. Hesitating, she glanced around quickly. She thought she had heard someone walking in the woods near her. She crouched down, feeling the damp moss beneath her hands as she steadied herself. She held her breath, not daring to make a sound, but nothing moved among the hemlocks and pines in front of her. Standing back up, she looked left and right nervously, trying to get her bearings. She knew Nelly's resting place was close by, but staying off the trails and navigating through the overgrowth was proving harder than she thought. She continued on, picking her way through the lichen-covered rocks and jutting roots that tried to trip her. Ahead, she could see a clearing. As she neared the edge of the clearing, she stopped again. She wanted to make sure no one else was there. It would be catastrophic if a member of the Butler or Hooper family saw her there.

In the year since George had left, everything had returned to normal. She no longer heard the voice. The fits had stopped, too. She could feel her parents almost sigh with relief. Reverend Crawford had even stopped coming to the house for his weekly visits with her. He was convinced that it was by the grace of God and his fine efforts that Lydia had returned from the brink of satanic possession. Whatever the reason, Lydia herself was glad to see her life set to rights. She had even seen her sister, Hannah, talking with Nelly's sister, Sally, in town the other day. So she was being overly cautious. The last thing she wanted to do was to start more trouble.

After making sure no one else was at the burial ground, Lydia slowly emerged from the darkened woods into the bright sunlight of June. She walked briskly toward the two black stones. She stopped only once, picking a few wild violets growing among the grasses. The violets, with their bright white flowers with just a hint of purple at the center, would have to be her offering. As she approached Nelly's grave, she slowed down. To her, it seemed as if the very hum of nature hushed as she approached. She stopped just a few feet from the stone and said a silent prayer. Bending down, she placed the handful of flowers up against the base of the stone.

"It's been a year," she said quietly. She heard the pines whisper in response. She looked up, expecting to see Nelly descending from a cloud. Then she shook her head at the ridiculousness of such a thought. She turned back to the stone.

"George left. But I guess you probably know that." She sighed and continued to stand there in silence. There was so much she wanted to tell Nelly about the voice, the fits, and how she knew things. She wanted to tell Nelly that she didn't mean for any of this to happen—it was just that, well, she knew she was supposed to marry George but Nelly had gotten in the way.

"Nelly," she started to say, but a gust of wind blew up from behind her. It blew with the violence of a thunderstorm, blowing her skirts up with such strength she had to fight to push them down. She looked around as the force blew around her and noticed that the trees on the edge of the clearing did not move. Whatever force this was, it was centered on her. She held onto her bonnet and tried to scream, but the wind seemed to suck the sound from her throat, silencing it before it could even escape. She fell to the ground and curled into a ball, trying to protect herself. "Nelly, I'm sorry!" she cried out.

Immediately, a bright white light appeared in front of her. It started as a small circle and then grew larger until the vision of a woman appeared within it. She was dressed in white and had the phospho-rescent glimmer of the sea at certain times of the year. She glowed with divine beauty and then was gone. Within seconds, the whirl-wind stopped, ending almost as quickly as it had begun. Eventually, the sounds of the earth around Lydia returned. Rising, she looked at Nelly's stone, her wild violets still lying there as if they had not experi-enced the violence she had just felt. Backing away slowly, as if from a worthy adversary, she could only say, "I'm sorry."

CHAPTER THIRTY-FOUR

Two-year anniversary of Nelly's death
June 13, 1799
Main Street, Franklin

Lydia hurried along, keeping her head down and hoping no one would see her. She had told her mother that she was going to town for more writing paper. She walked quickly past the stationery store, saying a prayer and asking God to forgive her for lying to her mother. If she could just reach the end of Main Street, she would be halfway around the bay and could head straight for Butler's Point. She was making her annual pilgrimage to Nelly's grave.

"Aye there!" a voice shouted out at her. "Lydia!"

She ignored it and kept her pace steady, but the young man would not be deterred. She could hear him running up toward her.

"I say, Lydia!" the young man exclaimed, breathing hard as he stepped in front of her. Sighing deeply, she stopped and stared at him. It was Asarelah Flint, known as Asa to his friends. He was a distant relation of her brother-in-law, Atherton. He was around eighteen or nineteen years old and had drifted up from Cumberland County to join other members of the Oakes clan. He'd been in town now for several months and had taken an interest in fourteen-year-old Lydia.

"Hello, Mr. Flint," Lydia said curtly.

"I've told you to call me Asa," he said, scuffing at the dirt with the toe of his boot.

"Calling you by your given name, Mr. Flint, would indicate that we were on a far more intimate level than we are," she said coolly. "If you'll excuse me, I have business to attend to." She tried stepping around him, but he jostled to the side and blocked her progress once more.

"Well, aren't we all hoity-toity today. What business do you have?"

"Private business," she said, staring hard into his eyes. "Good day, Mr. Flint." Again, she tried to escape from him, but this time he reached out and grabbed her arm.

"I mean no disrespect, Lydia, but you're a tad bit uppity. Won't you just consider giving a fellow a chance? I mean, you are a right fine-looking young woman." He smiled broadly at her, showing the decay that peppered his teeth. Standing this close to him, she could also smell his breath, and it made her stomach lurch. Lydia shuddered and shook her head slowly.

"I give chances to no one, Mr. Flint," she said. "Now, please let go of my arm, or I will let out a scream that will bring the entire town of Franklin down upon you." She flashed him a wicked smile and felt him release his grip. She did not move from her spot, instead waiting for him to retreat back the way he had come first. He did so, slinking back up the street like the sea urchin he was. She watched until she was certain he had returned to the area near the docks. Then she turned on her heels and quickly headed out of town. At the end of Main Street, she glanced over her shoulder just to make sure she wasn't being followed and turned down the old trail that was a shortcut to Butler's Point.

＋———＋

Lydia had left Asa feeling defeated. This was a feeling that did not settle well within him. He would not be bested by a girl. After reaching the docks, he doubled back behind the row of shops and hurried along in the direction he had seen Lydia go. He made it to the end of the buildings just in time to catch a glimpse of her white bonnet disappearing into the trees along the side of the road. What kind of business did she have in the woods? He walked on toward where she had disappeared, not wanting to draw attention to himself but not wanting to lose sight of her, either. Keeping his eyes on the side of the road, he almost missed the faint, old trail that she must have ducked down. He pushed past the overhanging branches and plunged in.

＋———＋

Lydia stood once more in front of Nelly's grave. Again, another year had passed calmly and uneventfully. She almost hadn't bothered to come. Was there a point to these pilgrimages? She knew from her experience last year that Nelly was not forgiving. She stood quietly for a moment before she proceeded to speak. "Nelly, I've come again to say I'm sorry." She almost whispered the words, fearful that saying them would cause something to happen. The forest around her remained calm, so she continued. "George is still gone. I'm afraid I have little news of him. What I do know I've only heard in town. Of course, it could be gossip." She held her breath, waiting, but again the birds continued chattering. She watched as a small white butterfly fluttered up and over Nelly's stone. Riding on the breeze, it continued away with no concerns.

"They say George is making quite the fortune for himself. I overheard some men speaking the other day. They were saying that George is a very wealthy man right now. He takes great risks, they said, and it pays off." Lydia could only imagine what kind of risks George was taking. Financial or physical, she did not know. She supposed he felt he had nothing to lose either way. A man with nothing to lose will risk everything.

"I hear that he has been seen as far north as York. He off-loads his rum to someone else to carry to Bangor. They say he will never come this way again."

She stopped to gather the rest of her thoughts, and as she did so, she saw the ground in front of her begin to rise up. Nelly's gravestone lifted so that Lydia had to raise her eyes to follow it. The ground rose and then fell, settling back to its normal level. This time, she backed up a step and watched as the stone and the ground around it rose and fell—like a living, breathing entity. Lydia was sure Nelly was listening to her.

<hr/>

Asa had followed Lydia all the way to Butler's Point. He was sitting on a small rock at the edge of the trees when he saw her walk into the clearing. He could tell it was a small graveyard. But who did she know that was buried on this side of the bay? All of her relations were on the eastern side. He watched as she stood there in front of one of the stones. To him, it appeared as if she was just standing there, as he was too far from her to hear if she were speaking. Graveyards gave him an uneasy feeling. He had never liked them after losing both of his parents when he was younger. If he had known Lydia was headed to a graveyard, he certainly would not have followed her. There were other, more pleasant ways to court a young lady.

He was just about to leave when he saw movement in front of Lydia's feet. His mouth gaped open as he watched the gravestone rise up and then settle back down. He glanced around the clearing quickly, as if looking for someone to explain to him what he had just witnessed. Had he truly just seen what he thought he had seen? He felt a cold chill run up his spine, and he slid off the rock. He leaned forward on his hands and knees, crawling silently forward to try and get a better look. He felt the softness of the pine needles beneath his hands. They muffled his progress as he made his way closer to where Lydia was standing. He watched as she backed up a step, and then he saw it again. The stone rose up, much like the rising of one's chest when you inhale deeply. With a burst of bright white light, there appeared a woman hovering just above the ground in front of Lydia. Dressed in white, she sparkled as if almost iridescent.

"Nelly, I'm…I'm…sorry," Lydia stammered, and just as quickly, the vision was gone and the stone fell like an escaping exhale.

Asa couldn't contain himself. He jumped up and burst from the line of trees.

"Jesus Christ!" he exclaimed, rushing out into the sunshine. Lydia, already on edge by the rising of the stone, let out a brief scream when she heard him but quickly stopped. She spun on her heels and started to run from the clearing.

"Stop!" Asa shouted. Running after her, he lunged, throwing his arms around her and tackling her to the ground. They both fell into the grass, and Asa heard Lydia cry out in pain as they landed. She struggled as he tightened his grip on her.

"Mr. Flint, for all that is decent, I demand that you let go of me at once," Lydia hissed. She felt trapped as she realized she was within earshot of the Butler homestead. There would be no screaming for help here. That would only bring acknowledgment that she had come to Nelly's grave. Asa was in full control. He quickly flipped her over and straddled her. Pinning both of her wrists to the ground, he leaned over her and stared into her face.

"What the hell is going on here?" he asked.

"I don't know what you mean," she replied.

"I was watching you. I saw that grave over there rise up like the person in it was trying to get out." He tossed his head in the direction of Nelly's grave as if Lydia didn't know which gravestone he was speaking about. Lydia tried to remain calm, realizing she had to try to regain control of this situation.

"Mr. Flint, I'm sure I have no idea what you are speaking about. Have you been drinking?"

"Drinking? Why, you..." He released one hand and slapped her across the face. It was exciting to be this close to her and have her in his control. He pushed himself hard against her. "Who is it, Lydia? Whose grave is that?"

"It doesn't matter, Mr. Flint. Please, just let me go." Lydia was starting to feel the panic rise within her.

Having slapped her once, he felt empowered to do so again. With the crack of his hand upon her face, her head lolled to one side and stayed there. She began to cry.

"Don't call me Mr. Flint," he growled. "Tell me who lies in that grave."

"Nelly Butler," Lydia said feebly.

Asa leaned even closer to her face, staring intently into her eyes. "Butler?" he asked. "Isn't that George Butler's wife?"

Lydia didn't reply, but she saw a slow smile creep across Asa's face.

"Atherton told me about you and George Butler," he said with a sneer.

"Please, Asa," Lydia uttered. "Please. I shouldn't be here. Please let me go."

"You shouldn't be here?" he asked. "And why is that?" When she didn't answer, he leaned down closer to her face.

"I know why you shouldn't be here. Atherton said you were sweet on George Butler. That you prayed to the devil to have him for yourself."

"I did no such thing!" Lydia spat out.

"Is that so? Then why did I hear you say you were sorry while you were standing there? Huh? And if you didn't pray to the devil, then why are the gates of hell opening up to come up through that grave? Jesus, I've never seen anything like this!" he exclaimed.

Lydia began to struggle again beneath him. "I have to go. It will upset my parents if they find out I was here. It will upset the Butlers. Let me go!"

The more Lydia moved beneath him, the more he wanted her.

"I want something too, Lydia." He smiled. "Why don't we make a deal? You give me what I want, and I won't tell a soul that I saw you here."

Lydia stopped moving. She sucked in her breath quickly. All of a sudden, she realized what he was suggesting. Shock registered all over her face.

His smile broadened. "It's exactly what I mean. I can take from you what I want right now. But if you were a bit more obliging, it would be more enjoyable."

"No. No, Asa, I can't. I won't." She began to struggle anew with an urgency that she hadn't exhibited before.

He leaned forward, pressing his forearm under her chin. He pressed hard on her throat, and she felt her airway collapse. "I'm taking it, then," he hissed.

Lydia fought to cover herself, to protect her feminine parts, to save something, but he was too strong. It was over and done with quickly, and he pulled away from her. She gathered her skirts about her, pulling her knees up to her chest. She wrapped her arms around her legs to protect herself and rocked back and forth. Her bonnet hung by its strings around her neck. Grass clung to her hair, and she could taste the dirt in her mouth. She started to cry.

He reached down and pulled on her chin until she was looking at him.

"Our little secret," he said. "You won't tell anyone what I did, and I won't tell anyone you were here or what I saw. Understood?"

Lydia nodded. She had no choice but to agree. It would devastate her parents to know she had been coming to Nelly's grave. But it would absolutely destroy them to learn she had been violated. She would be no good to a husband now. She would have to marry Asa or remain a spinster all of her life. No man would want her. George would not want her. She thought of the ring engraved with *George & Lydia Butler 1800*. She was six months from the year 1800, and now everything was ruined. She shouldn't have come here today. If she had stayed at home, safe on her side of the bay, none of this would have happened. She felt her stomach churning with anxiety, and she leaned to the side and expelled its contents into the grass.

CHAPTER THIRTY-FIVE

November 1799
Blaisdell Home

The sky had turned a steel gray, which matched Lydia's moods lately. Winter was coming fast. The days were among the shortest of the season now. Lydia sat out on the porch wrapped in her layers of wool clothing. The air had a chill to it, but she wanted to remain out-of-doors as long as possible. Once the snows came, there would be no more sitting on the porch. She looked across the bay and could see the Butler home bright white against the bare trees. Only two more months until 1800, and so much had changed since this summer.

Asa came to call frequently. Her parents thought he was courting her. Oh, if they only knew what had happened, they wouldn't greet him so easily. Although her parents weren't particularly fond of Asa, they knew their daughter had few prospects of an advantageous marriage. The Butler problem had insured that Lydia wasn't exactly first on anyone's list as a potential wife. Asa worked the docks making a decent wage. He would never be a wealthy man, but he could probably provide reasonably well for a family. Besides, Lydia must have feelings for him, they thought, as she let him keep calling.

Lydia laughed at this. Yes, she had "feelings" for Asa, all right. But they weren't the ones her parents thought. She despised Asa for what he had taken from her.

The sound of voices brought her from her musings, and she got up and went inside. Her father had just come in from being in town. She heard him utter the words "very ill."

Her mother looked up when Lydia walked in.

"Who's ill?" she asked.

Abner and Mary exchanged worried looks, but neither of them spoke.

"What's wrong?" Lydia asked, glancing back and forth between her parents. Abner sighed with resignation and then spoke.

"Moses Butler is very ill. They do not expect him to survive more than a few weeks."

"What?" Lydia exclaimed, sitting down at the table. "When did this happen? We just saw him at church."

"Yes, the last we saw him, he looked as healthy as an ox," Mary agreed.

"But the Lord taketh those He wants, when He wants," Abner said.

"Amen," Mary mumbled as she returned to her dinner preparations.

Lydia sat staring at the grain of the wood on the table. She traced the lines with her fingers as her mind mulled over this news. Moses was the head of the large Butler family. He had settled this area first. Built it to what it was. Butler's Point was like an empire, and he was the king. Who would that fall to now?

"George." The word escaped her mouth without her even realizing she had said it.

Abner and Mary both turned toward her in shock.

"What did you say, Lydia?" her father asked.

"I was just thinking out loud, I guess," she said, getting up from the table. "I'm going to take off these heavy clothes and get ready for dinner." She headed for the stairway that led to her room.

"He's on his way," Abner said.

Lydia stopped and turned around. She walked back into the kitchen and faced her father.

"Who's on his way?" she breathed in anticipation.

Abner sighed heavily. "George Butler. They sent word out on every ship leaving port from here to York to try and find him. He was in Boston. He'll be here in a few days."

Lydia sat back down in the chair she had just vacated. "George will be here in a few days?" she said incredulously. "That can't be. George said he would never return to Franklin."

"Well, young men say lots of harsh words they come to regret," Abner replied. "He probably thought his father would never die, either."

"Now, Lydia," Mary said soothingly to her daughter, "we don't need any repeats of the past. You must keep yourself calm." The worry was etched across Mary's face. "Asa Flint is a marriageable young man, but your fits would scare him off for sure."

"Asa Flint?" Lydia laughed. "I don't give one hoot about Asa Flint! I'd be happy to have him run off!" She realized the error of her outburst as soon as the words escaped her throat.

Taken aback, Mary stammered a reply. "What do you mean you don't care for him? He's been courting you since summer, and you've never told him to stop. Your father was just waiting for him to ask permission to marry you."

Lydia let out a laugh that shocked both of her parents. "Marry him? I would never marry him even if he were the only man to ever ask me! I've only been allowing him around because he's Atherton's relation," she lied. Even with the news of George's impending arrival buoying her spirits, she could never let her parents know the real reason why she tolerated visits from Asa.

"Oh, Lydia," her father moaned. "You should have never allowed that young man to get his hopes up. If you had no intention of marrying him, you owed him the decency of letting him know."

Owed him decency! There was so much Lydia wanted to say, but she knew that she had already let out too many of her pent-up feelings.

"I'm sorry, Father," she replied meekly, trying to regain composure and look contrite. "I will make sure I tell Mr. Flint exactly how I feel when the time is right."

"I hope so, Lydia," he said.

Gathering up her outer clothes, Lydia started again for the stairs to her room.

Against all odds, George Butler was returning to Franklin. The year 1800 was less than two months away.

CHAPTER THIRTY-SIX

December 1799
Butler's Point

G eorge had been home for almost two weeks now. Every day was a trial. They were all exhausted from the waiting as his father lingered on. Everyone had said their goodbyes. Reverend Crawford had come and prayed for the release of Moses's soul, and yet the old man held on. George was restless and anxious. He hadn't been ashore this long in two years. Every time he stopped at port, he made it a point to only be ashore for a limited time. His life was on his ship. He was safest on his ship. Now he was not only trapped on land, but on the land that he swore he would never see again.

The first few days after his arrival, he had been busy with his brothers. Poring over all of the papers in his father's study, they had made sure his affairs were in order and that the transfer of all the Butler holdings would go smoothly after Moses's passing. Nathan would take control of the sawmill. Peter would continue to expand the land holdings, selling those lots that his father had purchased years ago and reinvesting the funds into more profitable timberlands farther north. For his part, George wanted none of it. This decision had worried his brothers, but he told them to take his portion and divide it amongst their sisters. His wealth was vast on his own. The banks of Boston could attest to that. Besides, he had no need of an inheritance. His life was on his ship, and he wanted nothing more than that.

"He speaks!"

The call came from the head of the stairs. It was one of the house-maids they had hired to help with the drudgery as the family dealt with Moses's sickness. Chairs all over the house scraped across the wooden plank floors and footsteps pounded as everyone made their way to the stairs. George burst into the room first and saw his mother in her chair of vigil beside Moses's bed. Her eyes met George's.

197

"He asked for you," she said.

As the large family gathered in the room, George crouched beside the bed. "I'm here, Father," he said.

"George?" Moses struggled to open his eyes. His face was slack on one side, with the corner of his mouth drooping down. These were clear signs that the man had suffered a stroke.

"I'm here," George repeated.

"Must…" Moses struggled, swallowing once and then speaking again. "Must talk alone."

George glanced at his mother and then over his shoulder at his brothers hovering in the doorway. His mother kissed her husband gently as she rose, relinquishing the chair for George.

"We will leave George here with you, Moses." Her voice was but a mere whisper as she crossed the room silently and shut the door. When Moses heard the click of the latch, he tried to speak again.

"The drawer. A pouch," he said.

"Which drawer?" George asked, thinking of the chest of drawers in the room.

"The stand," Moses sputtered.

Turning to follow his father's gaze, George noticed a small candle-stand near the window that had a drawer in it. He stood and walked to it. Opening the drawer carefully, he spotted a small leather pouch with a rawhide drawstring.

"Is this it?" he asked, holding it up for his father to see.

Moses nodded. "Here. Bring it here."

George returned to his father's bed and held the pouch out for him. Unable to move his arms, Moses closed his eyes in frustration.

"Shall I open it, Father?" George asked.

Opening his eyes, Moses looked directly at his son. "I'm sorry," he said.

George again sat down in the chair next to the bedside. "Sorry for what, Father?"

Moses sighed deeply and closed his eyes before speaking. "Nelly's grave."

George looked down at the pouch he held in his hand. He felt his chest tighten, and his hands began to shake.

"You found this on Nelly's grave?"

"Open it," was all Moses would say.

With trembling fingers, George fumbled at the leather drawstring until he had pulled open the neck of the small pouch. Tipping the pouch upside down, he dumped its contents onto the bed linen. Landing softly and shining in the fading November daylight was the small silver ring from the posset on the day he had married Nelly.

George jumped back, knocking over the chair. "Jesus Christ!" he shouted.

Abruptly, the door swung open, and Peter stood there.

"What's going on?" he demanded. "I will not allow any of that shipboard language in this house as our father lies dying!" Peter's voice was filled with anger and worry.

"No, we're fine," George stammered, racing to close the door.

Peter reached out and held the door tightly. "Are you, George?" The two brothers stared at each other as they struggled.

"It's all right," George exclaimed. "Just let me be alone with him a moment longer." He stared intently at his brother until Peter relented and allowed George to close the door.

Smoothing back his hair, George turned to gaze at his father in the bed.

"Where did you find it? How did it get here?" he asked.

"Nelly," was all Moses would say.

"Nelly?" George repeated. He walked back toward his father's bed. "That's impossible. I threw that cussed thing into the bay the day I left Franklin for good."

"Second time," Moses said.

George knew this was the second time the ring had been thrown into the bay only to resurface. The first time, Lydia had somehow gotten in possession of it. Now he was supposed to believe that Nelly had somehow become involved.

"Ridiculous!" George said. "This can't be the same ring."

"Look," Moses muttered.

But George shook his head. He refused to believe, or he didn't want to see it again with his own eyes.

He knew what was inscribed on that ring. 1800. Time was running out. It was all too much. His father's illness and imminent death. His return home, and now the return of this ring. He sat down in the chair and stared at the silver band.

"Take it," Moses said. "It means something."

George looked at his father incredulously. "Means something? Father, how could you even think such a thing? That ring is the spawn of the devil if it is anything. But it surely holds no meaning!"

Moses closed his eyes and mustered all of the remaining strength he had left. Carefully, he began to speak. "You created it. Lydia possessed it. Nelly possessed it. Somehow, it is a sign."

"A sign? A sign of what? That I am to be tortured by that Blaisdell girl all of my days?"

"You must keep it. Do not rid yourself of it again."

"And why not?" George asked defiantly as the very idea of throwing the ring out the window crossed his mind.

"Nelly said you should keep it." Moses exhaled as if speaking had exhausted him. "Marry Lydia."

George stood, shaking his head. "No. No! So now you are going to tell me you conversed with my dead wife and she instructed you to make sure I marry Lydia Blaisdell? Have you completely lost your mind?" George's voice rose in anger.

The door to the room burst open, and Peter entered again, this time with their mother right behind him.

"George, I don't know what's going on in here, but it has to stop. You are yelling at your own father on his deathbed." He grabbed George by the shoulders, shaking him.

"What has gotten into you?" his mother exclaimed, righting the chair and resuming her spot next to her husband. She reached for his hand, and when she did so, she saw the ring lying on the bed. "What is this?" she asked, holding it up to the light so she could see it better.

George reached out, snatching it from her grasp before she could see the engraving on the inside.

"That is a ring Father wishes me to keep," he said, stuffing it into his pocket.

"Nelly," Moses muttered again from the bed. His color had faded greatly, and he was turning an ashen gray.

"No, Moses, no," Sarah cried as she realized her husband was nearing his end. "Peter quick, get the rest of the children."

Peter ran to the top of the stairs and called the rest of the family up.

"Nelly. Nelly. Nelly," Moses kept muttering as his remaining children and grandchildren filed into the room.

George stepped back away from the bed. Were these his father's last words, the name of his dead daughter-in-law?

"Shhh, Moses, shhh." Patting his hand, Sarah tried to quiet him. "Rest your mind. Go in peace, my love."

"George, keep the ring," Moses sighed. "Promise me."

Everyone looked at George. Peter and George exchanged looks, and then Peter spoke.

"What say ye, George? Will you keep a promise to your father as he dies?"

"Peter…" George struggled. Only George and his father knew that the inscription on the inside of the ring meant that George would be promising to marry Lydia when the time came. And that would be soon. To the rest of the family, promising to keep a ring seemed like a simple request. "You have no idea what you are asking of me." George pleaded.

"Promise me," Moses sputtered as his breaths grew raspy and spittle dripped from the drooping side of his mouth.

"George?" Peter said, looking at his brother for strength as they watched their father die. "He's dying."

The whole room stood silent as George mulled over his fate. If he promised this to his father, he knew he was doomed. What more evil would befall him? But if he didn't promise his father, here and now, in front of the entire family as the man lay dying, he would be reviled by his family forever.

With a sigh of resignation, George hung his head and uttered the words "I promise."

And with that, it seemed as if the whole room exhaled and the breath escaped out of Moses's chest with a great rushing sound. And he was gone.

George turned away and walked silently from the room. He felt his own breath caught in his throat. Felt the immense fear choking him, gripping him tighter and tighter as if he himself would die from the strangulation of it. His fate was cast.

CHAPTER THIRTY-SEVEN

January 1800
Blaisdell Home

Hannah struggled with the last basket of fleece as she shut the outer door with her hip. Stomping the snow from her feet, she set the basket down with a thud.

"It's freezing out there!" she said, blowing onto her hands as she looked over the dozen or so baskets of cleaned wool fleece scattered about the room. Mary and Lydia were already getting started. The carding of the wool was going to take the better part of the day, for sure.

"Sit, Hannah, warm your hands by the fire for a bit," Mary said, motioning for her daughter. "Lydia and I will do fine for a minute."

"Yes, Hannah, sit, sit," Lydia exclaimed, moving her chair a little farther from the fire to make room for her sister.

The room where they had set up for the carding was in the very back of the house. It was an unfinished room mostly used for activities such as this—carding, spinning, quilting, and so forth. With bare pine-board floors, lath on the walls, and a fireplace, it was built for utility rather than comfort. There was a small storage cupboard on the wall it shared with the kitchen, next to the door that led to that part of the house. There was also an exterior door on the opposite end of the room. This led out to the back of the yard and the entrance to the cellar. The room was large with Mary's loom standing as the central focal point. Two windows on either side of the loom gave the room its light. The cellar, directly under the floor of this room, was used mostly for storage of root vegetables during the winter. It had a dirt floor, was windowless, and was lined with shelves. The ceiling was low, but the cellar had the same large footprint as the room above it.

"It's a new year and a new century," Lydia said, reaching for a large handful of wool from a basket to begin her carding. "What lies in store for us?"

"All of this fleece," Hannah said with a chuckle.

"I pray that this new year brings us peace," Mary said when the laughter stopped. "We've had too many struggles of late."

It was true. Just in the last few weeks, there had been much tragedy. Hannah had lost her husband, Atherton. The ship he was working on had been lost in a storm and was never seen again. She had been crushed by the loss. With no body to bury, there had been very little closure for her. To try and ease her grief, Abner had purchased a stone for his son-in-law. Deeply carved to last for many years, it simply said ATHERTON OAKES—LOST AT SEA—1799. It stood in the cemetery next to the church among the other monuments to the others who would never return.

Lydia thought of her own struggles with Asa. She had refused his last few visits to her parents' home, staying upstairs in her room as her father tried to explain to the young man that she was indisposed at the current moment. Abner saw this as just a continuation of Lydia falsely encouraging Asa, which led to more tension between Lydia and her father. Lydia's mind, however, was on another family.

"Let's not forget the loss of Moses Butler," she said as she pulled the wool between the tines of her carding paddle.

Her mother stopped and looked at her sharply. "Lydia," she said with a tinge of caution in her voice.

"What?" Lydia asked. "I merely mention it because it is a loss for the community as well."

"Or could it be that you mention it because George has been unable to leave and return to sea?" Hannah said sharply.

Mary broke in between the two girls. "How the Butlers handle their affairs is none of our business," she said with the authority that only a mother has to bring her children into line. "Let's pray that the Lord will bless all of the families around the bay with peace this year."

The women sat without talking for a while, and the only sound was the passing of their carding paddles. The wiry bristles made a gentle swooshing sound as the pieces of fleece were pulled between them. Once the fleece was transferred from one paddle to another, it was lifted off and rolled into a cylinder shape, then placed in another basket. These rolls would be used when they were ready to do the spinning.

The silence of the room was broken suddenly by a knocking sound.

"What was that?" Lydia exclaimed, jumping up.

"What was what?" Mary asked.

"That knocking. It was so loud, I nearly felt it in my bones," Lydia replied.

"I heard nothing," Hannah said with just a tad bit of concern on her face. She noticed that Lydia's face had gone pale. "Lydia, you're scaring me. Sit back down. What's wrong with you?"

Lydia was certain she had heard a knocking. She couldn't sit back down. How could her mother and sister not have heard it? Not have felt it as she had?

"Mother, tell me honestly—you did not hear that?"

"No, child, I did not," Mary said. "Sit down—you are as pale as a ghost." She reached for her daughter to help ease her back into her chair.

As Lydia sat back down in her chair, her hands began to tremble. It was starting again, she knew it. Then she heard it again—a loud, powerful *thud, thud, thud* coming from the cupboard next to the kitchen door. It shook her so that her teeth rattled.

"Oh!" Mary exclaimed. "I heard it that time."

"Me too!" Hannah said, standing. She made her way to the cupboard and opened it. Nothing seemed out of place. The canvas bags of dried beans and crocks of pickled vegetables were all undisturbed. Hannah moved a few of the items this way and that way, sticking her head inside.

"There is nothing amiss here," she said.

The sound repeated itself just as Hannah was shutting the door. Lydia felt each jolt like a pain and groaned from her chair.

"I come as a voice in the wilderness," a voice said, echoing throughout the room.

"God's truth!" exclaimed Hannah. "Who said that?"

"I have no idea," Mary replied. "Check the windows, Hannah, and see if one of the boys is playing a prank on us."

As Hannah stepped to the windows, the voice spoke again.

"I come under the direction of God," said the voice, stopping Hannah in mid-stride in the middle of the room. It was the voice of a woman, sweet and lilting, with a slight melodious tone to it. The voice spoke with authority yet was gentle and pleasant to hear.

"Pray, Mother, pray," Lydia said as she buried her head into her mother.

"My heavenly day," said Hannah. "What is this all about?" Having checked all of the windows and not seeing anyone, she was confused as to the origin of the voice. For when it spoke, it sounded as if it were in the center of the room.

"Who speaks to us?" Hannah said, walking back to the kitchen door and looking that way for the source of the voice.

"I was once Nelly Hooper."

Mary's back stiffened. Lydia lifted her head and whispered to her mother in a trembling voice, "She was once who?"

"My dear Lord," Mary murmured, pulling Lydia closer to her. She closed her eyes and began to pray.

"Oh, this is ridiculous," said Hannah. Her pragmatism made her more puzzled than shocked by this turn of events. She marched across the room and opened the door leading out to the backyard. Lydia felt the rush of cold January air sweep into the room. "Who's out there?" Hannah hollered into the wind. There was no answer from the yard.

"I was once Nelly Hooper but died as the wife of George Butler," the voice spoke again from the very center of the room.

Hannah spun her head around and stared at her mother and Lydia. Seated in the room among all the baskets of now-forgotten wool, they looked shaken. She closed the door slowly and walked back to the center of the room.

"What do you want?" Hannah said. Clearly taking command of the situation, she would not allow her mother and Lydia to be tormented any longer.

"I have come for Lydia," the voice replied.

"No!" Mary screamed as she gathered her youngest daughter into her arms. "What kind of devil act is this?" Her fear was palpable.

Lydia shrunk back into her mother's embrace, trembling.

"Do not be afraid, Lydia," the voice said. "I do not come to take you. I come with a message for you."

Lydia looked around the room from her huddled position. "Where are you?" she asked.

Mary immediately hushed her. "Lydia, do not tempt the spirit."

But Lydia was already rising from her chair. She had seen Nelly before. "Show yourself," she said, "like before."

Mary gasped. "Before? Lydia, what are you saying? Has this spirit visited you before?"

Lydia stood, glancing around the room. But there was no sign of a glowing light.

"Twice, at Nelly's grave, I have seen a vision of a woman," she replied.

"Lydia!" Mary exclaimed, sitting down in her chair. "Can you not let this rest? You have visited that woman's grave? Not just once but twice?"

Lydia looked up at her mother, her dark brown eyes boring into Mary.

"I have tried, Mother. I wanted to be done with it. I wanted it to stop plaguing me. But as you can see, this is apparently my lot in life. You have heard the knocking." She turned and looked at Hannah. "You too, Hannah. You both have heard the knocking and the voice. I am not dreaming this. This is not the imagination of a child. This is real and must be dealt with."

"I was once Nelly Hooper. I died as Nelly Butler. I have come with a message for Lydia."

The return of the voice startled all three of them. Lydia stepped forward. "Then tell me. What is this message?"

"Send for George Butler. Bring him to me. So that I may tell him myself that you are to become his wife."

"No, no, no," Mary said, jumping up and speaking into the empty space in the middle of the room. "We will not. That poor man has suffered enough and does not need to be bothered by us with the workings of evil. Be gone, spirit! Leave now! I insist!"

"Send for George Butler so that I may tell him myself that Lydia is to become his wife," the voice said with urgency.

Lydia began to shake. Trembling, she said, "I cannot do that. I truly cannot do that."

"You must. For he is to be your husband."

"He would only scoff if I told him. He would not come. I am but a child to him."

"Send for George Butler."

"I honestly cannot do this thing that you ask. From God or not, I cannot do this." Turning, Lydia ran into the kitchen, slamming the door behind her.

The room fell silent as Mary and Hannah continued to stare at each other.

"Is it gone?" Hannah finally asked after a few moments.

"I'm not sure," Mary replied. "Spirit, are you gone?"

But there was no answer.

CHAPTER THIRTY-EIGHT

Later that evening Abner sat staring at his bowl of beef stew while his wife chattered on about knockings, spirits, and the voices of dead townsfolk.

"Are you daft, woman?" he finally grumbled. "You are telling me that the voice of Nelly Butler, rest her soul, spoke to you today in your carding room?"

"Yes, Abner, I am," Mary said indignantly. "Or at least she said she was Nelly Butler."

"Even worse, Father," Hannah interjected, "she wanted Lydia to go fetch George Butler and bring him here so the voice could give him a message."

Abner's eyebrows raised at this. "And what message might that be?"

"That Lydia is to be his wife," Hannah said, tilting her head and giving a slight snort. "If I had not heard it myself, Father, I doubt very much I would believe it."

"It's true, Abner. This isn't just Lydia's imagination. This is more, somehow connecting everything we have gone through with Lydia over the years. The fits, the unearthly voices, all of it. Hannah and I both heard the knockings. We both heard the voice." Mary reached over and clutched at Abner's arm. "It's true."

"George Butler's wife? Are you both mad?" He shook his head. "Let the poor lad be. His wife has been dead two years hence. He lost his father less than a month ago." Staring pleadingly at his wife, he said, "Let this be."

"I, too, begged Lydia not to start all of this again, Abner," Mary reasoned. "But this is not of Lydia's doing. This is something else. I'm not ready to say it's of God or of the devil. It's not like the other episodes, Abner. This felt different—not scary, more serene. But it is just as real as the other things I have witnessed."

Abner stared at his wife, this woman he had shared half his life with. He glanced at Hannah, levelheaded and strong from her trials. She nodded in agreement with her mother.

He was rising to get more stew from the pot hanging over the cooking fire when they all heard a knocking sound on the other side of the kitchen wall.

"Oh no," Hannah whispered.

"Lydia!" Mary shouted. Footsteps could be heard coming down the stairs and into the hall. Abner stood frozen in his spot near the fire, staring at the wall that separated the kitchen from the carding room. Three more knocks could be heard distinctly and loudly as Lydia entered the room.

"I think you're being called," Hannah said to Lydia as Mary reached out for her hand.

"No," Lydia said, backing up. "I don't want to do this anymore." This time, the three consecutive knocks were louder and stronger. Lydia turned pale.

Abner set his bowl down on the table. Pointing at Lydia, he said, "You! Stay right there with your mother. Don't touch a thing. Hannah, you stay there as well."

Taking a candle from the sconce on the wall, he opened the door to the carding room and stepped into the darkness. "This is preposterous," he muttered. "I'll get to the bottom of this." His candle cast shadows about the room that bounced off the baskets of unfinished fleece.

"Who is in here?" he shouted. Three quick knocks in succession were his answer.

"Show yourself, spirit or devil, whichever you may be!"

Again there were three more knocks, but this time they came from the wall with the exterior door. In quick strides, Abner crossed the room and flung open the door.

"Who goes there?" he shouted out into the winter darkness. "Who dares to disturb my family?"

"I come with a message from God."

Abner turned slowly, shutting the door. He stared into the dark room, holding the candle high to illuminate the room.

"Who speaks?" he asked.

"I was once Nelly Hooper," the voice replied.

To Abner, the voice sounded like the tinkling of crystals on a chandelier. It was light, airy, almost kind but full of authority. Yet there was a feeling of serenity with it. Gentle as the brush of a butterfly's wings.

"What kind of devil trickery is this?" He strode back into the kitchen. Mary stood with the girls close beside her. Lydia was crying.

"I told you, Abner," Mary said, trying to comfort Lydia. "We have nothing to do with this. It is a spirit of some kind that has come to this house."

From the carding room, the voice could be heard speaking. "Bring George Butler to me so I can tell him Lydia Blaisdell is to be his wife."

Abner inhaled deeply as if to steady himself. He looked once more into the carding room with the candle, then turned to Mary.

"We will need the strength of God to withstand this evil that has come upon us," he said to his family.

<hr />

Later that night, after everyone had gone to bed, Hannah was roused from sleep.

"Please. Please just go away. I cannot do what you ask."

She rolled over and saw Lydia kneeling on the floor before a white, glowing light. It was a floating orb, the brightest part of it being about the size of a summer melon. It floated about a foot or two off the floor.

"Dear God, Lydia!" She beckoned for her sister to come to her bed. "How long has that been there?"

"I don't know. I awoke because I heard the voice speaking to me. I thought maybe I was dreaming, but when I saw the light, I knew I wasn't."

Lydia scrambled up into the bed beside Hannah, and they sat and watched the orb gently lifting and dropping, as if it were inhaling deeply and then slowly letting its breath out. Its light filled the whole corner of the room where it appeared.

"Has it spoken?" Hannah asked.

"No—well, at least not since I awoke. I heard it speak to me in my dream. But I don't know if it was just in my mind or…" She dropped her head, covering her face with her hands. "Oh, Hannah, I don't know what is real anymore."

Hannah tried to comfort Lydia. Looking up, she spoke to the orb. "Why do you keep tormenting my sister?"

"Send for George Butler. Bring him to me," came the reply.

"Why? What good will that do? He is not interested in my sister. From what I hear, he is not interested in anyone since the death of his wife and child. He is a sad man."

"I was once Nelly Butler. I know of his loss and his sadness."

Hannah challenged the orb. "If you are truly Nelly, then I would think you would want to spare him further trouble. For certainly all of this will come to no good."

The orb expanded in size and floated closer to the bed.

"Lydia, I must speak to George. Bring him to me."

Looking up at the orb, Lydia spoke. "Why here? If you need to talk to George that badly, why can't you just go to where he is?"

"All things are done according to the ways of the Lord."

"What does that mean?"

"You must go and prepare the way for me."

"I hardly think George is going to listen to Lydia," Hannah smirked.

"George must show his faith in coming to see that of which he only hears about."

"I don't think anyone is going to believe this," Lydia sighed.

Suddenly the orb grew larger, and intense light filled the whole room. Slowly, from within the center of the glowing orb, the shape of a woman began to form. Her dress was the whitest of white with an iridescent shimmer to it. Her hair was covered by a flowing, transparent veil. In her arms, she held the shape of a baby. Her whole form lifted until it floated silently over the bed as Hannah and Lydia watched. Hannah gasped as she recognized the face of Nelly Butler looking down at her through the thin veil. As the form moved from one side of the room to the other, it spoke.

"Let your faith be bigger than your fear."

In an instant, the woman was gone, reduced to a pinpoint of light near the ceiling, and then it blinked out.

Hannah and Lydia were silent, both pondering what they had just witnessed. It was clearly Nelly Butler. There was no denying that. Both of them had seen her just as plainly as they had seen her at church meeting before her time had come.

"It would appear that none of this is going to end if we don't go talk to Captain Butler," Hannah said at last.

Lydia rolled her eyes. "There is no way he will talk to me. Even if he did, he would not believe a word of this."

"Well, maybe you shouldn't go. I'll go. I'll walk over to Butler's Point tomorrow and let him know that you would like to speak to him. If he comes, then the spirit will talk to him, and maybe you won't have to say anything. She said that all she wanted you to do was to bring him to her. She didn't say you had to talk to him."

Lydia thought about this for a moment. "You won't say anything to the Butlers about the spirit, will you?"

"No. I'm afraid they would think us mad if I did!" she exclaimed. "I'll just ask him to stop by the house the next time he is on this side of the bay, as my parents would like to express their condolences on the loss of his father."

"That might work," Lydia said. "It will be strange, but maybe it will put this whole thing to rest." Lydia hugged her sister tightly.

Hannah hoped this would work. She needed to protect Lydia, it was clear. The poor child had been struggling alone with this burden for too long.

＋————＋

First thing the next morning, Hannah stepped out the door, pulling her cloak tightly around her to ward off the cold January air. She could see Butler's Point off in the distance on the western side of the bay. The bright white of the main house shone against the gray bleakness of the winter sky. If this were summer, she would take the skiff and row across. Winters were a different story. The winds blew stronger and harsher, and she didn't want to try that this time of year. She would have to set out on foot through Franklin and then around to the point. With each step through the path of snow, she rehearsed in her mind what she would say. Pleasantries, condolences on the recent loss of Moses, small talk, and then the invitation to come to their home. It seemed like a solid plan. It had to be.

By the time she had left the main road and made the turn down toward Butler's Point, the sun had broken through the overcast skies and was shining brightly on the snow. She pulled the visor of her bonnet down to try and ward off the rays of sunlight slanting toward her as she faced directly east. Blinded by the rays of the rising sun, she did not see the man approaching her on the small narrow path she was traversing.

"Good morning, my lady," she heard a voice say. "What business have you this early?"

Squinting and shading her eyes with her hand, she looked up to see George's brother Peter facing her.

"Oh, Mr. Butler, what a pleasant surprise," she stammered. Her rehearsed speech was erased from her mind as she now faced a real person. "I, uh, have come to pay our respects and condolences to the family." She pulled off her bonnet so Peter could see her face and recognize her.

Peter eyed her suspiciously. He knew very keenly that the strain between the Blaisdells and his family was such that this seemed an unlikely scenario.

"Well, let me also express my condolences on the recent loss of your own husband, Mrs. Oakes." He bowed graciously, being the gentleman that he was. "I'm sure you and my mother will understand each other's loss more deeply than anyone else." He smiled, again maintaining his proper upbringing. His next question, however, betrayed his inner feelings. "It is not exactly the calling hour, is it?"

Hannah blushed, knowing full well this early morning visit was not the norm. She couldn't think of an appropriate answer other than the truth. Since she just wanted to get this over with, she sidestepped the question completely.

"I am looking forward to meeting with your mother. A widow's cross is a hard one to bear." She made movement to indicate she was done with the conversation and wished to continue on her journey toward the house.

Peter remained unmovable as he studied her. "Allow me to accompany you back," he said, offering her his arm as he turned to return in the direction he had just come from.

"Oh no, Mr. Butler, I do not wish to deter you from whatever errand you were on." Her heart sank at the thought of him escorting her the remainder of the way.

"Certainly not, Mrs. Oakes, there could be nothing more important than seeing a member of the Blaisdell family to the door of my mother's home," he replied with just a touch of sarcasm. Gripping her by the arm, he firmly but gently led her in the direction of the main house.

<hr>

Hannah sat politely at the table in front of George's mother. Peter stood leaning against the doorjamb, arms folded, keeping his eye on the women. Clearly, his earlier business was of little importance because he had not left his mother's side since Hannah had arrived.

"It is very kind of you to think of me so soon after your own loss," George's mother said to her.

"Well, I know it was a tremendous loss, not only to you, but to the whole family," Hannah replied. She had not seen any sign of George since arriving. She really needed to steer the conversation in his direction. "How is everyone coping?"

"Well, naturally, it was a great shock to all of them. However, my sons are strong, and they have resumed their father's businesses and affairs equally well."

"And…George?" Hannah dared to venture forth. "I have not seen him about lately."

Peter stiffened at the doorway, as if he knew this was ultimately her reason for being there. Before he could say anything, Sarah spoke.

"Mrs. Oakes, we are naturally thankful for your condolences on the loss of my husband. However, given the strained relation between our two families, I know I can speak for my whole family," she said, waving a hand in Peter's general direction, "when I say we find your visit this morning rather odd and your inquiry into George specifically alarming." She stared intently at Hannah. "What is the true nature of your visit? If I can be so blunt to ask."

Hannah shifted uncomfortably in her seat. This was not how she had rehearsed this. She had not prepared herself in any way for a defense from them. She had naively thought she could just walk in and ask for George to come to the house and everyone would agree.

She took a deep breath and plunged in.

"It would please us greatly if George could stop by our home." She could see the shock register on both Sarah's and Peter's faces.

Peter could no longer remain quiet. "George? Come to your home? For what preposterous purpose?" He had moved into the room and was standing directly behind his mother. He glared down at Hannah.

She realized his earlier demeanor of polite society was gone. "Well, of course we would like to express our condolences to him in person," Hannah explained. But she knew it wasn't enough. She thought of Lydia. She thought of the orb and the vision of Nelly she had seen. This would never end. Lydia would continuously be tormented if she didn't put a stop to this here and now. "Lydia would like to speak to George privately."

And with that, it was as if a lightning bolt had exploded in the room. Peter turned away and muttered a profanity or two under his breath.

"You have seriously come here to ask us to send George to see Lydia?" he yelled, turning back around.

Mrs. Butler, who had maintained her composure throughout the whole interview, spoke to Hannah directly. "Mrs. Oakes, it is well known that Lydia, despite being but a child, has caused much anguish for my son for many years. As his family, we have seen for ourselves the distress that even the mere mention of her name causes him to suffer. I find it very interesting…" She stopped herself as if rethinking what she wanted to say. "No, I find it actually disturbing that Lydia would choose this time, after the death of my husband, to make her attempt at an interaction with George. Do you not as well?"

"Of course she does not, Mother, otherwise she would not have come here to make such a ridiculous request." Peter had stepped back into the conversation. "Mrs. Oakes, I believe it is time for you to depart. Allow me the pleasure of escorting you back to the main road." He reached his hand out toward her.

Hannah knew this was her last chance. If she didn't take a stand, the cause would be lost. She would never get another opportunity to sit at the table with any of the Butlers.

"I'm sorry, but Lydia has a very important message she must deliver to George. He must come to her."

"Come to her? You are asking Captain George Butler to attend to a child, and not any child, but one who has been rumored to have a familiar spirit or a pact with the devil?" Peter shot back at her.

"Peter," his mother said in a soothing but chastising tone. "We will not repeat idle gossip in my home." She turned her gaze intently on Hannah. "It is none of our affair what the townsfolk speak of regarding Lydia, Mrs. Oakes. What I can say for certain is that I will in no way relate your request to my son for reasons that I have no intention of justifying to you. Good day." She turned in her chair and prepared to rise.

"Lydia has a message for George," Hannah repeated. "From Nelly." She had promised Lydia she would not speak of the spirit. She had agreed the Butlers would think them all mad. But at this point, it appeared they considered the Blaisdells mad, anyway. "Please ask George to attend on Lydia at his earliest convenience, as she has a message from Nelly."

Hannah had made her final and parting shot. The silence in the room was smothering. Peter and Mrs. Butler were dumbstruck. Both stood motionless, staring at her. She rose from her seat and walked toward the door. Peter's own words had proven they thought ill of Lydia. Let them also believe she was familiar with spirits, then. Brushing Peter as she went by, she said, "I will find my own way to the main road, thank you."

"Mrs. Oakes, what do you..." George's mother began.

Hannah turned to her, cutting her off. "Mrs. Butler, what I can say for certain is that you should relate this request to George, for reasons I have no intention of justifying to *you*." Turning on her heels, she walked from the room.

CHAPTER THIRTY-NINE

George sat across the desk from the attorney who had handled his father's affairs. The man slid yet another document toward George for his signature.

"This should be the last one," he said, showing the document to George.

"Excellent!" George said, signing the last bit of parchment with his flourishing signature. "I would like to be gone by the end of the week. If this weather holds, I can make it out with no problems."

George stood, thanking the man for all of his help. With these last few loose ends tied up, George had put his mother in a safe position financially. The businesses were secure, and Peter and his other brothers could handle that end. All he had to do now was speak with Reuben about gathering the crew and order provisions, and they could be gone within a few days. It was his intention to put as much space between himself and Franklin, and thus Lydia, before 1800 had advanced too far. He felt the days pressing on him as each one passed. The ring did not specify a date, just the year. So he had no idea if his time was running out or if he had plenty to spare. Better to be safe than sorry.

He stepped out the doorway of the solicitor's shop and right into the path of Hannah. She plowed into him, causing him to stumble backward slightly.

"I am terribly sorry, miss," he managed to get out as he gripped her by the shoulders to prevent them both from slipping on the snowy surface.

"Oh," she exclaimed, "it is all my fault…" She looked up and realized it was him. "George!"

Cautiously, he looked at her face under her bonnet. "Mrs. Oakes." He dropped his hands, feeling a chill run down his spine. "Forgive me. Are you all right?"

Hannah smoothed down her dress. "Yes, I'm so sorry. I had quite a bit on my mind and wasn't paying attention."

George stepped aside from the doorway. "Allow me. Are you here to see the solicitor?"

"Solicitor?" Hannah was confused, then realized where they were. "Oh, no. Actually, I was just returning home." With only a slight hesitation, she continued. "I have recently been to Butler's Point looking for you."

He was taken aback. "Me? You were at my mother's house looking for me?"

She moved in closer, so as not to be heard by any of the other people who were milling around Franklin that morning.

"You must come see Lydia. She has a message for you."

George felt his vision funnel down to one tiny spot in the snow in front him. He felt the ring, kept close to him in his breast pocket, burn hot.

Bowing his head slightly, he uttered, "Good day, Mrs. Oakes." He turned to walk away.

"Captain!" she shouted, which drew the attention of a few townspeople. "You must come see Lydia. It's very important."

George glanced around nervously. He could see that Hannah was prepared to play this out in front of the town gossips.

"Mrs. Oakes," he replied calmly, "my deepest sympathies on the recent loss of your husband. Please give my regards to your sister and the rest of your family." He touched the rim of his hat lightly as a sign of respect, although he did not feel like showing her any.

"Captain Butler, it is imperative that you speak with my sister, Lydia," she called out. "She has a message for you from Nelly."

George had walked several feet from her when the magnitude of what she had said registered in his mind. It had also registered with several passersby, who stopped abruptly to stare.

He could see a couple of the most notorious town gossips put their heads together in tight whispers. His blood ran cold when he realized that before nightfall, he, Lydia, and Nelly would be the talk of the town once again.

He stared long and hard at Hannah, but not willing to give anyone any more to gossip about, he turned away and hurriedly headed for Butler's Point.

+ —— +

Lydia saw Hannah coming up the lane. She flung open the door and ran into the January cold.

"Hannah! Hannah!" she shouted to catch her sister's attention. "Did it go well? Will he come?"

Hannah reached the steps and urged her sister into the house. "Land sakes alive, Lydia, let me get inside first." As she entered the hallway, she saw both her mother and father seated in chairs.

Lydia leaned in and whispered, "I told them where you had gone."

Abner, especially, looked stern and foreboding. Their mother looked more cautious with a touch of concern.

Hannah removed her coat and boots, leaving them both by the door.

"Come sit down." She urged Lydia toward the room where their parents were. "We all need to talk."

Hannah then described to them the meeting with Mrs. Butler and Peter, how it had turned exceptionally tense when she asked for George to come to their home. "It quickly got out of hand, and I'm afraid I said things we had agreed not to mention."

Lydia looked horrified. "You didn't mention the spirit, did you?"

"Well, not exactly, but I did tell them you had a message for George from Nelly."

"Oh, Hannah!" Her mother bowed her head.

"Mother, I had no choice after hearing the things they were saying about Lydia." She looked at her sister, feeling sorry for her. "It's not going to matter. It's truly not. And it may be the only way to get him to come." She also told them how she had seen George in town. She looked sheepishly at her father. "I may have spoken a bit too loudly when I told him that he needed to see Lydia, as she had a message from Nelly."

At this, Abner rose from his chair and paced to the window. Gazing out over the bay, he spoke without looking at his wife and daughters. "And I'm sure there were others who heard this pronouncement as well."

220

Hannah's silence was affirmation enough for him. He turned back toward his family. "We will prepare for the onslaught of disbelief and anger that will come toward us."

"Sally!"

Moses Wentworth's voice echoed through the house with such force that it frightened his wife, Sally. Nelly's sister dropped the sheet she had been folding on the bed and ran to the top of the stairs.

"Moses, I'm up here! What's wrong?" She heard her husband's footsteps returning to the front of the house.

"Please come down here now." Sally's feet barely touched the last step before he was pulling her into the front sitting parlor and shutting the door.

"Moses? What is it? You are frightening me," she exclaimed after he had shut the door.

"I have just come from Franklin. There is talk all over town," he gasped.

"About what? I don't listen to idle gossip, Moses, you know that."

"Nelly," he said, the one word reverberating in the room.

"Nelly? My sister?" She sat down. "What could possibly be said about Nelly?"

Moses knelt in front of her, taking her hands in his. "The Blaisdells are saying that Nelly has spoken to Lydia. She has a message for George."

"Ridiculous!" she shouted. "Moses, what is wrong with those people?" Sally felt keenly the loss of her beloved sister all over again. "A message? From the dead?"

"I'm not exactly sure, but the tongues in town are wagging like the tail of a happy dog with a new bone."

Sally shook her head. "George has no intention of acknowledging this, does he?"

"I don't know. Word is that Lydia's sister Hannah confronted him in the street, demanding that he meet with Lydia so she could relate a message from Nelly. He apparently did not reply and headed for the point. They say he has been secluded out there all day."

Sally thought for a moment. "Nelly has been gone nearly three years, and they wait until George loses his father to dredge all this up again. How cruel. What could they possibly have to gain from doing this?"

"No one seems to have the answer to that," Moses said.

"Do my parents know?" Sally asked.

"I'm not sure. It won't be long until they do, though."

CHAPTER FORTY

George sat behind his father's massive desk. The silence that enveloped him here was the only comfort he could find at the moment. Directly in front of him on the ink blotter lay the ring. It glowed with almost an unearthly shimmer despite the fact that no sunlight touched its surface. The light source coming from the ring itself pulsated as if the object were alive. This fact only added to George's realization that he was fighting a power greater than himself. He had been two, possibly three days from departing, and now he felt trapped. He had left before and been called back. Even if he had gotten away, what would have transpired then to force him back to Franklin?

There was a knock on the door that roused him from his thoughts.

"Enter," he said as his mother slowly opened the door.

"May I come in?"

"Yes, please do, Mother." He stood to show his respect for her and in doing so scooped up the ring and returned it to his breast pocket.

"Given the fact that you have been locked away in here most of the day, I'm assuming you have somehow heard of Hannah Oakes's visit to us this morning."

George nodded. "I heard it from Hannah herself. I ran into her, literally, in town this morning. She informed me that she had been here to see you."

"And?" she prodded. "Did she tell you the purpose of her visit?"

George sighed deeply, then indicated to his mother that she should sit. He, too, sat back down in his father's chair, folding and unfolding his hands multiple times before he spoke.

"Mother, I was mere minutes away from sending word to Reuben that he needed to assemble a crew. In fact, I was leaving the solicitor's office to do just that thing when I stumbled upon Mrs. Oakes. By afternoon, I would have had all of my provisions ordered and could have departed for a voyage within two days." He hung his head and started to cry.

Sarah rose and came around the desk. She enveloped her son in an embrace that only a mother can provide. She allowed him to cry it out against her breast as she made soft soothing sounds in an attempt to comfort him.

"George, you do not have to acknowledge this attempt at terrorizing from them." She patted his shoulders as his sobs subsided a little. "Let me send for Peter. He can get word to Reuben for you. At least start to assemble a crew."

George raised his head, trying to regain his composure. "I'm sorry, Mother. You should not have seen me be so weak."

"Nonsense!" she exclaimed. "I am your mother. No matter how old you are or how many people call you 'Captain,' you will still be my little boy." She laughed a little. "Did Hannah indicate to you what this message was that Lydia needs to tell you?"

"No," George said, shaking his head. "I did not really give her the time to tell me much of anything. She was clearly willing to involve as many people as possible. She was not quiet in her attempts to let me know I needed to see Lydia." He pushed back his chair a little. "With that in mind, I made sure that what everyone heard from me was respectful and acceptable. I bid her a good day and walked away."

As George began pacing the room, Sarah thought for a moment. "We have no idea what the message is, and they have thrown poor Nelly, God rest her soul, into the middle of it to entice you. What a conniving, scheming trick."

George watched his mother. Although several members of his family and Nelly's would remember the posset ring incident from the wedding, none of them knew the history of the ring since then. He alone knew that this ring had returned over and over, despite the numerous times he had tried to rid himself of it. Even his father had been pulled into it at the end of his life, but he was gone and could not share in this knowledge of the ring with him. No, he alone would carry the burden of the ring. To the others, this seemed like a trick. But George knew there had to be more to it than that.

Just then, there was another knock on the door.

"Enter," George said. His sister Mercy stuck her head into the room. "George, Mr. Hooper and Mrs. Wentworth are here to see you."

"Send them in, by all means." George rubbed at his cheeks, hoping to remove any evidence of his earlier tears before Nelly's father and sister could see him in this condition.

"George!" David said as he entered the room. He turned to address Sarah, bowing slightly and then taking her hands. "Sarah, please know I am so sorry about the loss of Moses." He kissed the back of her hand lightly.

"Thank you, David," she said.

Sally had also entered the room, her skirts dampened along the hem from where they had brushed in the snow. George threw another log on the fire and urged the two to sit close to warm themselves.

"What a pleasant surprise to have you visit us today," Sarah began.

But David got right to the point. "Sarah, George, I'm certain you're aware of what the Blaisdells have attempted this day."

"Yes, I actually had words with Hannah myself," George replied.

"What did she say to you?" Sally asked. "I mean about Nelly?" As appalled as Sally was by this whole incident, she longed for her departed sister.

"Nothing specific. I did not give her the opportunity. She was attempting to make a scandal of it, in front of the townspeople, of which I refused to be a part."

David nodded. "Good. We cannot allow them to control this situation—which is exactly what we have come here this afternoon to discuss. I want you to know, George, that you are not alone in this. We are here to support you in any way. I wish Moses were here. Your father was a very intelligent man, and we could use his guidance."

George, thinking of his father's parting words regarding Nelly and the ring, wondered what David would think if he knew what Moses had known.

"Thank you, David."

"We must be united against this effort to drag both of our families into a scandal," David continued. "I feel we should not acknowledge what they are trying to do in any way, despite the fact that they are using Nelly."

"I agree," Sarah interjected. "I think George should continue with his plans to prepare for his voyage and depart as soon as he can."

"Were you planning on leaving again, George?" David asked.

"Yes. In fact, I was just about to start my preparations when I had the confrontation with Hannah."

"Then your mother is correct. You should do so, and quickly. With you out of the area, it may again quiet down. I can only assume they have restarted this because you returned home for your father's illness."

"I agree with this, George," his mother said. "And I think your father would also feel it was the sensible course of action."

They continued talking, discussing how the others would deal with the situation, the gossip from the town, and the general difficulty of living in close proximity to the Blaisdells. George would send word to town to have Reuben come to Butler's Point. With the help of his trusted assistant, he could conduct all of his business from his father's study and not have to enter town until the day he would inspect his vessel and depart. They all agreed that they would provide a united, respectful front. They would continue to be cordial with the Blaisdells if faced with having to interact with them. However, they would all try and avoid contact with them if at all possible. And above all else, they would not acknowledge or discuss with anyone outside of the family any mention of messages from Nelly.

CHAPTER FORTY-ONE

Blaisdell Home

Reverend Archibald Crawford sat uneasily in the chair in the front sitting room of Abner Blaisdell's home. It had been three days of absolute turmoil in Franklin. Word of Hannah and George's interaction on the street had not only spread like wildfire, it had taken on a life of its own. The story had gotten embellished so much in the retelling that now it seemed almost unbelievable. Worse still was the appearance that Hannah herself was promoting this. In the three days since she had spoken with George, Lydia's sister had not only continued speaking to anyone about this message from Nelly that needed to be delivered to Captain George Butler, but she had actually encouraged those who didn't believe her to come to their home and wait upon the spirit's next visit. Several of the women were reporting that they had heard the knockings, but nothing more than that had transpired.

From his position in the sitting room, Reverend Crawford could hear the chatter of women in the kitchen. It seemed there were several women in there, and he suspected there were more women elsewhere in the house beyond his vantage point. At that moment, Abner entered the room. Archibald rose in greeting and shook the small man's hand. As usual, Abner's demeanor was one of contrition and humility.

"Reverend Crawford." Abner sat down in the chair opposite him. "I'm sorry to have kept you waiting." Abner had taken over many of the duties of his recently deceased son-in-law, Atherton, one of which was repairing the fishing nets. He spent most mornings restringing the nets so they would be ready for spring.

"Not at all, Abner. I've actually enjoyed the chatter of a busy household," Reverend Crawford said, indicating with his head the obvious activity level in the back rooms.

Abner turned only slightly to acknowledge the source of the commotion.

"I'm assuming you're here, Reverend, to discuss the unusual situation my family finds itself in."

The reverend nodded and added, "And your oldest daughter's intentional effort to create a public spectacle."

Abner appeared to be arranging his thoughts before he spoke. "I agree with you, Reverend, that Hannah has not maintained the level of propriety that one would normally see in dealing with a family issue." He paused but only briefly. "However, this is by far not your typical family situation. I agreed to let Hannah pursue this course in hopes that it will put an end to the scrutiny that my family has been under for several years now."

"She has your blessing, then?" the reverend asked.

"Yes, she does," Abner replied. "Reverend, you must understand how difficult of a situation this is for us. Particularly for me." He leaned forward. "I have always been a God-fearing man. Did I not seek out your guidance when I was first presented with the struggles Lydia has faced?"

Archibald nodded in agreement.

"And at your urging, did we not pray and read scriptures daily with the poor child in an effort to rid her of the evil that was gripping her?"

"Yes, Abner, you did—and it worked, did it not?"

"It appeared at the time that it had. However, it has returned, and this time I am not convinced that it is a demon or an evil spirit." He shrugged his shoulders. "I'm also not convinced that it is an angel or a messenger from God. I do not know what is happening."

Abner then proceeded to relate to Archibald all that had transpired in the carding room—the knockings, the voice, and the persistent and repetitive urging to bring Captain George Butler to see the spirit for himself. He also told the reverend of Hannah and Lydia's experience with the orb and how Hannah insisted she had recognized Nelly in the personage.

"It was after that evening that Hannah became almost militant in protecting Lydia through this ordeal," Abner said. "She came to us, her mother and me, explaining that if others outside of our family could hear or see this apparition, it would remove all doubt that Lydia was communing with familiar spirits or that evil had befallen our family.

In turn, if there were more people involved than just Lydia, Captain Butler would have to respond, deal with this spiritual manifestation of his wife, and thus hopefully remove it from Lydia once and for all."

Archibald rubbed his thumbs over his temples, thinking. "Abner, I must admit that your willingness to bypass the power of God in exchange for the assistance of the mortal souls of Franklin is a bit troubling to me."

"I see no other way out of this for my family," Abner replied. "Captain Butler must come here. Then Nelly will speak to him, and this will all end."

"Captain Butler is preparing to leave this very afternoon," Archibald informed him. "He has a vessel waiting now in the harbor."

"That is a shame," Abner replied. "Come with me."

Abner rose and walked from the room. Archibald followed him down the hall and into the kitchen area. There he saw Lydia seated at the worktable with several other women. However, Abner continued through the outer doorway that led to the carding room. He stopped and turned.

"Come, Reverend, this is the room where everyone gathers."

Upon entering the doorway to the room, Archibald was taken aback by the number of people that were there. Close to twenty people filled the room. It was women, mostly, but there were a few men. Some were seated in chairs, but most either stood or were seated on the floor along the walls.

"Reverend!" someone shouted. "Have you come to hear the spirit for yourself?" There was a low murmur of excited laughter.

Archibald nodded his head in respectful acknowledgment but did not speak.

"As you can see," Abner said, "the more the spirit manifests itself, the more people come to witness it."

Archibald was surprised to see Abigail Abbott seated in a small chair, her hands folded in her lap. It appeared she was fervently praying. She was a devout woman, and it shocked him to see her not only give credence to these tales of ghostly visitations but also participate.

He saw several of his parishioners among the group as well as quite a few of the local riffraff. Namely, he saw Asa Flint leaning up against the windowsill, his hat slung low, partially covering his face. He knew of Asa courting Lydia and how frequently the two were seen together. If there was something inherently wrong with this situation, something not godly but more worldly, Asa would be involved.

Archibald turned to Abner. Speaking low, he said, "I should not stay. I would not want my presence here to be construed as support or approval of this." He started to turn back into the kitchen, placing his hand on the doorjamb, when he heard a loud bang. It reverberated from the wall right next to him, and he felt it in the wood just as certainly as he had heard it. Within an instant, the chatter from both the kitchen and the room where everyone was gathered ceased.

"It has started," someone whispered.

Again a distinct and solid thumping sound could be heard, this time not from the wall but from the floor itself. Archibald could feel it in the soles of his feet. He scanned the faces of those in the outer room. Specifically, his gaze fell upon Asa Flint. The lad had not moved from his position near the window. He had only shifted his weight to his other foot and slid his hat back slightly so he could see better.

Lydia had risen from the worktable and was approaching the doorway where Archibald stood. She was deathly pale, and it appeared she looked right through him, so intent was her attention focused on the room. He stepped aside to let her pass, and she did not even acknowledge him as she walked by. Soon, she was standing somewhat in the middle of the room, as everyone had shuffled back to the perimeter as she had entered.

Archibald observed she had the pallor of someone who was very near death. He tried to remember if he had taken note of her countenance when he passed her in the kitchen. Had she been this pale then?

The knocking from under the floorboards continued, forcing those who had been seated along the walls to stand. It appeared that once everyone was standing, the knockings ceased.

"I come as one who speaks in the wilderness."

Archibald recoiled at the sound. Abner nodded slowly at him.

"Who speaks to us this day?" Lydia replied to the voice.

"I was once Nelly Hooper, but I died as Nelly Butler."

There was an audible gasp among those gathered. One woman arose and exited out through the rear door. Archibald saw Abigail clasp her hands even tighter, and he could see her lips moving in prayer.

"Have they not heard her speak before?" Archibald asked Abner.

Whispering so as not to disturb the spirit, Abner replied, "No, this is the first time she has spoken to anyone outside of our family."

"I come with a message for Captain George Butler."

"Spirit," Lydia cried out, "what have I done that I must suffer this? Why do you come to me?"

Archibald was struck next by the feeling that permeated the room when the disembodied voice replied to Lydia. Although the manner of speech had not changed, the feeling of intense gentleness and compassion that accompanied it was something he could not express in words.

"You have done nothing wrong, child," answered the voice, seeming to arise from the vacant space that surrounded Lydia where she stood. "Go up and sit with the others at the kitchen hearth so that this company may know it is not you who speaks but I."

Archibald watched as Lydia again walked past him, neither speaking nor acknowledging him or anyone else in the room. When she had returned to the kitchen, a small pinpoint of light appeared where she had stood. It grew increasingly larger and brighter until it resembled an orb floating just off the ground. At this moment, Archibald swore he heard the tinkling of crystals, although there were none in the starkness of that utility room.

"I was once Nelly Hooper, daughter of David and Joanna Hooper," the voice declared and then proceeded to call out several in the room by name—persons Nelly had known as a child or before her marriage to Captain Butler. The voice spoke of things that were familiar to them, things that no one else could have known. She called these things tokens and said that through them, they would know she spoke the truth.

"Do you see that I am who I say I am?" the voice finally declared. Several in the room nodded in agreement, but no one dared speak to the spirit directly.

"Then bring George Butler to me." The orb of light rose slightly as if to place emphasis on this point.

"For what purpose would it serve to bring him here, spirit?"

Archibald was surprised to hear Abner address the spirit, as he had remained quiet throughout this whole performance.

"I have a message for him."

"What is this message, spirit? Help those here in attendance know the importance of this message."

"Lydia Blaisdell is to be his wife."

There was an audible gasp in the room as the import of this information settled upon them. A couple more individuals bolted to the rear door. Archibald was certain it was not in fear this time. No, theirs was the wish to be the first to spread this juicy piece of gossip through the town.

"Bring Captain George Butler to me, that I may tell him that Lydia Blaisdell is to be his wife."

And with that, the light shrunk back to a pinpoint in the center of the room and blinked out. Everyone was silent for a moment. No one dared to move. Archibald took a quick account of who was there in attendance and who was missing. He noticed that Hannah, the ring leader of these gatherings, was not in the room. He also noticed that Asa had never left his position next to the window. Nor did he seem as shocked and surprised by this revelation as the rest. Archibald thought this strange, as he was under the impression that the young man had designs on Lydia himself. But there the young man stood, neither shocked nor in awe of what had just transpired in the room. Whereas everyone else was quick to discuss what they had seen, Asa remained aloof, almost unmoved by it all.

"Reverend?"

Archibald was roused from his thoughts by Abner.

"Do you not see how important it is that we share this burden with others?"

"'Tis certainly a burden, Abner," he replied. He walked back into the kitchen and saw Lydia sitting in a chair next to the hearth. Her color had returned but she seemed weak, almost sickly. He knelt down beside her.

"Child? Are you all right? Are you ill?"

She looked at him with that vacant stare and did not answer.

"She does not speak. The voice speaks through her." It was Hannah, who had appeared in the kitchen amongst the other women. "Reverend, your word carries more weight than anyone else's in this town. I beseech you. Go to George and tell him what you saw here. Tell him he has to come."

Archibald rose, staring intently at Hannah. Was she behind this? Could this be some kind of trick of light and sound? Would a woman know how to assemble a hoax of this complexity? He studied Abner. Or was Hannah just the cloak behind which Abner was hiding?

"Abner, is there a cellar under that room?" he asked, pointing back in the direction of the carding room.

Abner seemed perplexed by this question but readily offered that there was indeed a root cellar beneath it.

"I would like to see it, if I may. Will you take me there?"

"Of course."

Archibald followed Abner through the room and out the rear exterior door. Nearby, there was a small set of stairs that descended to the dirt cellar. Archibald bent over as he stepped inside the small doorway. Abner did not follow him in but allowed him to examine the cellar freely. Archibald was specifically looking for something that would have made the vibrations he had felt with his own feet and hands. He made his way over to where he felt he was standing directly under the doorway to the kitchen. He reached his hands up and felt among the rafters and timbers. But he found nothing. He examined the dirt beneath his feet but did not see anything that would testify to there recently being some kind of apparatus placed there that could have shaken the floorboards above.

"Reverend? Are you convinced?" Abner said from the ground level.

Archibald ascended the stairs and ventured back out into the light of day.

"Abner, I do not know exactly what just took place here. Like you, I am not ready to ascribe this to the devil or to God."

"Then find George Butler and bring him here. Only he can stop this and bring peace back to this town."

Abner gave a curt nod of his head and walked away, leaving Reverend Archibald Crawford alone in the yard. Across the bay, he could see the main house on Butler's Point. This would not end between these two families, of that he was sure.

+ ———— +

Asa watched as the room cleared of people. The women were quick to start retelling what they had just seen. Even among those who had witnessed the manifestation, they told differing accounts of what had taken place.

"I tell you, I saw Nelly myself, just as she had looked on her wedding day," one woman was insisting.

"Have you lost your mind?" said another. "There was nothing there but a beam of light. It probably shone through that far window." She gestured toward the window on the other side of the loom. "This was all a hoax, Martha. I won't be wasting my time by coming here again." She began gathering up her knitting basket.

Incredulous, Martha tried to convince her friend. "But you heard her. She said George must marry Lydia Blaisdell!"

"Oh, pish posh!" She pulled her shawl tightly around her shoulders. "Martha, this is nothing but a trick to get Lydia married off into that wealthy Butler family." She hefted her basket and rolled her eyes at her friend. "I can't believe that you think this some divine intervention."

The bickering continued as the two women walked out through the door at the far end of the room.

Asa was growing increasingly concerned over these new developments. Up to this point, he had been free to visit Lydia at his will, knowing that she needed him to keep quiet on what he had seen at the burial ground at Butler's Point. He had hopes of convincing her to marry him. But now, all of that had changed. Others had now seen the spirit. The Blaisdells were no longer hiding Lydia's secret. The balance of power had shifted. He needed to regain control of this situation.

He thought for a moment as he listened to others continue their discussions on what they had seen or heard. Perceptions were divided—some claimed it was a visitation from a heavenly messenger, while others were convinced it was a hoax perpetrated by the Blaisdells. And that's when Asa realized how he could turn this to his advantage. The Butlers had money, and lots of it. If half the town thought this was a hoax, an effort to trick George into marrying Lydia, then by God he was going to help further that perception. He would use his recent association with the Blaisdell family as leverage, and it was going to cost the Butlers a price for him to provide proof that this was all just a trick. How he was exactly going to do that, he hadn't yet determined, but he was switching sides. He smiled to himself as he began to formulate the plan in his head.

He walked into the kitchen and approached Lydia at the hearth.

"Are you all right?" he asked her.

She glared at him. "As if you truly cared," she spat.

Ignoring her barb, he lowered his voice. "They all know now, don't they? It's no longer just our secret."

With so much on her mind, Lydia had not even thought of how all of this would affect her relationship with Asa. She no longer had to keep him quiet. In fact, the exact opposite was happening now. Hannah had convinced her that everyone needed to know about this. As realization dawned, she sat up in her chair just a little straighter.

"That is true." She smiled at him. "Your presence here, Mr. Flint, is no longer warranted." She almost laughed with the feeling of empowerment that now washed over her.

Asa didn't take kindly to being mocked by her. Gritting his teeth, he leaned in close to her and hissed, "You are no longer of use to me, anyway." He blew softly into her ear, sending shivers down her arms.

"Get out," she whispered to him.

"Good day, Miss Lydia," he said, his honeyed voice loud enough for everyone in the room to hear.

Lydia's mother approached him. "Mr. Flint, will we see you again soon?"

Lydia felt her stomach churn as she waited for his answer.

"I will continue to call, Mrs. Blaisdell, as this performance has intrigued me." He turned and looked at Lydia. "But if one believes what happened here today, then it appears God has another suitor in mind for your daughter." He glanced at Hannah, who had also joined them. "And if not God, then someone else." He laughed sardonically and bowed to them. "Good day, ladies." He placed his hat back on his head and walked toward the front of the house.

CHAPTER FORTY-TWO

The Docks, Franklin

George was bent over the map spread out across the small, rustic table in his cabin. His first mate stood on the other side of him. George had created a master plan that he hoped would bring a good turn on his investment. He was just beginning to discuss this with Reuben when he heard the shouting. Cocking his head, he paused to listen. Reuben, too, had heard the commotion.

"What in the world is taking place out there?" he asked. "Sounds like quite a dustup."

"I'm not sure," George replied, stepping to the small window that faced the dock. He saw a group of men assembled on the passageway. He recognized them as members of his crew. There appeared to be quite a bit of jostling going on, and he would not tolerate fighting amongst his crew members, especially before they even set sail. Taking the steps from his cabin two at a time, he was soon on deck and shouting at the men.

"You there! Stop!" He leapt over the rail, with Reuben not far behind him, and dove into the fray. What had appeared to be a fight was actually more of a detention, as it became clear the crew was merely trying to prevent another man from gaining access to the ship.

"Captain Butler! Captain Butler!" a young man shouted, freeing himself from the grasp of a burly-looking seaman. Everyone had stepped aside upon George's arrival, and the man was now free to regain his footing.

"What is going on here?" George demanded.

The heavyset fellow who had placed the firm grip on the newcomer spoke up. "This man said he had to speak to you, sir. I told him you were not available, sir, but he tried to enter the ship on his own."

"Is that so?" George eyed the young man. "Who are you?" he asked.

"My name is Thaddeus, sir," he said breathlessly. It was clear that he was extremely agitated and unable to contain his excitement much longer.

"And Thaddeus, what is your business about my ship?" George asked him. "My crew is full, and I am no longer hiring."

"Oh, I do not want a job, sir!" the young man replied. "I was just in attendance at the Blaisdells." He turned and pointed down the eastern shore of bay.

George felt the color drain from his face.

The young man continued to babble on. "There was a great manifestation of the spirit at the place. I saw it for myself!" He turned to the other men standing on the dock and waved his arms about for added dramatic effect. "First, we heard knockings, and then a voice spoke to us from out of the air!" He was warming to his story as he continued on. "Then a light appeared! It came from nowhere and just appeared in the middle of the room. The voice spoke from within this light. The voice, it said it was Nelly Butler! Wasn't that your wife's name, sir?"

George felt like he had been hit with a boulder right in the center of his chest. He gripped the railing of the dock until his knuckles were white. Reuben surged forward and grabbed the young fellow by the lapels of his coat.

"What right do you think you have to come here with this hogwash tale?" he screamed into the man's face.

"Reuben," George hollered, thinking quickly of how his family, and Nelly's, had agreed not to increase the drama surrounding the town gossip. "Put the poor fellow down." He tried to sound calmer and less agitated than he actually was as Reuben settled the man back on his feet and stepped behind George.

"Young sir," George managed to say, "I ask you to leave at once. I am going to return to my ship, and neither you nor your gossip will follow me there." He eyed his crew. "And all of you will let this man leave quietly, unmolested. Am I clear?"

There were a few nods among the men, although some of them looked like they were itching for a fight.

"But, sir!" the young man cried out again. "I heard her speak myself. She asked for you, sir!" He was jumping up and down, trying to see over the shoulders of the men who had closed in around him as George walked across the deck of his ship.

"Sir! Sir!" he shouted, waving his arms. "She asked for you, sir! Said you had to come to her!"

The men were walking forward step by step, causing the young man to stumble backward as he was being indirectly moved off the dock.

"Captain! She said you were to marry again! She wants to tell you that you need to marry Lydia Blaisdell, sir!" he yelled.

Reuben saw George's shoulders slump as he walked through the door of his cabin and slammed it shut. If it were up to Reuben, he would handle the situation a little differently. George had said the man needed to leave quietly, and that's exactly what Reuben intended. He stepped over to the lad and with his strong arms quickly had him in a headlock with his large paddle-like hand covering the man's mouth.

"You will not repeat that story anywhere near the captain, do you understand?" Reuben said to him as he lifted him up and carried him to the end of the dock. He unceremoniously dumped the man into a bank of snow. He sank down so far that only his feet were sticking out. "And you'd do well to not repeat that rubbish in town, either!"

The rest of the crew cheered and laughed as Reuben walked back down the dock toward the ship and his captain.

Opening the door slowly, Reuben spoke as he entered George's cabin. "Captain, I disposed of the miscreant for you, sir." He glanced around the room, trying to locate George. He saw him lying prone on his bunk, his boots hanging half off the edge. He walked over, pulling up a chair. "Sir? George?" he asked. "It's time I speak frankly with you."

George rolled over and looked at his friend. Reuben took this as permission to continue, so he did.

"This is 'bout as near a fatherly talk as I'll probably ever give you," the man said. "No disrespect to your own father, who so recently passed. God rest his soul." He looked down at his hands.

"No disrespect taken, Reuben," George muttered. "I could probably stand for a bit of talking to at this point." He sat up, running his fingers through his hair. "Go on."

Reuben took a deep breath. "You must deal with this. It's not going to go away. You can run all you want, but this thing, whatever it is, it's going to follow you." He swallowed hard and then continued on. "I've heard the talk in town, probably more than you have. There are so many rumors swirling around. The child is familiar with spirits. The child made a pact with the devil. On and on, they are clucking like a flock of hens at pecking time. They haven't forgotten that posset ring and the spectacle at your wedding. They haven't forgotten the child setting the sheets on fire or any of the other bizarre happenings that have surrounded her since the day she landed a fancy on you." He stood and paced around the room. "And now this? Claiming that your sweet, departed Nelly has come back from the grave to decide who you marry next? And it's to be Lydia, no less!" He threw his arms into the air. "Damn that child to hell!" he thundered, worked into a frenzy by his own rants. "Damn the whole Blaisdell family to hell!"

George almost laughed to see the man so worked up. Normally so reserved and even-keeled, he rarely let anything rattle him, but now he was clearly aggravated.

"Reuben, sit down." George reached out toward him, but he snatched his arm away.

"No, stand and fight with me, man! Come on! What's wrong with you?"

George reached into his breast pocket and removed the ring. He tossed it in Reuben's direction, and Reuben caught it in midair.

"What's this?" he asked, looking at it.

"It's the posset ring," George said.

"The posset ring?" He seemed puzzled "But I saw you throw this in the bay."

George laughed. "I did. As did Sally at one point."

"Then how the…?"

"That's a very good question. Read the inscription inside the ring."

He watched as Reuben walked toward the little window so he could see more clearly. He saw his friend's lips move as he read it: *George & Lydia Butler 1800.*

He let out a slow whistle. "Jesus Christ Almighty," was all he could say. "Who put that there?"

"I have no idea, but I have my own set of bizarre happenings." He shook his head, almost resigned to the fate that had befallen him. "You are correct in one thing—I can't run anymore. I can't try to hide from this any longer."

+ ———— +

Asa Flint walked down the dock like a man with a purpose. "Hey there!" he shouted out to the men on the deck of a ship. "Is this Captain Butler's ship? I'm looking for Captain Butler."

"You and every other friggin' nutshell," one of the men murmured under his breath. Several of them laughed. "Be off with you, buddy. The captain is much too busy to address the likes of you."

"So this is his ship, then," he said, preparing to step aboard.

"Whoa, hold on right there, mister. No one comes aboard ship without the captain's permission." The big man stepped up to the railing. "And we've already run off one of you town gossips today. We'll not be dealing with another."

"A town gossip?" Asa asked, trying his best to act surprised. So the news had reached George Butler already. He wouldn't be the first to break the news, but he'd certainly make sure he had the best to offer. "What's the gossip about?"

"Aw, come on, man." The man rolled his eyes. "State your business and I'll see if the captain will see you."

"I've come with word of a hoax being attempted on the captain," Asa revealed.

Again the big man rolled his eyes. "And I'll only tell you one more time, the captain is already aware and is not meeting with anyone. Now be off with you."

"But I have proof it's a hoax," Asa shouted as the man turned away.

He stopped short and turned back. "Proof, you say?"

"Yes." Asa wasn't exactly sure what he could provide for proof, but if it got him in front of George Butler, he was certain he could bluff his way through a winning hand.

"And what's your name, man?" the crewman said with a sneer. "So as I can tell the captain."

"Asa. Asa Flint. I have intimate knowledge of the Blaisdell family." He almost chuckled to himself when he thought exactly how intimately he was acquainted with one family member in particular.

"Hold on."

The man disappeared beyond Asa's line of sight as the rest of the crew glared at him. He was almost certain he heard someone whisper, "Keep yer eye on him."

<hr />

The knock on the door startled both George and Reuben.

"Enter," George shouted more to relieve his tension than to be heard. The big crewman opened the door just enough to stick his head through.

"So sorry to bother you, sirs. There's another one of them town gossips here saying he needs to see you, Captain."

"Send him away, Beals," Reuben replied. "And keep everyone away. No one sees the captain!"

"Aye. But this one says he's got proof it's a hoax, sir," Beals replied.

George looked up. "A hoax?"

"Yes, sir, and he says he knows the Blaisdell family well."

George thought for a moment. "Did he give a name?"

"He did, sir. He said his name is Asa Flint."

George shook his head. "I don't know him. Dismiss him, like the other."

"Yes, sir." Beals started to retreat from the door.

"Wait!" Reuben said. "Flint, you say?" He looked at George. "Isn't that the fellow who's been spending a lot of time with Lydia Blaisdell lately?"

"Reuben, I haven't really been paying attention."

"No, I'm certain that's the name I heard flitted about town. They say he had designs on marrying her himself."

George sat up straighter. "Marry her? Well, then, it must have been quite the shocker to hear her say she was destined to marry me!"

"Jilted suitor comes knocking with an ax to grind, saying he's got proof of a hoax?" Reuben rubbed his chin. "Might be worth listening to him, George."

George nodded. "Beals, send him in."

＋———＋

It was an interesting yarn the young man was spinning. According to Asa, he had attempted to court Lydia on several occasions, only to be rebuffed. Undeterred, he had continued to call because Mrs. Blaisdell had seemed open to the idea and always let him in. Lydia herself seemed partially willing to accept his attentions. However, Hannah and Abner were both vehemently opposed to the idea of his being around—so much so that on the last evening he had been at the house, Abner had informed him that he need not return. There were other suitors for Lydia, he said. Shortly after being dismissed by Lydia's father, he had heard talk of a spirit. Intrigued with this new development, he had managed to sneak in the back of the room this morning and was present when the spirit appeared. He was not at all surprised when the spirit announced the reason for its visit—that Lydia was to marry George.

George remained silent for quite some time. The silence of the room was clearly making Asa uncomfortable, as he shifted his weight in his chair twice before George spoke.

"You are new to town, are you not, Mr. Flint?" George asked him.

"Fairly new, sir. Been here close to a year now."

"Then you must have heard the stories around town of Lydia's odd ways. Why would you consider her suitable for courting?"

Asa gave a sly smile. "Well, sir, I am but a poor man. My choices will never be as varied as yours." He indicated with a wave of his hand the obvious wealth that surrounded George. "If I may be blunt, I am a relation to Atherton Oakes, who had himself married into the Blaisdell family and was doing reasonably well before his death." He glanced down momentarily. "I have little to my name, sir. Nothing, really. A marriage to Lydia would have at least provided a roof over my head and three squares a day."

"So you have no feelings for the girl, then?" George prodded.

"No, sir." It was the most honest statement he had made all afternoon.

George sighed. "Mr. Flint, my assessment of you is that you are a man looking for a way up. So why have you come to me today? Clearly you have something to offer, and it will have a price, I'm sure."

Asa leaned forward. "You are shrewd, Captain Butler. I like doing business with men like that." Again he flashed a smile that unsettled George in a way he could not exactly pinpoint. "As I said, I believe this is the family's attempt to secure an advantageous marriage for Lydia with you, sir, by using the rumors of Lydia's odd ways to their advantage." Settling back in his chair, he crossed his legs. "I saw this spirit today. I believe it's a trick of light. There were also knockings that preceded it coming from the floor. Again, an easily done trick."

"Was Lydia present?" George asked, this being the first time he had heard any details regarding these supposed visitations from his wife. He was curious.

"Yes. She was at first, but the spirit sent her from the room, telling those assembled that she wanted them to see that Lydia was not the one speaking to them, that your wife was actually speaking."

From the dark corner of the room, Reuben mumbled, "Sounds like they are trying to protect her. Keep her looking innocent so she attracts sympathy in all of this."

"Exactly!" Asa got excited. He knew this would be a lot easier if he could get the two men to come to their own assumptions. "And Hannah wasn't there. She wasn't in the kitchen, either. I saw her arrive after the spirit had departed."

George sat up a little straighter. "Hannah wasn't there?"

"No. I saw her arrive in the kitchen when I was saying my goodbyes to Lydia. She just appeared, and I did not see from where."

Again, Reuben spoke. "What about Abner? Where was he?"

"Oh, he was there in the room where the spirit appeared. He had Reverend Crawford with him."

"Reverend Crawford." George thought of the kindly older man who had blessed and welcomed him and Nelly into the community on that fateful Coming Out Sunday. "Did he see the spirit?"

"Yes, we all saw it."

George was growing impatient. Now that he knew the reverend had been there, someone he respected far more than this riffraff, he was anxious to dismiss him and speak with Archibald directly.

"Again, Mr. Flint, what do you seek to gain from me in all of this?"

Asa could tell from George's posture he needed to close the pitch now. "Let me be your eyes and ears. I'm pretty sure this is a trick, and I will provide you with the proof of it."

"At what cost?" George replied.

"Land," Asa answered.

"Land?" George was incredulous. Land ownership made a man. Gave him rights that others simply couldn't attain. Asa could have asked for money. George was expecting that the lad would want a quick payment. But a landowner was something altogether different. This gave a man the right to vote, to speak up in discussions about his community, and elevated him to a different station—in short, it gave a man respect.

"Yes, I want land," Asa replied. "I understand there is quite a bit of timberland under your control. I'm interested in a portion of that. I do not want anything in this area. I'm ready to leave Franklin and try my luck somewhere new."

George thought of the posset ring, of his father's last words to him, of all the things that had transpired over the last five years. They were all real, were they not? Asa was offering the possibility of this being a hoax. Knowing what he knew, could it be? Then again, Nelly orchestrating his life from beyond the grave didn't seem plausible, either. He rubbed his hands over his face before responding to Asa.

"Mr. Flint, I think you are being opportunistic." Playing his cards close to his chest, George continued. "I'm not sure I see the urgency in this to prove anything." He could see Asa's facial expression fall.

"I am set to leave Franklin within hours. It matters not to me what tales the tongues wag in my absence. With that being said, I'm willing to give you a few days to gather this information that you claim you can find. If you can, in fact, beyond any doubt, prove that this is all a hoax put on by the Blaisdell family, I will honor your request for a payment in land."

Asa straightened in his chair, buoyed by the positive turn in George's response.

"If for nothing more than to save my family the continued annoyance placed upon them by the Blaisdells."

Asa jumped up, his youthful exuberance momentarily spilling out of him. He extended his hand in George's direction, "Thank you, Captain."

George did not reciprocate by shaking the hand offered him.

"A few days, Mr. Flint, and it better be valuable information." He eyed him strongly. "You are dismissed."

Asa knew enough to take this as a victory and exit. He bowed slightly at Reuben, who was stationed in the corner on a three-legged stool, and headed for the door.

After it was certain Asa was out of earshot, Reuben spoke. "What about the ring, Captain?" Reuben was clearly perplexed. "It would have to be some damn good hoax to explain that ring, sir."

George stood and gazed out the window as Asa retreated along the dock. "I know, Reuben. But a man can always hope, can he not? Besides, what if he can provide me with something of value?"

"Valuable enough for a piece of land?"

George turned toward his friend. "He said he wanted land. He didn't specify that he wanted good land."

Reuben raised his eyebrows.

"I've got a small piece up north of Bangor along the Kenduskeag. Mostly marsh, not worth a damn, and I'd be glad to unload it." He smiled and winked as he reached for his hat. Opening the door to his office, he stepped out into the cold winter air. "I'm going to pay a visit to Reverend Crawford. Keep the men working. I still want to pull out of here in the morning if we can."

Reuben stood in respect to George. "Yes, Captain," he said as George strode across the deck.

Archibald was just stepping up onto the granite step of his stoop when he saw George's figure approaching from the southwest. He sighed, knowing exactly what this was about.

"Captain Butler," he said, smiling, "what a pleasure it is to see you."

"Reverend," George replied, shaking the hand offered to him. "I wish this were a pleasure visit, but I'm afraid I have much to discuss with you."

"As I with you. Please come in."

Archibald opened the front door and stomped the snow from his boots. George followed suit, and both men retired to the study immediately off from the entryway. After the door had closed, George wasted no time in addressing the situation.

"Reverend, I understand there was a dramatization today at the Blaisdell home and you witnessed it."

Indicating a chair, Archibald spoke. "Sit, Captain, please." He took a seat himself across from the one he had offered George and inhaled deeply. "Yes, I was at the Blaisdells' when the manifestation occurred."

"Manifestation? So you believe this to be real?"

"I'm not sure, George. Truly, I am not. The Lord works in mysterious ways, and the scriptures are full of instances where ordinary people have seen or witnessed extraordinary events."

George stood and started pacing the room. He turned to the older man. "Do you believe it was my wife? Risen from the dead?"

"Goodness, no, George," Archibald replied. "She did not appear with a body of flesh and bone as the resurrected Lord did. But it was a manifestation of her spirit in some manner."

"Did it look like her?" George felt his heart lurch. His chest ached with the thought of his beloved Nelly.

Archibald nodded solemnly, not wanting to speak out loud the words that might crush George's already broken heart. He had indeed seen something that appeared to be Nelly.

George took a deep breath. "I was approached by Asa Flint just before coming here. He has offered to find proof that this is a hoax. Do you believe it is?"

Archibald thought for a moment. "That was my initial thought," he replied. "In fact, I thought maybe Asa was involved in some way. But I could not find any device or mechanism that could be causing the knocking. I searched the area beneath the room where this all transpired. Nor could it have come from the kitchen area, as that room, too, was occupied by people outside of the family. And then..." His voice trailed off.

"And then what?" George prodded him.

"As the spirit spoke—I call it a spirit for I do not wish to declare that it was Nelly—there was a feeling that permeated the room. A peace that one could not have created if it were a hoax, George."

George sat back down and looked at his hands. "This spirit asks for me, doesn't it? It has a purpose."

Archibald cleared his throat. "Yes. It says you are to marry Lydia."

George looked up with pleading eyes, begging for guidance. "That's preposterous, is it not?"

"I agree it is quite unorthodox, George."

Leaning forward, George stressed his concerns. "This child, Lydia, she has had an infatuation with me for nearly five years now. If, as you say, there was a 'feeling' in the room, then this cannot merely be a hoax to secure Lydia financially through marriage." He took a deep breath, thinking of the ring. "There has always been talk of her being familiar with spirits. Could this be something of her creation, then?"

Archibald looked perplexed. "Of her doing?" he asked.

George shrugged. "Yes, like some kind of manifestation of her energy. Or maybe she is working with the devil. Perhaps she sold her soul or some such thing."

"Oh, that would be troubling," the clergyman mumbled. "But I did not sense that from her when I saw her today. She appears to suffer when these happenings take place. Her father said they have feared on several occasions that they were about to lose her."

"Lose her? As in death?" George asked.

"Yes. According to Abner, it has happened many times before. But not with any indication that Nelly was involved."

"So this apparition that appears to be my wife is new?"

"Yes, at least according to Abner. Whether Lydia herself has been visited in the past by something appearing to be Nelly, he did not indicate."

George hesitated for a moment, then pulled the posset ring from his breast pocket. He handed it to Archibald.

Turning it over in his hand, the reverend looked at George quizzically. "What is this?"

"That," George began, pointing to the ring, "is the ring from the posset that Nelly and I had at our wedding. It is the very same ring that Nelly's sister Sally threw into the bay at the wedding after Lydia pulled it from her cup. It is also the very same ring that somehow again came into Lydia's possession after disappearing into the bay. It flew from her pocket during your sermon, inciting the uproar that caused Nelly and me to leave Franklin in the first place. In short, I have attempted to rid myself of that ring only to have it return again and again. Most recently, I was told by my father on his deathbed, no less—that I must keep it."

Archibald looked shocked. "Your father?" he asked as he adjusted his glasses to examine the ring closer. Seeing the inscription, he almost dropped the ring, as if it had burned him. "Land sakes alive!" He pulled his glasses off to look at George. "What kind of trickery is this?"

"Well, that is what I'm here to ask you, Reverend. You were there. You saw this spiritual manifestation. Is it my wife?" George's voice grew demanding. "Was it? Should I go to her? Should I marry Lydia as the spirit instructs? As this ring has foretold?" He gestured toward the ring that Archibald still clutched in his fingers.

Archibald shook his head. "I do not know, son. I do not know." He handed the ring back to George as if he wanted to rid himself of an evil. He closed his eyes, pondering the situation. Sighing deeply, he remained silent.

"So you have nothing to offer?" George asked him. The feeling of isolation was overwhelming. He had so recently lost his father, his most trusted counsel. Now Reverend Crawford had nothing to give him in the way of advice or comfort. Was it possible that his only hope lay with Asa Flint?

"I would tell you to wait," the man finally answered. "There is no reason to rush to action just yet. My advice would be patience. Let

Asa make the first move. Let him gather the information he believes is there that will prove this is a hoax."

"But is it?" he asked, raising the ring as an indication before placing it back in his pocket.

"Well, that will be my job. Let me look into the spiritual side of this. For it is either the work of God or the work of the devil. And I am a man familiar with both." He smiled slightly to lighten the mood.

"And what shall I do? I just can't sit around in town and pretend that my deceased wife's ghost isn't beckoning me to come to her," George exclaimed.

"Leave, then," Archibald replied.

"Leave? Like a coward who cannot solve his own problems or protect his family?"

"No. Like the dignified gentleman that you are. A man of means who cannot be bothered with the idle gossip and drama of the small-minded. A man who can rise above it and will make his decisions once all the facts have been gathered. Who will remain, always, Captain George Butler, a man of esteem among his peers."

George considered this. The reverend was correct. He needed to have patience and let all the facts be gathered before he committed himself to reacting to this.

"Very well. I will leave tomorrow as I had originally planned. Three months? Do you think if I return then that there will be some significant progress made?"

"Yes, I think that is very wise," Archibald replied.

George rose and extended his hand to the reverend, who grasped his hand firmly. "Thank you for your counsel, Reverend. It was desperately needed."

"You're welcome, Captain. Peace be upon your soul."

George left the Crawford home, formulating his plan. He'd have Asa report to Peter on word of the hoax. He was done dealing with the young man himself. He would head to York and try to pick up whatever he could that needed to go south. He'd go all the way to Florida if he had to as long as he was back here by the end of April. That would at least buy him more time from the inscription on that ring.

The following day, as Lydia stood upon the shore. She watched in disbelief as George's ship headed down the bay. How could this be? She scanned the deck of the ship, but she did not see him. Just his first mate stood at the helm. Maybe it was leaving without him. Was that possible? Could a ship sail without its captain?

Then he appeared, just as the ship passed in front of her. Strong and tall with the bearing of a man who knew he had mastered much in his life. She saw him approach the railing. He was staring right at her. She felt his gaze. She stared back at him. Although his ship stayed to the deepest part of the channel in the center of the bay, she felt that he was standing right in front of her. She could see his eyes, the embroidery on his captain's hat, the way his knuckles had turned white from his grip on the railing. Could he see her this clearly, too?

She slowly raised her hand, extending her fingers slightly, before pulling her hand back down to her side. It was a slight wave at best, and she wasn't sure he had even seen it. Until she saw him release one hand from the railing and raise it slowly as well. Her heart leapt in her chest. He had acknowledged her! He turned suddenly from the railing and was again gone from sight. She watched as the ship slipped past the small outlet islands and out of view.

⁎⸺⁎

"What do you mean he left?" Hannah was storming around the kitchen table. Lydia had just returned to the house and had informed everyone that she had seen George leave.

"I saw him on his ship, just now, when I was down at the shore. He's gone."

"He can't!" Hannah screamed. "This is ridiculous!" She threw her arms up in the air and sat down at the table. "Now what are we supposed to do?"

Their mother appeared in the doorway "What is this all about?"

"Captain Butler left!" Hannah said with anger in her voice. "He left, and now we are stuck with Nelly and her never-ending entreaties to bring him to her. How are we supposed to do that if he's not here?" She laid her head down on her folded arms on the table and began to sob.

Lydia rushed to her sister's side. "It's okay, Hannah. Nelly must know he is gone, too, so maybe she won't come anymore."

"Lydia has a point, Hannah," her mother said. "Maybe he left so that all of this will stop."

"But will it?" Hannah asked, raising her head. She nodded her head toward the twenty or so people who were stationed out in the carding room.

"They gather here daily now, Mother," she pointed out. "We are taxed beyond our resources most days trying to accommodate them."

"The Gathering Room," Lydia mused.

"The what?" her mother asked.

"The Gathering Room. That's what your carding room has become." She shook her head. "The townspeople have given it a name."

CHAPTER FORTY-THREE

Days went by, and then weeks, with no appearance of the spirit. There were no knockings, no voices. Slowly, the number of people that gathered in the room dwindled. The deepest part of a Maine winter locked the communities of Sullivan and Franklin in its grip. The snows came, and Lydia watched as the bay finally froze over. Even if George wanted to return, he could not do so now. He would have to remain at sea or at the ports farther south. Reverend Crawford came several times to talk to Abner. But as the weeks wore on and nothing more happened, even he, too, stopped coming. Asa, however, still managed to visit. He hung around the kitchen chatting with Lydia's mother. He asked all kinds of questions, and as the spirit visits appeared to be over, he alone increased his visits to the Blaisdell home.

Asa had become frustrated with the abrupt end to the spiritual visitations. He had followed George's instructions and had reported to his brother Peter at Butler's Point for the first few days after George's departure. But as time wore on and there was nothing new to report, Peter had told him to stop coming until he had something of value to say. Rebuffed, Asa had turned his attentions on the Blaisdell family. Asa was convinced that this was something created by the Blaisdells, if not a hoax in the true sense of the word. The visitations had ceased the minute Captain Butler had left. It appeared that no audience meant no show.

Instead, he made himself indispensable to Abner. Now that Atherton was gone, Abner needed another man around the place. Asa pitched in and worked alongside Abner. In doing so, he had access to every inch of the Blaisdell property from the root cellar to the boathouse to the public rooms of their home. He searched the cupboards and every nook and cranny looking for any apparatus that would have produced the trickery of light he had witnessed in the room that day, but he found nothing. Working with Abner, he prodded him with questions until he had learned all he could about him. Abner was deeply rooted in his Christian beliefs, and Asa began to think he couldn't be behind a hoax. The man was just too honest. Too God-fearing.

Asa hung around the kitchen as much as was proper, trying to overhear the women's conversations. Lydia was wary of him, naturally, but Hannah and their mother talked freely, and he never got an indication from their conversations that they were up to anything more diabolical than the household chores. In fact, Mary Blaisdell seemed almost pleased to have Asa around. She herself began suggesting that the courtship between him and Lydia, which had long been suspected but not openly confirmed, should be encouraged. Asa was inclined to agree with her. With no more evidence of the spirit and certainly no evidence of a hoax, he knew he would have nothing to offer George when and if he returned. That left him with only one option—he had to switch his alliance yet again. But he knew he couldn't approach Lydia about it. No, he would have to go directly to Abner and let him decide his daughter's—and ultimately his—future.

✦———✦

Abner was bent over the nets in the boathouse when Asa found him.

"Good morning, sir," he said.

Looking up from the nets, Abner seemed pleased to see him.

"I'm so glad you have arrived, Asa," he said, pulling on the netting. "I seem to be struggling with this larger one this morning. Give me a hand, will you?"

Asa bent down and pulled hard on the section that Abner was working on. The extra effort helped the mass to give way, and it was pulled free from the tangle it had gotten into.

"This one here is for Captain Miller," Abner explained. "It's the largest I've ever made, and I'm afraid I have overdone myself." He laughed as he sat down to rest.

Asa took up a stool next to him. "I was wondering if I could speak with you, sir, for a moment before we start work for the day."

Abner could see the seriousness in the young man's face. "Why, yes, what is this about?"

Asa took a deep breath. "I'd like to ask for Lydia's hand, if I may?"

"Her hand in marriage?" Abner asked.

"Is there any other kind?"

"Well, no," Abner replied, thinking before responding further. "You ask this even after all that has transpired?"

"Yes," Asa replied. "I am not afraid of Lydia's peculiarities, as one might call them." He jutted his chin out to show his authority. "I have witnessed them for myself, and they do not concern me."

"And this latest situation, this spirit proclaiming Lydia is to be the wife of Captain Butler—you do not find that troubling?" Abner prodded him further.

"Not at all." Asa took a deep breath. "Pardon me for speaking boldly, sir, but I believe what Lydia needs is a firmer hand. These fantasies of her childhood have been allowed to fester within her mind and have now taken on a life of their own. What she needs is to be set on a path of more mature womanhood. A husband could provide her with stricter boundaries and, of course, children." His gaze became more intense. "Being a wife and mother, having to care for a husband and children, will help her to forget these fantasies."

Abner was taken aback. "So you feel I have been too lenient with my daughter?" He attempted to control his anger. "Young man, if you are trying to win my favor, insulting me is not the way to go about it."

"Of course not," Asa interjected. "I only suggest that your deep belief in God may have shrouded your understanding of what was actually happening with Lydia." He softened his tone. "That maybe this is not the work of God or the devil but just the overactive imagination of a child."

Abner thought for a moment. "So you do not fear that by taking Lydia as your wife, you are defying God or His works?"

Asa sat a little straighter on his stool. "Absolutely not. I have seen nothing yet to prove to me that what has been happening here is truly the works of God. On the contrary, I don't believe anything has been proven one way or the other."

Abner took a deep breath and exhaled it slowly. "Why should I allow this? Let me speak boldly to you, sir." He leaned toward Asa. "You have nothing to offer me for my daughter's hand. You have nothing to offer my daughter as far as a secure future." His voice rose slightly. "You, sir, are even less desirable than your cousin Atherton, whom I allowed to marry Hannah." He settled back on his stool. "If I allow this to happen, you become one more mouth I have to feed along with any offspring you produce with my daughter. I do not see how I or Lydia will benefit from this prospect."

Asa had expected this. He knew he was not a man of means and would probably never become one. "Agreed, sir. I am well aware of my shortcomings in life." He paused for effect. "And yet, your daughter has no other suitors and is not likely to have any, given her history. Captain Butler clearly was not swayed by the spirit of his dead wife, as the man left town the very next day. Have we heard word that he plans to return? No. So if he were not swayed by the dramatics that played out, I doubt it very likely that he will return willing to marry her at some future date." He rose from his stool to walk around the small shed, turning back on Abner. "Is it not true, sir, that when George Butler is absent from Lydia's surroundings, she does not suffer?"

Abner nodded slightly.

"Then I, sir, offer myself to you and Lydia as the only option to release Lydia from her struggles. With me as her husband, Captain Butler will have no reason to be a part of her life, directly or indirectly. And he may even choose to stay away from Franklin for good."

He had played his last card, and he hoped his argument had been convincing enough. Lydia had no other options, just as he had none.

"I shall ponder it," was all Abner would say. He returned to the nets, handing the threading tool to Asa. "We have work to do."

CHAPTER FORTY-FOUR

March 1800

Lydia stood in front of her father's desk. Her mother sat to her right in a rigid, straight chair. Rarely had her father called her to him in such a formal manner. She wanted to sit, but he had not instructed her to do so nor offered her a chair. She watched him as he stared down at his hands, locking and unlocking his fingers in a gesture of nervousness. She could feel his tension fill the room.

"Father?" she finally said to break her own anxiety. Abner looked up at her, and she could see his own anxiety reflected back at her.

"Lydia, my child," he sighed. "I have made a decision regarding your future, a decision that I and your mother have determined is best for you." He gestured toward her mother.

Lydia was confused. Her future? What was he talking about? She knew her future. She was to be the wife of Captain George Butler. At some point, he would return and they would be married.

"What do you mean, Father?" she asked him.

He looked her squarely in the eyes when he responded. "I have given my permission to Asa Flint for you to become his wife."

Lydia felt something explode in her chest. She reached forward and gripped the edge of her father's desk.

"You have what?" she gasped out. She felt the room spinning around her. She could no longer see her father, just shots of bright white light flashing on a sea of blackness. She crumpled to the floor.

"Lydia!"

She could hear her mother saying her name over and over. Felt her patting her cheeks. Her eyes fluttered open, and she saw her mother's face.

"Mother," she murmured. Her mother offered her a glass of water, tilting her head so she could sip from the cup more easily.

"Lydia." Her father's voice was unusually stern. "Arise. There will be no more of this."

Her mother helped her to a chair. She turned her gaze to her father, who still sat at his desk, unmoved by what had just transpired. He continued to speak.

"I have prayed to God for an answer for your troubles. I have sought His guidance in the best course for you."

Lydia cut him off. "And God told you Asa Flint was the best course?" she said incredulously.

"Do not speak disrespectfully to your father," her mother whispered.

Abner held up a hand. "I understand your desires, Lydia. You have believed since you were a small child that your future was to be with George Butler. But it is time to put these childhood fantasies to rest. They have created so much trouble for everyone. Whether of God or of the devil, created by you or by the captain himself, no one can tell. Enough is enough. It must end."

He paused to take a breath. "Captain Butler lost his wife. Naturally, a man would be looking for another. And yet, he did not marry. He left Franklin. Left his inheritance, left everything behind. He only returned because of the death of his father. He had no intention of finding a new wife here. Then he was presented with the spirit of his dearly loved wife telling him to marry you. And what did he do? He left again, Lydia. He left."

The purport of his words sunk deep into Lydia, and she could feel herself being absorbed into her chair as if she no longer existed. She was a possession of her father's, and he would be making this decision. Clearly, his mind was made up.

"Given your history, you can understand that your options are limited. There is much talk in this town on whether you are sick of mind, possessed of an evil spirit, or involved in a pact with the devil—none of which attracts potential suitors."

Lydia felt her mother reach toward her and place a reassuring hand on her shoulder. These were all things they knew, but it was hard to hear them spoken out in the open.

"Asa has presented himself and offered to take you as his wife."

Lydia felt her skin crawl at this notion.

"Realistically, he has little to offer. Truth be told, he has nothing, not even a decent upbringing or name."

Abner rubbed his hand over his face. "Agreeing to this will actually be more of a financial burden to me, as I will have to care for you and him."

Lydia jumped on this, leaning forward in her chair, reaching out for his desk. "Then why, Father? Why? Please do not do this. I just can't," she pleaded, sobbing uncontrollably.

Abner stiffened his back. "You can and you will, Lydia," he said sternly. "By placing you under the care of a husband, making you a married woman, you will no longer be a child with a fantasy. I am in hopes that all of these troubles will end. Asa's offer is our way out of this dilemma."

Lydia continued to cry. "Father, please, no."

Abner glanced at Mary for help with this. She leaned toward her daughter. "Shhh, Lydia, it will be all right, you'll see. Soon you will have babies to care for, and you will forget all about Captain Butler."

This did not produce the loving maternal result that Mary had intended. Far from it. Lydia recoiled at the thought of Asa being physically intimate with her again. She felt the bile rise in her throat.

Her father rose from his chair. "Come, Lydia." He walked around his desk, reaching for her hand. "Asa is in the next room. Let us go to him and show some kind of joy in this decision we have made."

Lydia took his hand and rose slowly from her chair. She knew she could not fight him on this. But she would fight Asa. She would make him regret this course of action for the rest of his life. She may not have been able to refuse him before when he knew things that no one else had known. But as his wife, she would refuse him. Oh yes, she would. Husband or not, he was never getting near her again.

———

Asa stood when he saw the door to the room open. Abner entered, first followed by Lydia, who was being pulled by the hand into the room. Mary followed her in and shut the door. Abner indicated to Lydia she should sit on a chair, and once she had he turned his attentions to Asa.

"Asa, I have informed Lydia of our decision." He looked at Lydia's sullen countenance and realized he could not continue. The silence hung in the room like a pall.

Asa cleared his throat and walked toward Lydia. He reached out for her hand, which she snatched away quickly, glaring at him.

"Ah, Lydia, I see you do not find this plan to your liking," he stated.

"No, I do not," was all she said. She would have spit on him if her parents hadn't been present.

"Well, that is of no matter, as your father and I have agreed to it." He placed his hand on her shoulder, gripping it tightly. Looking up at Abner and Mary, he said, "I have chosen the end of April as the perfect time for a wedding. The snows should be gone by then, and spring has always been a time of rebirth, has it not? A fresh start." He slid his hand up to Lydia's neck and grasped her chin. Turning her face toward him, he forced her to make eye contact with him. "A time to forget the past, do you understand?" When he smiled, Lydia could see his browning teeth, and it revolted her. "You may choose the day, my love," he said with a sneer as he kissed her lightly on the cheek. Lydia pulled away from him and ran from the room.

Abner sighed. "We did not suspect that she would be happy with this decision. It is why I took so long to make it." He shook his head. "I pray that she will not trouble you too much as she settles down."

Asa laughed. "No, I shall have no problem taming her."

His tone caused Mary to bristle slightly, and she wondered if she had misread him on his many visits to their home. She stood and addressed Asa as she prepared to leave the room.

"Mr. Flint, I will do my best to prepare my daughter for her new role as your wife."

"Thank you, Mrs. Blaisdell." He kissed her hand reassuringly and smiled warmly at her.

"Now, if you will excuse me, gentlemen, I have a wedding to prepare for in less than six weeks!"

She hurried off, leaving the two of them alone. Asa turned to Abner.

"It will be fine. She will come to accept me over time."

Abner shook his hand firmly. "She will have to. She has no other choice."

<hr>

Hannah was walking up the path from town when she was nearly run over by Lydia running toward her. Lydia fell on her, sobbing uncontrollably.

"Heavenly day, Lydia! What is wrong with you?" she blurted out as she supported her sister.

"Asa." Lydia managed to get out in between sobs. "It's Asa. Father is making me marry him."

Hannah was stunned. "He is doing what?"

Lydia gathered herself and slowed her breathing. "Father and Asa made some kind of agreement that I am to become his wife."

"Wife? But that miscreant has nothing to offer! He was a hanger-on from the beginning. Even Atherton, his own kin, was not fond of him. What did he possibly offer to Father for your hand?"

Lydia was shaking. "He somehow convinced Father that if I were married, it would put an end to all of my experiences." She began to cry again. "That my belief that I am to marry Captain Butler is just a child-hood fantasy and if I marry Asa, it will all stop."

"Stop? And Father believed this? He saw the spirit himself. He heard it speaking." Hannah looked shocked by this turn of events.

"And then he saw it all stop as soon as Captain Butler left town," Lydia said. "He says he cannot be convinced any longer that what we saw and heard was of God or of the devil. Either way, it has to stop, and he believes making me a wife and mother will put an end to it. He says George has no intention of marrying me. If he did, he would have done so by now." She sobbed heavily. "And he says that Asa Flint is my only prospect, given the talk about me in town. No one else would ever want me."

"Oh, my poor Lydia," Hannah said, trying to comfort her. Holding her sister's head close to her chest, she cooed soothing words to her. "Don't lose hope—we will find a way out of this."

CHAPTER FORTY-FIVE

With the same speed that word of Nelly's spirit had spread around the town, word of the impending marriage of Asa Flint and Lydia Blaisdell soon was the topic on every lip. It did not take long for the news to reach Butler's Point, either. Coincidently, on the day word of it arrived, Sarah Butler was preparing to entertain Nelly's mother, Joanna, and her sister, Sally, from the other side of the bay. As she busied herself in her preparations, setting out the tea things and arranging the chairs, she was surprised to see Peter enter the room.

"Why, Peter, I thought you would have been up to the pond by now."

Peter had spent the winter clearing the land he had acquired from George after Nelly's death. Although the pond would always be known as George's Pond, Peter was preparing to build himself a fine home there and move his family from the point.

"I was headed there, Mother, when I heard news in town that I thought you should be made aware of."

"News? Of what sort?" she asked as she polished one of the silver spoons on her apron.

"The Blaisdell girl is to be married," he said.

Sarah lifted her gaze from the spoon and looked at Peter. "Married? Who in this town would consent to marry her after all that has transpired?"

"Flint. The very same that approached George claiming he could prove Nelly's spirit was a hoax."

"The scoundrel," she said, shaking her head. "Well, it sounds like he is well suited to that family then, wouldn't you say?"

"Yes. For he provided me with absolutely nothing as evidence of a hoax," Peter said. "I fear George was seduced by a wild talker and nothing more than that."

"And wild talk is the best way to describe the Blaisdells." Sarah thought for a moment and then spoke. "You know, Peter, this is actually a blessing for us."

"How is that?"

"If she is married, then her attention will not be focused on George any longer."

Peter smiled. "Then maybe we should thank Mr. Flint rather than feel sorry for him!"

Laughing, Sarah said, "Oh, I still think he has chosen a difficult path. He may yet still need our sympathy."

Peter kissed his mother lightly on the head as he prepared to depart. "Enjoy your visit with the Hoopers today." He paused as he neared the door. "Should we send word to George? About the Blaisdell developments, I mean."

Sarah shook her head. "No, I do not think that is necessary. His plan included returning in the spring, did it not? Perhaps by then she will be married off and George can be free of this nightmare once and for all."

"And our family as well," he said, placing his hat back on his head and leaving.

+————+

Joanna Hooper and Sally Wentworth arrived with the same news. Joanna said that Mary Blaisdell had been seen in town making purchases that were obviously related to the wedding. It appeared, she said, as if the Blaisdells were going to treat this wedding just the same as Hannah's wedding to Atherton. The gossips in town were calling that brash. It was felt, given Lydia's history and the public spectacle the family had become, that a quieter, more private ceremony would be more appropriate. Mr. Flint was certainly no man of character or esteem and did not warrant anything more elaborate than the magistrate pronouncing them man and wife and signing the papers. A celebration was seen as excessive. Talk also centered on Lydia's age. She was young, not unmarriageable young, but still young enough to set a few tongues wagging. It was felt that another year or two would have benefited her. This set off a debate about the timing of the marriage. If they waited too much longer, then the dramatic events that had surrounded her life might continue. Waiting also produced the very real possibility that she would never find a reasonable suitor and would remain unmarried for the rest of her life.

With the visitations abruptly stopping after George's departure, people speculated on the most likely reason behind Lydia's marriage to Asa. Perhaps the Blaisdells had finally come to realize that they could not trick Captain Butler into marrying their daughter and had suspended the trickery, settling for the only real prospect Lydia was likely to ever have. So it appeared that every camp was satisfied. Those who were still trying to figure out if Lydia's problems were the act of God or the devil seemed to be content with letting it go in favor of waiting to see how Asa would handle her peculiarities. Those who felt the Blaisdells had been behind the whole mess were satisfied that this would stop the harassment of the Butlers. The whole town would breathe a sigh of relief once Lydia Blaisdell was married.

CHAPTER FORTY-SIX

April 11, 1800
Castine Harbor

"Where you off to next, Captain?" the steward asked as George signed off on the last shipment to be unloaded from his ship. He had just docked in Castine Harbor with a shipment of board lumber up from Bangor. He had spent the past four months making short runs between ports on the southern east coast. Now that winter had loosened its grips and the ice had broken, he was headed north and was able to make his way farther inland to river ports such as Bangor and those along the Kennebec—securing valuable commodities that had waited all winter to be transported Downeast.

"Franklin," he said, dipping the quill one more time as he finished his signature with a flourish. "Home, that is. My crew and I are due for a break."

The steward took the paper back and then recognized George's name.

"Captain Butler, is it?" he asked.

"Yes," George said warily. "Is there a problem?"

"Oh no, sir. Just…well, the hauntings." He almost seemed embarrassed to speak it out loud.

"The hauntings?" George replied. He knew immediately what the man was talking about, but he did not consider what Reverend Crawford had described as a haunting. That word gave it a connotation of something dark, sinister, almost scary. Hadn't Reverend Crawford said he felt peace and compassion while the spirit was there? "Where did you hear of that?"

"Oh, everyone speaks of it, sir," the man stammered. "Word travels fast aboard ships. Faster than by land. You should know that." He scribbled a receipt and handed it to George. "So is it true?" he probed.

"Of course not," George replied, accepting the receipt without exhibiting the anger that he felt building inside. He tipped his hat and calmly walked back toward the ship. Let them talk all they wanted, but they would never be able to say Captain Butler was reactive in any way.

"Is it done, Captain?" Reuben called from the railing.

"It is. Set the men, and let's get going. We should be able to make it home before we lose too much daylight."

"Aye, Captain," the man replied.

George took his place at the helm of his ship and gripped the wheel, watching as the men unfurled the sails. Hauntings. The word echoed around his brain. Plural, the man had used the plural. So had Nelly's visits continued after he was gone? Was the whole town on fire with the excitement of it? He was eager to talk to Peter and learn of what, if anything, Asa Flint had been able to piece together to give him some hope that none of this was real.

He waited until the winds caught the sails and he felt the boat strain against the ropes holding it to the dock. "Release them, Reuben!" he called down and saw his men pull the large ropes from the pillars, working furiously to haul them in. The ship slipped effortlessly away from the dock. With fair winds, he would be home in record time.

"Storms farther out would be my guess," he heard Reuben say. "From the direction of the winds, I would say it's a spring nor'easter out there."

"Winter's last gasp at trying to stay relevant," George replied. "Not cold enough for snow, so rough seas and heavy wind for a few days is my guess. Franklin should be protected enough."

"Except for the high tide. Should I order additional ropes, sir?" Reuben asked. The bay always felt the brunt of nor'easters during high tide. The strong currents, pulled by the tides and then churned up by stronger storms out at sea, brought whitecaps to the bay and made keeping a ship at dock difficult.

"Yes, for now. If it becomes too much, I'll order you to take her farther down the bay and moor on the sheltered side of Bean Island. I don't know how long we'll stay this time, and I don't want to dock more than once if we don't have to."

Reuben nodded his head in agreement. "I'll have the additional ropes brought up from the hold, then."

"I need to speak with my brother Peter, and of course I want to see my mother," George informed him. "But if things have settled down and there are no further developments, I'd like to be gone again in a week." He turned the giant wheel of the ship as he watched the coast slip past him and directed the compass bearing northeast. "Give the men a short rest, restock, and we'll be on our way."

"If things have settled down," Reuben reminded him. "That ring says 1800, sir."

George scowled at his friend. "You are dismissed."

———

Pressed forward by the winds of the nor'easter, George's ship sailed quickly into the bay toward Franklin. The bright white sails cracked before the winds, almost announcing his arrival as he sped into view of the eastern shore first.

Abner and Asa were busily working the nets they had strewn across the beach. Each end had to be weighted with stones so they could be dragged behind the fishing ships. Together, the men gathered the small rocks from the shoreline and secured them to the edges of the nets. They were racing against time, as the seas had begun to churn. There was a storm out at sea, and the violence of it would change the shoreline. Many of the smaller stones they needed might be pulled out to sea.

Asa was bent over picking through the stones, selecting just the right size, and dropping them into his pail when he heard the first crack of the canvas. Glancing up, he saw the ship come into the bay.

"Well, look there," he exclaimed out loud.

Abner heard his soon-to-be son-in-law's voice and looked up. He recognized George's ship immediately. They both watched as the ship quickly glided past them.

"What has brought him back so soon?" Abner exclaimed.

"I doubt very much he has come to give Lydia and me his blessing," Asa snorted. His mind raced through the scenario he knew lay before him. He had hoped that George would return at some point. He felt he still had a card to play in extracting something of value from Captain Butler. Seeing the ship and knowing that George was going to be in town this very afternoon lightened his mood. "I think I shall pay a visit to Captain Butler," he smirked.

"I would advise against that," Abner replied. "Let this end, my son. Lydia is yours—in only a mere ten days, she will be your wife. George Butler will have no further influence in her life." He picked up Asa's pail and shoved it toward him. "Come, let us gather as much as we can before the storm takes it all away from us."

Asa looked at the pail and knocked it from the man's hand. "I don't think so, old man. I've got something to report to the captain, and it's time to collect my due."

"Your due?" Abner exclaimed. "What on earth are you talking about?"

Asa turned to him. "Don't you get it? My marrying Lydia releases Captain Butler from this whole situation. It sets him free. That has got to be worth something to him."

Abner was shocked. Not that he had thought for even a moment that the young man actually loved his daughter. He knew Asa was opportunistic, but he felt that his agreeing to marry Lydia was just to secure a modest future. He didn't realize the depths to which Asa would go.

"Extortion? Is that what you have planned?" Abner asked him.

"Call it what you will, but I am providing a great service to the captain. One that I hope will set me up pretty nicely." He bowed mockingly at Abner. "Thanks in part to your handing over Lydia to me."

He turned and began to run up the path. Considering the speed with which that ship was barreling toward Franklin, he knew he would have to make it quick if he wanted to catch the captain before he departed for Butler's Point.

+———+

Sarah Butler stood over her small garden plot imagining how it would be planted in the weeks to come. It was still far too early for planting anything, but with the warming days she enjoyed coming out here to pick through last year's remnants and plan for this year. It was a blustery day, and she could hear the sounds of the waves crashing along the shoreline below the main house. She tucked strands of loose hair back into her bonnet and walked toward the bay to get a better view of how choppy it was getting. It was then that she saw George's ship speeding toward the point. She grasped at her bonnet as a particularly strong gust plucked at it and began waving frantically with her other hand.

"George! George!" she yelled. She saw her son standing proud and strong at the helm, but with the winds she knew he could not hear her. His attention was fully focused on successfully guiding his ship up the bay, so it wasn't likely that he saw her, either. She turned and quickly headed for the house.

"Anna! Anna!" she hollered for her house girl. The young woman came out from the kitchen, wiping her hands on her apron. "Quick, get one of the boys to send for Peter. He's up at the pond. George is home!" She pointed at the ship that was just slipping out of view as it progressed quickly up the bay. Anna ran for the barns.

When Sarah turned back around, the ship was gone from view. "God help him," she muttered. She smiled and headed for the house. If her son was coming home, then she needed to get ready.

George ordered the sails pulled as soon as they had cleared Butler's Point. He had never returned to the bay with this much speed behind him. Even Reuben looked a little dubious as he awaited orders. Once George gave the order, the lines were pulled and the canvas dropped quickly. The ship slowed considerably but was still being driven forward by the strong current.

"Thought you were going to crash the dock, Captain," Reuben muttered as he took the wheel from George to prepare for the docking.

George laughed. "It was a bit of a ride, wasn't it? Don't think I've ever seen it this windy in here."

"Nor I, Captain, nor I," the older man stated. "An omen, maybe, sir?" he asked.

George scoffed. "Let's get the facts first, Reuben. Then we will make a decision."

The docks at Franklin were clearly in view. George could see his usual slip was empty. He instructed Reuben to bring her in nice and easy. Then he stepped down onto the decking and ordered the men to man the ropes. He could see the dock workers scurrying about, ready to grasp the ropes as they were thrown to them. They were still coming in stronger than he would have liked, but there was nothing he could do at this point. He felt the jolt as the ship banged into the dock. "Heave!" he hollered as the men threw the ropes. Those below made quick work of securing the ropes, but the deck continued to sway and bob beneath his feet. The bay seemed to be in turmoil.

As Reuben approached, George was still shouting orders to the men.

"Once they are done, pay them and release them," George said, pulling a leather pouch from his coat pocket. The coins within jingled as he tossed it to Reuben. "The remainder is for you. Thank you again for another successful run. You are indispensable, Reuben. Indispensable."

"And you, sir?" Reuben asked, avoiding the compliment with all the humility of a true Yankee.

"I'm going to set things to right in my office, lock her up, and then head for Butler's Point. Go home, Reuben. I'll send word in a week at the earliest about my plans."

"Aye, Captain." He eyed him warily. "But if you learn anything and need me, send for me."

George smiled and shook the man's hand, then stepped into his cabin and shut the door. He pulled the ring from his breast pocket and stared at the inscription again.

"And what have you planned for me on this trip?" he said, laying the ring on the blotter on his desk. The ship continued to heave as he began gathering his things.

<hr/>

Asa had nearly sprinted up the entire eastern shore, only slowing slightly when he came upon others on the path. Trying not to draw attention to himself, he slowed to a reasonable walking pace until he was past them and then sprinted onward again. By the time he came within view of the first buildings of Franklin, he was out of breath and sweating. The heavy breeze felt wonderful as he tried to calm himself for what lay ahead of him. He made his way through the main street and headed straight for the docks. He could see the masts of the ship bobbing up and down as the ship was tossed about by the winds and strong current.

He stepped onto the dock, looking about for anyone who might stop him, but the whole place appeared empty. Walking quickly, he made his way to the side of the ship. He could see the extra lines of rope that were attempting to hold the ship in place. He stepped gingerly over them and grasped the railing. Almost immediately, the ship rose, lifting him off the dock. He felt nothing beneath his feet and gripped with all his might as he struggled to get one leg up and over the railing. If he fell here, he would be crushed by the ship as it cascaded downward on the swell. Clutching to the railing with all of his might, he finally managed to slip over it and land sprawling on the deck of the ship.

"A less than graceful entrance," a voice said.

Sitting up, Asa saw George exiting his cabin.

"Captain," he said, standing quickly and trying to look as if he were at home on the deck of a ship. But the vessel's constant motion made this impossible.

"You certainly didn't waste time in getting here, Asa," George said. "Have you news for me?"

Asa smiled. "I have valuable news for you."

George turned and walked back into his cabin. He did not invite Asa in, but the man followed him nonetheless, sliding and grasping at objects along the deck to try and maintain his balance. Once inside the cabin, he scurried for a chair and sat down hard, almost rolling off the edge. George smiled at the man's inability to stay upright. He also noted that Asa was beginning to look a little green as the ship continued its constant motion.

"I don't remember there being this much movement the last time I met with you here," Asa said, swallowing hard.

"A strong storm out to sea is pushing the wind and current into the bay," George explained. He sat down. "Now, what do you have to tell me? I'm certain you didn't rush here to discuss the weather."

271

Asa swallowed again and then began to speak. "I did as you instructed. I investigated every member of the Blaisdell family. I searched their home and tried to learn all I could about their ability to perpetrate this hoax upon you, sir."

"And what was behind it? Who is responsible?" George asked.

"Well, that was the trouble, Captain. I could not find any proof at all of it being a hoax."

George felt his heart throbbing in his chest. He knew this was going to be the answer. He had resigned himself to this. The ring, it couldn't have been faked. Nor could the feeling that Reverend Crawford described after seeing the spirit. Nelly had indeed spoken. It was truly his beloved wife who had come for whatever reason and said he needed to marry Lydia. He would not fight this any longer, nor run from it. The time had come to speak with this spirit himself and prepare his mind and heart to take Lydia as his wife. He began to rise from his chair.

"Thank you, Mr. Flint, you may go." He indicated the door with his outstretched hand.

Asa was shocked that the meeting had ended so abruptly. "Go? Do you not wish to know more?"

"Is there more, Mr. Flint? The way I see it, you were unable to prove it was a hoax, therefore it must be of God or of the devil—either one, it doesn't matter. My fates appear to be tied to it."

Asa sat back in his chair, a smile widening across his face. "Please, Captain, do sit back down and let me shed some more light on this situation for you."

George didn't like the look on the man's face. But he slowly resumed his seat, wary of what Asa could possibly be prepared to propose next.

"As you described so well, sir, your fates do appear to be tied to Lydia Blaisdell and whatever evil she carries within her." He gripped his chair, leaning forward with an air of concern for George. "It is with all of this in mind that I have taken a most unusual step that I hope you will see as a gesture of pure humanity toward you, sir." His gaze fell as he tried to appear a most humble servant. Lowering his voice, he added, "And that I'm in hopes you will feel is worthy of the land we spoke of at our first meeting."

So that was it. Unable to provide George with proof of a hoax, Asa was now offering himself as the sacrifice worthy of payment.

"Speak plainly, man—I am anxious to get this over with and get to my family," George shouted at him.

Asa took a deep breath and plunged in. "I have offered myself as a husband to Lydia."

George felt the thunderous results of these words deep in his bones.

"Abner Blaisdell agreed with my reasoning and gave his daughter's hand to me. We are to be wed on the twenty-first of this month."

Shocked, George struggled to find his voice. "You? You are going to marry Lydia?" he stammered.

"That is correct," Asa announced, puffed up by his own imaginings of grandeur as the savior of Captain George Butler.

George felt the ring burn hot in his pocket. "But you can't," he said.

"And why not?" Asa replied. "It will release you from the grasp of the Blaisdells and that, I would think, should be worth something to you."

George's mind was a muddle of thoughts and emotions. He felt as if he were riding the waves like the ship being tossed beneath him. At one moment, he was despondent at the thought of having to marry Lydia himself. Then resigned to it and seeking the compassion he hoped Nelly could lend him. Then down again when he realized that another had supplanted him.

"And Lydia has agreed to this?" George asked.

Asa laughed scornfully. "Agreed? We hardly gave her the choice, sir. She is but a woman and barely into her womanhood, at that. She needs the guidance of a man. Her father and I both made her aware that this was the best course of action to put an end to all of the troubles. She is resigned to it, if not happy about it."

George shook his head, trying to assemble his thoughts. "And Nelly? Has the spirit continued to appear and ask for me?" His voice was one of almost pleading.

"Alas, no, sir. I'm afraid as soon as you left, the visitations ceased, causing many to believe that once you, the intended audience, were gone, there was no reason to continue the act." He paused for effect. "It also helps me to believe that once Lydia is forced to focus on a husband, and ultimately children, she will no longer be victim to these experiences that seem to plague her when she thinks of you."

He swayed in his chair as the ship rose on the current but still managed to maintain his contrite, humble countenance.

George leaned back in his chair. The spirit, if it were Nelly, had stopped coming. He closed his eyes, trying to make sense of it all.

"Sir?" Asa said. "As I said, I would think my act of charity toward you would be worth something."

George's eyes flew open. He could not deal with this miscreant now. Not with so many emotions flowing through him. "Get out," was all he could think to say.

"Sir?" Asa stammered. "Please, sir, I am doing this for you. For your peace and well-being. Can I not be rewarded for the burden I am releasing you from?"

"Get out!" George thundered, rising violently from his desk. He made as if he were going to lunge at Asa, causing him to lose his balance on the tossing ship and tip over in his chair. His legs sprawled out and his arms flailed about trying to find anything at all to grasp as the ship rose and fell. George stood over him, and Asa saw the rage in his eyes.

"Sir?" was all he could say before he felt George's strong hands grasp him by the collar of his shirt. His feet never touched the floor as George carried him to the still-open doorway. With a heave, George threw him out onto the deck, where he slid a bit before coming to rest against the mast.

"Get off my ship *now*!" George roared, slamming the door to his cabin shut.

Asa struggled to regain his feet. The ship rolled as if sitting on boiling water. He glanced around, hoping that no one had heard George's outburst. Realizing he was still alone, he started to back away toward the railing of the ship. He hefted one leg up and over, balancing himself while straddling the railing. Gripping it with both hands, he looked down at the space between the dock and the ship. He judged it to be a bit more than two feet across. He could see the kelp and seaweed growing thickly along the sides of the dock pilings, their leafy arms waving and lifting as the water roiled around them. Barnacles on the sides of the pilings stood out in stark white contrast to the dark green water below. He shuddered and glanced one more time toward George's cabin. The door was still closed. He had lost his chance. He must go.

He shifted his weight so as to allow him to stretch one leg out toward the dock. Just as he did so, a large swell tossed the ship heavily, raising it violently, and then the retreating tide sucked the ship back down. The ropes strained, and Asa could hear the tension in them. He lost his grip on the railing as the ship shuddered to one side, as if it were literally trying to toss him off. He felt himself falling. His right arm slammed against the edge of the dock as he went down in the very narrow space between the ship and the pilings. He heard the crack and knew it had broken.

With his good arm, he tried to grasp at anything as he felt the cold water wash over his head. He kicked with his legs, trying to raise his head above the water. Breaking the surface, he took in a gulp of air before the ship shifted again and he was pulled under by the current. He dug at the kelp that clung to the pilings, but it was too slippery to offer him any safety. He broke the surface yet again, inhaled again, and spotted one of the tie ropes that had broken off because of the strain placed on it. If he could just reach it, he might survive this. The cold water was beginning to numb him, and he struggled to keep his head above the water as he grabbed at the rope. His right arm hung limply at his side. He clung to the rope with desperation as the tide continued its relentless battle with the ship. Kicking as hard as he could, he shimmied up the rope, trying to get as high as he could. It mattered not, as the water still washed over his head with each passing swell, choking him and leaving him exhausted.

It was then that he heard footsteps above. He heard George close the door to his cabin and proceed across the deck. From his cramped position clinging to the broken rope, he looked up the sides of the ship and could see the daylight above. He watched in horror as George easily laid a plank across the space between the ship and the dock and walked across it. Of course there was a plank. Why hadn't he thought of that? Asa tried to call out to George, but the water rushed over his head at that moment, blocking his view and crushing his lungs with pain. When the water receded again, he looked up and the plank was gone. He knew George was gone as well.

Just then, the ship gave a mighty heave and listed to the dock side. Asa felt the barnacles dig into his back as the weight of the entire ship pressed him against the piling, crushing him. He felt his bones crack with the full weight of the ship. He gasped as pain shot through every inch of his body. His eyes rolled back in his head as he struggled with the last breaths of his life. His grip on the rope loosened and his cheek dragged along the wet kelp as he slid downward. When the ship eased back with the flow of the current, Asa was no longer there. He had been swallowed by the sea.

✦ —————— ✦

George heard the heave of the ship before he actually felt it. The groaning of the timbers and the singing of the taut tie ropes rang out, causing him to stop and turn around as he made his way across the dock toward town.

"God almighty, hold together, girl," he muttered as he watched the ship slam into the dock with the receding swell. The whole dock shook beneath his feet, causing him to stumble slightly. He'd have to send word to Reuben. They couldn't leave her tied there—the risk of damage to his ship and the dock was too great.

"Shall I moor her out, sir?" Reuben suddenly said, appearing from nowhere behind him, as the man was wont to do on occasion.

George jumped at the sound of the man's voice. "Reuben!" he exclaimed. He saw his first mate walking toward him. "Yes, it's probably the best decision. Can you get some men together and get her down there this afternoon?"

"I should be able to," the older man replied. "Are you all right, sir? You look a little distracted."

George looked around, expecting to see Asa still lurking nearby. But there was no sign of the man.

"Mr. Flint was just here," he said. "Didn't you see him?"

Reuben shook his head. "No, sir. I was up at the tavern paying the men and just now headed back here to see if you needed anything else before I left."

"But you should have passed him," George said, looking around again.

Reuben was not the least concerned with the disappearance of the shifty Asa Flint but more focused on why he had been there to begin with. "What did he want this time?"

"His land," George said.

"Did he have proof of the hoax, then?"

"No. He's marrying Lydia," George said, lowering his head and turning to walk away. "Moor up the ship, will you? I'll be at the point."

Stunned, Reuben reached out and grabbed George's arm.

"What do you mean he's marrying Lydia?"

George stopped. "Yes, he's marrying her, in less than two weeks, I believe. He wants the land as a reward for sacrificing himself for my benefit. By marrying her, he believes it will free me from the turmoil of her peculiar ways. He feels that is worth something to me, and he wants to be compensated."

Reuben stormed around the dock, muttering. "He's marrying her? What about the ring? What about the spirit? The spirit said she was to marry you!"

"Well, apparently the spirit stopped appearing shortly after we left. She hasn't been seen since, and that left open the door for Asa and Lydia's father to devise this plan of ending this drama once and for all."

Realization dawned on Reuben at that moment. "Ah, that's it! That damn Abner Blaisdell, he's going to get something from you one way or another, isn't he?" Reuben pushed back his hat so he could see George more clearly. "Look, sir, don't you see it? When they couldn't convince you to marry Lydia based on the so-called appearance of your dead wife telling you to do so, they decided on this second means of extorting you." Exhilarated by his own thoughts, he leaned in close to George. "It's the Blaisdells, sir! They are behind this whole damn thing one way or another!"

George stared at Reuben. He had to maintain stability and composure in this whole situation or he could see it spiraling out of control quickly. "I have thought of that myself," he said. Tossing his head in the direction of his ship, he instructed, "Take her down to the lee side of Bean Island until this storm passes. I'll send word later."

CHAPTER FORTY-SEVEN

Butler's Point

The next morning George sipped his tea slowly as he stood staring out the window toward the east. The sky was a milky gray, the lower-hanging outer clouds of the storm passing off the coast. He could see the Blaisdell property off in the distance, the small house with its attached utility room telescoping off to the south. Closer to the shore was the boathouse built by Atherton Oakes before he died. It was there that Atherton had envisioned building his fishing business with his father-in-law weaving the nets. Atherton was probably the best of that bunch, George thought. And that wasn't saying much. At least he'd had ambition for an honest day's work. What the Blaisdells were trying to accomplish with Lydia was abhorrent. He watched the house closely, wondering what the response had been yesterday when Asa had returned with news of his meeting with George. Would this marriage still take place if they couldn't get the financial compensation they were looking for?

He had talked at length last night with Peter and his mother. He had told them what had transpired between him and Asa. That there was no evidence of a hoax, per se, but that he still felt the Blaisdells were attempting something with this latest pronouncement of a marriage with Lydia and Asa's demand for a reward. His mother had seemed shocked by the realization that they could continue this.

"I truly thought that this marriage between Mr. Flint and Lydia was an attempt by the family to finally settle things down," she had said. "I'm saddened to think there is more to this."

"It's because you don't have an evil thought in your mind, Mother," Peter had told her. "Look, how could we have not suspected something like this to begin with? I've always felt that Abner Blaisdell hides behind his professed Christianity. How else can you explain what has taken place here?" He had pointed at the ring that George had laid out in front of them. "I tell you, they are using the devil to extract financial gain in this life."

The conversation of the night before had left George unable to sleep well. This morning, he had much work to do, and he shook his head to clear his thoughts as he sat down at his father's desk and tried to focus on his ledger books. Shipping was a financial boon for him, but it also required a lot more of his time than just sailing from port to port. As he worked the numbers of his most recent voyage, he stirred in his chair, shifting his weight. He seemed to be on edge, unable to focus on the task in front of him. Tossing his quill aside, he leaned back in his chair and locked his fingers behind his head. He leaned back and closed his eyes. His mind swirled around thoughts of Nelly, and he could see her laughing as they courted and strolled together. He saw her caring for Edna while they were in Bangor. Her joy when she had told him she was with child. And how she struggled to give life to that child, only to have it kill her in the end. He felt a tear trickle down his cheek.

George's thoughts were cut short as the door opened to his father's study and Peter rushed in.

"George!" he exclaimed, planting both hands firmly down on the desk in front of him and leaning forward. "Asa Flint's body was just pulled from the bay."

CHAPTER FORTY-EIGHT

Eastern Side of the Bay

A crowd had gathered to gawk as Reverend Crawford approached. Many of the same folks who just months ago had gathered to listen to the ghost of Nelly Butler were now staring down at the bloated, white body of Asa Flint that lay crumpled upon the rocks.

Have these good people nothing else to fill their time? Reverend Crawford thought.

"Stand aside," someone hissed as the bystanders began to realize he was there. The crowd parted slightly, allowing him to get closer, and he saw Abner Blaisdell standing nearby.

"Abner," he said, tipping his hat slightly.

"Reverend. I'm glad you came."

"What has transpired to cause this?" he asked, looking down at the expression of agony frozen on Asa's face. His eyes were wide open, staring blankly at those around him. He lay somewhat prone, his face pressed into the rocks. His right arm was bent at an ungodly angle behind him. His mouth gaped open, his tongue black and swollen. The back of his muslin shirt was shredded, his shoes were missing, and his stockings had gathered at his ankles. Any amount of bare skin that was exposed was gashed, the flesh torn in places. "It does not look like he came to a peaceful end."

"No, I'm afraid not," Abner muttered. "I last saw him yesterday. He did not return in the evening. I found him here this morning." Abner indicated his nets and the obvious work area nearby.

"I see," Archibald murmured. "Do we have something to cover him with? And we need to send these people home." He looked around at the crowd, seeing even more people making their way down the path toward them. He noted, too, that there was a small rowboat approaching from the western side. Sighing deeply, he called out to the crowd.

"Please go home, people." He waved his arms. "There is no need for you all to be here."

There were murmurs of dissent. Someone called out, "Does he have kin, Reverend? Shouldn't word be sent to someone?"

Archibald looked at Abner, who only shrugged. Turning back to the crowd, he assured them, "I will see that the man has a Christian burial and those he may have left behind are informed. Now please go." He moved toward them, speaking directly to those he recognized, urging them to go back to their daily tasks.

Abner had located a piece of canvas and was laying it over Asa's body just as Peter Butler beached his rowboat nearby. He and George disembarked and walked toward the men.

"Reverend." George shook the man's hand. "The body?" he asked, pointing to the now shrouded corpse.

Archibald nodded. "Abner found him this morning. The tide must have left him."

Abner approached at that moment. "Captain." He acknowledged George. "Did Asa meet with you yesterday?"

Shocked, Archibald turned to look at George. "You met with him?"

"It wasn't a planned meeting. He came to me unannounced," George explained. "But yes, I saw him yesterday." He rubbed the back of his neck. "How did you know that, Abner?"

"Asa was working with me yesterday when we saw your ship enter the bay. He was very animated with the idea of speaking with you regarding his upcoming marriage to my daughter Lydia."

"I see," George replied, glancing back at the canvas. "And did he tell you the nature of his visit to me, specifically?"

Abner kicked at a stone near his feet. "He said he wished to convince you that his marriage to Lydia had financial value to you."

Archibald gasped. "Extortion? Is that what you are saying, Abner?"

"Yes," he admitted, but quickly added, "I tried to talk him out of it. I begged him to leave you alone. To not bring any more attention to our family."

George eyed the man warily, trying to gauge the honesty within his statement.

"Truly, Abner?" he said. "Please forgive me, but for years now your family has been attempting to intertwine itself with mine."

"And yet a man is now dead and you admit you met with him," Abner shot back. "Were you the last to see him alive?"

George bristled at the attack, but before he could respond, Reverend Crawford stepped in.

"Gentleman, enough!" He reached out, placing a hand on each man's shoulder. "Let's just try and find the facts without adding more to this." He turned to George. "When did you see Asa?"

"He came to my ship shortly after we docked. My men had all departed, and I was alone in my cabin when he arrived. He told me of his upcoming marriage to Miss Blaisdell and demanded to be paid for his sacrifice, as he saw it."

"And Abner, this corroborates with your conversation with him?"

Abner nodded.

Reverend Crawford turned back to George. "Did you pay him?"

"Of course not," George scoffed. "I told him I did not care if he married her for my sake or for his. I wasn't paying him for it."

"No, of course not," the reverend replied. "And then he left?"

"Yes," George said. "I indicated that he should leave my cabin, and the last I saw of him he was standing on the deck of my ship when I slammed my cabin door shut."

"And you have no one to confirm this story," Abner sneered.

At this, Peter stepped forward, ready to defend his brother physically if need be.

"Mr. Blaisdell, I take offense if you are insinuating that I had reason or cause to murder this man." George swung his arm toward the canvas heap on the rocks. "I see no benefit to me that he is dead. Living he was of more value to me, as he would have married Lydia and removed that menace from my life." He saw Abner cringe at the description of his daughter.

George turned to address Reverend Crawford. "My first mate, Reuben, can attest to my whereabouts shortly around the time I saw Asa. He returned to the ship so shortly after Mr. Flint's departure that I was surprised he had not passed him on the dock."

Looking at Abner, he continued, "He informed me that he had not seen the man. This indicates to me that wherever Mr. Flint fled to after learning his plan would not be successful, he did so quickly."

Reverend Crawford nodded. He seemed to be satisfied with George's explanation.

"Abner, was there any indication on the body that his end befell him in any way other than drowning?"

"No, sir," he replied. "Drowning it seems to be." Sighing deeply, he glanced back at the body, speaking as if he was very tired from it all. "With his only kin that I knew of being Atherton…" His voice trailed off.

George saw the man's struggle.

"Reverend, get him a decent burial, though nothing more than a pauper's grave," he warned. "Send me the bill. I will take care of it." George stepped back toward the rowboat. "Mr. Blaisdell." He nodded at Abner.

"Thank you, Captain," Abner replied. "I am sorry, sir…" He paused. "For everything."

George did not respond, just walked down toward the water's edge. Peter had already made his way back to the seat in the rowboat. George grasped the vessel by the bow and gave it a mighty shove. It scraped along the gravelly shallows before finally becoming buoyant, and he leapt aboard.

✦———✦

Lydia sat at the window watching Peter Butler row his brother back across the bay. She had seen the crowds gathered along the shore. Everyone wanted to catch a glimpse of the body. Earlier this morning, when she had been collecting the eggs, she had seen her father running up from the direction of the boathouse. He had run all the way to Captain Miller's house next door to share the news and ask that someone send for Reverend Crawford. Coming back, he had told the rest of the family. She had bolted from the house and run down the path herself. He had followed her, yelling for her to stop. That it was not right for her to stare upon a corpse. She didn't care—she had to see him for herself.

She had stopped just short of the body, panting heavily. She saw his eyes. They were staring right at her. His mouth was grotesquely open. It was like she could hear him screaming at her. She had to look away from his face. Her attention focused instead on the one hand she could see. She remembered the way his hands had gripped her and held her that day, preventing her from escaping him. Now one of them lay with the flesh torn away. The whole palm of his hand was bloody and raw, as if it had been chewed by some creature of the sea. He clearly had drowned, and it had been a violent drowning. In addition to the wounded hand, his other arm appeared to be broken. She saw the scrapes along his back and several of his bones sticking through the puffy, bloated flesh beneath his tattered shirt. They were small bones, with just the ends jutting out. They must be his ribs.

"Lydia! Get back from there, child!" her father hollered. Grasping her by the arm, he pulled her away and made her go back to the house. "It is not well for you to see that."

Now, as she watched George disembark from the small boat on the opposite side of the shore and walk back toward the main house, she spoke her thoughts out loud.

"He is gone. You are here. She will come."

CHAPTER FORTY-NINE

Just as Lydia had predicted, the spirit resumed her visitations almost immediately upon Asa's death and George's return. The crowds again gathered in the utility room attached to the Blaisdells' kitchen. The knockings announced the coming appearance of the spirit, and she again instructed those gathered to bring George to her. As the visitations increased in frequency, Lydia became more and more drained by the experiences. So, too, did her family. The increase in visitors again began to tax the meager resources of the Blaisdells. For the next three weeks, well into the first part of May, visitors came from far afield. With spring and the increase in shipping traffic, word spread faster from port to port aboard the ships leaving Franklin.

George met with David Hooper, conferring on the changing situation across the bay. The Hoopers were still adamant that neither family acknowledge the spirit or anything that was being gossiped about regarding Nelly or Lydia. But George knew that soon, he would have to act.

He had not informed Peter of his decision but asked him to accompany him to the Hoopers'. There he would discuss with him and Nelly's father the decision he had made. As the two men slowly cantered their horses along the main street of Franklin, George heard someone call out to him.

"Mr. Butler! George Butler!" the voice rang out.

Turning in his saddle, he saw a finely dressed woman step into the street and head toward him. As the woman got closer, he recognized her.

"Peter, hold up," he said, reining in his horse and dismounting in a quick motion. Reaching the woman in just a few steps, he removed his hat as a sign of respect for her. "Mrs. Giddings," he said.

He was totally taken aback to see Nelly's friend and mentor from Bangor. It was while working with Lucy Giddings that Nelly had come to find Edna.

"George," the woman said, leaning in to allow him to plant a brief kiss on her cheek. "I was just asking someone how to find you." She indicated the group of women still standing clustered together at the side of the street.

"Well, here I am." He smiled at her. "But why are you here in Franklin?"

She leaned in close to him, whispering. "Word came to Bangor last week of a fantastical ghost story." She stopped when she saw George shudder noticeably. She placed her hand on his arm. "I'm sorry, I don't mean to upset you."

"No, no," he said, trying to reassure her and hide his feelings better. "It's fine. I just didn't realize word of that would have gotten as far as Bangor."

"Well, it has, and when I heard Nelly's name associated with it, I knew I had to come here myself." Leaning in again, she whispered, "Is it true? Is it her?"

"I do not know, Lucy," he said.

"So you have not seen this spirit for yourself?" She seemed shocked by this piece of news.

"No, personally, I have not seen the spirit. I have only been told that it speaks and asks for me."

"I see," she said, glancing down a bit. "I remember Nelly telling me you were reluctant to return home because of a young girl. It was this Lydia person wasn't it?" When George nodded in agreement she continued. "I intend to call on the Blaisdells this afternoon." She again indicated the group of women behind her. "I have a near relation in these parts who has let me stay with her and says she can introduce me to them." She took a breath and stood a bit taller. "I know Nelly as if she were my own daughter, bless her heart. If this spirit is really her, I will know."

"I'm sure you would," he said, smiling. "If you'll excuse me now, I do have business to attend to."

"Oh yes, please, do not let me delay you." She touched his arm again. "It was good to see you, George, you look well."

"Thank you," he replied, touching the brim of his hat slightly. Placing his foot back in his stirrup, he easily swung his leg over the horse and mounted with grace. "I hope you find what you are looking for at the Blaisdells." He slapped the reins on his horse slightly before he pulled away from her.

She returned to the group of ladies, shaking her head.

"He is very sad," she said to the women. "Very, very sad." She watched him and Peter ride out of sight. "I hope this doesn't destroy him."

✦———✦

George and Peter sat with David Hooper in chairs on the front porch of his home. George remembered sitting on the porch in those early days with Nelly, on days just like today.

"So what brings you all the way out this way?" David asked the men. "Your mother is well, I hope?"

"Oh yes," Peter quickly responded. "She's fine. Everyone in the family is fine." Looking at George, he waited for him to respond.

"David," George said, inhaling deeply, "I came out today because I've made a decision and I wanted to inform you of it first."

"And that decision is?" David asked.

"I'm going to the Blaisdells." He watched as both his brother and David registered shock on their faces. "I've thought about it, and I feel it is best that I confront this specter. To see it for myself and decide what to do from there."

Outraged, David stood up. "Are you turning your back on us, George?" he asked. "Willing to forget we consider you family and allow yourself to be submerged into some kind of trickery!"

"I'm not turning my back on you, David," George pleaded.

"Yes, you are," the older man replied. "We agreed to present a united front. That both of our families would stay above all of this and let the Blaisdells drag themselves through the mud. If you go there, George, you will be acknowledging their trickery. Giving it merit and validation."

George placed his elbows on his knees and hung his head forward. He heard Peter scrape back his chair and stand.

"George," he said, "I'm afraid I agree with David on this. You absolutely cannot go there."

George reached into his breast pocket and grasped the ring before pulling it out slowly. Opening his hand, he let it lie flat on his upraised palm for both of the men to see.

Peter plucked it from his hand. "What is this?" he asked.

"The posset ring. From our wedding." Speaking barely above a whisper, he added, "Read the inscription."

Peter tilted it, saw the writing, and then handed the ring slowly to David, who did the same.

"How did you come by this again, George?" David asked, recalling the last time he had seen the ring.

"Father had it," George said.

"He gave it to me as he lay dying." George stared at David directly. "He said Nelly had given it to him." He paused for effect. "After she had passed away."

David was still holding the ring as he stared at George.

"I'm not turning my back on you, David. On you or anyone else in your family or mine." He glanced at Peter. "But I can no longer believe this is trickery on the part of the Blaisdells. I've begun to accept that whatever is driving this whole situation is far greater than any of us." Swallowing hard, he continued. "And I have got to see this spirit for myself."

"And do what?" Peter interjected. "If you take that step, George, are you also willing to marry Lydia Blaisdell if you believe the specter is real?"

George remained silent, staring vacantly out at the meadows that surrounded the Hooper's property.

His silence enraged David. He handed the ring back to George. "Maybe I can't explain that ring. But I can tell you I in no way believe that God allowed my daughter to die so that she could then reappear in the house of the Blaisdells and tell you to marry Lydia." He shook his head. "That I cannot accept. And if it's not of God, it's certainly of the devil." His face was red with anger now. "And if it's of the devil, I will not support any of it. Do you understand that?" he pressed George. "Is your mind set on this course of action?" he asked.

George turned back toward his former father-in-law. He remembered how much his own father had admired David Hooper. How they had served together in the war and come to this bay together, the two men struggling to build this community through sacrifice and hard work until they were two of the most prominent men in the area. And the joy when the two families were united in the marriage of their children. Was he willing to disrespect all of that for what he felt he was being compelled to accept?

Standing up, he placed the ring back in his pocket. "My mind is set, David. I'm going to see it for myself."

The two men stood facing each other for a moment. David turned toward Peter, his eyes showing the sadness he felt deep in his heart. "Give my best to your mother, Peter," he said. Turning to face George again, all he said was, "Get out," before he stepped off the porch and walked away.

CHAPTER FIFTY

Blaisdell Home

A large group had assembled in the Gathering Room, as Lydia now called it. She avoided the area, staying mostly upstairs in her room. She had pulled up a chair to the only window in the room and opened the glass to let in the fresh spring air. It was here that she first spotted George approaching. He walked slowly, unaccompanied, and carried nothing with him. He made his way along the path that had previously been narrow and winding, but now, due to the increase in visitors, it was wider, and people could walk two abreast.

Sucking in her breath at the sight of him, she rushed from the room and quickly descended the stairs, grasping at the banister to catch herself so she wouldn't tumble the whole way down. She tore into the kitchen, where she found her mother.

"He's coming!" she blurted out.

"Who's coming?" Mary asked, concerned that Lydia was suffering from another visitation.

"Captain Butler," Lydia said breathlessly. "He's coming down the path!"

"Oh my!" her mother said. "Quick, go get your father. He's down at the boathouse." She pushed Lydia out the side door of the kitchen. Smoothing her apron and running her fingers through the sides of her hair, she stepped into the hallway. She walked slowly toward the door, waiting for the knock she knew would come. But when it did, she jumped nonetheless. Reaching for the doorknob, she turned it and opened the door slowly.

"Mrs. Blaisdell," George said politely.

"Captain." She nodded demurely.

"May I speak with your husband?" he asked.

"Yes, of course." She stepped aside to allow him entrance into the hallway. "Please wait here." She indicated that he should take a seat in the small room adjacent to the doorway.

It was the very room he had been in on his last visit to their home—when Lydia had collapsed into a fit and objects had flown around the room. He eyed the candlesticks warily as he chose a seat close to the doorway. Shortly, although it seemed to him to be hours, Abner entered the room followed closely by Lydia.

George rose, nodding at Lydia. Abner walked into the room, taking the seat opposite from George. Lydia quietly slipped into a chair off to the side.

"Captain Butler," Abner said, "I must say I am surprised to see you in my home."

George took a deep breath. "Abner, I'm here to see the spirit, if possible." He swallowed, looking at Lydia. "I'd like to settle this problem once and for all."

Abner thought for a moment before speaking. "The spirit does not appear on demand. I have no control over its visit. If you are insinuating otherwise, you would be gravely mistaken."

"No, I understand," George replied. "I am not accusing you of anything, Abner." He sighed heavily, and Lydia could see his shoulders rise and fall with the effort. "I've come to see if what appears here is truly my wife."

"And if you begin to believe for yourself that it is truly Nelly, then what? Are you prepared to follow the directions of the spirit?"

George glanced at Lydia. Her face was partially hidden from his view by her hair, but he could see she had turned a bright crimson.

"Yes," he said quietly.

Lydia felt her blood surge. She thought for sure that she would faint, slip from her chair, and lie sprawled on the floor in front of the captain. She didn't dare look at him and kept her eyes turned downward.

"Then your intentions are of one seeking the truth?" Abner continued to prod him.

George nodded.

"Then you are free to wait here with everyone else." He rose from his chair. "Please, follow me."

George rose as well but indicated that Lydia should exit the room before him.

"Please," he said, bowing slightly to allow her to pass by him.

"Thank you, sir," she said quietly.

"Please, there is no need for so much formality now," he whispered. "You may call me George."

She nodded. "All right. George," she said, almost choking on the word but giving him a small smile.

They both followed Abner down the hallway and through the kitchen. George observed that Hannah and Mary were both present there. He nodded slightly at each of them.

Crossing the kitchen, Abner stepped down into the Gathering Room and George followed. The light chatter ceased as soon as he and Lydia entered. There were several gasps as people in the room recognized him. Abner spoke to the crowd.

"Everyone, as you can see, Captain Butler has joined us. I ask that despite this turn of events, you all continue to wait humbly upon the spirit."

A gentleman along the wall stood immediately and offered George his chair. "Sir," he said as he rose.

George stepped slowly across the room, taking the seat offered to him. After settling himself, he began to take note of those around him. Immediately, he recognized several people from church meetings. So the God-fearing were here. But he also saw some of the more tawdry members of their community—those who were quick to share this story far and wide, he was sure. He noticed, too, that Lydia did not sit down. Instead, she stood near the doorway, watching him. He felt himself shrink a bit under her gaze.

"Welcome, George," the woman seated next to him said, and he realized for the first time it was Lucy Giddings, who he had encountered in Franklin the day before. Smiling at him, she whispered, bubbling over with excitement. "I'm glad you are here, for it is truly her, George, truly." She reached out and pressed his hand.

"You have seen her?" he asked.

"Yes." She nodded enthusiastically. "Just yesterday, she appeared after I arrived in the afternoon." Her eyes filled with tears. "She knew me, George, she truly knew me. Spoke my name directly."

George felt a sudden burst of fear. Although he was quite certain he was prepared to see the spirit and try to determine if it was, in fact, Nelly, the thought had never entered his mind that the spirit would know him and call him out.

"How wonderful for you, Lucy," he managed to choke out.

She patted his hand some more. "It will be fine, George, you'll see. Just rest your mind and be prepared."

He leaned back against the wall, closing his eyes and trying to block out the attention that he knew was focused on him. He could hear the slow murmurs of conversation. As his mind began to slow down, his thoughts stopped racing and he could feel his breathing slowing. It was then that he noticed the inexplicable feeling that permeated the room. It was of a higher kind, a deep, engulfing feeling that seemed to encompass all of mankind—a sense of calm and peace like none he had ever experienced before.

He wasn't exactly sure how long he had sat there. Maybe he had drifted off to sleep, he couldn't exactly tell. But suddenly, he felt as if he had been pulled back to the interior of the room, jolted back to awareness. There had been a knocking. It was very loud, but he couldn't quite tell where it came from, just that it filled the room with its presence.

Lucy leaned toward him. "It's starting."

George first sensed that the knocking was from under the floor directly beneath him. He lifted his feet in response to it. Then he heard the knocking coming from the wall across from him. It banged there loudly, echoing within his ears. Then it quickly shifted and came from the wall to his left, the one that was shared with the kitchen. The sound was loud enough, but he also noticed the weaving shuttles that were tacked there rattle and shake from the vibration of it. He no sooner registered that the sound was indeed coming from that direction when it seemed to jump across the room, coming from near the doorway that led outside on his right, startling the gentleman who had just entered that way and still held the doorknob in his hand.

Just as quickly, the sound returned to beneath his feet and then shot out again to encircle the room. Round and round the sounds came, picking up speed in their repetition so that he could no longer follow them. The knockings were encircling the whole room in a rapid-fire succession of sound. It was when the knockings appeared to be at their zenith that George saw Lydia enter the room.

The first thing he noticed about her was that she stared blankly straight ahead. Her eyes held an eerie, vacant look, and her face was exceedingly pale. She stepped down into the room and walked forward until she stood directly in front of George. The knockings ceased the minute she approached him. Everyone in the room appeared to be holding their breath. George shifted slightly in his chair, unsure of what was about to happen.

"He has come."

In the stillness that filled the room after the knockings had stopped, the sound of the voice made George jump in his seat. Lucy reached out and touched his arm in reassurance. He stared at Lydia, but she had not spoken it. He had not seen her lips move, but even if they had, he was certain it was not her voice. It didn't sound like a normal voice. It tinkled, like crystals, but was hushed and delicate like one would imagine the breath of an angel. Otherworldly was the only way he could describe it.

"Who has come, spirit?" It was Abner. He was standing in the doorway to the kitchen and spoke out into the room.

"George Butler."

George felt the sound of his name wash over him. He had no idea that sound could make a physical impression, but this did—he actually felt as if the sound were brushing against his skin. It wrapped around him like a veil, sheer and airy. He closed his eyes as he felt it, as if by removing the sense of sight, he could focus more on the feeling of the sound. And what a feeling it was! Never in his life had he felt anything like this. He was completely and utterly at peace.

"Who are you, spirit? What is your name?" Abner asked.

George watched as Lydia, still standing in front of him, began to move. Slowly, her arms rose slightly from her sides until they were outstretched, her palms turned outward in a gesture of supplication.

"I am Nelly Butler. I was once the wife of George Butler."

Again, Lydia's mouth did not move, and her eyes continued to stare blankly ahead. George was not even sure she could see him.

"Speak to her, George," Lucy said, nudging him.

George opened his mouth, but he could not form a word. He could not speak. Shaking his head, he tried to maintain his composure. As if reading his mind, the voice spoke again.

"Fear not, George. It is truly I."

George saw a pinpoint of light appear to Lydia's left. It hovered near the ceiling before growing in size and bouncing slightly up and down until it was at shoulder height. Suddenly, it appeared to burst right in front of him. He flinched and covered his face to shield himself from the brilliance of it. The light filled the entire room, startling everyone. Several of the women shrieked. The man who had entered through the rear door just as the knockings started bolted out.

George looked up and saw a shower of iridescent sparks falling upon him, but when he held out his hands to feel them, nothing was there. When the light receded, what remained was the vision of a woman, dressed all in white, her bare feet showing delicately beneath her dress. She hovered still, no more than a foot or two off the floor. Her hair fell loosely around her face, but when she lifted her head to look at George, what he saw made him suck in his breath.

It appeared to be Nelly in every sense. Her eyes were just as he remembered them when they had gotten married. That blissful way she gazed at him filled with so much love and joy at the thought of being his wife. He saw the curve of her beautiful, tender lips and remembered how they felt when he kissed her. She tilted her head in that way that Nelly often did when they were alone and she spoke softly to him, the way a wife does, as if no one else were in the room with them.

"Can you see that I am who I say I am?"

"Yes." The word escaped his lips without his realizing it. Tears ran down his face as he was overcome by the grief that had been hidden within him. He stood, walking toward her, wanting to feel her, to hold his wife one more time. "Nelly," he sobbed, but as his hand reached into the light that surrounded her, he felt it burn, and he pulled back quickly.

"You cannot touch me, George," she said, "for I am not with you any longer."

Recoiling from the sting of the burn, he cried out as he collapsed back in his chair. "Why do you come?" he exclaimed, rubbing his temples with his hands. "Here of all places," he said, gesturing around at the room full of people. He looked up at her, pleading. "Why have you not come to me when I am alone?" He dropped his shoulders, angered that his emotions were being revealed in so public a setting. "I have wanted you. I've needed you. Why do you not come to me privately?" he sobbed, hanging his head.

The vision moved from the center of the room toward where he sat until it was mere inches from him. Within the light, Nelly appeared to kneel in front of him, crossing her hands upon her chest in a gesture of earnest pleading.

"George." Her voice dripped with the love she had for him and was full of compassion for his suffering. "I am but a servant to a power greater than us all."

George raised his head to look at her. "And what is the purpose of these visits, Nelly?" he asked, knowing full well what the answer to his question was going to be.

Nelly rose from her kneeling position and floated back to where Lydia still stood motionless in the room. As if inhaling, the light that surrounded Nelly lifted her higher until she hovered close to the ceiling. All eyes looked up at her.

"Lydia Blaisdell is to be the wife of George Butler." She spoke outwardly to all of those in the room, spreading her arms wide before looking down upon George. "Do you accept this?"

Every eye in the room turned to George.

Adrift and helpless against this power he felt had taken control over his life, George gave the only answer he felt he could.

Quietly he whispered, "I will."

And with those words, Lydia collapsed in a heap in front of him. Instinctively, he bolted from his chair and rushed to her side.

"Come," Nelly spoke from above them. "Leave her there." Looking up, George watched as the light descended downward and moved toward the rear door. "I must walk among you without Lydia so that all will know that it is not she that declares this."

With that, the rear door swung open as if by a gust of wind and the vision departed. Quickly, everyone stood and followed her out into the bright spring sunshine. George hovered over Lydia's body for a moment before Abner approached him.

"Go. I will stay with her," he said. "Go!"

His urgency startled George. Rising, he followed the rest of the group outside. Even in the sunshine, the vision of Nelly could be seen with the same intense brightness as it had displayed in the Gathering Room. Nelly had instructed everyone to form a line behind her, and all of those in attendance stood two abreast behind her.

"Send George to me."

All eyes turned on George, who stood alone in the Blaisdells' side yard.

"Come," she said, reaching out one hand as if she would hold his hand in her grasp.

He walked to the head of the line and took his place beside her. She began to move forward, walking along the shore path toward the center of Franklin. George glanced down and noticed that although her legs moved as if she were walking, her feet did not touch the ground and the grasses remained untouched with the passing of her gown.

They first began to encounter other people not far from Captain Miller's house. Mrs. Miller was hanging laundry on her line when the group passed. She paused, the wash all but forgotten, a clothespin dropping from her grasp. Lifting her skirts, she ran back toward the house.

"James! James!" she hollered, rushing inside. Soon, her husband joined her in the yard as the procession stopped directly in front of them.

"I was once Nelly Butler. Hear me." The spirit spread out her arms wide. "Lydia Blaisdell is to be the wife of George Butler."

George felt like shrinking as he realized James was stepping toward him.

"George!" he thundered. "What is the meaning of this spectacle?"

Stammering, George looked upon his friend. "You can see it for yourself, James." He sighed deeply. "I have no explanation."

"James!" his wife shouted from the porch, waving an arm frantically. "Get back from there!" She was clearly frightened.

Captain Miller stared hard at the vision of Nelly.

She spoke to him directly. "So that all may know," she said, smiling at him.

Scoffing, Captain Miller spit on the ground in front of George.

"Either you have lost your senses, George, or you have given in to the devil." He grabbed George by the arm. "Which is it?"

George remained expressionless as he replied. "I don't believe it's either, James. But I'm powerless to stop it."

With that, the vision of Nelly began to move forward. The group following her continued to do so, but George could go no farther. He stepped aside and let them all pass. James eyed him warily.

"What has happened to you, George?" James said.

George looked at his friend intently before answering. "James." His voice cracked a bit, and he cleared his throat before he resumed. "James, you saw her. It's truly her, don't you think?"

"For the love of God, man!" his friend said. "What have they done to you?"

"But you saw her. She spoke to you. It's her."

"No. No, it's not, George." James reached up and grabbed him by both shoulders, shaking him hard. "Those damn Blaisdells have somehow concocted one hell of a trick. I don't know how they have done it, but it's a trick, George! A trick. You cannot let them deceive you like this."

George slumped in his friend's grasp, exhausted from the ordeal of it all. His legs buckled beneath him. James tightened his grip to keep George from completely falling to the ground.

"Christ almighty," he exclaimed. "I've got to get you home."

James rowed George across the bay to Butler's Point. He met with George's mother and told her what little he knew of the goings-on at the Blaisdell house. He informed her that he had seen the specter himself.

"Mrs. Butler," he said quietly after George had been put to bed, "I cannot explain it, but I do not believe it one bit."

"Well, how could one?" she replied.

It was a tale that had now become too fantastical to be believed.

<hr />

The procession led by Nelly's spirit had continued into Franklin after departing the Miller house. Later, reports would state she had walked over a mile in broad daylight with up to one hundred people seeing her. Reverend Crawford had stood in his own doorway and watched as the procession marched by his home. The sight of it had frightened him. Not because of the specter—he had already seen her for himself—but because of what this meant for his community. This was no longer contained within the walls of the Blaisdells' home. This was now out in the open for all to see, even for those who wanted no part of it. What troubled him the most was that this vision of Nelly proceeded alone, without Lydia. Ever since the first reports of the visions had emerged, talk had centered on Lydia being the conduit. The people who felt it wasn't a hoax—and there was still considerable disagreement about that—felt that Lydia was in some way instrumental in providing the portal for this ghostly appearance from another realm. Yet here walked the ghost of Nelly Butler, speaking to believers and nonbelievers alike, without Lydia present.

Lucy Giddings was among those in the group who had followed the vision of Nelly into Franklin that day. She had returned to Bangor shortly after, taking her tale with her. So it was not surprising when a week later, Reverend Crawford found the story featured in a recent broadsheet, *The Whig & Courier*, published out of Bangor. There in bold type were the words: "Pause reader, and consider a few moments, what evidence would convince you of the existence of a specter?" The story was spreading like wildfire.

He read it all with increasing concern. Captain George Butler's life would never be the same.

CHAPTER FIFTY-ONE

Nelly's sister, Sally Wentworth, could feel her anger rising with each turn of the carriage wheels.

"Moses, can you please drive faster?" she asked her husband. The man remained silent but did tap the reins lightly on the rump of the black mare so that she increased her pace a bit. As the carriage drew into the clearing at Butler's Point, he finally spoke.

"Sally, just be patient."

As soon as the carriage stopped, she disembarked without any assistance. She turned and looked at him. "The time for patience has passed, Moses." Gathering up her skirts, she walked briskly toward the front door. Before she could even knock to make her presence known, George's mother opened the door.

"Sally!" she exclaimed. "What a surprise. Come in, come in." Sarah swung the door wide open as Sally, followed by the reluctant Moses, entered.

"I'm here to see George," Sally blurted out. "And I'm afraid my visit is not a pleasant one today, Mrs. Butler."

Clasping her hands together in front of her, Sarah remarked, "There isn't much pleasant in any of our lives lately. Please come in and be seated." She led them through into the next room. Sally perched on the edge of a finely carved settee while Moses stood resolutely nearby. "I'll get George," Sarah said.

Within a few moments, George entered, shutting the door behind him. Nodding at Moses, he turned his gaze upon Sally.

"I know why you have come," he said quietly.

"I'm sure you do!" Sally thundered at him. "George, your name is on the lips of everyone from here to Boston and possibly beyond—and with it, the name of my sister. Do you know the dishonor you have brought to us all?"

For the next several minutes, George sat silently as Sally berated him for going to the Blaisdells' home after both families had agreed to remain silent and ignore the issue. She told him how her father had been plunged into a state of melancholy after George's visit a few days ago, and they were doing their best to shield him from this latest dramatic turn of events.

"So you are to marry Lydia Blaisdell?" she asked him point-blank. "That is what we are hearing. That you spoke it in a room full of people. Is it true?"

George raised his head to look at her. "I am only doing what Nelly asked me to do."

Sally bolted from the settee. "How dare you speak of my sister in that way!" she cried, coming at him. Moses stepped forward and grabbed her. He held her fast, preventing her from getting to George. "Nelly is dead, George. She is dead. She could not have told you anything of the sort."

"That's not true, Sally. You have not seen what I have seen." His voice softened. "I beheld her with my own eyes. It was the very likeness of her. She spoke to me in the same manner that she had when she was with us." He swallowed hard, trying to find the words to help Sally understand. "It was more than just seeing her, Sally. It was a feeling. There is a feeling around her that convinces you of the truthfulness of the things you are seeing."

Sally wiggled free from Moses. "Let go of me," she exclaimed with irritation. Moses removed his arms from around her but did not move away.

"You've been duped, George. Tricked. Coerced. I don't know how it's being done, and at this point, I no longer care. I'm just here to try and get you to see reason. You cannot marry Lydia Blaisdell."

George could see how visibly upset Sally was by this. Her hands shook, whether in rage or in fear, he wasn't sure. He reached out, taking both of her hands in his.

"I have seen things you have not, Sally. I have spoken with my wife. Do you hear me? My wife. She has told me I must do this. Nelly said she is only a servant of the one who directs this. I don't completely understand what is happening or why. I only know that I can no longer fight it." He saw her facial expression change from one of anger to one of frustration.

"So Nelly told you to marry a child? For she is but a child, George. How old is she? Twelve? Thirteen at the most?"

"She's fifteen," he replied. "Certainly old enough to marry, but that's not the point. Sally, please come to the Blaisdell house. See Nelly for yourself."

Sally yanked her hands away from George's grasp. "I most certainly will not! I will not be a party to any of this."

Sighing, George walked to the door and opened it. "Then we have nothing further to discuss."

Shocked, Sally replied, "So you will not change your mind?"

"No," was all he said. He looked from her to Moses and then to the door.

Moses reached out and touched his wife's arm. "Come, Sally. We are finished here."

Sally smoothed her skirts slightly and then reached for the bonnet she had discarded on the settee. She followed Moses out the doorway but paused as she stood in front of George.

"Your father would be so disappointed in you, George," she spat out. "So very disappointed."

After she had walked through the door, George slammed it hard behind her. Leaning his head against it, he pounded his fist several times against the hard oak. He felt the tears warm against his cheeks.

He felt absolutely powerless to stop the storm that was gathering around them all.

CHAPTER FIFTY-TWO

Over the next several days, George's decision to marry Lydia Blaisdell set an already divided community on fire. It was proving to
be such a problem that Reverend Crawford finally sent word by letter
to his friend and mentor Reverend Abraham Cummings in Freeport.

May 8, 1800

My Dear Sir,

In my last correspondence with you, your judgment was most helpful in providing relief to a very difficult problem that had surfaced among my flock. I am therefore encouraged to ask your further attention in an affair that has developed from the same source.

I speak of the family of Abner Blaisdell, specifically his youngest daughter, Lydia, who you will recall was suffering from what we perceived to be at that time a possession of some sort. I heeded your advice and was pleased to see great results.

Currently, the same young woman has begun to exhibit other manifestations. Some call it the Blaisdell Specter, others the Ghost of Nelly Butler. In any event, they are one and the same, and word has flown from here in Franklin with such speed and veracity that one can only imagine how far this tale has been spun. If you have not already heard of this, I'm sure you will shortly.

I myself have witnessed this spirit. I have seen it with my own eyes and heard it speak. It proclaims that young Lydia is to be married to Captain George Butler, a well-to-do seafarer from a prominent family. The captain has agreed to follow the promptings of this spirit. Many in my community are of the opinion that the good man has been deceived by trickery, while others hold still that this is truly direction from the unseen world, if not from God directly.

In the ensuing weeks since the first proclamation by this spirit, Captain Butler's reputation has been made to suffer. And yet, I perceive that my own may also perish along with his, as I am of the side that believes this is a communication from beyond our understanding. I feel that the Blaisdell family is being unjustly censured along with those who vindicate them.

I seek your advice in this matter. If I were to preach from the pulpit on my belief in the truthfulness of this spirit, I fear I would lose half my congregation. However, if I continue to avoid taking a stand on this vital spiritual matter among these people, I risk losing the other half.

Yours in the service of our Lord,
Reverend Archibald Crawford

CHAPTER FIFTY-THREE

George strolled down to the water's edge. Looking out across the bay to the Blaisdell property, he felt a shudder run through him as he thought of all that had taken place in the past few weeks. He needed to clear his head and try thinking some of this through. Turning, he walked along the shore, carefully picking his way over the granite and avoiding the slippery rocks covered in seaweed. In time, he found himself within sight of Bean Island, and he could see his ship, still moored on the leeward side—silent, unmanned, and almost forgotten in the rush of events that had taken place since he had returned home. He sat down on the rocks and stared at her. Her dark brown decking stood out in contrast to the deep greens of the hemlocks, spruce, and pines that covered the island. She sat on water that was almost still at this time of the morning. A few seagulls had perched on the boom, and he thought first of the droppings that would need to be swabbed up. Then he realized he had no idea what the future would hold for the ship—or for himself, for that matter.

He was going to marry Lydia. That he had come to realize. There would be no large wedding gathering like he had had with Nelly. Something of that nature was not appropriate in this situation. But after that, he was unsure about everything. He could not leave Lydia and return to sea. He could not leave her here to face all the repercussions herself. He would have to stay in Franklin with her. Where would they live? He could not see his mother allowing Lydia to reside at Butler's Point with the rest of the family. Nor would Lydia feel comfortable there. He had sold his land up near the pond to Peter. So that was no longer available. He had thought about returning to Bangor, but his reputation was now in tatters. Entering into business again was out of the question. His judgement would consistently be questioned. And thoughts of Nelly and Edna were too raw in that place. He could not build a life with a second family there.

A second family. The thought of it made him shake his head. Marrying Lydia also meant fulfilling all aspects of his role as husband to her. As much as he told himself she was old enough to be married, she was still a developing young woman. Would he be able to find her desirable? Or would he forever see her as the child he knew she was? Could he follow through with all of this? Picking up a stone, he threw it with a heave out into the water with all the power of his frustrations behind it.

"Be at peace, George."

He had heard a voice speak to him. Spinning around to see who had approached from behind him, he saw no one. He looked up and down the rock-strewn beach, and still there was no one who could have spoken. He looked out over the water, sensing that maybe someone was approaching that way, and again, there was no one. Then he saw it—a brilliance of light against the dark greens of the island. It was a small orb, about the size of a pumpkin, hovering over the water just off the stern of his ship. Suddenly, it bounced along quickly, skipping over the water like a stone but leaving no ripple. Before he could even register that it had changed locations, it hovered directly in front of him.

What he noticed first was that there was a slight hum to it, like the sound of the rushing wind and yet almost undetectable. It was perfectly circular in nature, and its surface was smooth and glassy. From within it swirled light that shimmered and reflected hues of pink, blue, and green, like a rainbow had exploded inside of it and was in constant motion.

He reached up his hands, cupping them and placing them gently underneath the orb. It settled slowly within his grasp, and he held it there for several minutes. Almost immediately, he felt an intense sensation run through his whole body—not physical in nature, but deeper. It was a spiritual experience that left him feeling the same sense of love and acceptance he had felt within the room at the Blaisdells'.

The orb rose again from his palms, and as it did so it grew bigger until George began to see the form of a woman within it. He easily recognized it as Nelly, not that he was expecting anything different at this point. But surprisingly as her shape became clearer, he noticed she held a baby in her arms. She was dressed in the same white dress he had seen her in before, and the child lay cuddled against her, swaddled in a white winding-sheet.

"Behold your son," Nelly said to him, looking down at the child with utter devotion.

George stood to get a better look at the baby. The child appeared to be sleeping, his eyes closed, his long eyelashes lying against his cheeks.

"He sleeps," George muttered. "But did he ever wake?" He thought of Nelly's agony as she labored to bring the child forth. He had never known if the child that died within her was a son or a daughter.

"He woke in the service of his God," was her reply.

Just then, George saw another personage begin to form within the orb. Smaller, but also dressed in white, it stood beside Nelly. He saw her look down past the baby in her arms and see the child who stood near her. It was Edna. Her blond curls shone like gold and bounced as she tilted her head and gave George a smile that nearly broke his heart.

He tried to reach out to her, but as he did the orb encircling them lifted just out of his reach.

"Please, Nelly," he begged her. "Please, cannot I not touch her? You?" He choked down sobs as he looked at his son. "Him?"

" 'Tis not to be," she replied.

The orb settled back down as George leaned against the rock in supplication. His sadness engulfed him completely, and he sobbed. His family stood before him. The vision of all that he had had in all the world. All that he had lost so quickly.

"You must build another," Nelly told him.

"Another family?" he asked her.

"Yes," she replied. "With Lydia."

George sighed heavily. "Is it that you know my thoughts, Nelly?" he said, thinking of his earlier concerns.

" 'Tis your duty," she said as George hung his head.

"My duty?" he asked her, his voice husky with the shame of it. "Is it not enough that I have lost everything that was dear to me in this world?" He gazed again upon sweet little Edna, who smiled and hid slightly behind Nelly's skirts. "My reputation has been shredded. My very character is in question in some quarters. The banks are calling in my notes out of fear that I've lost my mind and will not repay them. I am afforded no credit anywhere now Nelly. I am judged as a mad man. I've lost the respect of my family and of your own family. I'm nearly ruined." He took a deep breath. "Must I also lie with her and complete my destruction?"

"You must fulfill your part."

"My part in what, Nelly?" he cried out. "Please speak to me as you once did. I cannot tolerate one-sentence answers anymore. Talk to me. Explain to me what is happening." He grabbed at the seagrass that lay near him, ripping it from the ground in his frustration.

"Do not lay your heart upon things of this world," was her reply. "It matters not the thoughts of men."

He watched then as the orb began to shrink away. Leaning forward, he crawled across the stones, trying to reach her.

"Nelly, please. Wait! Please don't take them!" he cried.

The orb lifted higher until he almost lost sight of it against the blue sky. He heard a loud rushing sound and then the words "It is to be so." And then it blinked out and was gone.

George rose, and in his anger, he kicked at the loose stones near him. "Aargh!" he yelled out, the sound of his voice echoing back at him. He spun around and tore his way back up the shoreline. Running, he made it back to the point and leapt into the rowboat tied to the shore. He pulled hard on the oars, trying to release his anger with each stroke. He felt the boat beach near the dock in town. In long strides, he covered the distance to Reverend Crawford's house, where he found the older man just stepping off his porch.

"Captain?" he exclaimed, shocked by George's disheveled and harried countenance. "Is everything all right?"

"I must marry her today," he blurted out.

"Today? You want to marry Lydia today?"

"Yes." He sat down on the steps at the man's feet. "There is no reason to wait. I am ruined already. Waiting will not correct that." He looked up at Archibald. "Nelly has appeared to me."

"Without Lydia present?" the reverend asked.

"Yes, just now. Farther down the shore." He pointed in the direction he had just come from. "She had Edna with her," he sobbed.

Archibald squatted down beside him. "Oh, George."

"And my son." He choked on the words. "My son, Reverend." He looked at Archibald with so much sadness the man's heart almost broke for him. "She held my son."

"I'm sorry. It's so hard to be reminded of one's loss," he said.

"I will get the papers made up at the clerk's office," George said, gathering himself up. He spoke with the authority that he normally commanded as captain of his vessel, a leader of his men. "Will you inform the Blaisdells that I will be there this evening?" After a slight pause, he added, "To get this done."

The reverend nodded.

"I want no fanfare. I would like you present as we sign the papers. There is no need to send for the magistrate. You can attest to our union."

"I will go at once and let Abner know," Archibald said.

"Tell her…" George stopped, swallowing hard on the words. "Tell her I have no place for her to stay. I have no plan for our future. I have nothing to offer her but my…" He stopped again, then regained his composure. "I have nothing to offer her but myself." He stood, looking intently down the bay at the small white house he could see on the eastern shore.

"I will tell her." Archibald rested his hand on George's arm. "It will be all right," he said.

George wasn't sure if he believed him, but he strode off in the direction of the town clerk's office with the air of a man who was committed to his fate.

CHAPTER FIFTY-FOUR

Lydia's mother rushed into her room. "Come, child," she said hurriedly. Lydia and Hannah were sitting together on the bed they shared. It was a rare spring afternoon when all of their chores were done and they had a few minutes to themselves. Hannah had recently borrowed a new book from a friend, and they were taking turns reading aloud to each other.

"What is it, Mother?" Hannah asked.

"Lydia, you must come down and speak with your father." She reached for Lydia to pull her from the bed.

"Why?" Lydia was slightly alarmed by her mother's anxious tone.

"Just come. Reverend Crawford is here, and he said he has news for you."

Lydia slid off the bed, her bare feet touching the smooth wood of the floor. She followed her mother down the stairs to where she saw Reverend Crawford talking quietly with her father.

"Ah, Lydia," her father said when he saw her. "Come, sit down." He motioned for her to take a seat next to the reverend. Lydia was suddenly aware that she had not put on her shoes, and pulling in her toes, she tried to cover her bare feet with her skirts. After she was seated, the reverend spoke to her.

"Lydia," he said, his voice soft and reassuring. "I have just recently spoken with Captain Butler."

Lydia felt her heart beat faster at the mention of George's name. She had not seen him for nearly six weeks, since the day he had come to their home and seen Nelly's spirit for himself. She had heard, for she had no memory of Nelly's visitation, that he had told Nelly he would marry her, but he had not been to see her or discuss this with her.

"How is Captain Butler?" she asked. "I understand he conversed with the spirit while he was here a few weeks ago."

The reverend bowed his head. "Well, he has suffered much because of that experience, Lydia."

Much for my sake, she knew he was thinking. She shifted in her chair. "He is not unwell, is he?"

"Oh no," Archibald replied. "It is his character that is under attack from many sides."

"So it is because of me that he suffers?" she asked.

Archibald glanced at Abner and Mary. "Yes, I'm afraid so."

"I see," Lydia replied, folding and unfolding her hands in her lap.

Archibald reached out and patted her knee. "But he is determined to make this situation right." Again, he looked at Abner and Mary before he continued. "For your sake, Lydia."

"What do you mean, Reverend?" Mary asked.

Sitting up straighter, Archibald told them of George's visit and his wish to marry Lydia that day.

"Today?" Mary cried out.

"Yes, when he left me, he was headed directly to the clerk's office to get the marriage banns written up. He will be here this evening," he said repeating George's wishes. "He wants no announcement. No great gathering. Abner, you and I will be witnesses, and that is all."

Lydia saw her mother relax a bit at this.

"Furthermore," he continued, "he wishes me to inform you, Lydia, that he has no place for you to live as of yet." Turning his attention to Abner, he stated, "In fact, he has no plan of any kind on how to provide for your daughter, Abner. He has informed me that the banks in Boston have called in all of his notes. He will have to sell the ship to pay them off. He has been refused credit even at the general store in town. He has nothing."

Abner looked grave. "I see."

" 'Tis no different than the situation with the Flint boy," Mary murmured. "It will be fine."

Abner let out his breath in frustration. "It's not the same, Mary," he grumbled. "This is Captain Butler we are speaking of. I'm sure he has resources that he could pull from."

"He is making a huge sacrifice in marrying Lydia," Mary said, eyeing Abner sternly, "and I think that will be enough."

"Very well." The reverend rose from his chair and looked down at Lydia. "Although these circumstances are far from ideal, young lady," he said, a smile spreading across his lips, "I'm sure a pretty dress would still be appropriate."

Lydia glanced down at the floor. Just the tips of her bare feet were sticking out from under her day skirt. Her apron was stained and unwashed. "Yes, Reverend, I will find something."

"Very good. I will return this evening with the captain."

As her parents moved away to walk Reverend Crawford to the door, Lydia felt herself swoon. Within a few hours, she would be married to Captain George Butler—just as the voices had always said. She had never lost hope. Never doubted that she knew things that others did not.

＋———＋

As the afternoon sun slanted through the windows George stood straightening his waistcoat in front of the looking glass in his father's study. His mother was walking by the open door when she noticed his movements. Looking in, she saw him in his full captain's dress.

"Why, don't you look fine," she remarked. Her heart lifted at the sight of him. "Making preparations to return to sea?" she asked.

George looked down at the floor. "Not exactly, Mother."

"Then why the full regalia?" she asked playfully. She picked up his hat, the yellow plume bouncing lightly as she reached up to place the hat on his head. He bent forward slightly so that she could reach. "Are you going to a party?"

"I'll be out for a while," was his only reply. He kissed her lightly on the cheek and turned to leave.

"Do not make the mistake of marrying that Blaisdell girl," his mother said.

George turned slowly. "What makes you say that?" he asked her.

"A mother knows." She reached for his hand. "Please, George, do not give in to this madness."

"Madness? Is that what you think I've sunk to?" George watched as his mother remained silent. "It is, isn't it? You think I've gone mad."

"George, please." His mother reached out toward him. "You don't have to do this."

He thought of Nelly, of the way she had looked at the Blaisdells' home. How she had spoken to him, and how he was sure beyond any doubt that it had been her. "Yes, Mother, I do," he said, walking from the room.

CHAPTER FIFTY-FIVE

May 9, 1800
The Marriage

George removed his hat as he entered the front room of the Blaisdell home. He bowed slightly to Mrs. Blaisdell and then spotted Lydia seated on a small straight-backed chair near the window. She looked frightened and more like the child he thought her to be than the woman he was about to take as his wife. He swallowed hard as the reality of what was about to take place began to sink in. Reverend Crawford was speaking to Abner, but George wasn't listening. His whole being was focused on Lydia. He watched as she gripped the sides of the chair with both hands until her knuckles turned white. She was very small in stature, like her father, and her feet barely brushed the floor. She was dressed in a rose-colored dress with a fresh, crisp white apron over it. She wore black shoes with no heel, and her hair was pulled back tightly and wound into a knot at the nape of her neck. Her face was freshly scrubbed, and her cheeks were pink from the effort. She stared at the floor in front of her, glancing up at George only intermittently. He could tell this was as difficult for her as it was for him.

"Shall we?" he asked her. Reaching out for her hand, he helped her rise from the chair. Her hand, so tiny, disappeared within his own. He closed his eyes, drew in a deep breath, and then turned toward where Archibald and Abner were standing. There on the table next to them were the marriage banns, prepared just that day by the town clerk. Archibald was holding out the quill toward him.

"You first, Lydia," George said, taking the quill and handing it to her. He watched as she took it, her hand shaking with the effort. She looked pleadingly at her mother, who nodded encouragement to her.

"Sign here, Lydia," Abner said, pointing down at the bottom of the parchment. Lydia's hand shook so violently that she struggled to get the quill into the inkwell. Pulling it out, she dripped drops of black ink across the words that would forever state that she was the wife of Captain George Butler. When she saw what she had done, she glanced nervously at Reverend Crawford.

"I'm sorry," she muttered, the mistake only making her more nervous. She leaned over the document and slowly wrote out her name in the letters her mother had taught her.

Straightening, she handed the quill to George without looking him in the eye. She kept her head lowered, her gaze solidly on her feet. George took the quill from her and dipped it in the inkwell. With a quick flourish, he added his name to the document next to hers.

And with that, they were married. No ceremony. No religious pronouncement. No happy family to witness it all. Just the simple act of signing their names, and in doing so, George took responsibility for Lydia and, ultimately, committed to starting a new family.

George handed the quill to Abner and watched as he and the reverend signed their names as witnesses. No one spoke. George looked at Lydia, who still stood beside him with her eyes to the floor. Gently, he reached out and placed his hand beneath her chin. Slowly, he raised her face until she was looking at him. Her eyes were as pale as her skin. Her features were so small and delicate, like a fairy's, he thought. And then he stopped himself. He could not let his thoughts go there. She was a girl, a young woman of flesh and blood. She was not a sprite, a fairy, or anything else fanciful like that.

"I have something for you," he said to her. She continued to stare at him as he reached into his breast pocket and pulled out the ring. "I believe this belongs to you."

She gasped. "The ring!"

Abner and Mary stepped closer. Lydia took the ring from George and showed it to her parents. She turned it so they could see the inscription inside: *George & Lydia Butler 1800.*

"What is this?" Mary asked.

George took the ring back from Lydia. Reaching out, he raised her left hand toward him. He easily slipped the ring onto her finger. It was as if it had belonged on her finger all along.

"This is the ring from the posset at my wedding to…" George stopped, the words choking in his throat. "From my wedding five years ago," he finished. He went on to explain to Abner and Mary how he had been given the plain little silver ring for the posset and how Lydia had managed to choose the cup that contained it.

"It's the same ring?" Mary exclaimed. "Wasn't it also at the center of that melee at the church?"

"Yes," George said, nodding. He then went on to tell them the journey the ring had taken over the years and how he had come to be in possession of it again. "My father had it."

"Your father?" Abner asked. "Where did he find it?"

George looked down at Lydia, who was watching him intently. "He told me that he had gone to Nelly's grave to pay his respects. That she had appeared to him, told him that I was to marry Lydia and had given him the ring."

Mary sat down quickly on a chair. "Captain Butler, you have had this ring for five years?"

George could sense her frustration. If he had possessed this ring that foretold the future, then why had he forced the Blaisdells to go through all that they had?

"Yes." George was still staring into Lydia's eyes. "So you see, I had no choice but to accept what fate has apparently set in front of me." And then he added, "I'm sorry it took me so long to accept it."

He held Lydia's gaze for what seemed like an eternity until she finally spoke. "I see," was all she said, but she reached out and took hold of his hand. They stood there holding hands, neither one of them moving.

Reverend Crawford cleared his throat before speaking to break the silence. "Mrs. Crawford and I would like to offer our home to you for the next few weeks, Captain Butler."

George was shaken from his thoughts. "What? Your home?"

"Yes," Archibald said. "We have been wanting to travel over to Machias to visit our daughter, and this seems like a good time to go. You and Lydia can have the home to yourselves while you get your affairs in order."

"Well, that is very kind of you, Reverend," George said.

"Mrs. Crawford is already packed and staying with her sister this evening. I will be joining her there. So if the two of you would like to…" His voice trailed off as the awkwardness of the conversation became too much for him.

"Ah yes," George stammered, realizing that this was his cue to take command of the situation. Speaking to Lydia, he said, "Why don't you go put a few things together and we can get on our way."

She blinked shyly and hurried from the room, her mother quickly following her. George could only imagine the words that her mother would try to say to her in an attempt to prepare the young girl for her wedding night. George felt the bile rise in his throat at his own thoughts of what this evening might entail.

Reverend Crawford placed his hat on his head and bid them all good night. "It will all be well now, George. You will see. God is pleased." He shook hands with Abner and left the two men alone in the room. They stood there staring at each other in silence before Abner finally spoke.

"So what are your plans? If you have to sell your ship you won't be going to sea then?"

George thought for a moment before speaking. "No I'll be selling the ship to pay off the notes. And I sold my farm at the pond to my brother after Nelly's passing. I'm afraid this story has spread so far that I could not enter business in Bangor or anywhere else for that matter."

Abner was thoughtful before he spoke. "I could still use help here with the fishing nets." He looked at George. "But only if you felt comfortable doing so."

"Thank you, Abner," George said. He knew the older man had struggled since losing Atherton and the fishing fleet on the eastern side of the bay had only grown. The work was plenty and the money good.

There was sound from the hallway as Lydia and her mother descended the stairs. Lydia stopped in the doorway with a shawl now draped over her shoulders. She had changed out of her best dress and back into an everyday dress. She had a satchel at her side. "I'm ready," she said.

"Why, yes. Yes, you are," George stammered. He reached for the satchel and took it from her. Taking a deep breath, he addressed Abner. "I will be in contact with you shortly on that suggestion."

Abner nodded.

George turned back to Lydia, offering her his arm. "Shall we? I'm sorry we will have to walk."

She smiled at him. "It's all right. It's not that far, really." Turning, she kissed her mother on the cheek and then took George's arm. He led her from the parlor and out the door into the world that would now have to accept them as husband and wife.

CHAPTER FIFTY-SIX

Neither of them spoke a word on the walk up the path toward town. They passed several homes and felt the glaring eyes of the curious upon them. Once into Franklin proper, George quickened his pace to get to the reverend's house to avoid running into anyone who might recognize them. His efforts were for naught as they were spotted by Mary Card, Nelly's old friend. She came hurrying over, her skirts bustling around her.

"Why, Captain Butler and Miss Lydia Blaisdell," she jeered. "Out for a walk together, I see."

George remained polite as always but did not stop. "Good day, Mary," he said, steering Lydia around the woman and heading straight for Reverend Crawford's home.

"Well, aren't you two in a hurry," she said, turning to watch them depart.

George felt Lydia increase her grip on his arm and then heard her whisper, "But she will see us go into the house together."

George knew there was no way to avoid this. They couldn't stay inside the reverend's home as prisoners, never going out. There was no hiding from this. He had taken Lydia Blaisdell as his wife, and he had to show all of them that he was not ashamed of this decision.

He stopped and took a deep breath. "My apologies, Mary," he said with a gallant bow of his head. "My wife, Lydia, and I have much to do." He indicated Lydia with a slight nod. "I'm sure there will be a time when Lydia will be able to call on you." He smiled his best smile. "Please excuse us." Turning to walk away, they could hear her sputtering.

"Your wife? Call? Call on me?"

Lydia heard her retort. Whispering to George, she said, "It's unlikely that anyone will let me in to call on them." They had just stepped up onto the reverend's front porch, and George stopped. He looked down at her.

"It's true that Lydia Blaisdell was scorned and ridiculed. Talked about in whispers," he said. "But now you are Mrs. Captain George Butler, do you understand?" He waited for her to nod in agreement. "For what is left of that name, we will hold it with honor." Sighing deeply, he continued. "We will rebuild from here. Let the tongues wag, but we do not need to be concerned with it. Hold your head high, Lydia, and we shall get through this." He reached for the doorknob and swung the door open, allowing her to walk through first. "We begin now to start something new." He closed the door on Mary Card's prying eyes.

—

Lydia sat on the very edge of the bed. They had chosen as their room what appeared to be the obvious guest room in the house. This was all awkward enough without thoughts of Reverend Crawford and his wife running through her head.

She straightened slightly to see if she could see George out through the window. He had left her to use the privy, he had said, although she knew this was his excuse for leaving her alone to get settled for the evening.

They had spent their first few hours in the home quietly avoiding any deep conversations. It wasn't that George was ignoring her—rather, he appeared to be very selective in what he discussed with her. She found the whole thing troubling and wondered if they would ever get to a point where they could converse with each other in a relaxed way. George had spent most of the early evening writing a letter. He did not tell her whom he was writing to. It was only after he had folded the paper and sealed it with wax that he told Lydia to prepare for bed.

She heard the door downstairs open and then shut. Her heart began to beat faster as George's footsteps fell on the stairs. He carried a small oil lamp in his hand, and she saw the flicker of the light along the hallway walls before she saw him. She swung her legs up onto the bed and settled herself against the pillows just as he entered. In the flickering, mellow light, she felt her breath escape her as she watched him enter the room. He was tall and ruggedly built. Not scrawny like Asa had been. George's tawny hair was no longer tied back, but rather it fell to his shoulders in slight waves. She had never seen him in this more informal appearance. He sat down on a chair near the bed and slowly removed each boot, placing them carefully next to each other. Rising, he began to untie his breeches. Lydia looked away, ashamed to be watching him. He noticed this and responded.

"It's fine, Lydia. You are my wife," he said quietly, almost sighing with the effort. "We don't have to do this tonight if you're not ready." He looked at her deeply and ran his fingers through his hair. "Hell, I don't know if I'm ready." He let out a little laugh to break the tension.

She swallowed hard. "Can we talk about it first?" she asked.

"Talk about it?" George sat up straighter. "What kind of talk, Lydia?"

She jutted her chin out slightly. "There is something you need to know if you are going to be my husband," she said.

"And what is that?" he asked.

"You are not the first." She reached down and grasped both of his hands with hers. Interlocking her fingers among his, she squeezed hard.

She saw the realization of what she had just said register on his face. "What do you mean I'm not the first?" He sat up straighter, boring his gaze into her. "Who else in this town have you been with, Lydia?" She could hear the anger building in his voice. He yanked his hands from hers. "Will this trickery never end?" he roared.

"I'm not tricking you!" she shouted back at him. "Is that what you think? That all of this is some kind of trick?"

He jumped from the bed. "Well, what would you call this, Lydia? The spirit of my dead wife supposedly comes back and tells me to marry you!" he shouted, pointing his finger accusingly toward her. "*You*! And now I find out that you aren't…pure." He shook his head as if to rid himself of the thought. "You're fifteen years old, for Chrissake!" He kicked at the chair, causing it to sprawl across the floor and knocking over his boots in the process. "Your parents knew this. Knew no one else would want you," he screamed at her, spittle flying from his mouth. "That's why they persisted in this even when they knew my money was gone. Because no one else would take you." His words flew at her like daggers.

"Stop it! Stop it!" she shouted. She ran to him and grabbed at his arms. "You had the ring," she yelled at him. "The ring! How could that be a trick?" She held onto him as he tried to pull away from her. All of his energy drained as he realized what she was saying. She waved her left hand in front of his face. "How could this be a trick?" Slowly, he sat down on the side of the bed and she stood in front of him. "My parents don't know I have been with someone," she said, her words laden with emotion. "I didn't trick you, George. This is hard for me, too."

He took both of her hands in his. "Who was it?" was all he said.

"Asa Flint," she replied. Her voice was cool and unfeeling.

"Ah, I see. You two were betrothed, were you not?"

She laughed slightly and crawled back up on the bed.

George turned around to face her. "Just couldn't wait until the wedding night?" he asked.

She drew in a deep breath. For a moment, she thought she could leave it like this. Let George think what he wanted. That she wasn't soiled because she had lain with the man who was intended to be her husband. But she couldn't start her marriage with a lie. "No, it wasn't like that at all."

She lay down on her side with her head on the pillow, staring at him. "I never gave Asa permission," she said.

George could sense the seriousness of her words. He lay down, facing her. "What do you mean?" he asked.

"Asa saw Nelly," she started to explain. "Well, actually, he saw Nelly appear to me long before anyone else did." She raised her arm and pointed toward the west. "At the burial ground at Butler's Point." Then she waited.

George looked perplexed for a moment. "You were at Nelly's grave? When?"

"I went every year on the anniversary of her death." She closed her eyes, her long lashes resting on her cheeks briefly before she opened her eyes to look at him again. "To say I was sorry."

"Sorry for what?" he asked.

"Sorry that she died. For as long as I can remember, I truly believed that you were to be my husband. I heard voices, George." Her voice rose slightly to emphasize her point. "I heard voices my whole child-hood." Swallowing, she continued, "I knew I was supposed to be your wife, not Nelly. Then when she died, I felt like it was all my fault."

George rubbed his hand over his forehead trying to comprehend all of this before reaching over and touching Lydia's cheek. "You poor, tormented child. It was not your fault that Nelly died. Do you under-stand that now?"

She nodded. "Yes, I know it's all part of a plan for us in some way."

George sighed. "So you were at Nelly's grave, and she appeared to you," he reiterated. "And Asa had gone with you?"

She shook her head. "No. He had followed me there, but I did not know that he had. Nelly's spirit appeared, and he saw it, too. I was afraid he would tell everyone."

Realization began to dawn on George. "So he blackmailed you?"

Ashamed, she closed her eyes. "Yes."

He reached over and rubbed her shoulder. "That wasn't your fault, Lydia." She opened her eyes to look at him as he continued. "Asa came to me saying he could prove this whole thing was a hoax. Did you know that?"

Lydia was shocked to hear this. She shook her head in disbelief. "What did he want from you?" she asked.

"Land," George replied. "He wanted land as payment for bringing me information that this was all a trick to get you married off to me." Pausing to think briefly, he continued. "I find it very hard to believe his whole story now that I know he saw Nelly for himself. Asa Flint was an opportunist, Lydia. His loyalties fell to whoever he thought could give him the best advantage at that time."

"Well, he certainly used me to his best advantage," Lydia replied.

"Did he hurt you?" George asked with concern in voice.

She shrugged not knowing what the best response would be.

George watched her in silence for a while. She could see that his emotions were torn. First he had thought of her as a child, but now she was a child who had been hurt.

"Lydia, I…" His voice trailed off.

She knew what he was going to say. He was going to leave her, in this bed, alone. He wasn't going to be able to be a true husband to her. At least on this night.

She leaned forward and kissed him long and hard on the lips. Pulling away, she whispered breathlessly into his ear, "Please don't think of anything else tonight." Her hot breath spread down his neck, and she felt him shudder slightly. Leaning back, she gazed at him. She reached over and gently brushed the hair from his brow. The dappled light from the oil lamps played shadows across her skin as she stretched out next to him. "I'm fine." As she reassured him, she watched something inside of him change. "I'm Mrs. Captain George Butler, remember?" she laughed. She watched as the slightest smile spread across his lips.

"And that you are."

"Then I will do well as Mrs. Captain George Butler," she said smugly.

George laughed. "I should say you will."

CHAPTER FIFTY-SEVEN

Butler's Point

George's brother Peter strode through the door of his mother's home with so much force that he knocked over a chair on his way through the kitchen.

"Mother!" he shouted as he reached to set the chair aright. One of the house girls stuck her head out of the pantry, nervously eyeing him. Peter spotted her cap-clad head.

"Do you know where my mother is?" he asked her. The girl shook her head quickly and ducked back into the pantry. Peter pushed on the swinging door that led out into the hall. "Mother!" He checked his father's study and the front sitting room, then headed for the stairs. When he could not locate her there, he stormed back through the kitchen. He yelled into the pantry. "Where in the name of God is my mother?"

The poor, frightened girl could only stammer. "I heard her say something about the Hoopers."

Peter turned quickly and headed outside. He mounted his horse and pulled hard on the reins. The animal was still slightly winded from its fast-paced dash out to the point from George's Pond. Now Peter pushed her at breakneck speed toward the Hoopers'.

It was a lovely spring day, and Sarah Butler and Joanna Hooper were sitting on the front porch enjoying tea when Peter's horse came thundering into the yard. Both women stood up quickly and dashed from the porch, Sarah leading the way to her son's side.

"Peter!" she exclaimed. "What on earth? What is wrong?" She could sense the tension in him as he dismounted from his horse. Reaching into his coat pocket, he pulled out a letter and handed it to her.

"He has married the little demon," he spat out. "And he intends to reside with the Blaisdells."

Sarah's face turned ashen as she looked from Peter to the letter. He could see his mother reading the words for herself.

"George?" Joanna asked.

Peter nodded. "He married Lydia yesterday." The anger in his voice was evident. "He says that Abner has offered him a place to live and work so he will be staying there."

Joanna gasped. "He married her?"

Sarah leaned against Peter as she finished reading the letter. She covered her mouth to stifle the sob that was escaping. "He has given up everything now, even his family," she cried.

"Tricked by the devil," Joanna added.

———

News of George and Lydia's marriage spread like wildfire around the bay and beyond. That Reverend Crawford had left town only added to the gossip when it was learned that he had, in fact, encouraged the joining of the two individuals. Strongly worded letters from several quarters were quickly sent to Bangor and to Boston requesting a new minister for the area. It was clear in the minds of many that Archibald Crawford was no longer fit to lead his flock. As a man of God, he had fallen and was now an instrument in the hands of the devil. Half the town demanded his removal, the Butlers and the Hoopers being chief among them.

David Hooper himself traveled to Bangor to speak with several of the leading clergymen there. He told them of his daughter, her life, her marriage to George, and her death. He expounded on the evil deeds perpetrated by the Blaisdell family, how they had twisted George's mind and succeeded in securing a marriage between him and their daughter. Reverend Crawford, he said, was an explicit player in this deception and needed to be dealt with accordingly. His words were met with grave concern, and a committee was assembled to look into the allegations. David left Bangor with reassurances that someone would be arriving soon in Franklin to take the pulpit from Reverend Crawford. A letter from Abraham Cummings came swiftly.

May 14, 1800
Freeport, Maine

Dearest Reverend Crawford,

Word has reached my ears of troubling news from your quarter. I have been told that the visits of a specter have continued unabated for the past few months in Franklin. That this specter was able to convince a God-fearing man from a prominent family to marry a young woman of dubious character.

As troubling as this talk is, I am more perplexed by the news that you, sir, as a servant of the Lord, actually supported the belief in this possible demonic apparition! That you were even present when this couple signed their marriage banns and gave them use of your home for their wedding night.

Because of these outrageous tales, and with this seemingly so out of character for the man I remember you to be, I am coming myself to Franklin. I will speak with everyone who is involved in this situation and determine for myself if it is of God or the devil.

I will be on the next ship departing this location for the Downeast.

Yours truly,
Abraham

True to his word, the Most Reverend Abraham Cummings came and took depositions from all of those involved. He sat through tellings and retellings of the appearance of the ghost of Nelly Butler. How the knockings had led to the appearance of the orb, the bright lights, the feelings of peace. He heard of how the ghost had walked in the open field to Captain Miller's house in broad daylight with people following her. He heard how the Blaisdells were not well placed and the belief of many that it was all a hoax, although no one could explain exactly how they had pulled it off.

In the end, Abraham Cummings left town with his case full of testimonies, unconvinced one way or the other.

"Archibald, this is a troubling set of circumstances," he said as he shook the reverend's hand before boarding his ship to depart. "Very troubling. The council will meet and go over all that I have recorded. We'll let you know of our decision."

Archibald nodded, knowing that either way, he was going to have to move on. His role in this had damaged his credibility with nearly half the town. It was time he found a new flock to lead.

There were also many in town who supported George and Lydia as they tried to forge a new life together. Many of these individuals had seen Nelly's spirit for themselves. They had heard her speak and believed the union to be God's will. Although there were no more manifestations of a spiritual nature or knockings heard in the Gathering Room, people still came. They came seeking. They sought out Lydia and begged her to speak to them of things she knew from the spirit realm. Could she talk with this one's dead husband? Or that one's sister who had died young? Lydia was overcome by their requests. She tried to explain to them that she could not speak to the dead at will. Abner stepped in, trying to assuage the throngs that continued to arrive. He read scriptures to them and spoke the words of God in an effort to bring peace to those who were searching for answers. Eventually, the crowds dwindled when Lydia exhibited no more odd abilities.

George settled into his work with Abner on the fishing nets. It was physically demanding work. He could see now why Abner had suffered so with the loss of Atherton. George found himself developing a bond with Abner as they worked together. The older man needed him, and this gave George peace of mind that he had made the correct decision in coming here. As for his decision to marry Lydia, with each passing day he was more and more assured that he had done the right thing. His bond with her was also growing. Living with her made him realize she wasn't the child he had envisioned. She was a woman in every sense of the word. During the day, she worked harder than he had ever seen his mother or sisters work. She and Hannah toiled endlessly in the garden planting and weeding to ensure that the family would have enough to eat long into the winter. She also stood for hours at the loom. She was becoming an expert weaver, and the cloths that her mother took to town to sell were beautifully designed.

In the evenings, when George was alone with her, she transported him to another place. He could never get enough of being with her. The first few months that they lived together as husband and wife had been a learning experience for both of them as they came to terms with what they had done. As spring turned to summer and then summer to fall, the intensity of their physical relationship helped ease them both through the transition.

CHAPTER FIFTY-EIGHT

October 1800

George felt Lydia get out of bed. He peeked out from under his half-closed eyelids. The room was still dark, but he knew she was going out to milk the cow, as she did every morning. He rolled over, grunting with the effort of shifting his weight on the mattress that had just recently been stuffed with new straw. He wiggled around until he could get comfortable again. After settling down, he opened his eyes and saw Lydia struggling with her dress.

"What on earth are you doing?" he asked her.

She tugged and pulled on her dress, trying to get it on over her head. "I can't seem to get this on." Half her dress still covered her face, and the rest bunched up around her waist.

George sat up slightly and reached to help her when he noticed the problem. A smile spread across his face.

"Um, Lydia," he said, not taking his eyes from her. "I know what the problem is."

Lydia mumbled from inside of the dress. "You do?"

He pulled on the top of her dress until it came off her head. Lifting her up in his embrace, he squeezed her until she let out a squeal. "Stop that!" she whispered. "We'll wake the whole house." She laughed.

"Why didn't you tell me?" he asked, looking down at her belly that was rounded and protruding slightly.

"Why didn't you notice earlier?" she fired back with a smile.

He rubbed his hands over her stomach, marveling at it. "When?"

She looked thoughtful for a moment. "After discussing it with Mother and Hannah, they think sometime in March."

George nodded in satisfaction at this and then added, "You're so small—will you be all right?"

Lydia rose from the bed in indignation. "I'm not small, I'm petite. But yes, Mother said that small women have smaller babies, that's all."

331

George's mind ran back to Nelly as she lay writhing in pain on her deathbed. The baby was lodged inside of her, unable to come out until it finally took her life. Nelly had been a full-grown woman in her mid-twenties. Lydia was only sixteen.

Lydia reached into the cupboard and pulled out a larger dress. "Mother made a few of these for me," she told him with a smile as she easily pulled it over her head. "She said I would know when it was time to wear them." Laughing, she caught her hair up in a knot and tied her cap around her head. "I guess it's time." She bent to kiss him before she left the room.

George stopped her by grabbing her hand. "Be careful," he said. She smiled and skipped from the room.

He lay there as the morning light grew brighter. He thought of all the emotions that had flooded him when Nelly had told him she was with child. The hopes for the future. The idea of a son to raise into a man. The start of a large family that would fill the empty places on Butler's Point and solidify his father's legacy. None of those things entered his mind now. The future, he had learned, could twist and change on you in a moment. He didn't care if it were a boy or a girl now, just so long as it lived. So long as Lydia lived as well. What good would a son be to him now, anyway? He had nothing to give him. His life at Butler's Point was gone.

He closed his eyes tight as a wave of grief swept away the joy he had just felt at the news he was going to be a father again. He felt tears streaming down his face and onto his neck.

Suddenly, the room seemed brighter than the morning light should be. He opened his eyes to find a glaring bright light filling the room. Raising his arm to shield his eyes, he saw an orb floating just above the foot of his bed. He sat up, pulling the covers close to him to cover his naked chest.

The bright white orb floated and bobbed slightly. His first thought was to shout for Lydia, but he realized she was out in the barn and would not hear him. If he shouted, it would only wake the whole house. So he sat still, watching the orb rise and fall until he realized it was synchronous with his own breath. He tried slowing his breathing, and the orb slowed. He sped up his breaths, and the orb quickly bobbed up and down in response. He could hear the tinkling of crystals, the same as he had heard when Nelly had come to the Gathering Room.

"Nelly?" he spoke to the orb. Slowly, the orb began to grow larger, becoming a swirling iridescent ball that glittered and sparkled. The figure of a woman began to take shape inside the orb.

"It is you," George spoke quietly.

"It is I."

The voice he heard was Nelly's, and his heart skipped a beat at the sound of it. He swallowed hard and leaned forward toward her.

"I married Lydia," he said. "Just like you asked me to."

"I know," came her reply.

He waited, but she didn't say anything else. She was dressed in white as she had been when he had seen her before. She did not have their child with her this time. Instead, her hands were at her sides. She looked at him, but it was more like she was looking through him, and he was unnerved by it.

"Should I get Lydia?" he asked her.

"No. I come with God's word for you, George Butler."

He was taken aback at her formality. As before, he wished that the spirit, which looked so much like his beautiful wife, would act like Nelly had acted. She had always been so energetic and happy. This manifestation was none of those things.

"What is it that God needs to tell me now?" He watched as slowly the spirit raised her arms outward, as if beseeching him. Her gaze became more intense, and he felt as if she were seeing him in the room for the first time. She stared right at him and he connected with her, feeling that warm, intense burn within his chest as she spoke.

"Lydia will die as I did."

The words hung in the room. George could not comprehend them.

The look on Nelly's face softened, and her apparition suddenly seemed to be only inches from his face.

"Lydia will die in travail with the child." With a sudden whooshing sound, the vision was gone and the room returned to the light of the early autumn dawn.

Stunned, George could not move. He stared blankly at the space at the foot of the bed where the specter had appeared. His mind ran back over the memories of Nelly struggling through her travail, crying out in pain until there was nothing left of her. Until it had killed her.

"Lydia!" He spoke her name in desperation. Jumping from the bed, he dressed quickly and descended the stairs in such haste that he nearly slipped, grasping at the banister to stop his fall. He ran across the yard and out to the small barn the Blaisdells kept behind the house. He saw Lydia sitting on the milking stool, gently pulling on the cow's udders, talking quietly to the animal as she did so. The milk made a pinging sound as it hit the sides of the pail. His bursting into the barn so suddenly caused the cow to jump, which startled Lydia, and she turned around to see him.

"George!" she exclaimed. She was shocked to see him, but his countenance scared her. His hair was standing nearly straight on end, as if he had run his hands through it several times. His clothes were all disheveled, and he stood in front of her barefoot.

Grabbing her, he pulled her from the stool. Bringing her up close to his face, he spoke in an urgent whisper. "Are you really with child? Is it true?"

She laughed and tried to get him to let go of her. "Of course it's true!" She eyed him suspiciously. "What is wrong with you all of a sudden? Put me down."

George would not release her. Instead, he continued to hold her near him. Their faces were so close that their noses were nearly touching. He stared at her intently.

She could feel his grip tightening on her shoulders. "George, put me down," she repeated.

Slowly, he lowered her to the ground, smoothing the sides of her shawl as he did so.

"Honestly, what just happened?" she asked him. "I left you mere minutes ago, and you were blissfully happy. Now you act like you've seen a ghost or some…" Her voice trailed off as she realized what she was saying. "Did you?" she asked, cocking her head slightly.

George only nodded and then sat down heavily on a bale of hay nearby.

"Was it Nelly?" she asked.

"It was." His voice sounded husky and hoarse.

Lydia sat down beside him, reaching for his hands. "What did she say?"

George turned his head to look at his child bride. So small, yet so full of life. A life that was soon to be gone. Months, that's all she had left to live. He could not tell her. Could not steal her joy from these last precious days she had left.

He forced a smile. "She told me to love you." It was all he could think of to say.

CHAPTER FIFTY-NINE

Autumn turned to winter along the Maine coast, and everyone burrowed in for the duration. The days were short, the nights were long, and the child within Lydia grew. George watched as Lydia truly blossomed with impending motherhood. Confident in herself, in her role as his wife, she fought for her place in the community that had long been denied her.

Those who whispered gossip and cast glances askew were silenced by the sheer force of Lydia's determination to be accepted. As the child within her grew as a symbol of her new life, she moved among the townspeople as if her past belonged to someone else.

As Lydia's light began to shine more brilliantly, George's began to dim as he became more and more burdened with the knowledge that Nelly had shared with him. He worked alongside Abner, but he was despondent most days or only slightly gloomy on others. He stopped his intimacy with Lydia altogether. She did not say anything to him, and he assumed she thought it was because she was with child. The reality, though, was that he had neither the strength nor the desire to complete the act. Whereas other men could enjoy their rights as husbands fully, doing so had only brought him death, loss, and sadness.

———

In February, Sarah Butler had heard enough of how her son was suffering, and she sent word that she wished George to come to see her.

"Will you go?" Lydia asked him as she set the letter down that he had handed to her.

Dark circles had formed under George's eyes, and he looked positively ghastly. He only shrugged his shoulders.

"I think you should," she said quietly.

"You really think I should go?" he asked.

"Yes. It's been nearly a year since you spent time with your family." She thought of the brief encounters that had taken place in town since their marriage, when they had inadvertently crossed paths with Sarah, Peter, and—on one occasion—the Hoopers. There had been awkward silences followed by the respectful acknowledgment of the well-bred and then a quick retreat. "I think it might bring some life back to you." She brushed at one of his fallen locks of hair. "You seem to have lost your way," she whispered.

Lydia had not failed to notice that George's mood had changed the day that he told her he had seen Nelly. The same day she had told him of their child. She had hoped that by sharing her joy and happiness at the thought of giving him a son, it would lift his spirits. Instead, it seemed to have the opposite effect. On several occasions, she had seen him almost cringe when she laughed at a funny story Hannah told or cried out in excitement when the baby kicked her.

"Then I will go." He rose from the table where he had been reading the letter. "But I wish for you to come with me." He kissed her ever so gently before adding, "I need your strength."

＋———＋

So it was that during the very last week of February, George settled a heavily pregnant Lydia into the front of the sleigh and buried her with quilts and bearskins. Taking his place beside her, they carefully made the trek around the bay, passing through Franklin and continuing on down the western side to Butler's Point. Lydia had not been this far down the point since George had married Nelly nearly six years ago. Her ventures to Nelly's grave at the family burial ground had not afforded her a view of the bay as she saw it now from the side yard of the Butlers' home. She glanced at her own home across the bay, observing how ordinary it seemed compared to the grand Butler home. She walked through the door of this home for the first time as George led her inside. Stomping the snow from her shoes on the straw mat by the door, she took off her cloak, her outer jacket, and her winter bonnet with George's help. She smoothed down her skirts and adjusted her curls around her shoulders.

Presently, a young house girl appeared, and when she saw George her eyes grew wide in surprise. "Captain Butler!" Her voice rose in excitement before she remembered her place and quickly covered her mouth with her hand.

"Margaret," George said, nodding at her. "Will you kindly tell my mother that I am here to see her? My wife and I will be waiting for her in the front sitting room."

The young girl nodded quickly, and George guided Lydia effortlessly down the hallway as Margaret scurried away to alert everyone that George was here.

Sarah Butler entered the front sitting room without so much as a rustle of skirts. Her sudden appearance startled both George and Lydia, who had been sitting on the settee, both lost in their own individual thoughts.

"Mother," George said, rising to greet her. He grasped her by the hands and kissed her briefly on the cheek.

His mother was startled by the sight of him. The dark circles aside, his face was drawn and gaunt. He had clearly lost weight, and his hair had thinned. "You do not look well," she said, speaking with the concern only a mother can have for a son. "You're so pale." She reached up and touched his cheek, almost afraid that the paper-thin skin would crack under her touch.

"I'm fine, Mother," George tried to reassure her.

"No, you are not. Anyone can see that." She glanced down at Lydia, clearly blaming her for her son's condition. "I have heard reports from several sources that you were close to death. I did not believe them." She placed her hand at the base of her throat and stared at Lydia. "As I was certain that someone would have sent word to me if my son were dying." She held Lydia's gaze only briefly and then looked back at George. "You may not be dying, but you certainly look as if you are." She urged him to sit down. "What has happened?"

George returned to his place beside Lydia on the settee. "Nothing has happened to me, Mother." He placed his arm around Lydia. "As you may have also learned, we are expecting your grandchild soon."

Sarah's back stiffened. George could only imagine what she was thinking.

"I can see that, George," she said sternly, followed by absolute silence. Lydia shifted her weight nervously but also to find a more comfortable position. "Is your time near?" Sarah asked her.

"I believe so," Lydia said, her voice cracking slightly. "My sister, Hannah, said she thought the child would come the first part of March." She cleared her throat to try and sound more assured.

Sarah pursed her lips together into a tight line. "So you will be having the child soon and your husband, my son, looks as if he will faint under the effort of just sitting there." Her words cut into Lydia.

"This is the reason I encouraged him to come see you today." Lydia spoke strongly and firmly, and the shift in her confidence unsettled Sarah.

"You encouraged him?" Sarah asked as she turned toward George. "You needed encouragement to come see your mother?"

George looked exceedingly tired all of a sudden. "It has been a difficult time, Mother." He sighed. "Lydia and I thought that maybe, by now, your anger would have subsided over the course my life has taken." He tried to rise from the settee but faltered a bit. Reaching back, he steadied himself. Lydia leaned forward to assist him, concerned with his frailness. He straightened as he spoke. "But I can see that we were mistaken. You still appear angry that I chose to marry Lydia." He reached out to offer Lydia help in rising from the settee. "We should go." Suddenly, his eyes rolled back in his head, and he crumpled to a heap on the floor.

"Oh!" both women shrieked. Lydia slid off the settee onto the floor beside George. She patted at his face, trying to revive him.

"Margaret!" Sarah shouted. "Send for help!"

Lydia looked up at Mrs. Butler. The two women stared at each other, each fearlessly preparing for a battle of wills.

"You did this," they said in unison.

＋———＋

The doctor had been sent for, and George had been placed in an upstairs room. Lydia had settled into a chair in the corner where she could keep an eye on him. His mother had been in and out with basins of water and more blankets, but neither woman said a word to the other. The doctor had declared it simple exhaustion.

"How hard has he been working over there?" Sarah's words felt like projectiles hitting Lydia. But before she could answer, the doctor interjected.

"He's clearly not in any physical shape to be doing any kind of strenuous work. My guess would be mental exhaustion. Has he had a lot on his mind lately?" He glanced at Lydia's protruding stomach.

She shifted under his gaze, placing a hand protectively over the child kicking furiously inside of her.

"He has not been himself since we found out I am with child. His despondent mood has only deepened as my time gets closer. When word came today that she wanted to see him," she said, indicating George's mother, "I thought this might be a good thing for him. Might lift his spirits." She frowned at Sarah. "But she did not make his visit a pleasant one, and it clearly taxed him further."

"Indeed!" Sarah exclaimed. "I asked my son to come to me because I had heard that he was suffering. Instead of coming home to me alone so that we could speak privately of his situation, he brings you!" Her face was turning red with anger.

"I am his wife," Lydia retorted. "Or have you forgotten that?"

The doctor spoke up. "Ladies, ladies, none of this is helping George, who I believe you both care about. He needs rest and a resolution to his problems." As he tightened the buckle on his leather bag, he looked at Lydia. "The worry over the child will resolve itself in due time, as I'm sure he is troubled by the memory of losing Nelly." His words were gentle and reassuring. He then turned to Sarah and spoke a bit firmer. "The loss of his family has clearly been felt keenly by him. My advice to you and the rest of the family is to let his choices be his and to accept him back into your good graces."

Lydia folded her arms smugly, watching Sarah's reaction. George's mother was a woman of great grace. Lydia watched as she lifted her chin slightly and then slowly nodded in agreement to the doctor.

"As you see fit, Doctor," was all she said. She cast one last look at Lydia before walking resolutely from the room. Her footfalls receded down the hallway.

The doctor smiled at Lydia. "She is a good woman. Stubborn, but good," he said.

"Thank you," Lydia replied. "What should I do for George?"

"He'll need to stay in bed. I'll be back in a few days to see him again and will decide then if he can travel."

"A few days? But I want to go home now."

"Well, he's not going with you." The doctor stood in the doorway, looking at her.

"I cannot be away from him." She began to ring her hands. "My time is too close. I don't want to be clear across the bay and have him here."

"Then I will tell Mrs. Butler that you will be staying." He winked at her. "I'll be back in a few days."

<hr />

Sarah and Lydia settled into a rhythm. They were respectful to each other but still did not discuss or address their mutual feelings of distrust. They took turns caring for George, managing to do so without ever really interacting with each other. Peter came, spending several hours alone with George. It made Lydia's heart soar when she heard their hearty laughter from the other side of the door. It seemed that Sarah, too, had finally accepted that George had done what he felt was right. On several occasions, Lydia saw her leaving George's room, dabbing a handkerchief to her eyes. A mother's love is strong, and Lydia knew that, ultimately, Sarah truly did love her son. Maybe not her daughter-in-law, but she did love her son.

Lydia had sent word to her mother that she would be staying at Butler's Point for at least a week as George had taken ill. Lydia's saving grace was the house girl Margaret. She had gotten Lydia settled into a room of her own and shown her around the grand home so that she knew where things were—most importantly, the privy. She was close to Lydia's own age and naturally had heard all of the stories about Lydia.

"Did you really see a ghost?" Margaret asked her one day as she helped Lydia prepare a soup for George.

"I don't think of it as a ghost," Lydia told her. "They were more like visitations. Someone who once lived just coming back in another form."

"But you saw her," the younger girl prodded. "Captain Butler's first wife."

"Yes, I saw her, but I don't remember much about it." Lydia picked up the spoon Margaret had been washing and set it on the tray she was preparing to take upstairs.

"I was here when she died. She suffered so." Margaret looked away. "Made up my mind then that I would never get with child. It's too dangerous."

Lydia didn't like the way this conversation felt. "Many women have babies, Margaret. Not all of them die."

"Oh, I know." She shuddered at her own memory. "But it was so awful. That babe stuck inside of her. The pain wracking her body over and over until she just could not go on living."

Lydia cleared her throat and picked up the tray. "Let's keep cheerful thoughts, Margaret," she said, leaving the girl alone in the kitchen. She made her way to George's room and found him sitting upright in bed.

She smiled as she entered his room. "I brought you some lunch."

He smiled back at her as she laid the tray on his lap. It was then that she first felt the pain. It cut across her stomach like a slow wave of cramping but more intense. She straightened up quickly, not wanting to alarm George. He certainly didn't need to know that something might be wrong.

"Are you feeling better today?" she asked him in a clipped tone.

"Yes, and I'm ready to get out of this bed and get back to the eastern shore," he grumbled. "Has anyone sent for the doctor?" He began in earnest on the soup. "I'm not waiting much longer, Lydia," he mumbled with food in his mouth.

"He should be here this afternoon." Lydia sat down in the chair and placed her hand against her abdomen. She had been feeling tightness for the past few days, but this was different. This was true pain.

George continued to chatter on about how he and his mother had come to an understanding. "Although I don't think she'll ever be overly warm to you," he said, looking up at her. It was then that he noticed the pain written across her face. "Lydia, is something wrong?"

She stood up. The pain had eased off. Perhaps it was just something in passing, maybe the child kicking her wrong.

"I'm going to fetch your clothes." She leaned over to kiss him and felt him place his hand on her stomach. She saw the worry return to his face. "I'm fine," she reassured him.

But she wasn't fine. The waves of pain continued. She kept her struggles to herself as she helped George dress to greet the doctor. His assessment proved satisfactory to George. They were given the go-ahead to travel back home. Peter arrived with his large brood of a family just as the doctor was leaving. With fences mended between George and his mother, she insisted on a big family meal before George and Lydia departed. So while Peter and George played with the children, Lydia stepped into the large kitchen to help with the meal preparation.

"Is there anything I can do to help?" she said just as another wave of pain washed over her. She reached back to grip the sideboard and gritted her teeth. And then she felt it—a feeling of something letting go inside of her and warm fluid running down her legs. "Oh!" she cried, looking down. There was a large puddle forming on the floor at her feet. She spread her feet apart and lifted her skirts.

Sarah noticed it first, dropping the pan she held in her hands. It clattered to the floor, getting everyone's attention.

"Dear God," she said. "Your time is here, Lydia."

CHAPTER SIXTY

Someone helped Lydia to a chair. Whatever progress Sarah had made in her reconciliation with Lydia and George was swept away at the realization that Lydia was going to give birth in her home. Sarah stood silently, the pan she had dropped still resting near her feet. She felt her heart sink inside of her. She did not want this child born in her home. Let it be born anywhere else, it was a part of George's world elsewhere. In due time, she would come to accept the child—and possibly its mother. But she wasn't ready now to see it welcomed into the world in her own home. The ties that were binding them were still too thin. She wasn't ready to think about what this child could be. The thought that it might have demonic tendencies like its mother tore at Sarah's mind. She stared at Lydia, who was struggling with another wave of pain. She could not turn them out at this point. Silently, she walked from the kitchen down the hall to where George and Peter were, her hands folded tightly in front of her.

"What's going on in the kitchen?" Peter asked his mother. "Did you drop something?"

Staring directly at George, she said, "Lydia's time has come."

George's face fell immediately. He rose and ran to the kitchen. There he found Lydia doubled over in pain.

"George!" She was scared at what lay before her and the fact that she was surrounded by people she did not know and could not trust. "Send for my mother," she cried, and tears began to run down her cheeks as she reached up and wrapped her arms around his neck. He lifted her carefully from the chair.

"Shhh," he soothed her. "I will, but let's get you settled first." Holding her in his arms, he looked around frantically at the women. "Where can I take her?" he shouted.

Everyone turned to look at Sarah, who stood silently in the doorway. George's eyes narrowed on his mother, but she remained silent, her hands still folded in front of her. It was Margaret who spoke up.

"Here, sir, bring her to my room." The young girl walked toward the back door, stopping to see if he were following her. George spun on Sarah.

"Mother?" he said. "Surely you will find a place for her."

His mother stood resolutely. "Margaret's room will be fine." She turned and walked from them. The room fell deathly quiet.

"Sir?" Margaret urged him, waving her arms. George glanced around at his sister-in-law, his cousins, and the other women of his family, but none would make eye contact with him. "God damn you all to hell!" he shouted as he carried Lydia out the back door and across the yard.

He stooped as he walked through the low doorway of the small log cabin that Margaret shared with another house girl. There was only one bed, so he laid Lydia on it and covered her with the quilt. Margaret was busy trying to start a fire.

"It will warm up soon," she said, trying to reassure both of them.

Lydia gripped at her stomach and cried out in pain again. "George!" she yelled.

He rubbed her hands with his. "It will be all right, Lydia." His mind was flooded with Nelly. The sound of her voice calling out his name as she felt the pains of childbirth wash over her. He turned to Margaret. "I don't think any of the other women are going to help." There was fear in his voice. This is how Lydia will die, he thought, at the hand of his mother! If he went for help, would she live? Could he himself stop Nelly's prophecy?

"I'll sit with her, sir," Margaret said as the fire roared to life in the hearth. "At first, that's all she'll need. Just someone to be here. But as time goes on, we will need someone who has delivered a baby before."

George nodded and thought back to how long Nelly had spent in travail. Although he knew Lydia would die as Nelly did, he did not know when. Maybe she would die sooner. He had to get her mother here.

"I have to go and get her mother."

"Yes! You should go at once." Margaret reached under the covers and felt Lydia's wet clothing. "I will get her undressed and have everything prepared for when you come back."

George leaned down and kissed Lydia on the forehead. "Margaret will stay with you," he said. "I'm going for Hannah and your mother."

George ran to the barn and found the Blaisdells' horse. As he prepared to place the saddle on her, he saw Peter entering the barn.

"Not now, Peter," he said angrily. "I've got to get to the Blaisdells'."

"I'm sorry about Mother," Peter said. "I just tried to talk to her. She's pretty set in her ways."

George pulled hard on the straps of leather until he was certain the saddle was secure. Placing his foot in the stirrup, he swung his leg up and quickly mounted the horse.

"She will die," he said, looking down at his brother.

"Who will die?" Peter asked, confused at the direction the conversation had taken. "Mother?"

"Lydia." George said her name softly. "Lydia will die today."

Peter smiled gently, placing his hand on his brother's boot. "Ah, I understand your worry, brother, but it's not necessarily so. You lost Nelly in childbirth, but it does not mean Lydia will follow suit."

"Nelly told me Lydia will die." His words fell on Peter like a cold rain. He watched as his brother's face reacted to what he had just said.

He pulled hard on the reins of the horse, causing her to rear back. "Yah!" he screamed as he forced the horse to bolt from the yard. He had to get all the way around the bay as quickly as he could.

✦━━━✦

By the time George returned with Lydia's mother and Hannah, things had progressed quickly. Even Margaret was a bit frazzled from dealing with it all on her own. George's mother was still resolutely refusing to assist in any way and apparently was not allowing any of the other women to help, either. Peter had packed his family up and headed back to the pond, not wanting to be part of what was taking place. He had left a brief handwritten note for Margaret to give to George. She handed it to him as soon as he entered her cabin.

Brother:
If what you told me is true, may God comfort you.
Peter

George crumpled the note and threw it in the fireplace. He looked down at Lydia, her hair plastered to the sides of her face with sweat. How much longer? he wondered. He was just about to ask Hannah when Lydia's mother touched him on the arm.

"This is no place for men," she said quietly.

"I'm not leaving her," he said. "Not this time."

Mary Blaisdell glanced at Hannah before responding. "Then step outside while I look things over, and then you can come back in."

Looking one more time at Lydia, George opened the door and stepped out.

Shortly, Mary called him back in. She was smiling, which gave him some comfort.

"She is doing very well," she said. "Here, sit." She had pulled a chair up to the bed near Lydia's head. "It may get unpleasant for a moment, but it won't be much longer." She guided him to the chair and smiled again as he sat down somewhat befuddled.

Hannah rolled her eyes and whispered to her mother. "This is really unorthodox. He shouldn't be here," she hissed.

Mary leaned her head in toward Hannah. "Show some sympathy. He lost his first wife on a day very similar to this one."

George reached out and took Lydia's hand in his own. She smiled up at him. She looked so small lying there in the bed. He could see she was struggling, but it was not the kind of struggle Nelly had endured. When he had left Lydia, she was in near panic, but now with her mother and sister there, she seemed to be calmer. Stronger. He continued to hold her hand as the waves of pain grew closer and closer together. With each one, she squeezed his hand with the strength of a thousand men.

George watched as the shadows on the walls began to fade and Margaret scurried around to light what few lamps there were in the cabin. He was stiff from sitting in one position for so long and was just about to stretch when Lydia cried out more than normal.

"It's coming!"

George bolted upright in his chair, completely and totally unprepared for the birth of his child. Nelly had said Lydia would die as she had died, and yet here Lydia was still alive and about to bring his child into the world.

Hannah and Mary quickly lifted the blankets from Lydia's waist. Mary helped her bend her legs, and as she spread Lydia's legs open, she made a surprised sound. "Indeed!" She clapped her hands in joy and then set to work.

Hannah pushed George aside as she wedged in behind Lydia, propping her up slightly. "We're going to push when Mother says to, okay?" Hannah instructed her.

Lydia nodded as Mary said "Push!" and George watched as Lydia's face turned bright red as she groaned and bore down on the child trying to escape her body.

George felt Margaret at his side, and she gently guided him toward the foot of the bed so that he could actually see the birth happening. He saw Mary's hands covered in her daughter's blood, but he also saw the small head of his child appearing between Lydia's legs.

It seemed like Lydia pushed dozens of times. The head showed and then retreated back inside her body only to reappear again the next time Mary said to push. Finally, the baby's whole face was exposed— its little eyes were clamped shut, its nose was purple, and its whole head covered in what looked like white, lumpy cheese. Mary wiped it quickly with a rag Margaret handed her and told Lydia to push again. It was small, like Lydia, but it was a child.

George marveled that Lydia still lived. He began to wonder if his vision of Nelly had been the workings of his own imagination. Born of his own fear once he knew Lydia was with child. He was dragged from his thoughts as Mary told Lydia one more push would do it, and with one final effort, the child slid effortlessly from Lydia's body. She fell back against the bed completely and totally exhausted, yet alive. Mary was wiping the child quickly and rubbing its back. He could hear her murmuring to it.

"Breathe, child, come on, breathe."

It was then that he noticed the child was very purple all over, not just its nose like he had noticed before.

Margaret was hovering nearby. "Is it stillborn?" she asked.

George looked quickly from Margaret to Mary, then to Hannah, and finally to Lydia, who lay exhausted on the bed with her eyes closed. He went to her side.

"Lydia," he said, and she turned her head to look at him. She was alive. He could not believe it. He had made himself sick for all of these months over nothing. Nelly had been a vision of his own creation. His heart was bursting with joy.

Mary was swiping out the inside of the baby's mouth with her finger, wiping the fluids on a rag. Suddenly and without any warning, the child coughed and screamed. It startled everyone, and then there was laughter. Mary wrapped the child up and handed it to George. Smiling, she said, "It's a girl." He took the bundle from her and held it close to his chest. It was oh so tiny, coughing and sputtering in his arms.

He bent down to show the child to Lydia when he noticed a strange expression cross her face, then her eyes rolled back in her head. Her arms stiffened at her sides, and her legs went rigid. Gurgling noises came from her throat. Mary and Hannah leapt to her side.

"The fits!" Mary cried out. "No, not now!"

But Lydia continued to thrash about on the bed. The afterbirth half expelled from her, oozing blood in every direction.

Margaret screamed and ran from the cabin, leaving the door open in her wake. The cold evening air rushed inside, causing the flames of the fire to flicker and thrash just as Lydia's body was. Still holding the baby, George reached over and kicked the door shut. Mary and Hannah were struggling to hold Lydia still.

"What is happening?" George screamed at the women.

"It's one of her fits," Mary cried out. George saw tears staining the woman's face.

George watched as Lydia's face contorted in ways he had never thought possible. Her mouth hung open, and the guttural, other-worldly sounds that he had heard when he had first witnessed Lydia having a fit six years earlier filled his ears. And just as before, items in the room began to fly about. The curtains were ripped from the windows. George ducked as a broom flew past his head. The basins of water and bloodied rags all upended, spilling their mess upon the floor.

Every sinew in Lydia's body was straining. Tiring from the effort, Mary and Hannah were losing control of her. Lydia slid from the bed, collapsing in a heap on the floor. She thrashed about on the floor while George watched in horror as blood and tissue from the recent birth were smeared into the floorboards.

"Stop!" he screamed. "In the name of God, stop!"

Suddenly, Lydia's eyes flew wide open and the thrashing stopped. He saw her limbs relax, and then she was still. Mary had come around the bed and was on the floor pulling Lydia up to her chest.

"Lydia! Lydia!" she screamed. The blood that was splattered all over the lower half of Lydia's body now seeped into Mary's skirts. She slapped at her daughter's face, but Lydia was gone. Her eyes stared lifelessly at the ceiling.

George felt his heart break within his chest. She was dead. Just as Nelly had foretold.

"No!" he screamed as he sat on the floor next to the women. "She can't be dead. Please, no!" he sobbed, tears running down his face.

Hannah reached out and touched his arm, trying to comfort him in some way.

"George..." she started to say, but there were just no words for the unimaginable grief that this man was facing yet again.

George was mumbling and rocking back and forth, still holding his daughter. His eyes were focused on the lifeless form of Lydia as she lay beside her mother. Mary, too, was crying silent tears of grief over such a violent end to what should have been a joyous day.

"Mary," George begged, "explain to me what just happened here."

The woman looked up, her face wet with tears and smeared with the blood of her daughter. "I don't know, George, I truly don't know," she cried.

George looked down at the daughter he still held in his arms only to realize that in the melee, she had stopped breathing.

"My God!" he exclaimed, ripping the blanket from the baby and shaking her. "She's not breathing! Mary, she's not breathing!" he yelled.

Hannah took the child from him and began to rub its back. She tried clearing its mouth again with her fingers. But it was too late. The child was gone. Both of them were dead.

George stood as if to back away from something that revolted him. He looked at Mary with Lydia and then at Hannah holding the child.

"What is this?" he screamed. "What have you done? What has she done?"

What he had just witnessed crushed his soul. Everything inside of him turned cold.

The women were startled by the harshness of his words.

"What have we done? George, are you mad? We had no control over this. How could any of us have predicted this would be the outcome?"

"What on earth do you mean?" Hannah shouted at him.

"Look at this scene before you, woman!" he shouted back. "That!" He pointed at Lydia. "That is but a demon in a child's body. She beguiled me! Tricked me with visions of my beloved Nelly!" His breath came fast, and he kicked at the chair that was overturned. "This whole mess was nothing more than the devil trying to destroy my very life."

He was no longer capable of believing that what he had seen was actually Nelly. No, this could not be the work of a loving God, his loving wife, or any force that had compassion for mankind. No, this had to be the work of the devil. "That familiar spirit Lydia conjured up to destroy me. That spirit knew this would happen," he said to them.

Mary struggled to stand, laying Lydia gently on the floor. "What do you mean the spirit knew?" she asked.

"It came to me in an orb," he said with sarcasm so thick it was clear he was mocking them. "The day Lydia told me she was with child. It came to me and told me Lydia would die in childbirth just as Nelly had."

Recognition registered on Hannah's face. "So that is why you have been so sullen these past few months. You knew!" she yelled at him. "And you didn't say anything to anyone? You didn't alert us so that we could have protected her in some way?" Her tone was accusatory as she glared at him.

"Protect her?" he yelled back. "She has clearly sold her soul to the devil!" He picked up a washbasin that had recently been flying around the room. "How are you going to protect her from this?" he shouted, throwing it into the corner, where it landed with a crash.

"That child!" he yelled at Mary and Hannah, pointing again at Lydia's body. "That child is possessed, as everyone believed! I was crazy to have fallen for her lies!" He stopped short and glared at the women. "For your lies! All of you Blaisdells! I don't know what kind of evil lives behind that pious front you put on for everyone to see, but look at what you have wrought!" he screamed. "She set her mind long ago to have me as her husband, and she clearly made a pact with the devil to have it happen." He glanced one last time at Lydia's lifeless body crumpled on the floor. "And she clearly paid for that deal with her life." He spat onto the floor. "Wrap them up! I'll send a wagon to take you all away from here!" He strode out the door and across the yard toward the main house.

Mary ran to the door, leaning through the entryway. "George, wait," she shouted. "You can't possibly expect us to go tonight!"

Turning around, he glared at her. "I can and I do. I want this evil removed from Butler's Point immediately."

CHAPTER SIXTY-ONE

George sent two of his father's stablemen around to the cabin with a wagon. He gave them explicit instructions to make sure the bodies of Lydia and the child were taken as quickly as possible to the eastern side of the bay.

"I don't care if they have a place to bury them or not," he said coldly. "Dump them from the end of the wagon if you have to. And send someone to alert me straightway when you have departed." He handed each man a fistful of coins as compensation.

Upon entering the house, he found Margaret in the kitchen sitting at the table, still shaking. His mother was with her, trying to soothe her with tea.

"What on earth happened out there?" his mother asked.

He only shook his head. "It was evil of a kind I do not wish to talk about," he said. "Lydia and the child are dead."

"Dead?" Sarah exclaimed in shock.

Margaret raised her head off the table. "I will never be with child. I will never be with child," she repeated over and over. Sarah tried rubbing her arm to shush her.

"You will not be able to go back to that cabin," he said. "Is there anything of a personal nature that you or Susanna need?" He directed his question to Margaret, but she just shook her head. "Very well." He turned to walk from the room when his mother spoke.

"But George, where is Lydia?"

"In hell," he said as he walked out.

+ ——— +

Within the hour, George received word that Mary, Hannah, and the bodies had been loaded into a wagon and were on their way up the road. Then and only then did George leave the safety of his childhood home and venture back outside. In the darkness, he made several trips to the barn, gathering pitchforks full of hay that he threw into the cabin. When he felt he had enough, he shoveled a hot coal from the hearth and laid it on the straw next to the western wall. He watched as the straw caught and flames jumped until they were also catching the bark of the logs along the wall. He reached into the hearth and shoveled out a few more hot coals, throwing them at the blood-soaked bedding before exiting. Leaving the door open behind him, he stood back and watched the room quickly brighten with flame.

+———+

As the wagon pulled into the yard of the Blaisdell's home, Mary and Hannah sat solemnly in the back. At their feet lie the bodies of Lydia and her baby, both wrapped together in a makeshift shroud. The baby nestled in Lydia's arms. Abner came out quickly when he heard them arrive.

"What is all of this?" he said, seeing his exhausted wife and the shrouded corpse.

"Lydia," was all Mary would say as she began to pull on the body. Abner reached up and took Lydia from the wagon. He had no sooner retrieved his daughter's body when the driver cracked the whip on the horse and pulled away. Abner stumbled slightly until he could adjust Lydia's weight in his arms.

"What in the name of God?" he said, looking at Mary. "What happened?"

"She's dead, Abner!" Mary screamed at him. "And I'm inclined to believe what George was saying."

"Mother!" Hannah shouted. "You cannot possibly think that!"

"It has to be true," Mary replied, turning to her husband. "Abner, it's more than possible that our daughter made a pact with the devil to gain George Butler as her husband. We all have been a part of this evil undertaking!" Mary looked at the form of her daughter resting in Abner's arms. "She got what she wanted. A husband. A few months of wedded bliss. A child." Mary choked on that word. "But she paid for it with her life."

Abner was stunned. His wife had long protected the child. Had said that a child couldn't be possessed by evil. Something truly awful must have happened for her to now think otherwise.

"Mary…" he started to say when he was distracted by the light flickering across the bay in the early morning dawn. As his voice trailed off, Mary and Hannah both turned to look at him and they, too, saw what he saw.

On Butler's Point, fire now consumed the entire cabin. Flames shot several feet into the air. The roar and crackle of the fire could be heard clearly all around the bay. George stood watching it burn. And with it, he hoped every bit of evil that had consumed his life since Lydia had come into it.

Abner, Hannah, and Mary stood transfixed on the eastern shore. The smell of burning debris drifted toward them. Across the bay, behind the Butler home, flames shot up into the sky.

"He's burning the cabin," Hannah said as she turned and walked into the house, exhausted from the whole ordeal.

Abner still held Lydia's body in his arms. "Mary," he pleaded, "why is he burning the cabin?"

An exhausted Mary replied, "So we would know." Sighing deeply, she continued. "So everyone would know. It was all of the devil, Abner. Every last bit of it." She slowly walked into the house, leaving him alone in the yard.

Abner looked down at his daughter's body. She was wrapped in a simple piece of muslin. He took in the shape of her head, the drop of her shoulders. He could see the contours where her arms were folded across her chest, and then what he saw next almost made him drop her.

"God save us!" he cried out as he watched a small black spot grow bigger on the fabric. Smoke began to rise as the hole grew larger, expanding outward from the center, the edges scorched and hot. Soon all of the cloth had burned away. What was left, bare and exposed, shining in the early morning sunlight, was the posset ring on Lydia's left hand.

AUTHORS NOTE

Whenever I finish reading a work of historical fiction, my first reaction is to find out what really happened! So for anyone who would like to know the facts about George, Nelly, Lydia, and how this story impacted the town of Franklin, Maine, I urge you to read *The Nelly Butler Hauntings: A Documentary History* edited by Marcus LiBrizzi and Dennis Boyd, published by the University of Maine Press. I first read that book on a Halloween night in 2015. In the weeks that followed, I became obsessed with this story. Although *The Nelly Butler Hauntings* does a great job of presenting the historical record, it is just a snapshot in time. It focuses on the appearance of Nelly's ghost and the controversy it brought to the town in late 1799 and early 1800. I wanted to know how George, Nelly, and Lydia found themselves in this situation in the first place. When I couldn't find any evidence of their relationships before the appearance of the ghost, I decided to create it. Everything I have written prior to the appearance of the ghost is one hundred percent fictional.

The historical record contains the testimonies of those that saw the ghost of Nelly Butler. In those depositions, which were taken by the real Reverend Abraham Cummings, what is recorded is that the ghost spoke in cryptic sentences. I have tried to use as many of those exact words as possible. It is also recorded that the ghost walked in broad daylight for over a mile and that people from as far away as Bangor came to witness it. To that I have also tried to stay true. Many of the names of secondary characters in this work are the real people who gave their testimonies. Others are completely fictional. In the historical record it is stated that the knockings and the appearance of the ghost took place in the Blaisdells' dirt floor cellar. I changed that location to a back room of their house.

It's important to remember that some of the individuals in this story were real people. And although Nelly and Lydia both died young, George went on to marry again and fathered eleven children with his third wife. To his descendants, I wish to say that I hope my imagination of how this story unfolded is taken in the vein that it was intended: a fictional portrayal of a recorded event. I tried to remain respectful to a man who must have struggled through a truly bizarre situation. He must have struggled emotionally. The same holds true for the Blaisdells. Although it was important to the fictional story to imply that they were of dubious character, I hope I left enough ambiguity and balance to reflect that we truly don't know much about this situation. To this day we still don't know what really happened. Was Lydia a clairvoyant? Was this a spiritual manifestation? Or is this simply a tale of folklore?

ACKNOWLEDGMENTS

This book would not have been possible without Darla Pickett, former editor of the *Morning Sentinel* in Waterville, Maine. I will never forget the day she walked up to my cubicle in the advertising department. She dropped on my desk the story I had written and submitted to be published in a special Veterans Day section where they had asked readers for story submissions. She looked me straight in the eye and said, "Why aren't you writing?" I smiled. "I don't write," I said. "I sell ads." In our following conversations she gave me the confidence to believe enough in myself to pursue writing this story.

I also owe a debt of gratitude to my husband, Craig, who has believed that I could do this from the very beginning.

And finally, I need to recognize the efforts of Jill Huard, who pleaded with me to continue writing when I hit a slump. Her constant encouragement got me through that slump so that I could finish the story.